Handful of Purpose

Sarah Hale

ISBN 978-1-64079-445-0 (paperback)
ISBN 978-1-64079-446-7 (digital)

Christian Faith Publishing, Inc.
832 Park Avenue
Meadville, PA 16335
www.christianfaithpublishing.com

Printed in the United States of America

I would like to dedicate this book to my sister Cathy for ALWAYS pushing me to pursue my dreams. To my parents George and Jane and brother Tim I say THANK YOU for giving me the best life imaginable.

Note to readers: As much as I would like for you to read and enjoy my book; I want you to know reading and spending time in God's Word should always be top priority.

Dakota Territory 1880

A lone horse stood quietly on the ridge. The rider, a Sioux Indian, sat like a statue atop the golden palomino. His gaze was fixed on the scene below. His eyes narrowed as he watched three men on horseback advance on a running Indian youth. Guns in the air they shot in attempt to frighten the boy. When he kept running without so much as a stutter in his step one of the men retrieved the rope from his saddle and lassoed the boy dragging the lad over rock covered ground. Peals of laughter came from the trio as they shouted at their prey.

The Indians legs tightened around the sides of his horse. The beast neighed ready to charge down the terrain as it had done so many times before. A sudden motion in the copse of trees caused the Indian to subdue his horse. Something shiny had caught his eye. He knew from years of fighting the barrel of a gun, even from this distance. A sudden shot rang out severing the rope between man and boy. As a gunfight ensued. The Indian boy blended into the environment as his people had taught him. He watched as the lone gunman fought a very strategic battle against his three opponents.

A few of his people now dotted the ridges around them. It took the three men several minutes to see the Sioux braves with their ponies pointed to descend. The trio retreated leaving a cloud of dust behind them.

The brave on the palomino heeled his mount cautiously down to the valley below. The Indian lad made his appearance to face his father. At the meeting of their eyes, the youngster bent his head, bracing himself for his father's reprimand. Lone Eagle's eyes softened at his son's reverence. His hand rested on the shirtless boy's shoulder surveying for any injuries.

A rustling in the brush was a reminder father and son were not alone. Spotted Hawk's savior emerged from his cover only to fall unconscious at Lone Eagle's feet. The man had been shot. Blood oozed from the wound just below his collarbone near his left shoulder. Another hole was spotted in the left thigh.

Wordlessly, Lone Eagle and Spotted Hawk lifted the man onto the prancing palomino. Lone Eagle effortlessly jumped astride the beast and set at a rapid pace down the valley path. Spotted Hawked took the opposite path by foot.

What a day! Feeling as if she accomplished so much in a short period of time, Maggie eased down in the rocker on the front porch. She loved this time of day. The orange sun melting into the rich blue hues only found in the Dakota sky. The smell of golden clover filled the air. A gentle breeze carried the sent to the porch where Maggie sat folding clothes she had just taken off the line.

Gus, her trusty companion, lay beside her chair. They had been together for years. Gus showed up the day after her grandfather died. As much as she tried to discourage the dog from staying in those first few days she is now thankful the canine was so stubborn. He was her only source of companionship most days. The dog sensing her thoughts turned his eyes to meet hers.

"Yes, boy, you won," the dog's head went down his muzzle resting on her bare feet.

She had inherited this little farm when her grandfather passed suddenly two years ago. She and her grandfather came to Dakota during the gold rush. Not necessarily for gold but for the adventure. It was an adventure but not quite what either of them expected.

Her father had died shortly after her birth. Her mother never completely recovered from the devastating loss and spent her life in and out of hospitals. Her uncle took custody of her until he decided to marry. Merry's grandfather had to be located before she could be shipped to Denver where her grandfather was living.

Merry Margret Quinn brought her lively Irish heritage to the rough Dakota Territory, and found a peaceful life. Always feeling somewhat like an orphan, Maggs, as her grandfather called her, had settled into the role of farmer, landowner, and now spinster. At thirty, she had proved herself to be quite capable of handling anything that came her way. She only needed a little help with the farm from time to time and her closest neighbors, the Hasketts, let their son Tommy work for her.

Tommy Haskett, a sweet eight-year-old, was always willing to lend a hand as long as he got some of Maggie's famous cookies. Tommy had helped her today, and they had finished mending all her fences. A yawn escaped Gus and Maggie agreed she was ready for bed as well.

The sound of horse hooves stopped Maggie in her tracks. Gus's lack of barking indicated the person on horseback was not a threat. Maggie turned just in time to see a man being dumped from the front of Lone Eagle's horse. The Indian's piercing brown eyes captured Maggie's, and for a brief moment, she thought he was going to dismount. Instead he nudged his horse and went with lightning speed toward the prairie.

The man's crumpled body lay at the foot of her cabin steps. Gus was circling the man, sniffing and nudging. No response. Maggie rolled him over to see his face. The night shadows made his features difficult to make out. Was the man alive? What was she supposed to do with him? His left shoulder had been dressed with bits of buckskin and twine. His left thigh had a rather dirty bandage wrapped haphazardly. His upper lip had a thin line of perspiration covering it.

Removal of his hat showed the same perspiration at the temples. The man was ill, to be certain.

Maggie got behind the man's shoulders, attempting to somehow will him to sit up. The movement stirred the man and a moan escaped his dry lips.

"Can you sit up?" she asked in a pleading tone.

His slow movements were purposeful but of little help. He struggled as Maggie pushed and prodded until she was able to get under the man's good shoulder. With all his strength, he rose to his feet, stumbled, and nearly fell, taking Maggie with him. She steadied the man. With great merit, she led him into the house.

Once inside the small dwelling she coaxed him to her grandfather's bed that lay just to the left of the tiny kitchen. The room only sported a bed and a curtain hung separating the two rooms. She herself had been sleeping there since her grandfather's death. Her room up in the loft had become a storage area for her lost and broken dreams.

Every movement seemed to affect the man. He fell onto the bed with great force and Maggie could see the pain on his face. His face, tanned by the sun with a white strip across his forehead where his hat had been. He had a few days' growth on his face but that did little to hide the thin jagged scar that went down the right side of his jaw to the base of this throat. She wondered for a moment what must have happened to the man to cause such an injury. She was afraid to let her mind take off with any kind of wild thought.

What kind of man might he be? And here she had brought him into her home. Why didn't she think to take him to the barn? *No, he is too ill,* she thought. She couldn't take proper care of him traveling from the barn to the house. She did the right thing, didn't she? *What is done is done*, she reasoned. *I will get him better and get him out.*

Just then the man's eyes popped open. The eyes were like glass looking directly at her. She could tell he was consumed with fever and wasn't sure what was going on around him. She had never seen eyes that color on a man. They were an unusual shade of blue. She remembered once seeing a wolf that had one brown eye and one blue it looked like ice and that was exactly what was staring at her. The hair on the back of her neck stood at attention.

As quickly as they opened, the man's eyes shut. His dark eyelashes lay fanned out over his face. They too were unlike any man's eyelashes. They were extremely long. Maggie determined that he was probably a very beautiful child and was often times mistaken for a baby girl. She wondered about the man's childhood then, her mind going over all the possibilities of the kind of life he had lived.

"Has it really been that long, Maggie," she said aloud to herself, "since you have had human contact that you are creating such stories in your head?" The man moaned then and Maggie was brought back to the task at hand.

She had a bit of laudanum she got the man to take. As soon as he was out she began assessing the gunshot wound. She first tore what was left of his shirt away. Lone Eagle had done a fairly good job at dressing the wound but a probing indicated the bullet was still present. With heated water and a knitting needle, she "dug" the bullet out.

The wound began to ooze and she quickly doused it with alcohol. The man's shoulder twitched and he moved slightly in response to the painful process. Once the bleeding had stopped she dressed it and removed the man's shirt. If she could have seen herself she would have noticed the flush of red that started at her neck and engulfed her face. Her ears were a fiery mess.

Broad shoulders stretched out on the white linen. His chest had scars here and there of different sizes. One was obviously a knife wound. She had stared so long at his chest that Gus jumped on the bed and nudged her arm, as if to say, "Get on with it, times a wasting." The dog laid his head on the man's chest watching Maggie's movements.

"His pants," she mumbled to herself. "How am I going to get to his leg wound?" She sighed and draped a quilt over his body. With closed eyes, she unbuckled the belt around his waist, went to the foot of the bed, and began to tug. With great effort and several minutes later the man's pants lay in the corner.

The second bullet was lodged in the outside muscle of his thigh. This wound seemed to be a few days older. Maggie was certain with the size of the muscle there was no way the bullet hit the bone. She heated her knitting needle and began to dig. This one was a little harder to retrieve and the man struggled against her. With one last poke and a coating of alcohol the chore was done and the man seemed to relax.

Maggie washed her patients face using a tepid cloth to relieve some of the effects of the fever. She had brewed some tea and tried to get the man to take a sip. He did with unconscious effort and drifted back into a restless sleep. His hair lay in a wet mass around his face. She tried to imagine what the man would look like if he was fit and healthy. She decided his thick dark, nearly black hair had a slight wave to it. It curled slightly near his ear. She was certain he kept some sort of a beard to hide the scar. After all, who would want that to show? People would surely stare, or maybe he didn't care. Maybe he is an outlaw? Her mind went wild with thought. One thing for certain he was ruggedly handsome and that unnerved her. She wanted him out of her house as soon as possible.

The man slept off and on through the night mumbling and moaning. The fever seemed to rage on. Gus would not get off the bed and Maggie would not leave his side. Something inside compelled her to care for the man.

This was her life, taking care of strays, tending the sick, visiting the poor, and staying away from town and the "going ons" that did not concern or interest her. She was an outcast so to speak, not the kind that was dishonest or of ill repute. Merry Margret Quinn just did not fit in. Anywhere! Her friends were limited to four people in town—Doctor Ezekiel Lapp and his wife Liddy, Sheriff Dan Bullock, and Pastor Joshua Gray.

The younger women in town barely spoke to her referring to her as "Old Maid Quinn," the men in town were much nicer and called her just "Quinn." The schoolchildren sometimes called her "Mag the Hag," not to her face, but Tommy had let it slip one day. He felt awful about letting her know and his Norwegian complexion boasted a red stain of embarrassment she had never seen. She laughed it off and tousled his hair. She made the face of a hag until he joined her in the merriment, but still it hurt.

She had accepted her lot, after all that is what everyone had told her she had to do.

"It is just your lot in life, Maggie," her uncle had said when her mother became too mentally ill to care for her. He said it again when he shipped her out west. Her grandfather used it several times when her feelings were hurt at the teasing of the children growing up. She learned quickly to hide it all away and mask her face into a portrayal of a confident independent woman.

She would have loved to be silly and feminine and look like other girls but it was not her lot. Her height was too tall for a girl, her bone structure was too large, and her feet too clumsy. Her grandfather used to tell her she took after her father. "A large strong Irishman he was and came from large stock." It was meant to impress Maggie, but it did nothing to shield the years of personal torment.

The gray light coming through the kitchen window promised a day of overcast skies. It fit her mood perfectly and the uneasiness she had about the stranger intensified. He had awakened with some work on her part just long enough to take some cool water. His brow was less hot but when he opened his eyes for a fleeting moment she could tell the fever was still present. Those eyes haunted her. He would look at her but it was as if he was looking past her. Maybe he had a mental disorder. Her mother use to stare at her the same way.

She heard Tommy at the back door and quickly closed the curtain between the rooms. There was no reason for Tommy to get involved. She grabbed a piece of paper and scribbled a note to Dr. Lapp. She would send Tommy to fetch the doctor then send him home. There would be no working today.

Ezekiel Lapp, MD, had just poured himself a cup of coffee and began to stock his medical bag. The strong brew permeated the air. His wife Liddy came from the bedroom complaining. She was not a coffee drinker and the smell in the morning always woke her up.

"Brewing more medicine this morning, Dr. Lapp?"

Ezekiel kissed his wife's forehead. "It is the only way I can get a morning kiss, Mrs. Lapp. If I did not make my coffee, you would sleep until noon."

This was not the case but the doctor liked teasing his wife just to see her smile. The couple had no children of their own but had fostered many of orphan infants until suitable homes could be found. Tommy Haskett was one of those children. They were delighted to see Tommy come up the walk even at such an early hour.

The boy was out of breath when Dr. Lapp opened the door.

"Tommy, my boy what brings you into town so early?"

Tommy stopped to catch his breath. He was bent over at the knees gulping in large amounts of air.

"Tommy, is something wrong? Do your folks need me?"

Tommy's head swung from side to side. "N-n-no, s-sir. Miss Q-Quin sent . . . t-this." Tommy's stuttering was always worse when he was upset. He handed the doctor the note. Liddy joined her husband reading over his shoulder.

> Doc,
>
> I need you to stop by today. I am all right but I need you to bring the sheriff too. Send Tommy home and tell Liddy not to worry.
>
> MMQ

"I am going with you." Liddy scurried to gather supplies.

"Now hold on, Liddy. Tommy, you go on home now and don't say a word about this, you understand?"

"Y-yes, s-sir." Tommy did as he was told and the doctor shut the door.

Liddy had continued as if her husband had not spoken.

"Liddy!" His voice was firm. "The letter was to me not you. I need you to stay here. Do you understand?" His eyes were pinning her to the spot where she stood.

"Zeke, if that girl is in some kind of trouble I need to know about it. She has no one."

His hand went out to catch his flitting wife. "You will stay until I see what this is about."

"Don't use that doctor tone with me, Ezekiel Lapp," she snapped with a strain in her voice her husband knew all too well. When one of her own, and Merry Margret Quinn was one of her own, was in need nothing could stop Liddy Lapp except Ezekiel Lapp. He was out the door before Liddy could protest.

Sheriff Bullock rubbed his jaw as he read Maggie's letter. "Best git out there and see what is going on." The sheriff grabbed his gun and put his hat on his balding head. "I don't like this. The last time she asked for the both of us we had a real mess on our hands."

The doctor followed him out the door. They set a quick pace to the Quinn place. The skies opened up just as they reached the corral and they both ran up the porch to Maggie's open door. The smell of coffee and alcohol wafted out the door.

Reading the looks on their faces prompted Maggie to put her hand up.

"I'm fine, but I have a very sick house guest." As she ushered them in she told them the whole story. They both had a lot of unspoken questions and the quiet man in the bed was not going to answer them anytime soon.

The doctor examined him, telling Maggie she did the proper thing. He left some medicine for the man, and as bad as he hated to tell her, he felt the man shouldn't be moved just yet. The sheriff didn't like the idea but there was little he could do.

"Did the man have any belongings on him?" the sheriff asked. "Has he talked any?"

"Have you spoken with Lone Eagle?" the doctor questioned.

Maggie could feel her stomach churn. The coffee she drank without any breakfast was making her nauseated. "No, he just dropped him off."

She should have told them she felt Lone Eagle did not see the man as a threat or he would have never brought him there but neither of the men understood her relationship with the Indian. She wasn't sure she knew herself and their history was too complicated to explain.

The men promised to come back the next day. Hopefully the stranger would be awake enough to answer a few questions.

He did wake up later that morning. She had just finished the breakfast dishes when she heard a commotion behind the curtain. The man was trying to brace himself to sit up. His unsuccessful attempt left him frustrated and mumbling.

"Good morning," she said in a hushed tone. His eyes moved to take her in but the movement made him dizzy so he shut them. With barely a whisper he tried to speak.

"Where am I?" It seemed to take all his strength as his facial muscles began to twitch.

"Dakota Territory," Maggie replied.

"What happened? Oh," he grimaced as he touched his shoulder. "Gunshot wound," he said so low she could only read his lips. His hand went to rest on his thigh and suddenly his eyes shot open and pinned her. One eyebrow went up in question "My pants?" Well, she heard that clear as a bell.

Her face took on the all too familiar crimson hue. For the first time, she understood how Tommy felt as her words tried desperately to get past her tongue. She focused her eyes on his. "I had to remove them to treat your wound." She braced herself for his censure or his rude comment. Neither came instead she saw the slightest nod of his head. "What is your . . . name?" she asked, but it was too late, he was out again.

The low murmur of voices drifted through the curtain. One had to strain to hear the whole conversation.

"I tell you, Merry Margret, this is not a good situation." Liddy's face was taught with concern as she sipped her tea.

"What was I to do? He was too sick to turn away. I couldn't let him just lay out there until morning."

"No, I suppose not. I would have done the same thing but I have a man in the house and you are out here all alone."

The man in the bed reached to scratch his head. Where in tar nation was he? The last thing he remembered was . . . *his pants*! He was held up somewhere recovering from a gunshot wound . . . or two.

He heard the scraping of a chair on the rough floor and the clanking of cups and knew there was movement behind the curtain. He closed his eyes in the pretense he was still "out" but he heard the door open and the women leave the cabin. If only he could find his haversack.

Maggie bid Liddy good-bye and went to work in her garden. She caught movement out of her right peripheral vision. She knew it wasn't Tommy. She saw someone slip around the barn. Caught between the garden and house she wasn't sure which way to go. Gus who normally stirred and barked when strangers were afoot only set at the edge of the garden wagging his tail. It had to be Lone Eagle.

When Liddy's wagon was out of sight, Lone Eagle made his presence fully known.

"You scared me," Maggie said as she smoothed the hair back from her forehead.

"You did right, Morning Dove, by acting as if you did not notice. Staying alert is always good. You make fine Indian."

Maggie smiled at the man. He had been a good friend to her and always referred to her as Morning Dove a high honor to be given an Indian name.

"I hung buffalo meat in barn for you, you have a hungry man to feed."

"About that, do you know anything about him? How did you come to be in custody of him?"

"You have many questions, Morning Dove, and many more in the depths of your eyes. I know the man did honorable in the sight of the Lakota. That is all I know."

His hand went up as if to brush her cheek but stopped in midair while his eyes caressed her face. He let out a whistle and his Palomino quickly and quietly appeared. In one swoop, he was up on the mount.

He tossed a saddlebag down to her. He did not tell her that her guest had witnessed the whole thing from the window of the bedroom.

How can one describe such an Indian? The man was nothing but pure muscle. No fat just a lean muscular corded structure. From the lack of a shirt one didn't have to guess about the strength of his back and shoulders. In all his travels the man sitting on the side of the bed had never seen an Indian quite like this one, and he had seen a lot.

It was all starting to come back to him. No wonder it seemed like an effortless motion that put him on the back of that Palomino two nights ago. It was effortless for such a species. What prompted the Sioux to help him? He had assisted in freeing the boy caught by the trio. Perhaps he was part of the tribe and they felt honor bound. And, he had never seen an Indian so "familiar" with a white woman. She was not the least bit scared of him nor did she comprehend the fact that he had almost kissed her.

Would it be dishonest to look through his bag? The thought was dancing all through Maggie's head. *If it will help me find out who he is or where he came from it would be all right*? She reasoned. *Make a decision already Maggie*! She scolded.

She sat down on an old tree stump and opened the worn leather bag. There were three initials stamped into the leather TJS. When she opened the sack, she found a bit of food, a small knife, and a gun. The initials TJS were stamped on the handle. There was a bible and a pocket watch that was engraved inside with the inscription "All my love, Abby." A picture of the man with a lovely woman and a tidy sum of money were at the bottom.

Maggie deduced the woman in the picture was Abby and Abby was undoubtedly his wife. She closed the bag and headed into the house. She needed to get word to this Abby as she would be sick with worry for sure and for certain.

She slipped behind the curtain prepared to put the bag under the bed. She was stopped dead in her tracks when she noticed the man was sitting up. The sheet lay just below his breast bone and he made no move to cover up. Instead he was looking at the bag and then to her face.

"Did you go through it?" he asked not in an accusatory tone.

"Yes, I did," she answered as if she had every right to do so.

"Did the Indian bring it?"

She dropped her jaw then closed it. The familiar flush crept up her neck. "Yes" was all she could get out. Her mouth was a husk. He just nodded and leaned his head back.

"Hungry?" she croaked out.

"Yes, ma'am." His throat must have been a husk also as he barely got the words out, although his was not due to embarrassment.

In just a few minutes she arrived with some ham a few biscuits and coffee. "It is probably best if you don't eat too much too early," she warned

"Yes, ma'am, this will be fine." She poured a cup of water for him and started to leave. "Thank you, ma'am, for everything."

She stared at him for a fleeting second and then remembered to ask his name. "What is your name?" If it was not something that began with initial TJS, she could be sure he was a dishonest fellow. She sized him up as if ready to throw him out at the first misstep.

"Thaddeus James Sheridan, ma'am. Most people call me Thad."

"Okay, Mr. Sheridan. Better get some rest the doc, and the sheriff will be out to see you later and they will have a heap of questions for a man such as yourself."

Thad was taken aback. *A man "such as yourself." What did she mean by that? She stands there and judges me before she knows me.* He thought he left that kind of prejudice back in Charleston.

Maggie was right, by his watch, it was three o'clock, and the doc and sheriff had just pulled a couple of chairs in the room. The doctor was assessing his patient when they both turned as Maggie entered the room and leaned against the wall.

"Now, Maggie," the sheriff began. "You can't stay in here."

"The man is staying under my own roof. I have a right to know what he is about. I'll not be leaving."

What he is about? Thad's inner voice repeated to himself. *Of all the nerve.*

"She can stay," he said, with more calm than he was experiencing. Much to the men's chagrin, they let her stay.

Thad recounted the story for the sheriff.

"So you were following these men for some time? Why?" the sheriff questioned.

"I was suspicious of them, thought they might have stolen something off of a friend of mine," Thad answered but the sheriff wasn't buying it. "I was just following them and watching them. They didn't even know I was there until the gunfight."

"You say they had lassoed a young Indian boy? Must have been Spotted Hawk. That would be the only reason Lone Eagle would save your hide."

Maggie unconsciously cleared her throat and Thad caught her pushing the hair back from her forehead as she did in the garden earlier that morning with Lone Eagle. Evidence of a nervous habit she had. His eyebrow went up in a questioning manner and she left the room.

"She is too sensitive when it comes to Lone Eagle and Spotted Hawk, people are starting to talk." The sheriff was looking at the doctor. "You need to have Liddy talk with her."

The doctor was taking Thad's' pulse and he never looked up but grunted from beneath his beard.

"A lot of good that would do," the doctor added. "Head like a rock, that girl." Both men chuckled. The sheriff winked at Thad and left the room.

"I still don't want you to move, son. You're not out of the woods yet. Understand?" He left the room on Thad's nod.

Thad could see the sun sinking in the western sky. He would love to be out of the bed and camped out under the stars on a night like tonight. There was a gentle breeze and coffee was filling the cabin. His stomach had started to growl; he was starving. As if she read his mind Maggie brought a tray in.

"Doc said you could have whatever you like. Buffalo okay? Boiled potatoes and some greens? I suppose it will have to be since that's what I fixed, no need really asking your opinion, I guess."

"No, ma'am, I will eat just about anything, I am at your mercy." Thad's mother would have scolded him if she had heard his tone. It would seem Maggie barely noticed.

"I have biscuits left over from lunch. Would you like some?"

"Yes, ma'am, if it is not too much trouble. They were very tasty."

She went for the biscuits but Thad stopped her. "Ma'am." He was going to apologize for putting her out the way he had but a huge sigh left her lungs and she turned on him.

"My name is Merry Margret Quinn, you can call me Merry Margret, you can call me Maggie, you can call me Mag the Hag. Call me anything for all I care, but for Pete's sake stop calling me ma'am!" Her eyes snapped at him and she left the room not to return until morning.

"I'd call you sassy," he said to himself.

After he ate his fill and slipped the tray to the other side of the bed he laid back and thought about his hostess. If he wanted to let his mind run, and tonight he did, he would say Merry Margret Quinn was a glorious woman. She was unlike any female he knew. She was tall and vivacious. The women in Charleston were all cookie cutter in nature. They manipulate their figures with stays and corsets, so they all looked the same. Their bodies were contorted out of the natural curves God had given them. A man didn't know what he was getting.

He remembered Abby's coming-out party, was it a shock to him. His long-time companion in crime came down the stairs powdered painted and molded into what society demanded a young lady should look like. His sweet baby sister was now out to catch a husband. He knew whoever married his sister would get a wonderful girl but when the layers were peeled away there would be the same stick thin girl he grew up with.

Merry, not so much. He liked to think of her as Merry instead of all the other names she suggested. "Mag the Hag." Nothing could be further from the truth. Oh, he supposed some men would not find her build, especially her height, very appealing. She did not dress to show her curves but yet tried to conceal them with full skirts and baggy shirts. Try as she may to be "unattractive," she was very attractive, wildly attractive.

Her thick brown hair had an auburn sheen to it. When the sun hit it, there were flecks of gold. It wasn't overly long, but barely flowed just past her shoulders, resting on her chest, or at least that is what he remembered from the first night when she helped him into the cabin. Her eyes matched her hair perfectly brown with flecks of gold. Her skin surprisingly a creamy white in spite of her time spent outdoors. *Stop*, his mind protested. Stop this train of thought.

He would have been surprised at "Merry's" train of thought.

"I have got to get him out of here as soon as possible. I want my life back to normal. I have so much work to do and I can't do anything until he is gone." She checked herself. "Lord, I know this has to be your will, help me to put myself in the proper place and do what is right." She too let her mind go to her house guest.

He obviously had lived a rough life. He was vague when the sheriff was questioning him. She did not buy his entire story. He was hiding something. She knew he saved Spotted Hawk that part had to be true. Lone Eagle's action supported Thad's declaration.

Those eyes were so . . . so . . . mystical and beautiful! When he looked at her it was if he was locked in on her soul. He made her feel like he knew something about her she did not know herself. She supposed some women may find his eyes unattractive, she mused, but they haunted her dreams. *Stop*, she reprimanded herself. *Stop this train of thought.*

Chapter Two

Maggie overslept the next morning. She had been sleeping in a rocking chair in the corner of the kitchen in case Thad needed something but last night she slept up in the loft. It had been a while since she slept in her old bed. She had forgotten how peaceful it was to go to bed with the night stars shining through the window. The sky invited her to do some thinking and praying, so much that it was almost morning when she finally drifted off.

She scurried down the ladder and headed to apologize to Thad.

"Sorry I over slept breakfast will be ready in a few minutes. She barely took time to look at Thad.

"Don't trouble yourself Merry, I have missed meals before please don't feel you have to wait on me. Keep with your daily routine. I am fine."

He was sitting on the side of his bed. His worn Bible lay open beside him. The sheet wrapped around him. So many things flooded her mind. She had pitched his clothes they were so damaged. Why didn't she think? She had no clothes for him. He was much larger than her grandfather. He couldn't go around in a sheet today.

"Merry?"

She was staring at the man trying to figure out an answer to this problem.

"Merry!" Thad tried to draw her out of her trance. She was not hearing him. Holding tight to the sheet he started to try and rise. The movement got her attention

"*Don't stand up*!" Panic was in her voice. He dipped his head to hide his laughter.

"You'll . . . you'll hurt your leg, open up the wound." She whipped around the curtain and Thad heard the slam of the back door and watched through the window as Merry walked briskly to the hen house. He couldn't help but smile that was until he noticed the pain in his thigh.

Breathing heavy, Maggie headed into the hen house. Her heart was beating out a fast pattern. She could hear it pounding in her ears and feel the flush from her neck to her scalp. Why hadn't she thought of his attire before she destroyed his clothes?

"Miss Maggie, you okay?" Maggie jumped out of her skin at Tommy's greeting.

"Tommy, you scared me half to death"

"S-s-sorry, M-m-miss M-Ma-Maggie."

The boy was so sweet with his gentle way. She really loved him dearly. "Oh, it's okay, Tommy. Boy, am I glad you came by today. I have two jobs for you."

Tommy's face was eager to hear what she had to say.

"I need you to go into town and tell Dr. Lapp when he comes to visit today I need some clothes."

Tommy's face held a quizzical look Maggie expected.

"I know it is an odd request, Tommy, but the doctor will understand, okay?" Tommy nodded. He would do anything for Maggie, he loved her.

Once you run to town and deliver the message, I was wondering if you would go fishing for me. I would love to have fish tonight for supper."

The boy's face lit up. If there was one thing he loved more than his friend Maggie, it was to fish, even if he didn't like to eat them. With a wide smile, he was off.

When her heart rate evened out Maggie's mind picked up the pace. What did he call me? Merry? No one calls me just plain Merry.

Somehow the way he said it . . . all velvety, made it sound not so plain. It sounded soft. Not like the harsh "Merry Margret" her mother used to scold her.

He was so kind about breakfast. Was that a smile on his face? How dare he make sport of my embarrassment? He did that on purpose. I bet he is howling with laughter. Well let's just see how funny no breakfast is and lunch too for that matter.

Maggie had stewed for a good part of the day. She stayed out of the house, she was too furious to return. She had lost all track of time when she saw Doc's buggy headed her way. It looked like sheriff Bullock was right behind them.

She met them at the front of the porch. Gus was barking so happily it was hard to hear the afternoon salutations. She was glad Liddy was with them she needed the presence of a woman, but something in Liddy's face put Maggie on high alert. The trio was up to something.

"Passed Tommy on our way, he's got a string of fish. Line so heavy he is carrying it with both hands," the sheriff reported. "I am awful fond of fish, one of my favorites." He winked at Maggie.

"I guess that means you'll be staying for supper?"

He smiled at her and headed into the house. When she and Liddy started in the doctor blocked the way.

"Ladies, I am going to have to ask you to stay outside. We need to talk with Mr. Sheridan." Maggie's head was going to explode. How can he kick her out of her own house? Before she could speak, he put a hand on her shoulder.

"And the boy needs to dress."

Boy, ha! she told herself. *That is no boy*. She continued her internal dialogue. *That is every bit a full-grown man and, well, you know it, Ezekiel Lapp!* She refrained from speaking the thought out loud. But, oh, she wanted to.

The doctor nodded to his wife and she guided Maggie down the porch.

Thad heard male voices and knew what was coming. The sheriff promised he'd be back and Thad had better have some answers. His sigh was met with the doctor's frown.

"You in a lot of pain son?"

"No, sir, it is tolerable."

"Yes, I can see that by the strain on your face." The doctor began his assessment and midway through the sheriff came around the curtain.

"There is no coffee. Not like Maggs not to have a pot of coffee on."

He was looking to Thad for an answer. He wanted to say she got her bloomers in a bind and hadn't been in the house all day but his southern upbringing wouldn't allow him.

"I think she got a late start this morning and things just went south from there." The sheriff nodded and pulled up a chair. They had some serious things to discuss.

The doctor stopped the sheriff before he could even start his inquiry.

"Let the boy get cleaned up a bit. At least let him dress." The doc produced a pair of trousers and a denim shirt.

"Hope they fit, hard to tell just how big or small a man is when he is lying in bed."

He assisted Thad as he dressed. It took both the doc and the sheriff to complete the task. When it was completed Thad felt humiliated and a little woozy. He supposed it was going from sitting to standing that produced the sway or maybe the lack of food.

"Could I sit in a chair for a while? I think I would feel a heap better if I could do that."

The sheriff gave up his seat and Thad's dizzy head cleared.

"Do you normally wear a beard Sheridan?" Thad rubbed his furry face and shook his head no. He didn't mind a day or two growth but this was too much. The doctor pulled a razor from his bag doused it with alcohol and handed it to the sheriff. Between the two of them Thad had a good shave.

"Suppose you tell us your story and let's start with that scar." The sheriff was pointing the razor at Thad's face and it made him a little nervous.

"This," he ran his finger down the painful reminder. "This was compliments of a Confederate soldier."

"You a Yankee?" Doc Lapp looked stunned.

"Not exactly."

"Meaning what?" Doc's tone was harsh.

Thad kicked his legs out to stretch them. "Pardon me but if you'll not interrupt I'll tell you what you need to know." They both agreed and Thad exhaled a long breath.

"I grew up in Charleston, South Carolina. My father owned a very profitable lumbermill and I grew up on a plantation. When I was of age I was sent to Boston to study law. During my time at school the War between the States broke out. I chose to stay in Boston. Needless to say, my father was not pleased with my decision to stay. He was further angered when I became a Yankee soldier. I am not going to discuss politics with you fellows but I'll let you know why I went against everything I knew. I never liked slavery and found the union political platform was better suited to my beliefs. I did what I felt was the right thing to do." The men looked at one another then back to Thad. They wanted more.

"After the war I had no place to go. My father had disowned me so my law degree was never completed. I could not go back home." He eyed them. "I had disgraced the Sheridan name and had forsaken the great South. I stayed in the army for a while until I took a job with the Texas Rangers. Six months ago, I quit the rangers. I have become tired of fighting."

The sheriff stood and poured himself a glass of water. "I thought your name sounded familiar, looked through all my wanted posters. I was sure you'd be on one. Just so happens I came across a case file of a prisoner that was temporarily jailed here about a year ago. The arresting officer was TJ Sheridan, Texas Ranger. You've brought some pretty rough characters to justice."

"Yes, sir, and I have the scars to prove it."

"If I was a betting man, I'd say you got some people after you. Maybe those three who tried to rope Spotted Hawk?" Thad didn't answer, his eyes were looking out the window. Was Merry crying?

"Liddy, surely you don't believe that?"

"All I am saying, Maggie, is the talk in town is that Lone Eagle is seen around your property very often and you do not seem to discourage him. I know there is nothing going on and I know he is your friend but the people in town do not know you like we do. The sheriff, Ezekiel and Pastor Gray just think you shouldn't give them reason to talk."

Maggie's heart pounded. No one understood her bond with Lone Eagle and Spotted Hawk. How do you tell people you can trust a Sioux? People can make friends with others different than themselves. This would be contrary to the people of Rudolph they hadn't wanted to be her friend since she arrived many years ago. What did they know and when did she ever care what they thought?

"Oh, but it is okay to have a strange man holding up in my house. That makes a lot of sense." By this time, Maggie's hands were flailing. She felt the warmth of tears forming in her eyes. She always tried to do the right thing and it seemed to always bring her trouble. She wanted to rail at her friend but knew she could not. Liddy was too kind of a soul and did not deserve her wrath. The two men in the house, however, was another story.

Spotting Tommy coming down the lane his small hands trying to carry his plunder broke Maggie's tension. "He is a keeper, that one there." She motioned and Liddy turned her head with a smile.

"Yes, he is."

"Tommy, you did a good job. These are big and beautiful. Did you have a good time?"

"Oh . . . y-y-yes, M-Miss Quinn. Loads."

"I know you don't like fish Tommy but would you like to eat supper with us. I will have other things too." He shook his head and his smile took up his whole face. You run home and ask your Mamma. If you don't come back, I'll know she needs you home." The boy went trotting through the pasture to his own home.

Supper, she had better do some preparing. She hadn't been in the house all day and she was expected to cook for three hungry men. The spirit checked her. One of those men had not had anything to eat since last evening.

She entered her own home but felt like she was intruding. Laughter coming from behind the curtain annoyed her. She began banging pots and pans and the odor of the fish flushed the men out.

"Anything we can do to help you Maggie?" the doctor asked.

"As if you could do anything but make coffee Ezekiel Lapp." Mrs. Lapp was playfully scolding him. They were always so much fun to watch. Sometimes they flirted like newlyweds. Sometimes they fought like the old married couple they were. It was the only marriage Maggie had ever witnessed. It seemed a lot of hard work but it had its rewards.

Doc Lapp surprised his wife by slapping her backside as he went out the door. Her face flushed more in embarrassment then anger. His chuckle was heard all the way to his wagon. The sheriff had a grin on his face as well.

"Dan Bullock, go arrest that man for assaulting a good woman, Liddy demanded.

"Keep me out of this, Liddy." He rubbed his chin. "Can't say as I blame him."

Thad listened behind the curtain. That conversation would have never taken place in the plantation parlor. He never saw his folks so much as kiss on the cheek. It would appear his parents' marriage was one of convenience. It was the only view of marriage he had ever seen.

He smiled to himself. If his father had slapped his mother's backside he'd been out on his, Hester his mother's slave, would have seen to that. She put up with no shenanigans as far as Mrs. Sheridan was concerned. She was a very devoted friend.

Thad shook his head to dispel the memories of his parents. He hadn't seen them in years. He wasn't even sure if they were still alive. He had written Abby but the letters came back to him. He smiled at the thought of his Abby. He missed her friendship.

The smell of fried fish and biscuits baking made Thad's mouth water and his stomach growl. He knew hunger and had gone without meals longer than one day but in all the times he was hungry during the war he was never tempted by the smell of something cooking just outside his reach. He wondered if he would be allowed to eat tonight. He chuckled to himself as he recalled the look on her face when he moved to stand. He was trying to get her attention, he reckoned he did and also got her furry.

"Sheridan, you think you can make it to the table with a little help?" The doctor peered behind the curtain. "That is, if you're hungry."

Was the man kidding? He would have crawled to the table. Thad braced himself and made it to his feet. Still a bit dizzy but he wasn't letting on. He had tasted those biscuits and he had thought about them all day.

Maggie was in for a surprise. The man that came around the curtain was not the man she had heaved into her house a few nights ago. This man was . . . was . . . clean. No, that wasn't the right word. This man was striking. His hair was neatly combed, his face clean shaven. The denim shirt only set off his eyes. Maggie wasn't the only one gaping at him. Liddy was surveying him as well. It was the sound of the doctor clearing his throat that brought his wife back to the here and now.

Maggie scrambled to put the food on the table. Only Tommy continued to stare. Taking in the scene Thad was amazed at the flurry of activity in the woman's wake. He looked at Tommy stuck out his hand and introduced himself.

"Hello, I'm Thad." Tommy's hand came out and Thad's swallowed it up. Tommy was speechless.

"Are you Tommy the great fisherman I have heard about?" Tommy's head bobbed up and down a shy smile on his face. "Smells pretty good, doesn't it?" Thad was talking to Tommy like he was the only one in the room and Tommy was eating it up.

After dinner and a few cookies, Tommy was sent home before dark. He didn't need to know that Thad was staying in Maggie's house. She told him she wouldn't need him tomorrow and she would see him Sunday at church.

The sheriff left also and it wasn't much later Maggie and Thad were left alone. "Would you like another cup of coffee Mr. Sheridan?" She was beginning to feel the effects of her temper and felt sorry she had not feed him breakfast or lunch.

"No Merry, I think I will head to bed, supper was delightful. Thank you."

"Mr. Sheridan, I am sorry about today." Those eyes caressed her face. She could feel them. They felt like cool water on her overheated face. He just nodded.

The next morning Maggie was up early. She put coffee on and gathered the eggs. She made a big breakfast to make up for yesterday and Thad ate heartily. She also set bread to rise and with a basket set out to pick some berries for a pie.

She had a lot of work to do around the farm but she couldn't do any of it until Thad Sheridan was safely out of her house. The doctor said last night Thad could be moved to he and Liddy's house by tomorrow. What a relief that would be, to both of them to be sure. She expected it to be awkward in the house with him but for some reason it had not. He had an air or grace about him she had not witnessed in a man.

Thad was pretty proud of himself. He was able to pull his pants on with minimal pain. The shirt was giving him some trouble. He was only able to button it about half way and he couldn't get it all the way tucked in. He thought if he could sit at the table and prop his bad arm on the table he could finish the buttons. He had stood up, got his bearings and limped to the edge of the curtain.

When he opened the curtain, he was met with the sourest face he had ever seen. A woman with a slender build, yellow gray hair braided in a crown around her head stood with eyes wide.

"I am looking for Maggie." The shock on her face was enough to make Thad howl with laughter but he knew this spelled trouble for Merry so he refrained.

"She stepped out for a moment. Is there something I can do for you?"

"Oh, no, just tell her I stopped by."

"All right, and your name, Miss?" Thad asked appropriately. The woman seemed a little put out as if Thad should have known who she was.

"I am Mrs. Elmer McPherson, coproprietor of the Rudolph General Store." Her hawkish nose went up in the air and she left swiftly.

"Good day, Mrs. McPherson. I'll tell Merry you stopped by."

"Was Liddy here? I thought I heard a woman's voice."

Thad rubbed his jaw. "A Mrs. Elmer McPherson was here to see you."

Maggie's eyes slid shut. It was all that needed to happen. The town's moral compass had just witnessed a man in Maggie Quinn's home. Her eyes opened and she took in his half-buttoned shirt hanging loose about his waist. It was more than Maggie could take. She turned to the sink and her head went down and her shoulders slumped. Thad stood behind her.

"Merry, I'm sorry."

Why did her name spilling out of his mouth seem to soothe her? His hand rested on her shoulder. She whipped her head up and pumped some water into a kettle.

"What is done is done. We can expect a visit from the preacher and the sheriff before long. If I know Zelma she will go right to pastor Gray." She turned and unconsciously, as if cleaning up a mess, buttoned up the rest of Thad's shirt.

Maggie washed the raspberries she picked and started on her pie crust. She was nervous and baking always seemed to settle her down. She had helped Thad onto the front porch. When he was settled with his Bible and Gus by his side she stepped back into the house.

She dusted, beat the rugs, put fresh sheets on both beds anything to take her mind off the conversation she knew was headed her way. It was late afternoon when Pastor Gray made his way up the steps.

"Good day, sir." He put out a hand to Thad.

"Good afternoon." Thad tried to stand without help but he had sat too long and struggled to get out of the rocker.

The pastor motioned. "Please don't get up, Mr. Sheridan." The pastor took the seat next to Thad. "Sure is a beautiful day."

Maggie heard all the small talk going on and she just wanted to get it over with. He is probably here to ban her from the church without knowing the facts. With the talk about Lone Eagle being circulated, she was sure this conversation was not going to be to her benefit.

She fixed some lemonade and put cookies on a tray and walked confidently onto the porch. Both men started to stand.

"Don't trouble yourself." She served the lemonade and cookies.

"Best cookies around, Mr. Sheridan, best cookies."

This was maddening. Why didn't he just get to the point?

"You'll need a couple more glasses, Maggie. Doc Lapp and Sheriff Bullock are on their way."

Thad took a drink of the Lemonade and was almost choked by the sour bitter taste. Merry had forgotten the sugar, or was she trying to get rid of her company. He drank the liquid as if it was the thirst quencher it was meant to be keeping one eye on the pastor. As Maggie went through the door to retrieve more glasses, the pastor went to the railing and spit. Thad kept hold of his glass and continued to drink as if nothing was wrong.

Doctor Lapp and Sheriff Bullock positioned themselves on the porch. Dan leaned on the door frame and Ezekiel sat on the railing.

"Maggie, the reason we are here—"

She cut Pastor Gray off. "We all know why you're here. Zelma McPherson has jumped to conclusions. Surely you have talked to Doc and he has told you what's been going on."

"Yes, I know what has happened and believe me, Maggie, I know of your innocence . . ." There was a pause and Thad knew the "but" was coming. "But in light of some other issues surrounding you, people would question your character. Your reputation gets a little more tarnished with each incident."

Maggie knew this was hard for Pastor Gray. She truly liked and respected him but right now her hurt and anger overrode her sympathy.

"What am I supposed to do? You know Zelma would not believe a word I say. She forms her own opinions and ideas. You remember, Doc, when Lone Eagle's woman died giving birth to Spotted Hawk and I kept the baby for a time the awful things she said, not only about me but about the baby."

Now Thad was getting angry. What kind of town doesn't stand behind someone like Merry?

"Don't get all upset, Maggie." The doctor had come to stand beside her. He lifted her chin and looked her in the eye. "The Lord will make a way." His words were comforting but she really didn't care what the town's people thought of her anymore. Each time something happened she became more bitter toward them.

The conversation for the next thirty minutes centered on the best way to salvage Maggie's reputation. There were several options on the table. All had plausible appeal but seemed lacking. Maggie kept insisting she did not care what others thought but the three men knew better and were thinking of her.

"You've remained awful quiet Mr. Sheridan." Pastor Gray had drawn him out from his silent reverie.

"Marry me."

There was dead silence except for the rocking chair Thad was sitting in and the thud of Gus' tale. Thad looked to Merry. Her mouth was open lips formed to speak but nothing would come out. After a pause three yeses and one loud *No* echoed off the porch. When she finally found her tongue, it was definitely unbridled.

"Are you all out of your minds? This is the most absurd suggestion. Don't you see that will confirm exactly what Zelma thinks she saw?" Maggie felt this was obvious and couldn't believe the conversation was happening.

"Now wait. This might work," the sheriff said.

"No!" Maggie replied but no one was listening.

"It all hinges on what response you gave to Zelma this morning, Pastor."

"No!" she tried again. It was if she wasn't on the porch and she was sure they wished she was not.

She wasn't about to leave nor let them dictate her life in such a high-handed way.

"It's a funny thing, now that you mention it, my response was very vague. I first encouraged her not to be a busy body in others matters." This was met with more than one chuckle by the men. "Then I simply said Maggie's life was her own and if she wanted to share any news with the town she would do so in her own time. I don't know what caused me to say it in just that way. I was rather taken aback by her accusations and wanted to give Maggie the full benefit of the doubt. Zelma kind of looked at me strangely but let it drop."

"I call that divine intervention pastor, divine intervention," the sheriff crowed.

"No, are you listening to me? I said no!"

"Maggs."

"Don't 'Maggs' me, Ezekiel Lapp! This whole thing is absurd and you know it. There is no reason for this. I will simply tell the church what happened and they can believe me or not." The sheriff moved to stand in front of her.

"So, you are going to tell them Lone Eagle dropped this man at your door step one evening with two gunshot wounds and a raging fever. You brought him into your house dressed his wounds which would be questionable. Then you waited until morning to summon me or the doc."

Maggie's eyes flamed "Well, I wouldn't tell it in such a vulgar way."

"No but they will form their own story." Doc added.

"Maggie, we are only thinking of you and your reputation."

She turned to Thad. "Why would you offer such a thing?"

Thad shifted in the chair so he could see her face. "I got you into this mess, Merry. I would like to make it right."

"But it's *not* right! You don't just up and marry someone for the sake of reputation." When he looked at her this time it was as if the others on the porch had faded into the dusk.

"It's called integrity."

This was her undoing. She promptly turned on her heals and stormed through the cabin and out the backdoor letting it slam behind her.

She heard footsteps coming up behind her. "I will not go through with it." She didn't care who stood behind her. It was her closest friend Dr. Lapp.

"Maggie, when your grandfather passed on I made a promise to him that I would look out for you but I see you working so hard every day without any help and I feel like I have failed my old friend."

"I get by just fine," she spoke through a broken whisper.

"Getting by was not what your grandfather wanted for you. It is not what I want for you."

"Oh, but you want me to marry a man I know nothing about, nor do you, I might add."

"I know enough Merry Margret. I know he will work hard and treat you well and in time will come to love you." His arm was around her shoulder. "He could help you make a go of this farm, repair some things you haven't been able to get to."

"So I marry him for what I can get out of him?"

"No, marry him because it is the right thing to do."

While Doc Lapp was talking with Maggie the sheriff thought he ought to give Thad some words of advice.

"You sure about this Sheridan?" The sheriff's face was very stern. Lawman to lawman he understood intimidation and its uses but there was no need for it now. It got Thad's hackles up but he cooled down quickly his face never giving his anger away.

"I'm sure."

"That girl has had a rough way to go probably more than any of us know." Thad nodded. "You better understand one thing. You marry her you get the Indian."

Thad had not expected this. His head shot up.

"Uh huh, thought that would get your attention."

"What do you mean by that?"

Lone Eagle has made himself Maggie's protector. I am not sure he is going to give that up."

"I see. Why is that, Sheriff?"

"You'll have to discuss that with your wife, if Doc can talk her into it. Never knew Doc Lapp not to be able to talk a body into doing what was best for it."

"What if he is already married? I have heard of some men having more than one wife in different places." Her mind flashed to the picture in his haversack and the watch inscription.

"What makes you think he is married?" the doctor asked.

Maggie countered with "What makes you think he isn't?" Her chin went up.

"I asked him," was Doc's reply.

"Oh, and you just believe a stranger?"

"Everything the man has told us has checked out as the truth."

"Well, he has a sweetheart somewhere I know that for sure."

"That may be the case but he must be willing to put that aside." Yes, Maggie thought it will be easy for him to put her aside too after a short while. She didn't know if she should be glad or sad.

It made perfect sense. They could marry he could stay until he was back on his feet, then leave. Her reputation would be saved and things could go back to normal. She would no longer be Old Maid Quinn but the woman whose husband left her. Either way she was going to be ridiculed or pitied depending on the personal character of the one deciding.

"What do you say, Maggs?" Doctor Lapp squeezed her shoulder.

"I'll do it for you, Doc."

"I was hoping you would do it for you."

"I have something to say," Maggie announced when she reached the kitchen, the doctor following behind with a look that said what Maggie herself was about to say. The men had moved to sit at the table.

"I will marry you, Thad Sheridan, and I thank you for your kindness."

"Merry, I—"

She stopped him. "There will be some conditions and understandings before we make it official."

He knew what was coming and knew there would be no negotiating any terms. He put his hand out and motioned for her to continue. "When you are back on your feet you will be free to leave. You can just walk away whenever you wish and I will sign any papers annulling this marriage, understood?"

Yes, he understood. He understood that day would never come. He also understood he could not tell her that right now.

Pastor Gray stood before Merry Margret Quinn and Thaddeus James Sheridan and pronounced them husband and wife. The "until death do you part" phrase stuck in Merry's mind. She silently asked the Lord to forgive her and promised to honor the marriage even after Thad's departure.

"You may now kiss the bride." Surely he was kidding. Merry's face showed her astonishment.

"It is part of the official ceremony." The pastor smiled.

Dan and Ezekiel were having a hard time hiding their mirth. Thad was having none of it. He gently raised the hand of his wife to his lips and kissed it. There was only kindness in his eyes as they met hers. She pulled her hand away gently, as if she would break some magic spell. This was her wedding day and yet this was not her wedding day. She had stowed away many dreams of how this day would be. Marrying in a field of golden clover just as the sun was setting. The sun was setting somewhere behind a thick covering of clouds. The skies threatened to open up at any time. Her heart felt the same, dark, gloomy and ready to dump the tears that she no longer could contain.

"We better get a move on if we want to beat the storm back to town," the ready sheriff spoke and all three men said their good-byes.

"I hope we did the right thing," the pastor spoke to his two companions.

The doctor turned and headed back in the house. "Thad, I want to see you in my office day after tomorrow. Maggie, you come too. It will do well for the town's people to see you two together. I will have the pastor tell Zelma the man was your new husband. By next Sunday the town will all know and you should be able to attend church with Maggie, Thad." The couple agreed and the doctor left. "It is all going to work out," he told the others.

Merry fixed supper and for some time they ate in silence. Thad wanted his wife to be his friend but her emotions were so raw right now he didn't know how to approach her. He always went for the straightest shot but women were different creatures. He didn't have to make a move because Merry was eying him and spoke first.

"What will Abby say about your marriage?"

Where did that come from? Thad wondered. He had not spoken of his sister, had he? He thought back. "I think she will understand."

Merry frowned. "Must be an incredible woman." She forked some potatoes into her mouth. She bet Abby would not be as understanding as he thought.

"I think so," he replied.

Her head shot up and it dawned on Thad that Merry did not realize Abby was his sister but had gotten the idea Abby was a sweetheart of his. Now, what to do with that information? Should he tell her or let her go on believing it? He decided he would answer her questions honestly but not come right out and tell her who Abby was.

"If you want to write her we could mail it Monday."

"You think I should?" He was goading her and it probably wasn't a wise thing to do but he couldn't help it.

"I guess you could keep it from her but you should at least let her know you are okay."

"Probably should do that." The conversation was over and so was the meal. As he drank his coffee in silence Merry washed the dishes. When she was finished, she turned and asked if he needed help to his room. He said he could make it and she headed up the ladder to the loft.

Merry set on the side of the bed. There was so much to take in. Everything happened so fast. A few short days ago, the man sleeping below was dumped into her life and she was now married to him. She knew women who came out west as mail order brides. She always felt those women were desperate to be married so they took the only offer they could. Had she been desperate? Desperate to save her reputation, desperate to please a town that really didn't care for her.

She began to brush her hair. She couldn't describe exactly how she was feeling. Guilty was about the closest she could come. She was married to a man who was loved by another woman for the sake of integrity. She asked herself again, what kind of man does that?

Thad stayed up and read his Bible for a while. He had been thinking about the story of Ruth. His sister loved the book. "Oh, Thad, it is the greatest love story I ever read," she would gush. He would tease her about it from time to time but tonight he saw something in it beyond a great romantic story. The stories focus for him had been shifted from Ruth's good fortune to that of Boaz. Boaz might have let Ruth have a handful of purpose but in the end Boaz received the handful of purpose when he became part of Christ lineage. Thad had been given his own handful of purpose sleeping above him and he was going to make sure good came from this marriage.

The next morning the smell of coffee woke Merry up. At first, she thought she was dreaming but she caught a whiff of something else. Was that ham she smelled? She quickly dressed remembering she was no longer the sole person living in the house. When she reached the ground floor Thad greeted her with a smile.

"Good morning Merry, coffee?" he poured a cup and handed it to her. In all her adult years, she had never had a man wait on her like this. She eyed him suspiciously.

"You don't have to wait on me, Mister . . ."She started to call him Mr. Sheridan but somehow the look he gave her made her think better of it. "Thad."

"I know that, Merry. I was up and there was no reason why I couldn't start some breakfast."

She looked at him with a frown. "Well, you're doing it all wrong. Just sit down."

"I beg your pardon?" He wasn't moving. There was not one thing wrong with what he was doing. She just had her back up.

"I said you're doing it all wrong." She pushed past him and looked at the perfectly cooking ham.

"The skillet is too big."

"What? The skillet is fine. I plan on cooking the eggs right next to the ham in the same skillet."

"You can't do that."

"Oh, I can't? Watch me." He cracked the eggs with one hand and dropped them beside the ham. The popping and cracking sealed the eggs fate and when they were just right he flipped them over. In a few minutes, he had breakfast cooked.

He stood behind her reaching around her he put the plate in front of her. "Your breakfast, my lady." If she cared to admit it, it smelled wonderful and she didn't have to cook it. He brought over some bread he had heated in the same skillet. It had a nice crispness to it, he spread butter and jam on a piece and laid it to the side of her plate. Without asking he took her hand and said grace over the meal.

The feel of his hand slightly, softly griping hers brought back the thought and feel of his lips atop her hand last evening as they said their vows. She let the warmth wash over her. It felt good, so why was she in such a foul mood. When he said amen he removed his hand and began to eat.

"Do you always make such strong coffee?" Why was she treating his kindness with such venom? She didn't know.

"Are you always this cheery in the morning?" Thad could tell that was the wrong thing to say. "There is nothing wrong with the way I am in the mornings."

"Well then have I done something to rile you Merry?"

Why did he always have to use her name like that, like a blanket around her on a cold night? Her ears loved hearing it. Her mind had to put a stop to it.

"You taking over my kitchen riles me. You taking over my house riles me. Your presence here riles me." If she thought she would surprise or hurt him his face didn't show it. He did look at her until she bent her head to finish eating.

"I suspected as much," he said. "Since my presence here isn't going to change anytime soon we should come to some type of agreement about how things are going to work." He paused and she looked up. Her cheeks were full of the "awful" breakfast he had fixed. He wanted to laugh at her but knew better.

"I will stay out of your kitchen, but until I can be outside working I would like to help you inside. I feel I need to earn my keep."

"Just keep your bed made and stay out of my way." She downed her "too strong" coffee and started to wash the dishes. Thad moved to the curtain to make his bed.

Thad had an idea. He grabbed his Bible and went in search of his wife. It was Sunday and since they couldn't go to Church yet he wondered if Merry might like to read and study the Bible together. He hoped it would lift her mood, except he couldn't find her. She was not on the back porch or the front. There was a small sitting room just near the front door but she wasn't in there.

Using the cane the doctor brought for him he worked his way off the porch and out into the blazing sun. It felt good to be out. He headed to the barn to look for Merry. Once inside the barn he noticed his horse in one of the stalls. He just assumed the horse was either part of the Sioux stock or gone for good. The black beauty recognized her long-time companion and began to prance in the stall.

"Hello there, girl. Somebody has been taking good care of you." The horse whinnied and stuck her nose into Thad's upturned hand. Sensing he was not alone in the barn, and from years of experience, his gut told him it was Lone Eagle.

"I figured you would have kept her." He said referring to the horse.

"Good horse flesh but one man horse." The man responded.

"Thank you for seeing to her."

"Not me. Spotted Hawk and Morning Dove have been taking care of her."

Thad turned to face the Indian. "I wanted to thank you for not leaving me out there in the brush."

The Indian relaxed a bit. "You put my son before your life; I thank you. You warrior?" Lone Eagle pointed to the scar on Thad's face. Thad weighed his options on how to answer.

"I have battled," he spoke.

The Indian grinned. "You battle in there?" he pointed to the house.

"Yes, I battle in there."

The Indian exited the barn.

Merry rose from her bed. She hadn't planned on falling asleep. She just meant to lie down, and get out of the foul mood. The position of the sun told her it was past noon. Thad was probably hungry and after the way she lashed out at him, he probably was afraid to go into the kitchen.

When she reached the downstairs, he was not in the kitchen. She heard his voice on the front porch. He was combing Gus and carrying on quite the conversation with the animal. The screen door squeaked as she made her way onto the porch. He smiled and she returned it. Gus made his way over to her for some attention.

"I don't think he is my dog anymore. You have won him over. He even sleeps under your bed." She said scratching the dog's ears. "Traitor," she scolded the dog.

"Who is Morning Dove?" Thad innocently asked. Lone Eagle said Spotted Hawk and Morning Dove had been seeing to his horse. He knew Spotted Hawk's mother was dead. Maybe Morning Dove was a daughter or new wife. The silence prompted him to look at his wife. She cleared her throat.

"Why do you ask?"

"Lone Eagle said his son and Morning Dove had been taking care of my horse Grace."

She looked a little panicked and the palm of her hand went to push back the hair from her forehead. He knew immediately that Merry was Morning Dove.

"W-w-was Lone Eagle here?" Her eyes scanned the horizon.

"Yes, Morning Dove, he was."

She blanched then turned red. "It's not what you think," she spat.

"We haven't been married long enough for you to know what I think, Merry." He resumed brushing Gus, but his irritation was evident. Gus left the porch as did Merry.

He didn't handle that very well. He told himself he would find a way to work through the Lone Eagle situation if he only knew what the situation was. He had been Merry's protector but why? This went against every grain of the Indian and white man relationship. He was thinking about this after dinner.

He had just finished off the raspberry pie and was drinking his coffee. Lost in his own thoughts he didn't see the storm cloud brewing in Merry's eyes. Mistaking his stillness for the longing of Abby's companionship instead of her own she blurted out what was on her mind.

"You should write to Abby so we can mail it tomorrow." His eyes met hers.

"You think I should write to Abby, do you?"

"Well, of course. At least so she will know you are okay. You don't have to tell her everything. Although I would think she should have the right to know what's going on and what your plans are."

My plans, he thought to himself. Maybe you would like to know my plans Merry Margret Sheridan. He liked the thought of that and would love the sound of it if he could only say it aloud.

"I'll tell you what Merry, I will write to Abby and tell her my plans and you can talk to Lone Eagle and tell him your plans."

He waited for the tongue lashing but it never came. Instead with tears in her eyes she quietly spoke.

"You don't understand. No one does."

He rose from his chair to kneel in front of her. He lifted her chin, so they were eye level.

"Make me understand." His soft plea did funny things to her stomach. It was like butterflies had been set loose and they were taking their flight stealing her breath.

She darted nearly tripping as she ran out of the house. Thad was left on his knees. He hadn't meant to hurt her. He took advantage of his position and began to pray. He didn't know how long he had been praying but the sound of the rocking chair told him Merry was on the front porch. Through the screen door he saw her profile. He didn't go out on the porch but through the screen he made his apology.

"I'm sorry, Merry." He saw her head nod and he took himself off to bed.

Chapter Three

Conversation about the day's schedule was done over breakfast. Thad was to see Dr. Lapp and even though it was not her regular shopping day Merry was to accompany him. Dr. Lapp was adamant about that, as was Pastor Gray. She did look forward to tea with Liddy.

She had a pencil and paper out making a list of what she needed.

"Did you want to add something to the list?" she asked Thad. He had stood to get more coffee and leaned over her shoulder to look at the list.

"I need a razor and a few more clothes. If you want to put that on the list, you can but I think I can remember."

He was too near her. She did not like people in her space.

"Something wrong?" he asked noticing the all too familiar hand to forehead.

"You're in my space, I don't like it." Her voice had a hint of exasperation.

"Bother you, does it?" he had a measure of glee in his tone that did not sit well with Merry and he did not move. She turned her sternest, coldest look toward him. Before she could, he spoke first. "Merry love, in such a small dwelling from time to time I will be in your space. I suggest you get used to it."

He picked up the pencil an under the list entitled Merry's List he wrote "space" and under Thad's list he wrote "patience." She made no remark as she went to finish the morning chores before they left for town.

Thad had managed to hitch up the team. If he held his arm and leg just right the pain was bearable.

"You are doing too much, Doc's not going to like it," Merry said as she put her shopping basket in the back of the wagon.

She had a pretty dress on. Thad thought. It was light blue with tiny white flowers. Her hair was pulled up but hung down in the back. She had a straw hat with yellow flowers perched on her head. He would have told her how nice she looked but he was sure it wouldn't go over well.

"Did you hear me?" she asked as she came to help him finish.

"I'm a grown man Merry, or haven't you noticed?"

She'd noticed and so would the women in town. She wished the doc would have left the razor for Thad. He had a scruff on his face that reeked of manliness. She dreaded the trip to town.

He knew better than to take the reins. He couldn't just walk into her life and take over all the things a man should do when she had been doing them for so many years that would be unfair. He did however sit as close to her as possible, just to get in her 'space'. He rested his left leg on the side of the wagon.

"How long of a trip to town?"

"About twenty minutes."

"Does he always follow you into town?" Her body tensed, Thad could feel it. She followed his eyes to the ridge where an Indian trotted along. She turned in the seat.

"Oh, Gus. He usually goes a little ways then turns around." Who was she fooling, certainly not him and not herself but she was in hopes it would work.

Thad let out a large laugh, threw his hand up and waved to Lone Eagle. Lone Eagle waved and turned the horse around and disappeared over the ridge. Thad made up his mind Lone Eagle was not going to ruin every day of his life. Sometime Merry would have to open up about the man.

Doc Lapps office was empty when the Sheridans arrived, Thad was ushered in and Merry went to find Liddy.

"Well, don't you look pretty. I haven't seen you wear that dress in a long time." Liddy hugged her friend. "Married life agrees with you I have never witnessed such a glow on you."

Merry eyed her friend to see if she was making a joke or if she was serious. It was not like Liddy to be cruel.

"I mean it Maggie you look wonderful."

Merry removed her hat. "Are you terribly busy today, Liddy?" Her voice sounded like a child's clamoring for a mother's attention.

"Oh, no. Come, let me make some tea and we can visit and you can tell me what's on your mind." A rich deep laughter came from the office and Merry wanted to scream 'that's what's on my mind' she couldn't bear the thought of Thad and the doctor's laughter being induced at her expense. She was being too emotional and on the verge of paranoia. Liddy looked toward the office and smiled.

"So how are you and Thad getting along?"

How would she answer that? She wasn't sure how they were getting along. She was downright hateful at times and he didn't fight fair. He wasn't going to be pushed around yet he countered every one of her moods with some form of kindness, more of his integrity she reckoned. She did not know how to handle him. She hadn't realized the tears were streaming down her face. Liddy rushed to her taking her into open arms.

"Oh, sweet Maggie, it will be okay." Liddy pulled back to see Merry's eyes. "He isn't hurting you, is he?" Liddy didn't think Thad was that type but she had to ask.

Merry's head shook through a veiled whisper, "He's so kind."

It was this scene Thad and the doctor encountered. Thad had an immediate lump in his throat. So much he couldn't speak, Liddy looked at her husband and shewed the men away with a smile. Thad couldn't move. Doc grabbed his shoulders and pushed him out the door.

"Best let the womenfolk work this out. She's fine, son, just needs her mama."

Thad trusted the doctor but he also couldn't imagine what he had done to cause her tears at least to cause them at this particular time.

"You go on and do your shopping. Maggie will find you when she's ready."

His mind racing, he tried to walk slowly around town. His thoughts were drawn to a similar scene when his sister had her first crush. He had found Abby in the arms of his mother. Mother had shewed him out in much the same manner. She told him later Abby was experiencing one of those times in life when love did not make sense. He found great comfort in the memory.

The town wasn't very big and it did not take long to walk all over it. He reached McPherson's mercantile. He wished there was another store in town. He didn't care for Zelma McPherson and didn't care to give her any of his hard-earned cash. The doctor had told him he could do whatever his body would allow and for him to be the judge. The steps of the mercantile looked a little steep so it took some extra effort to get his left leg up.

Outside the store stood a group of females window shopping. He didn't mean to listen in but the young women were talking rather loudly.

"Did you all hear Old Maid Maggie got married?" A somewhat attractive girl had her hands on her hips, head in the air as if she knew more than the others.

"Yes, Iris, we all know that. Can you just imagine what *he* looks like?"

"I know, I know," a short redhead was laughing as she spoke. "Probably eighty years old, missing a couple teeth, and three feet shorter than her." The group all laughed.

The one called Iris spoke again "I am surprised anyone would have her."

Suddenly the group noticed Thad and boy did they notice Thad. Eyes batted, smiles were coy, hair was tossed and a handkerchief was dropped. He had experienced it all before. In his younger days, a woman like Iris would have been right up his alley. Not anymore. *When I was child, I did childish things,* he mused.

He was livid at how they had talked about Merry. He picked up the handkerchief like a gentleman and handed it to the redhead. "Ma'am," he said as he entered the store. The entourage followed at what they thought was an inconspicuous pace. He overheard the proprietor tell a customer that Mrs. McPherson was home with a headache. Good he thought, she deserved it.

Thad moved around the store the girls following him. Every so often they would try to make small talk or ask him to hand something down from the top shelf. He could hardly get his own shopping done.

He had gotten his razor and a cup. Picked out a couple of shirts and pants, and picked up or asked for everything on Merry's list.

"Mighty strange concoctions of things you're purchasing there." Mr. McPherson was just as annoying as his wife. Thad just looked at him. He noticed all female eyes were on him.

"I am certain my wife will add a few more things when she gets here." There was a collective hard sigh from the women in the store.

"You folks new in town?"

"You might say that."

Merry braced herself as she entered the door of the mercantile. She had already spotted Iris Shoemaker and Ellen Grigsby and she knew Laura and Leah Myer were sure to be lurking around the store. As soon as she walked in, Thad turned and smiled.

"Honey, I think I have got everything on your list but you better come double check."

Merry made her way over to the counter. Thad's arm rested on the small of her back, placing her just in front of him. He kept his hands on her as she looked into the box. She couldn't think. His hands were firm and warm on her back. His face was just next to hers. He smelled of sandalwood. Her head was swimming.

He leaned in and whispered in her ear, "I'm having a hard time finding that space you wanted." She blushed and everyone saw it.

"Yes, you got everything." Her voice was a little higher pitched then normal. No one but Thad noticed.

"McPherson, can someone take this to my wagon? I would like to take my wife to lunch."

"Certainly, I will have Peter take them."

"Thank you, and good day." Keeping his hand on Merry's back he escorted his wife past the staring female crowd. "Ladies." He tipped his hat and Merry nodded. Once outside, he took hold of her hand as he led the way to the café.

"Seat yourselves," the waitress shouted from behind the counter.

Merry moved to a table in the center of the room. Thad grabbed her hand and led her to a table in the corner. The chairs were situated very close. *He is pushing this space issue too far.*

He pulled her chair out and helped her get seated.

"Did you and Liddy have a nice visit?"

"You didn't have to do that."

He looked at her in puzzlement. "Do what?"

"What you did in the mercantile."

"What is it you think I did?"

"Make our situation look honest."

"What?" his voice was a little louder than intended but their situation was honest. What had she conjured up in that hard head of hers? The conversation was temporarily halted as the waitress approached with two cups of coffee.

"Do you know what you want to eat?"

Thad was furious and tried to contain his emotions. He deferred to Merry her eyes focused on the sheet in front of her.

"I'll have the special," she said. Thad nodded his choice as well and the waitress was gone.

"What makes you think our situation is anything but honest Merry?"

"I just meant you put up a front to save face and you didn't have to."

"I didn't behave any differently than any other husband trying to please his wife." His tone was unpleasant.

He sighed, took a deep breath and reined in his anger. "Did you and Liddy have a nice visit?" he thought he would try and start over.

"I wasn't crying over something you did if that is what you are wondering?" Why was she making this so difficult. He wanted to snatch her up and haul her home. He remembered what he had written under *Thad's list*. "I am having a hard time finding the last thing on my list as well, Merry Sheridan." The rest of the meal was eaten in cold silence and the ride home didn't warm up any.

Tommy showed up just after breakfast. He smiled when he saw Thad.

"Hello, Tommy." Thad opened the door to let him in. The boy's face lit up at the sight of Thad. Animals and kids had always been his specialty.

"Is M-M-Miss Q-Quinn home?"

"She is, come on in. How about some breakfast?" Tommy nodded and Thad got him a plate and a glass of milk. The boy ate like he hadn't had anything for weeks.

Merry came down the ladder from the loft "Good morning Tommy and how are you this fine day?"

Thad would like to hear that kind of greeting in the morning. Tommy's mouth was too full to speak. Merry messed his hair and sat down across from him.

"Tommy, I was going to shod the horses today, you want to help me?" Thad asked. The boy took a swig of milk to wash down his pancakes.

"Y-yes, s-sir."

"Okay, come out to the barn when you're done, you don't have to hurry."

Tommy was enamored with Thad. Merry had only met Tommy's father briefly. He was very quiet and seemed introverted. Tommy's mother was very sweet and didn't seem to mind Tommy spending time at Merry's. He will be spending even more time now with Thad around. It will break Tommy's heart when he leaves and Merry will be there to pick up the pieces.

Tommy made a beeline, out to the barn. "Ever shoe horses before?" Tommy's head went side to side.

"Nothing to it once you learn, but you have to be very careful. You must do everything I say so you me and the horses stay safe, you understand?" Tommy nodded again. Thad wished Tommy would understand his stuttering didn't bother him. He wished the boy would talk.

After they shod the horses they put them in the corral and mucked out the stalls.

"You're a good worker, Tommy. I bet you're a big help to your pa."

Tommy tilted his head and looked at Thad. "My P-P-Pa cries sometimes."

"I reckon most men do that sometimes, done it myself." Thad was careful not to make light of what the boy was saying.

"S-S-Sometimes he makes M-M-Ma and m-me get in the cellar." This caused alarm in Thad. He kept silent and let the boy talk. "H-He hears things. H-He has sc-scars like you."

It was starting to make sense to Thad. "Your pa in the war?"

"Yea, be-before I c-c-came along."

"Well, Tommy, sometimes war does things to a man. He sees a lot of sad things. Has to do a lot of things that is not in his nature. Think your pa could use a friend?"

Tommy ran to Thad and hugged him around the waist. This was a picture that would be embedded in Merry's mind as she walked toward the barn to get the two for lunch.

"Tommy lunch is on the table why don't you go in and wash up." The boy did as he was told.

"What was that all about?" she asked Thad turning back to watch Tommy run to the house and race up the stairs.

"What do you know about Tommy's folks?" Thad was walking to the pump. He leaned underneath the cool water and drenched his head and washed his neck. He swung his head to get the hair out of his face and washed his hands. Running his hands through his hair he looked to Merry for an answer.

"Uh, not much, Melissa is very nice. Hank keeps to himself. I have met him once or twice."

"Think we could invite them over for supper sometime soon?"

"Sure." She felt herself wanting to put her arms around his waist as Tommy had but the realization that he would eventually leave tugged at her mind. He headed to the house and she followed.

Thad walked Tommy home that night. Listening patiently as the boy told him all about his room and toys at home. Melissa Haskett was taking clothes off the line when they approached. Tommy raced to his mother.

"Th-This is Thad."

"Hello, Mrs. Haskett I am Thad Sheridan, Merry Margret's husband. Tommy's mouth dropped open and Thad winked at him.

"I had no idea Maggie was . . ." She had no more words.

"We recently got married."

"Well, congratulations."

"Thank you. Tommy here is a great help to us, if you don't mind we would like for him to keep helping out if you and your husband can spare him. I will pay him."

"Oh, he loves Maggie, and her cookies, that's pay enough."

"No, cookies are a bonus."

Mr. Haskett came from the barn. Slow steps brought him to Thad.

"Honey, this is Thad Sheridan, he and Maggie were recently married." The man stuck out his shaking hand "Nice to meet you."

"Thank you, I was just saying what a great worker Tommy is and if you can spare him I would like to have his help. I would pay him." Tommy's father's head was shaking like his hand. The man drank, Thad would bet his last dollar on that.

"He is a good boy, he can work for you when you need him. I don't want him getting in your way though, understand, boy?" He speared Tommy with a look.

"Yes, s-sir."

"Merry and I would like for you to come to supper Thursday." Mrs. Haskett looked at her husband. She was so much younger than she appeared. Years of worry were etched in what was once a beautiful face.

"Hank?" There was an urging in her voice encouraging him to pay attention to the request.

"Be obliged, Sheridan."

"All right. Tommy, I will see you tomorrow and we will see you all Thursday."

Early Thursday morning Thad went hunting. He wanted to put a good meal on the table for the Hasketts. He felt he could help Hank but it would be a slow process. Sitting up against a tree, waiting for some game he began to pray.

He was humbled at what the Lord had done for him, delivering him from a wretched life. He wasn't worthy of God's love yet it was bestowed upon him through the acceptance of Jesus Christ. A lump formed in his throat, that a man would give his life to save him was more than he could comprehend but he tried. He tried every day to please his master.

He wasn't worthy of Merry's love either though he desperately wanted it. He would learn to be content with the Lords will. He prayed silently that he would be whatever the Lord needed him to be for Merry. Two rabbits suddenly sprang from their hiding and dinner was served.

The Hasketts arrived promptly at six. Tommy had his Sunday best on and his hair all slicked back. This was the first time the family had been invited anywhere for supper in years.

"What a good-looking family has come for supper tonight, Merry." Thad said as he opened the door. "It's Hank and Melissa Haskett but I'm not sure who this handsome young man is with them."

Merry joined him at the door. She put one hand on her hip and one finger tapped her jaw. "Hello sir, are you visiting the Hasketts?" Tommy's face was full of delight. His big blue eyes shone like Merry had never seen.

"I-It's me, Tommy."

"Well, so it is." Merry turned to Thad. "Have you ever seen a more handsome man?"

"Every day in the mirror, but I reckon he'd be a close second?" He winked at Tommy and Merry punched Thad in the arm. There was gentle laughter as the Hasketts were welcomed into the Sheridan home.

Merry fixed a hearty meal. Rabbit and potatoes, beans and corn from the garden. Homemade bread with jam Melissa had brought. The two rabbits were completely gone. There wasn't left one scrap for Gus who wasn't the least bit happy so Tommy took him out to play.

After supper coffee was served and conversation revolved around crops and weather. Thad noticed Hank slowly withdrawing from the conversation. His eyes darted around the room as if he was looking for something. Melissa gently touched her husband's arm.

"Hank, would you like more coffee?"

The rapid eye movement continued. He had not heard his wife but looked right at her. She tried to hide her fear but it was impossible. Suddenly Hank stood up, knocked over his chair and went to the kitchen window. Standing just to the side and peering out he ordered the men to get into position.

He busted out the kitchen window and Melissa screamed. Merry silently looked to Thad. "Melissa," he whispered. "What rank was your husband in the army?"

She looked at Thad with a blank look. "Sergeant," she mouthed.

Thad stood. "Sergeant Haskett, dismiss your men immediately the enemy has retreated."

Thad's voice rang out as a commanding officer. Merry had a shocked look on her face and Melissa was in tears. Hank Haskett suddenly came to himself. When he saw the destruction and Melissa in tears, he knew his mind had left him again for another place and time.

"Let's go for a walk, Hank." Thad put his hand on Hank's shoulder and the two went out the back door. Merry's eyes never left her husband the integrity he had must be as big as the Dakota Territory. She envied his ability to discern how and when to use it.

Melissa Haskett had her head in her hands. The shaking of her shoulders told Merry she was still crying. Merry put her arms around the woman and held her in a comforting embrace.

"I'm sorry, Merry, we ruined your evening."

"Nonsense. It was a lovely evening, Hank didn't know what he was doing, that was obvious. Melissa, he is sick and it couldn't be helped." Melissa couldn't say anything, she was too overcome.

The women cleaned up the kitchen and by the time they were done the men were back.

"I think we better be going Melissa it's getting dark. Mrs. Sheridan I apologize."

"For what Mr. Haskett? I don't know of one thing you need to apologize for it was a lovely evening and I hope we can do it again sometime."

He nodded and did something outside of his nature he kissed Merry on the cheek. His eyes had a mist about them when he turned to his wife. "Where is our boy?"

Tommy was curled up on the porch sound a sleep with his head resting on Gus. In the dimming light, Merry could see wet streaks on the boy's cheeks. Hank lifted his son and carried him to the wagon. It was obvious he had witnessed the whole scene. When he laid him in the wagon Hank Haskett wept like a baby. Thad closed the door and Melissa drove her husband home in tears. Thad quietly went to his room and Merry to hers.

The next day Thad was not himself. His mind was preoccupied with Hank Haskett and how he might help the man. He wanted to talk to Doctor Lapp but that would have to wait until Sunday. He and Merry were to have Sunday dinner with the Lapps after church. He would do what he could for Hank but he wasn't sure how much good it would do. War did strange things to a man. Merry was quiet too. He could tell the evening had taken a toll on her as well. The vision of the grown man crying over the sleeping boy had almost been Thad's undoing. He couldn't imagine what it would do to a woman's caring heart.

He stopped working for a minute to look for his wife. He spotted her in the garden bent over hoeing. She appeared to love her garden. He watched for a while enjoying the sight of her and thought about what it might be like to just hold her.

Suddenly she raised the hoe and brought it down with a mighty force. The snake didn't have a chance. She got rid of the garden intruder and turned to a prairie dog that was scooting out of her way "and that's what will happen to you if you try to get into my garden too mister." The prairie dog waddled away and disappeared into the nearest hole. It made Thad rethink his previous thought about holding her. She caught him staring and shrugged her shoulders. He laughed and she smiled. How little they knew about one another and it was if Merry didn't care to know anything about him. He would have to work on that.

It was unusually warm for this time of year and working under the blazing sun could be draining. Thad was working on the barn roof. He and Hank were going to repair and reinforce the structure starting Monday so he wanted to have it in shape to be worked on. He had removed his shirt and climbed on top the barn. His arm still ached a little but he pulled and tugged to remove the damaged boards.

The sun was high above his head and he knew it was close to noon and thought about lunch. Suddenly he had a brilliant idea. He went down the ladder and headed toward the clothesline where Merry had just hung up the last article. He should put his shirt back on but frankly he was tired of treating his wife like she wasn't his wife.

Merry saw him headed her way. His gait was easy so she knew nothing was wrong.

"Hot out here today."

She shaded her eyes with her hand, partly to block the sun but partly to block the view of her very handsome husband. "Sure is, wonder if it will be like this all summer?"

"Let's take the afternoon off, go to Tommy's fishing hole and get cooled off. Maybe take some lunch."

Merry's heart was beating out of her chest. She stood silent for a moment her mind in a muddle. She wanted to go but every time they were alone they either fought or her heart got a little more involved.

The silence was killing him. He wasn't an amateur at wooing the fairer sex but Merry was different. He would try anyway. He ran his hand down her arm and clasped her hand pulling her toward him.

"Come on Merry. I want to get to know you." She found herself mere inches from him and it was hard to find her words.

"Your heart and eyes are saying yes." He said in a knowing tone. "Won't be long until the head agrees." How could she say no to that?

"All right, you win," she said as she went to move but he still had her hand in his. He raised her hand and kissed it like he did on their wedding day and released her. "I did win," he said to himself. He pulled a clean dry shirt off the line and hitched up the team.

When they reached the creek bed Thad helped her out of the wagon. She felt awkward at having to be helped out but knew it was what a gentleman was supposed to do. She moved to stand under a big shade tree.

"Here?"

He shook his head no and went a little farther down. "Let's cross here and go over under those big trees." He grabbed the picnic basket in one hand and Merry's in the other. He maneuvered them across some stones in the creek to the other side.

Two trees had bent toward one another making a canopy. "This is a perfect spot," he said as he placed the basket down. Merry turned her face up to survey the tree's her eyes closed and a cool breeze whipped at her hair. It was refreshing from the hot sun.

"I brought my Bible Merry, would you mind reading it together before we eat."

"I would love it." Thad saw a smile he hadn't seen before and was thankful reading the word pleased her so much.

She bent down and removed her shoes and stockings. Sitting at the creeks edge she plunged her feet in. "Oh, that's colder than I thought." Thad followed suit, and for the next forty-five minutes they read passages in the book of John and discussed them. They nearly forgot about the food until Merry's stomach growled. They moved in under the trees and Merry brought the food out.

"Would you like some lemonade?" Merry asked without looking Thad's way. "Don't worry, I remembered the sugar this time. I can't believe you drank that and never said a word." They both had a good laugh.

After they ate almost everything packed, they sat back in comfortable silence.

"Merry, tell me about yourself." Thinking there was not much to tell she didn't know what to say. His eyes were perusing her face wanting something from her.

"My father died when I was just a baby. My mother never really got over it and ended up not mentally being able to care for me. I lived with my uncle until he sent me out here to live with my grandfather. I was about nine or ten and I grew up in the cabin, that's pretty much it."

Thad saw a hurt and a longing in her eyes. It almost killed him. He just wanted to crush her in his embrace and tell her he wanted her even if she felt like no one else did.

"What about you?"

He sighed. "Grew up in the South. My father sent me to law school back East. When the war broke out I joined the army. The Union army." He chanced a look at her. Her face was in total surprise. "Yeah, I bet that's the look that was on my parents face when they heard. I guess I was a traitor but I just felt that slavery should end."

"You must have had been raised in a strong Christian home, surely your parents understood."

"Well, that's where you would be wrong. I wasn't raised in a Christian home I was raised in a rich, prideful plantation home and what I did disgraced the family."

The look of surprised was back on her face.

"After the war I stayed in the Army for a while then took a job with the Texas Rangers."

Merry released a pent-up sigh.

"That was a heavy sigh." He looked at her for an explanation.

"I was just thinking about the scars all over your . . ." She paused and her face flushed. She pointed. "That scar, it . . . I . . . well . . ." He let her stammer on. She usually didn't have any trouble speaking her mind. "Well it just explains a lot," she said, frustrated. "I wondered for a while if you were an outlaw, it's good to know you're not."

"I am no outlaw Merry but I'm no angel either. I have had to do a lot of things I'm not proud of."

He stretched back and pulled his hat down over his eyes.

"Will you return to the Texas Rangers?" he eyed her from beneath the hat.

"No, I gave that up. It was time to settle down."

"Oh, Abby," she said it so softly he barely heard her but hear her he did. He pretended not to.

The gentle flowing of the creek played like soft music and Thad found himself lost in the sound. The cool breeze beckoned him to close his eyes. Before long his breath evened out and Merry knew he was asleep.

She watched him for a while, looking at his chest rise and fall. He was a pretty fast healer. It wasn't that long ago he was nearly dead on her doorstep and look at him now. *Yes, look at him. No, don't look at him,* she told herself but her eyes did not follow the command.

She looked at his face half hidden by the hat. His strong jaw and chin relaxed in slumber. His muscular lengthy frame stretched out in peacefulness. Soon he would be gone, back to Abby but he would take her heart with him. The realization stung her pride and tears welled up inside of her. She stretched out beside him and willed herself not to cry. She clinched her eyes shut so tight in an effort to remove him from her mind but it wasn't working. Everything about him filled her thoughts.

Something tickled Thad's face and his shoulder was beginning to hurt. He had dozed off. It didn't take him long to understand why his shoulder hurt or what woke him up. Merry was sound asleep nestled nicely right up against him.

Her head was resting on his shoulder and her hair was in his face. There was no way on earth he was moving from this spot. He laid there quietly as not to disturb her. This felt so right. He was pretty certain she hadn't intended to fall asleep, and when she woke up she'd be red from her neck to her forehead.

With an abrupt movement, Merry sat straight up. Thad did not move. He kept his eyes closed. He did not want to cause Merry embarrassment and he certainly didn't want to hinder anything like this from happening again.

She looked down at him, he could feel it then he heard her leave the blanket and begin cleaning up. He propped himself up and smiled.

"Guess I was pretty tired. Not much company this afternoon. Sorry, Merry." He stretched and yawned then rose to help her clean things up. She didn't say two words on the way home.

Sunday's were a quandary for Merry. She loved church and worshiping but she didn't like going to church with some hypocrites. Pastor Gray had encouraged her to attend church for the Lord and no one else. Some Sundays it was a challenge. Today would be her first service with Thad. She wasn't sure how the church would treat her new husband.

Thad was speaking to her but she didn't hear him. His back was to her so he didn't realize her mind was elsewhere. After a few seconds of silence, he turned. "Do these baskets need to go into the wagon?"

"I don't know how they will treat you?" She said words rushing out.

"Well, let's go find out, shall we?"

"If your leg is bothering you we don't have to go."

"One thing you should have figure out about me is I don't back down from a challenge." He motioned with his hat to the door. She didn't move.

"Merry I will throw you over my shoulder and carry you to the wagon if you don't get a move on." Her eyes went wide in anger.

"Care to challenge me?" He raised his eyebrows and took a step toward her.

She marched by him. "You are a bully, Thad Sheridan." He laughed out loud, smacking her backside with his hat as she went by. She didn't dare turn around because a smile tugged at her lips.

Pastor Gray greeted them at the church entrance. Those who normally sought Merry out made their way over to congratulate the couple. The handful that gave her the most grief stood in a clump whispering.

Thad's hand that ushered her in the church remained at the small of her back as they entered the pew. Once they were seated his arm went around her resting on the back of the pew. How many

Sundays had she looked out over the crowd of couples and dreamed of being in this spot. She would cherish this feeling even if it was only for a few months. No one could take the memories of Thad from her. Not even Thad.

Thad was pleased with the church service. He enjoyed the message and gained some insight into the scripture. The people, for most part seemed welcoming. There was a cluster of people he wouldn't waste his time worrying about. He hoped Merry wasn't dwelling on their looks.

After the service, Pastor Gray announced the recent marriage of Merry Margret Quinn to Thad Sheridan and welcomed them into the church. Thad noticed Peter McPherson, son of Zelma and Elmer, whispering to a young man beside him. Thad knew the comment made was about his wife. Thad didn't take kindly to what he saw. Prayer was given and church was dismissed.

Outside the church the newlyweds were further congratulated. Some of the children had commandeered his wife's time so Thad went to ready the wagon. Walking past the side of the church he heard Peter McPherson's voice.

"Oh, Mag the Hag finally got hitched."

"Yeah," another voice chimed in "Merry MOO-gret found a man to marry."

"I thought she belonged to that ole Indian."

Thad was livid!

"Hey, you guys better hush, her husband, did you see him. He looks like an outlaw. I wouldn't want him riled up."

Smart boy, Thad thought.

"I'm not afraid of him," Pete replied. Thad was just about ready to break up the ring when he heard Sheriff Bullock calling him.

"Sheridan, would you like to do a little target practicing with me and the doc before dinner."

"Doc a sharp shooter?" Thad asked.

"Listen, boy, he is the second best shot around. You just wait. You have a gun with you?"

"Never go anywhere without it."

"What's Merry think about that?"

"Don't know that she knows, don't know that she would care." His tone was a little more edgy than what he intended.

"Little gal not warming up to you." The sheriff clapped Thad on the back as they headed toward the wagon.

"I wouldn't say that, I think there has been a couple of days we didn't clash. Which one of you said she had a head like a rock?"

The sheriff grinned "Could have been either one of us, I figured you to be a faster worker."

"I'm not discouraged, I see a glimmer of the real woman Merry is every now and then."

"See much of Lone Eagle?" The sheriff's curiosity had gotten the better of him.

"He's around" was all Thad said.

"Say, Sheriff, do any of the boys come to the target practice?"

"They come but they are not allowed to participate, what's on your mind Sheridan?" The sheriff knew mischief when he saw it.

"Just thought Peter McPherson may want to watch today, you care if I ask him?" The sheriff sized up Thad with one eye closed.

"You get your gun and Peter can show you where we shoot."

Thad went to tell Merry where he was going and pulled his gun from under the wagon seat. She had no idea it was there and stared as he strapped it around his waist and headed in the opposite direction to McPherson Mercantile.

Thad approached Peter who was sitting on the front steps whittling. "Peter, do you know where the doctor and sheriff target practice at?"

The boy eyed Thad's gun and recalled what one of the boys said earlier. "Sure, it's just past Doc's to the right about one hundred yards."

"Would you like to join us?" The boy's face lit up.

"Yeah," he hollered into the side door and told his parents where he was going. Didn't ask, just *told* them. The boy needed taken down a notch and that was about to happen.

The doctor shot first and was really good. All six shots were within a half inch of the center of the target. The sheriff's aim was equally as good in fact a little better. His shots were within a quarter inch of the target. Thad took his turn. Standing stock still he fired off the six bullets each one following the previous one through the center of the target.

The next few minutes were spent giving Thad different challenges. He shot a stone the sheriff threw up in the air and kept it from hitting the ground with the next five shots. They timed his draw response. Peter stood watching pretty sure Maggie's new husband was an outlaw.

Thad was wiping off his gun as he headed toward Peter.

"That's really good shootin. How'd ya learn to do all that?"

"Years of practice," Thad responded. "Say, Peter, you seem like a smart man. Will you do me a favor?"

Peter became all puffed up with pride at being called a man. "Certainly."

"Word has gotten to me that some of the boys around town have been referring to my wife in an unkindly manner, having nicknames for her." Peter's face went ashen. Thad lifted his gun into the sunlight to inspect his cleaning job.

"Can you see to it that stops *today*?" Peter could only nod. Thad returned the gesture and headed back to the sheriff. Shaky legs took Peter back to his whittling.

"It is about time you men got here. If that chicken is cold I don't want to hear any complaining, Zeke Lapp." If there was one thing Lydia Lapp couldn't abide, it was a ruined meal.

"Liddy, have I ever complained about one of your meals?" She started to speak but he was correct. Early in their marriage she burned everything and never a word from her husband.

"The town of Rudolph has a new sharp shooter. Maggie, this man of yours can handle a gun better than any I've seen," the sheriff declared.

"I would hope so," she said rather abruptly, considering the fact he was a Texas Ranger.

Both the Lapps frowned at their Maggie. What had gotten into her? Thad took it all in stride.

"Something sure smells good, Mrs. Lapp."

"Now you call me Liddy, Thad, and have a seat over there by Merry." He took his seat next to his wife. When they all were seated, Doc Lapp bowed his head to offer up the prayer. Thad reached for Merry's hand that was resting in her lap. He always did that when there was a prayer. Why did he feel the need to do that? When the prayer ended, he did not release her hand but rested the entangled fingers on his thigh. It wasn't until he was asked to pass something that he relinquished the hold. He was maddening. Why did he insist on doing those little things?

The sheriff had to make some rounds leaving just after dessert was served. Thad and Zeke had moved into the sitting room. Thad took this opportunity to discuss Hank Haskett.

The women had cleaned up the kitchen and were discussing recipes over a cup of tea.

"I am a little disappointed in the way you treat Thad, Maggie," Liddy said as she poured the boiling water over the tea leaves. Merry's face never lifted.

"No man likes to be cut down in front of other men by his wife." Merry's look was defiant now as she reached for the milk. "Mark my words Maggie, if you don't start being nice to that man he is going to leave."

Sadness had settled in Merry's eyes. "Either way, he is going to leave, what difference does it make?"

What makes you think he is going to leave?"

"Abby," it was barely a whisper.

"Who?"

Merry relayed the whole story to Liddy. "I know, Liddy, as soon as she writes back he'll be gone. His obligation was fulfilled today and as soon as he feels like he has paid me back, that will be the end."

"So, Merry Margret Sheridan is going to build up a huge wall and insulate herself from love, right? If I don't get involved, I won't get hurt?"

"It's not like that. I don't want to keep him from the woman he loves and I don't want his pity."

"No, you would rather have your own pity." Liddy was harsh but she felt that was what Merry needed to hear. It was obvious Thad

had feelings for his wife, and with a little encouragement from Merry, the marriage would work.

"Have you thought about giving him some reasons to stay, if he is in fact thinking about leaving? Maybe do a little fighting for his love."

Merry had lain awake all night thinking about that love, rather it would work or not. She had decided to prepare herself the best way she knew how for his departure. Maybe she had gone about it all wrong but she had to keep distance between her heart and her head even with Liddy's disapproval. She took her tea into the doctor's waiting room and curled up on the couch. She soon found the sleep that eluded her the night before.

On the way home, Merry asked about what doc thought might help the Hasketts. Thad told her of his conversation and by befriending the Hasketts doc thought they were on the right track. There was no medicine to help ease the man's mind.

Out of nowhere she blurted "Liddy was upset with the way I treated you today. She thinks I was disrespectful to you especially being there were other men around."

Was that supposed to be some form of apology? He wasn't sure.

"I've been dressed down in front of a whole platoon by generals. I reckon a misspoken word by Merry Sheridan won't devastate me."

"So you think I was rude?" she asked flatly.

He should choose his words carefully. "Since I am not given to lying, I guess I would have to say you were a little on the rude side."

"I am sorry," she spoke.

"Did you apologize to Liddy? She seems more offended than me."

She looked at his profile. "No, I was so tired I went to sleep. I will talk with here the next time I am in town."

Chapter Four

For the next few weeks, the Hasketts and the Sheridans spent a lot of time together. After the barn roof was finished, Hank offered to help out some more and the house also got a new roof. One of those days Tommy had spent helping Merry bake cookies. He was a much more animated boy than before and she credited it to Hank feeling better and Thad's playful attention.

They were just finishing up when Thad entered.

"Tommy, I am sending you and your dad home. It's a good day to fish and picnic."

Tommy almost jumped out of his skin with excitement.

"Maybe Merry can send along some of those cookies you just made."

"What a great idea. Hank if you will give me a minute I will fix up a basket for you all so Melissa won't have to."

"She'd appreciate it." He smiled. She loaded him down with food.

"Careful of the Lemonade, sometimes she forgets the sugar." Thad winked at Merry.

"There's sugar in it. Tommy can testify to that."

"Come on son, let's go surprise your ma."

Thad went to the sink to wash his hands and snag a cookie. The pastor was right 'best cookies around'.

"Tommy tells me that Peter has told the kids to stop referring to me as Mag the Hag and Merry MOO-gret. Says my outlaw husband threatened them."

Thad was smiling around the cookie.

"I never threatened anyone. I just ask Peter to see that it stopped."

"This isn't funny, why can't you stay out of my business." She was extremely outraged.

"I didn't realize it would upset you so but I am not sorry I did it. There's a way to handle such situations. By putting Peter in charge of seeing the behavior stops, I know it will stop."

"But Peter is the main offender."

"Exactly, you cut the head off the snake and the snake dies."

"And you didn't think I knew how to handle the situation? Well I did I ignored it because it doesn't bother me." She was yelling.

"Well it bothers me." His voice was louder than normal.

He was getting his belly full of her ill-timed tongue lashings. He calmed himself down as she moved about the kitchen gathering a basket and her hat.

"Going in to town?" he asked in a much calmer manner.

"Yes, and I don't need any company and I don't need you to protect me." Venom pure venom dripped from her lips.

"No, I suppose you don't. You have Lone Eagle for that." Cold, the room was cold as he hard footed left the house. It wasn't long until she heard Grace exit the corral at a lightning pace.

Thad couldn't remember when he had been this angry. He let Grace have her head and she took off. They headed for the prairie at full speed. He didn't notice the other horse until it passed him on the ridge. Lone Eagle and his palomino flew past, he motioned with his hand and Thad and Grace gave chase. He knew there was very little chance his horse could win but he heeled her on.

Lone Eagle slowed his mount when Thad approached and he did the same.

"Only one thing make a man ride a horse like that." Lone Eagle was staring at Thad

"And what would that be?"

"Woman." Lone Eagle showed a full set of white teeth with his smile.

Thad chuckled.

"Morning Dove hard woman to understand."

"Aren't all women?" Thad asked and the big Indian grunted.

They rode a little farther before either spoke. "Spotted Hawk is eager to meet man who saved his life. Wishes to understand white man's way of learning. Wants to read and write." Thad was astonished at the admission.

"Morning Dove say she teach him but he not interested until you come to live with her."

"I'm sure Merry's offer still stands."

"What do you say?"

"Fine idea."

"Come to my encampment." Lone Eagle nudged his horse down an incline and Thad followed.

"How did you and Merry become . . ." What were they? He wasn't sure how to ask the question. He didn't have to.

"Morning Dove was out in field working when Yellow Flower time came. It was too early and we were trying to get home. Yellow Flower fell from horse and Morning Dove came to help. Took Yellow Flower to house and tended to her. Late in night she sent Grandfather for doctor. Too much blood. Morning Dove delivered Spotted Hawk but Yellow Flower spirit gone. Spotted Hawk more Morning Dove child than Yellow Flower."

Thad said nothing, just listened to the Indian. It explained the relationship. He was not prepared for Lone Eagle's next statement.

"Lone Eagle love Morning Dove, want for wife. Your people and my people make impossible."

"I see," Thad said.

So that's the way it was between his wife and Lone Eagle. Lone Eagle sensed Thad's ire.

"You only hear half." The Indian jerked Grace's reins to get Thad to look at him.

"I said Lone Eagle love Morning Dove. Did not say Morning Dove love Lone Eagle." At that point, the Indian rode ahead into the village.

Spotted Hawk came to take the horses. He removed the saddle and groomed the animals. When he was done, he would be introduced to Thad. After some very strong coffee and conversation, Spotted Hawk joined them.

Several Indian women had come close speaking in the Lakota tongue. Thad looked to Lone Eagle.

"They say your eyes that of night wolf. This is true. I call you 'Night Wolf'.

Thad gave Spotted Hawk his promise they would teach him to read and write and anything else he wished to learn.

It was well into the evening when Thad returned home. Merry had just arrived home shortly before he did. She had placed his mail on the table. The lovely script that had addressed the letter had to be that of Abby. This is what she had dreaded. Why was she so mean to him this morning? Why did she drive him away at every turn? She looked at the letter, that's why she said to herself.

Thad entered and treated Merry as if nothing had happened. He was even humming.

"Did you have a good day?" he asked as Gus came from under the table to catch some of Thad's attention. "Hey, boy."

"You have some mail there on the table." Thad looked at the table but made no move to retrieve the letter. He was scratching Gus' belly. The dog would let him do that all night. Why isn't he opening the letter?

"What's going on in town, anything exciting?"

Why the small talk, just open the thing her mind raced. She was reminded of something Liddy had said today "Merry, do you not see that Thad always puts your needs before his. He cares more about what is going on with you then what he is doing?" he was doing that right now, asking about her day.

"Nothing new in town. Liddy has a summer cold. She is hoping to be rid of it before the celebration on the fourth."

"What goes on at the celebration?" Thad looked like he really cared.

"Everybody gets dressed up and we eat together. There are games for the kids. Contest for the adults. A dance."

"What kind of contest?"

"Baking mostly for the women, best pie, best cake, things like that. For the men, there are ax throwing, log sawing, and sharp shooting."

"Sounds like something I would enjoy, looking forward to it."

Not after you read the letter, you'll be gone as quick as you can she thought to herself.

"Come on Gus, let's go outside and get you brushed." Thad rose and the dog followed.

"Don't you want to read your letter?" She handed it to him.

On the front porch after Gus had been tended to Thad opened his letter from Abby. He had been a little afraid of what she might have to say. The last letter he received from his mother had not been all that kind.

Dearest Thad,

How splendid to hear from you. I must say I was afraid you were dead. It sounds as if you have the beginnings of a wonderful life in Dakota. So someone finally snagged my handsome big brother. Many of hearts are breaking all over the South at the news. She must be quite the woman to slow you down. I look forward to meeting her sometime. I don't know how much you know about the family. Papa died about five years ago. I tried to find you but letters just kept coming back. Mama is getting a little more feeble each year but her mind is still sharp. I think sometimes she mourns more for you than for papa. I am married to Jackson Lorton now and you have two nieces Anna Beth is five and Patience is three. Believe me we named her correctly because she has tried mine. Jackson and I are going to be close to Dakota Territory July 1 and 2, would love to see you. I will bring a few things of yours with me just in case you're able to come. We are staying in Denver.

All My Love,
Abby

Denver was about a two-day ride from here. The date was June 28. He would have to leave first thing in the morning if he was going to make the trip. He had to make the trip. He needed to see his sister. He also needed to tie up some loose ends and Denver was just the place to do it.

He went back into the house. Merry was headed up the ladder to her loft.

"Merry, I need to leave first thing tomorrow."

Here it comes, the conversation she knew would happen and the time she had dreaded. She stepped down into the kitchen.

"The letter was from Abby, I take it."

"Yes, would you like to read it?" He held it out to her. She saw "All my love, Abby" at the bottom and she had seen enough.

"No, I don't need to read it," she said.

He folded the letter and put it on the table.

"I promise I will be back for the celebration."

Sure he would, with annulment papers. "What time you figuring on leaving in the morning?"

"I will take care of the animals before I go."

"Tommy's coming tomorrow. We can take care of the outside chores, don't worry about that."

He smiled at her. He was happy, she could tell. His eyes were sparkling.

"Good night then," Merry said as she went up to the loft. Her heart was so heavy she felt it was making the climb up the ladder impossible.

Thad was up early moving around downstairs. Merry had been up for hours trying to shake her blue mood. She didn't want the last thing Thad to see was her mope around. She fixed a big breakfast and as he saddled Grace she packed some food for his journey. He came back in to get his saddle bags and she walked out with him.

"I made you some food." She handed him the sack stuffed with food.

"Cookies?" He smiled.

She smiled back. "Of course."

"Cinnamon and sugar?" These were Thad's absolute favorites.

"Would I dare put any other kind in there?"

"You're a peach," he said as he fixed the bag to his saddle.

She stepped to the bottom step of the porch. It brought her eye level with her husband. She kissed him on the cheek. Her hands went around his neck in a tight grip and her head lay pressed against his shoulder.

What was this? Thad wondered as his arms pulled her as close to him as he could. She pulled away and kissed his cheek again and went running into the house. His first inkling was to go in after her, but somehow he knew he should not. He promised himself when he returned he would make many opportunities for Merry to be in his arms.

As he was riding out he passed Tommy on the road.

"Tommy, you look after Merry. I am going to be gone a few days but I will be back before the Fourth of July celebration." Tommy said he would and patted Grace's head before Thad was off again. Lone Eagle was perched on the ridge. He watched until Thad was out of sight.

Thad thought about what the Indian had said. He loved Merry. How does a man deal with another man being in love with his wife? Did she love him? After this morning's good-bye, he would say no. Merry did not love Lone Eagle. Merry genuinely seemed upset that Thad was leaving.

When Merry was sure Thad was gone, she hitched up the wagon. She needed to see Liddy. She decided to take Tommy with her so after seeking permission from Melissa, she and Tommy headed to town.

"Where is Thad going?"

"I don't know, Tommy." He looked at her kind of strange.

"Tommy, I'm not sure he will be back." Again, a strange look covered his face.

"He'll b-b-be b-back, h-he s-said s-so."

"You talked with him?"

"Saw h-him on th-the r-road, s-said he'd b-be back b-b-by the fourth."

She let the conversation drop. *So help me, Thad Sheridan, if you lied to that boy*, she thought to herself and pushed the horse a little faster.

"W-Why d-d-does the Indian h-hang a-around s-s-so much?" He pointed to Lone Eagle who was heading his horse toward her. Tommy grabbed her arm.

"Don't be frightened, Lone Eagle is my friend." Tommy's grasp relaxed.

"Where is Night Wolf off to so fast?" The Indian handed her a container full of honey.

"Night Wolf, how did he get that name?"

"Lakota women say he has eyes like night wolf. They very fond of husband. Say he make good brave." When did the Lakota women see her husband? She felt what could only be jealousy of a group of women giving her Thad the name of Night Wolf.

"I don't know, he didn't say. Just that he had to leave."

"He return, he warrior." He flicked Tommy a piece of buffalo jerked meat and was on his way. Tommy chewed the meat and found it very tasty. "W-What did he mean h-he a w-warrior?"

She wished she knew.

Tears spilled down Merry's face when she told Liddy Thad was gone.

"What? Surely not for good." Merry just nodded and continued to cry.

"I don't believe it. Did he say he wasn't coming back?" Merry choked back another sob.

"He said he'd be back for the fourth, but he will see Abby again and he won't be able to leave her, not a second time."

"Nonsense. If he said he was coming back he will come back."

"No Liddy we fought terribly the day before he left. I told him I didn't need him to protect me."

"Oh, Maggie, no!"

"He said he supposed I was right because that job belonged to Lone Eagle."

Liddy sunk in the chair.

"Maggie, I have warned you about your relationship with Lone Eagle. Does he know the full story?" Merry was crying beyond the point of reason but Liddy saw her head shake indicating the answer as no. Liddy just held Merry. After a while the tears became occasional gulps and she had calmed down some. Liddy made some chamomile tea to help sooth Merry's raw nerves.

She and Tommy stayed for supper. It was a very blue Mrs. Sheridan that crawled into her husband's empty bed that night. She could not stand the thought of him being gone so she snuggled down into the pillow, hoping it would comfort her and she could feel his nearness. The smell of his shaving soap was on the pillow and she turned her face into it. She thought about what life would be without him and she didn't know how she would live through it.

July second the women of the community met to prepare for the upcoming Fourth of July festivities. Several people commented to Liddy on Merry's lack of enthusiasm and somber mood. No one knew Thad was gone.

"I bet she's expecting, some women get with child first thing, it will be hard on her at her age." Liddy just smiled. She knew better.

"She just isn't herself, something must be bothering her," another one commented.

"She is fine, ladies, she and Thad just work too hard."

"Not getting any younger," someone thought they should add.

It was a clear case of pinning away.

Liddy had instructed Merry that when Thad returned she had better change her ways, rein in her tongue and pay him some attention. Merry promised *if* Thad returned she would do just that. She was certain the only communication she would have with Thad Sheridan would be in the form of legal papers.

Every lamp in the house was burning when Thad drove up in the new wagon he had bought on his way back from Denver. He had purchased a new horse as well. Grace didn't like being tied to the back of the wagon and let Thad know about it every inch of the way home. At first, he thought something was wrong, then he spotted Merry's silhouette at the stove and the smell of something baking coming from the cabin.

Gus followed him to the barn where he fed and cared for the horses. He partially unloaded the wagon. Abby had brought him some things from their childhood home, some things that belonged to his Father. His Mother had sent some things too, things for Merry.

It was a very surprised woman that stood in his kitchen, flour on her face and hands and stray hairs surrounded her face that had come loose from their clip. What a sight. He had missed her. There were cookies everywhere. Cookies on the table, cookies on the bed.

"'You're back," she croaked out.

"I said I would be back for the fourth." He smiled at her and his eyes traipsed a slow path from her head to her toe and back up again. Her hand went to her forehead to push the hair back.

"I must look a mess." He was about to tell her how good she looked and his arms ached to hold her but she had moved on.

"I bet you're hungry, let me get you something to eat. How was the trip? Everything go okay?" She just wouldn't stop moving or talking.

"I could eat, that's for sure and for certain." He had started to pick up some of Merry's Irish ways.

She set a plate in front of him and poured some coffee.

"What? No cookies."

She passed a whole plate his way.

"I bought some things on my way home from Denver. I bought a new wagon. The one we have now isn't going to hold out much longer." She looked surprised

"You're not going to fret over the money, are you? I had some savings tucked away."

No mention of Abby or how things went.

"I have some things for you too." He went out onto the porch and came back with three packages.

"These are for you. This one," he handed her a big package wrapped with twine, "is from Abby."

Her fingers stopped playing with the twine and her head dipped just a bit. Thad lifted her chin with his curled index finger.

"My sister."

Merry lost her breath. Right there she stopped breathing. Her chest was so tight she was sure her heart was going to cease beating.

"I know I should have told you, but you are such a stubborn, hardheaded woman that I just let you think what you wanted. So go ahead and give me the tongue lashing I deserve."

She was so overjoyed that Abby was his sister she couldn't contain her joy.

"Well, when you put it that way, it takes all the fun out of it."

She started to open the package and immediately saw it was unmentionables.

"Oh." She shut the package back. "I will look at these upstairs." The blush on her face was enough to stop Thad from making the comment that was on the tip of his tongue.

"This is from me."

She opened the small box and found a set of hair combs and a bottle of cologne.

"The combs are beautiful and the cologne smells . . . expensive."

"Abby tells me it is French perfume and it is all she wears. I know you have lavender water you use and I am not insinuating you smell or anything. I just thought you might like it."

She had such a bitter tongue in the past that Thad had to make an apology in case she took the gesture the wrong way. She had a lot of repair to do.

"No, I love it, I really do. Thank you for thinking of me."

That's all I have done, he wanted to say and he wanted to ask if she thought of him.

"This last gift is from my mother."

"Did you get to see her?"

"No, she is still in Charleston. She sent it with Abby."

Merry peeled back the paper to reveal a small box. Inside the box was a beautiful necklace. It was silver with a blue stone dangling from the chain. Merry's mouth was dry. She looked at her husband and held the necklace up. The stone matched the color of his eyes.

"I am speechless, it's exquisite."

She turned so he could help her put it on and went to find a mirror.

"Oh Thad, I have never had anything so precious."

Neither have I, he said to himself, thanking the Lord above for the direction his life had taken.

They talked as he helped her clean up the kitchen. "You sure have made a lot here."

"This is nothing. I am headed to Liddy's in the morning to help bake cakes and pies."

She felt a little disappointed. She wanted to spend the day with her husband. Hear more about the trip. If he was disappointed, and he was, he didn't show it.

"I guess I will just meet you at the celebration then? What time does it start?"

"We start around two in the afternoon."

A yawn escaped Thad and Merry knew he must be exhausted.

"You better get some sleep you look beat."

She went to the door and called for Gus. "He has been moping around here for days, looking down the road whimpers at night."

The dog wagged his tail and headed for the bedroom. If the dog could talk, he would have told Thad he wasn't the only one looking toward the road and whimpering at night.

Merry headed toward the ladder then stopped. She called Thad's name and he came out from behind the curtain.

"I am glad you're home," she said and kissed his cheek then kissed it again. He leaned in for a little more but she scurried up the ladder with her packages.

The bed felt good to Thad. He had slept under the wagon last night on the hard ground. He was getting too old for that he reckoned. Just as he drifted off to sleep he noticed the aroma of lavender on his pillow. No, it was in his head. He picked the pillow up put it over his face and inhaled deeply, yip lavender. Someone had been sleeping in his bed. He was smiling when he fell asleep and smiling when he woke up.

The smile didn't last as Merry was not in the house. The note on the table said she didn't want to wake him and she left breakfast in the warmer. He would have to wait to see her a little longer.

If ever a day dragged it was the fourth of July. Merry had made pies and cakes until she couldn't stand it and it was only noon.

"I think that is enough," Liddy proclaimed as she took the last pie out of the oven and set it to cool. Merry poured them some water and they ate a bite of food.

"What are you wearing to the celebration, Maggie?" Liddy asked in a coy way.

"What I have on." She had her best dress on and Liddy knew it.

"Oh, no, Merry Margret Sheridan, you come with me."

Liddy led her upstairs and opened the bedroom door. The most beautiful blue dress lay on the bed.

"That's what you're going to wear."

Merry's mouth opened and shut a couple of times as her eyes moved from the dress to Liddy.

"Where did you? How?"

"Don't just stand there try it on."

Liddy helped her into the dress.

"Liddy, this will never fit."

"Be still I have never misjudged in all my sewing days it will fit." And it did, like a glove which bothered Merry just a bit. It clung to her figure a little too nicely.

"It's perfect, perfect length, perfect fit, perfect color, and perfect woman," Liddy declared. Merry hugged Liddy for a long moment.

"Now, you take that dress off and I am going to fix you a nice bath to soak in. We are going to have you looking like a queen. Today we are putting 'mag the hag' out to pasture."

Merry soaked in the fragrant water and washed her hair. Liddy had left a robe by the tub.

Once secured away in the bedroom Merry gazed at the dress. Never had she had anything so nice. Liddy joined her and she brushed Merry's hair out.

"You said you brought some things you wanted to show me." Merry's face had a small blush on it.

"Thad's sister sent me some things and to tell you the truth Liddy I am not sure what they are."

She reached for the package and Liddy opened it. She first pulled out a chemise that was a silky fabric with tiny ribbons and lace with a matching pair of pantaletts. There was another set that was not as fancy and made of cotton. Underneath it all was a beautiful night gown with a matching robe.

"Surely you know what this is?" Liddy smiled.

"Yes!" Merry snatched it form Liddy's hands.

"The other stuff, I have never seen anything like it."

Liddy felt ashamed. She had never realized how much Merry did not know about being a woman, and that was Liddy's fault. Tears filled Liddy's eyes.

"Maggie, I feel like I have let you down all these years." Merry went to her dearest friend and put her arms around her.

"No Liddy! If I had cared about such things I would have asked? Please don't take this on yourself."

Liddy got a look of determination on her face. "Today, Merry Margret, is you're coming out party."

Liddy set to work and before she was done Merry had been pampered in every conceivable way.

Standing in front of the mirror stood a real beauty. She would rival any of Thad's southern belles. The necklace her mother-in-law sent accented the dress beautifully. It was the only jewelry she needed. Her thick hair was pinned and styled. Thad's gift was placed at her crown. The perfume took only a drop to fill the room with its sweetness. Merry glowed.

Making his way to the center of town Thad remembered why he shied away from wearing suits. His neck itched for one and the tie felt like it was cutting off his air. Tommy looked just a miserable but everyone dressed up for the big celebration. When they got closer to the excitement Tommy asked if he could go play. He had come to town with Thad and planned to stay all-night with the Lapps. It was a tradition and he did it every year. July 5 was the yearly anniversary of the Lapps giving Tommy to the Hasketts and they took him every year on an overnight picnic fishing trip.

Thad gave Tommy the go ahead and went to join the men.

"Who is that with Doc Lapp's wife?" One man asked and all heads turned.

"Can't rightly say, doesn't look familiar to me."

Thad knew in an instance that was his Merry. "That'd be my wife fellas."

He surprised the men as he made his way through the group and headed toward the Lapps wagon. He snuck up behind her and caught her about the waist.

"Man would have to travel pretty far to find a woman as beautiful as you, Merry." He whispered in her ear, took a deep breath inhaling the smell of the cologne and kissed her neck, all right out in public. Her elbow nudged him a little.

"Isn't my face red enough Thad Sheridan?" but she was smiling as she tried to hide her face and he liked it. She turned and handed him a load of pies to carry to the table.

"Make yourself useful." She scolded.

He leaned in close to her face. "I was trying to." With a wink he was gone.

People couldn't stop looking and talking about Merry. She felt a little nervous. She never really liked attention, or did she? She so rarely got it. When the music started, people began to dance. Merry went to make sure the tables were filled with plenty of snacks. She usually stayed at the table during the dancing part. No one ever asked her to dance.

The sheriff approached the table.

"Can I get you something, Sheriff" she asked.

"I had a hankering for dance." Her eyes became wide.

"You never dance." She said dismissing his request.

"Never seen a gal worth dancing with, until tonight." His rough hand clasped hers and he led her to the other couples.

"Thought that man of yours would have you in his arms first dance."

"Tommy had a little problem with his pants so Thad was taking him to Doc's to change."

The dance ended and another started. Merry thanked the sheriff and was on her way to return to the food table when Peter McPherson asked her to dance. His face was all red and his voice was squeaky. She took pity on him and followed him. There was silence.

"You dance rather well, Peter," she complimented.

"Thank you, Mrs. Sheridan." He acted as if he was going to say more but a look of panic spread across his face. Thad was approaching and tapped the young boy on the shoulder. Peter couldn't leave fast enough.

Thad took her in his arms.

"I'm gone two minutes, and you're in the arms of another man."

She snickered "I don't think he's quite yet a man." She sobered "I do think he had something he wanted to say."

"Probably the same thing every other man wishes to say to you tonight." Her look was one of puzzlement.

"And what would that be?" he looked at her for a fleeting second, as if she should know.

"Merry Margret Quinn, we should have known." She still looked puzzled, and her eyes questioned him

"Never mind," he said as he moved around the makeshift dance floor. He thought to himself, *I knew right away what a beauty you were.*

He couldn't keep his eyes off of her nor did he wish too. Everything about her had so permeated him he couldn't imagine life without her.

"You really shouldn't hold me this way," she interrupted his thoughts. "It's," she hesitated "inappropriate," she whispered.

His eyes traveled to the other couples. Those not married were a good distance from one another. Those married were closer than he and Merry; it was her space issue he supposed.

"You're right, my dear, I should be holding you more like we're married than courting," and pulled her closer to him, their faces were so close she could feel his breath on her cheek.

"You're impossible," she spoke as her heart pounded out of her chest. She was sure he could feel it they were that close. She was losing the space battle.

The celebration ended, and the Lapps asked the Sheridan's to spend the night. It looked as if it was going to rain and they didn't want them getting caught in it. Merry's mind raced if they stayed the spare room only had one bed it would cause her great conflict, so she was pretty adamant about going home.

"I think we can beat it home," she told Doc.

"But, Maggie, we have room, and it's getting late."

You have one room, Merry thought. Thad was looking at Merry and saw the sheer panic on her face.

"It's whatever you want to do, Merry."

I want to go home, she thought. As if he read her thoughts he turned to the Lapps.

"We best head home. Tommy, you have fun tomorrow, and I want to hear all about it when you return." Tommy shook his head as he held Liddy's hand. Thad had just taken care of the whole ordeal without so much as a word from the Lapps.

It did start to pour down rain half way home and did not let up. By the time the couple got home, they were soaked. The rain had caused the night to be unseasonable cool. Thad pulled as close to the door as he could get.

"You better get that dress off and into dry clothes, or you'll be sick. When I get in I'll start a fire."

He helped her down, and she went in. He hurried and unhitched the team, gave them a brushing to get the water off and fed them. It took him longer than usual because everything had been thoroughly soaked. Including himself.

When he reached the house Merry was standing in the middle of the kitchen trying to start a fire. Her dress was still on and making a puddle in the middle of the floor.

"Merry I said I would start the fire; you need to get out of that dress."

She turned sad eyes on him. "I can't get out of it." She pivoted and only about four buttons were undone. The rest were out of her reach.

His hands slowly traveled down her back unbuttoning what seemed to be hundreds of tiny buttons. The rain had done nothing to diminish the smell of the French perfume, and it filled the space around them. He wanted to speak, but his throat felt numb. She turned and touched his cheek lightly with her lips, twice again and made her way up the ladder.

Sometime during the night Merry had a bad dream she was thrashing in the bed and yelled out. Thad pulled on his pants and was headed toward the ladder when he saw her coming down.

"You okay?" It was still raining, and a flash of lightning illuminate Merry's face, fear was what met him in the dark confines of the kitchen.

"Merry, what is it?" she went to him, and he engulfed her in his arms. She was shaking.

"I need to tell you something."

He didn't move only placed a kiss on her forehead.

She moved and lit a lamp. Sitting down she motioned for him to sit across from her. He did so. She reached and grabbed his hand like he did when they prayed together.

"About six months after my grandfather died two men came riding up to the farm. They said they were lost and asked for directions to a town I never heard of. I tried to put them off and told them how to get to Rudolph and that someone there may know the town."

Thad did not like where this story was headed.

They got off the horses and tried to get friendly." She wouldn't look at him. "They grabbed at me, both of them just kept touching me. She clenched her hand tightly around his. I tried to push away but they started to get rougher, tearing my dress."

Thad had a knot in the pit of his stomach. He raked his hand over his face as he held fast to Merry's with his other, she continued.

"They knocked me to the ground. I tried to scream, I remember trying to scream and nothing was coming out." She now looked at him, pain and fear in her eyes. "All of the sudden I saw both men drop to the ground with an Indian arrow straight in the heart. They were dead."

Tears were streaming down her face. "Lone Eagle was kneeling over me, just talking in soft tones. He carried me into the house and sent Spotted Hawk to get the Sheriff, Doc and Liddy. They would have . . ." She paused, closing her eyes.

Thad stood, bringing her into his arms.

"Shh," he was murmuring over her head kissing her hair and holding her gently but protectively against him. He knew what the men had intended to do and his anger boiled. Thank God for Lone Eagle.

She continued.

"When the sheriff got here he identified the men as a pair hanging on wanted posters in his office. It was decided between him and the doc they would take care of the bodies and leave it at that. Lone Eagle was free to go and none of us would discuss it. Doc gave me some medicine and I slept for hours. Liddy stayed by my side and Lone Eagle came daily to check on me. You understand now about Lone Eagle, don't you? I love him, Thad, but not in the same way I love you. Please tell me you understand."

Did she just say she loves me? The pause caused her to look up at him

"Sweet Merry, I understand."

She loved the way he spoke to her, always so soothing.

"Is that what you were dreaming about?"

"Yes, I haven't had the bad dream in a while but tonight I was thinking about it before I fell asleep. I was thinking about how to tell you. I guess I was thinking a little too hard."

"Did I do something to cause you to start thinking about it?" he remembered his lingering fingers when he unbuttoned her dress and the snide comment about Lone Eagle being her protector.

"No, I just knew I needed to tell you." She clung to him shivering.

"Here, sleep in my bed tonight it will be warmer. I will build up the fire so you can get warm."

He pushed her toward the curtain and she willingly crawled in bed. He stoked the fire, grabbed a kitchen chair to sleep in and returned to make sure Merry was tucked in. She was lying on the far side of the bed with the covers turned back on his side. Her tear stained face looked up at him.

"Please don't leave me," she said as her hand reached for his.

"I'm not going to leave you."

He stretched out beside her and gathered her in his arms holding her until she fell asleep.

An empty side of the bed greeted Merry. She sensed it the minute he moved to leave. It was early morning and chores needed to be done. She remembered how kind Thad was to her. He didn't judge her or make her feel bad over the information she had shared with him, instead with his ever-present integrity, he simply held her all night, letting her emotions exhaust themselves. He was a true gentleman.

She knew one thing she wanted to be with him as much as she could. She wanted to draw strength from his strength. She wanted to learn from him and she wanted to love him. She laid there a little longer praying and thinking. Life would be different now and she wanted it to be the best it could be.

He had left her some breakfast but she wasn't hungry. She dressed and combed her hair. She didn't feel like putting it up so she left it draped to one side and loosely tied. She found her husband in the barn unloading things from the new wagon.

"Where did all this come from?" she asked.

There were a couple of trunks and several crates of items he had purchased.

"My sister brought some of my things from home. I think that trunk over there are my law books. There are some books in there to help teach Spotted Hawk how to read and write. He wants to learn you know."

Merry seemed a little shocked.

"I thought he had given the notion up."

"Must have decided otherwise. He wants to start at the end of summer. You up for it?"

Merry was delighted. She so wanted to see Spotted Hawk learn. He was a smart boy. She squealed with delight and Thad turned to look at her.

"If that's all it takes to make you happy, Merry. I am in good shape."

"I am pretty easy to please." She jumped up in the wagon and begin going through the trunk her legs dangling off the edge.

"Hmm, what's this? She began to read."

> For my beloved brother Thad, perhaps this book of poetry will help you with the ladies since you have such trouble keeping one. Love, Abby.

"Give me that." He reached for the book but Merry drew it out of his grasp.

A few pictures fell out of the book of girls from Thad's past.

"Have a little trouble wooing the girls?" She asked a smile tipping just the corners of her mouth. She was trying to keep a straight face. He approached her and the book went behind her back. His hands rested on either side of her.

"I can assure you I had no trouble with the ladies." His eyes pinned hers.

She placed her hand on his chest to hold him at bay as she brought the book out.

"Some of these pages are marked." She giggled.

"There marked because Abby marked them."

"Uh huh."

He looked a little embarrassed. Merry thought he looked like a school boy. She reached her hand around his neck and brought his lips to hers. She kissed him once and then twice. It was difficult to break the kiss but she did.

"Is there a reason why you always kiss me twice?" He wanted to know.

"Isn't it obvious?" Her head tilted to one side.

He raised both hands in a questioning manner.

"One isn't enough," she said as if it was common sense.

"Well then," he put his forehead on hers, "do you foresee a time in the near future when two won't be enough?"

He went to kiss her but she hit him in the chest with the poetry book.

"Maybe this will increase your chances." She slipped away from him and glided to her garden.

He shook his head and smiled. All men like a chase. She liked playing with him. All those far away dreams started to resurface and slowly they were coming true.

Merry spent the afternoon in the kitchen. She made a mouth-watering supper. Chicken and biscuits, mashed boiled potatoes with a little cream and butter, vegetables from her garden. She made a chocolate cake for dessert.

Thad declared himself too stuff to eat a piece of the cake at the moment and suggested a walk. They walked hand in hand around the property checking the fences looking at the livestock and ended in Merry's beloved garden.

Thad noticed Lone Eagle and Spotted Hawk racing on the ridge. When they had slowed, he gave a shrill whistle and the two turned. He motioned for them to come down. They came down the ridge and eased their horses to the edge of the garden.

Thad invited them for coffee and some chocolate cake.

"Night Wolf lost mind?" He said to Merry. She smiled.

"You're always welcome in our home Lone Eagle."

His Morning Dove was happy he was happy.

"We go," he said and Spotted Hawk looked crestfallen.

"Wait," Merry said. She left the men to get some cake for Spotted Hawk to take with him.

"You take care of Morning Dove now." The big Indian was staring at Thad rather seriously.

"Yes, but I like the thought of having you around," Thad confessed. Lone Eagle's gaze never left Thad's, as if he were measuring him.

"You unlike other men, is it your God?"

"Yes," Thad said. "I would like to tell you about him sometime."

Merry returned with a couple of pieces of the chocolate cake and handed them to Spotted Hawk.

"I am looking forward to helping you learn, Hawk." The boy's eyes looked from Merry to Thad and then to his father and back to Merry. He nodded and inhaled the cake. The adults laughed and father and son headed home.

The couple had their cake and coffee on the front porch, with much conversation and laughter they watched the sun drop behind the black hills and the sky become dotted with stars. It had been a wonderfully peaceful day. Gus, who was enjoying having his belly scratched, let out a big yawn signaling the end of the day.

"Look who's tired, slept on the porch all day?" Merry reached to grab the dogs muzzle. Standing she stretched. "It was a good day, Thad. Thank you." He was taken aback.

Why was she thanking him? His face must have showed his bewilderment.

"I feel like a weight has been lifted off of me since you've come and last night, getting what happen out of the recesses of my heart makes me feel new again. I have purpose back in my life. You did that Thad Sheridan." He was overwhelmed with her words.

She bent to kiss him good night and she didn't stop at two.

The sun was just coming up and peeking through Thad's bedroom window. He lay with his left arm securely around his wife's waist. The smell of her hair, he inhaled, lavender was the last thing he remembered before he drifted off. He liked it being the thing that woke him in the morning.

Chores weren't going to get done with him lying there. He started to shift but she grabbed his arm tucking it beneath her head until her cheek rested in his palm.

Half asleep, she muttered, "It's too early, go back to sleep."

He could do nothing but put his head back down and enjoy the time cuddling with his wife.

It was a wonderful summer that led to a bountiful fall. Merry was certain this had been the best harvest ever. Not only did the crops produce nicely her marriage had turned out to be such a blessing.

For the first time in her life she didn't dread the coming of winter. She had begun teaching Spotted Hawk and couldn't believe what a fast learner he was. Lone Eagle would join him once a week and he and Thad would discuss religion in the barn. Lone Eagle was Thad's mission. It was hard to get the Indian to understand the concept of sin and the need for a savior, but he felt he was making progress.

Hank had been invited but he had yet to attend. His episodes of outburst were fewer and farther between but he still drank.

Melissa and Merry were planning a nice Thanksgiving dinner if one of the men were able to get a turkey. Hank and Thad had planned to take Tommy hunting and the boy was beside himself with excitement. It was all he could talk about. Unfortunately, Hank was having a bad day, and Melissa and Tommy came to say he wouldn't be hunting. Tommy's face showed his disappointment.

"Melissa, do you think it would be okay if I took Tommy hunting?"

"Oh, would you, Thad? He has had his heart set on it."

Thad was happy to do it. In the back of his mind he thought maybe he should ask Hank's permission but Tommy's enthusiasm urged him on with the plan. It was a mistake.

When he and Tommy returned emptyhanded, Hank met them in the yard. He took a swing at Thad. The act caught Thad by surprised and Hanks fist made contact with his jaw. Hank was in a rage about Tommy being his son and he would take him hunting and he didn't need Thad showing him up.

Thad calmly tried to reason with Hank but his eyes were wild. He was itching for a fight and Thad was in no mood to engage him. Hank had obviously been drinking and began to rant and through the slurred speech Thad caught some insinuation about Lone Eagle and Merry, not taking kindly to Hanks accusations he harshly encouraged him to stop. Hank did not and came at Thad a second time.

Thad had him subdued in a matter of minutes and escorted Hank back into his house. Once inside the house he released him.

"Get yourself together Hank. The liquor is going to cost you more than you can ever imagine if you don't end this behavior now."

Hank started to rise and Thad pushed him back down.

"Don't come after me again, Hank." Thad's words were stern and Hank knew he meant it.

Outside Tommy stood holding onto Gus, his face buried in the dog's coat. He turned to look at Thad with clouded eyes. What must the boy be thinking? Melissa who had tried to stop her husband but was pushed aside apologized for her husband.

"If you ever feel unsafe Melissa you and Tommy have a place with us." She nodded and Thad and Gus headed home.

He did a lot of praying along the way. He had befriended Hank and the whiskey had come between them. Many men had lost everything over the disgusting stuff.

When he returned home he relayed the whole, well almost the whole, incident to Merry. He left out the insults Hank had made toward her. Maybe he was trying too hard to be an influence on Tommy. He just wanted him to see a man who served God instead of drink.

Merry was very reassuring that when Hank sobered up things would right them self again. He prayed she was right. With no turkey and no guest the Sheridan's celebrated Thanksgiving alone, which was not a hardship on them. After the noon meal of stew the two sat in the small sitting room and chatted.

The room was a little chilly so they curled up under the wedding quilt Liddy had made for them. Merry was grinning to herself and was trying to suppress the laughter bubbling inside.

"Are you going to tell me what has got you giggling like a school girl?"

"I was just thinking about Abby's last letter."

His kid sister was notorious for silliness even by mail.

"What has she written now?" He asked with a sigh.

"She asked if your book of poetry had any effect on me, and if so I would be the first."

"Funny thing, Merry, with you I don't need the poetry." He looked at her with a sideways glance.

"And what is that supposed to mean?"

"You and Abby seem to have all the answers, why don't you write and ask her?"

"You think I am a pushover, don't you?" She moved away from him and he laughed.

"A good fight does better than poetry with you." She started to get up and he reached for her pulling her on his lap and she willingly complied.

"See?" His eyes caressed her face. She touched his jaw.

"You're impossible."

"So I've been told."

Chapter Five

December started off extremely cool, Merry was sure they were in for a bad winter. They plan to head to town and stock up for the winter. It was not uncommon to be snowed in for weeks at a time. Thad hadn't been himself. Merry was sure it had to do with the fact neither Hank nor Tommy had been in contact. She on the other hand was excited about her first Christmas with Thad.

She thought of going to Hank and Melissa herself but Thad had been adamant about the next move being Hanks. Stubborn man. She frowned.

"What's that frown for?" Thad had hitched up the team and came in from the cold blowing on his hands.

"I was just thinking about how stubborn you can be."

"Me!?" His eyes were wide

"Yes, and don't argue with me. Tommy is missing out on all the holiday spirit because—"

He interrupted her. "Because he has a father who won't take responsibility and I can't change that."

"Your—"

He interrupted her again. "Impossible, yes, I know."

"I just don't see what it would hurt to swing by and test the waters."

"Merry, do you trust me?" His look was serious. "I said do you trust me?"

"What is this about?" She asked.

"It's about you trusting me to make decisions. The right decisions."

"I trust you but I don't understand."

"A man's pride can rule him. In certain situations, that can be an asset in others it will kill him. Hank is vulnerable and he drinks the two make him volatile. It has to be his resolution."

He was finished and she knew she should let the matter drop. They were headed to town and she needed to see about Thad's Christmas present. Her excitement returned.

The Sheridans headed to town. The skies had the hint of snow and Merry moved closer to her husband. He wrapped his arm around her and rubbed his hand up and down her arm.

"I know you miss Tommy, Merry, I do too but I don't want to fuss about this."

"Do we fuss?" Merry placed her chin on his shoulder and nuzzled his cheek giving him her customary double kisses separated by some very sweet words whispered in his ear. His grip got a little tighter.

After winter supplies were purchased Thad dropped Merry of at the Lapps and he went to the livery. Merry was eager to see Liddy she had something to discuss with her.

"Liddy I think I am pregnant." She just blurted it out.

Liddy's face showed pure delight. "Well let's find out for sure."

She led Merry into Dr. Lapps office and in a few minutes Zeke Lapp joined them. After talking with Merry and an examination Zeke confirmed Merry's suspicions. Dr. Lapp gave Merry all the information about what to expect. He frightened her a little by talking about all the things that could go wrong during the pregnancy and Liddy saw Merry's face.

"Zeke you're scaring the poor girl."

"Maggie, you'll be fine." He patted her shoulder. "Thad know?"

Her smile was wide. "No, I am waiting until Christmas so please don't mention it."

He kissed her cheek "he'll be thrilled. I estimate you're probably a couple months along, due sometime around first of June.

The wagon was loaded down with supplies and Thad had one more stop to make. He headed into the post office. There should be a package from Abby waiting on him. He had asked her to send him two gold bands. He wanted to surprise Merry with a wedding ring. Abby in her customary manner had sent her own set of gifts along with the rings.

It was almost impossible for Merry to keep her secret. She wasn't sure she would make it. Just one week until Christmas. She would stare at her husband at strange times wondering what his reaction would be when he heard the news.

She had an ill thought. What if he didn't want children? They had not really discussed it. He thought the world of Tommy why wouldn't he want his own children? She was watching him through the window now. She hoped their baby had his eyes, and his smile and well she hoped the baby looked just like him. Could she love another person as much as she loved Thad? Would the baby change that love? Yes, it would and she hoped for the good.

He noticed her watching from the window. There were several inches of snow on the ground and more falling. He motioned for her to come out. She joined him out in the snow and they went for a short walk.

"You ready to be snowed in for a long winter?" she asked her arm in the crook of his.

"It's all I've been thinking about." His lips touched hers.

She pushed back a little. "You know we'll fight."

"Looking forward to it." Why was she talking when he wanted to be kissing? He pulled her back to him.

"I have your Christmas present." Thad gave up. Merry was in the mood to talk.

They continued walking. "Oh, that's right. I better make a trip into town before long." She slapped his arm playfully.

"Don't you want a hint?" she asked. It would be her nature to just blurt it out but she was sure she could hold out a few more days.

"I like surprises, I can wait."

"Well, aren't you going to offer me a hint?" Merry stopped the procession into the house.

Thad's expression was way to serious and Merry felt a bit alarmed.

"Merry." His arms went snuggly around her. "You have Mr. Impossible and I just can't see you needing anything else." He was smiling.

She broke away and reaching for a handful of snow off the porch railing showered her husband's face with flakes. He caught her before she went through the door and before he was done her face was as wet as his.

An aching in her back interrupted Merry's sleep. She was trying to think what she had done to cause the pain. Other than taking the walk with Thad she had done no physical exercise. She tossed and turned for a while and dozed off. Suddenly the pain was a little worse and had moved to her abdomen. Perhaps her supper did not agree with her. The doctor said food sometimes becomes an issue with pregnancy.

She got up and went into the kitchen for some water. The pain was similar to the cramping she would have with her monthly cycle only a little worse. She tried to lie back down but it seemed to be intensifying.

She put on her robe and shoes in between the pain maybe a trip to the outhouse would relieve some of her pain. Thad heard her stirring around.

"You okay?'"

"I think it is just something I ate. Go on back to sleep." He looked at her with the expression "Are you sure?" "I'm fine, go back to sleep." He closed his eyes and turned over.

Merry made her way through the kitchen grabbing a lamp. When she reached the back porch, the pain doubled her over. She was perspiring in spite of the chilly air. She didn't think she could stand the pain. Suddenly she felt the warmth of fluid running down her leg. In the dim light, she saw the snow turn to red. She was bleeding.

The pain continued and the blood was coming faster. It hit her full on she was losing the baby. Doc Lapp had included this in his discussion. It happened sometimes he said but you can't go through your pregnancy worrying if it is going to. She chose not to worry and now it was happening.

The pain was so bad she couldn't get her breath she tried to holler for Thad but she couldn't get enough force behind the words. There was a break in the pain and she knelt down in the snow.

"Thad!" the shrill scream woke him up immediately.

He bolted out of bed and headed toward the call.

"Thad." This time there were tears in the words.

He arrived on the back porch and found Merry on her knees hands clinched resting beside them. There was a substantial amount of blood on and around her. He had no clue what had happened to her. He reached her and she grabbed him. The pain began again and she let out an agonizing groan. He didn't say anything but lifted her and brought her into the house.

"Merry what happened?"

He couldn't understand what had transpired. Merry with tears streaming down her face uncontrollably and gasping between the pains she spoke in a barely conceivable murmur.

"We both know what's going on."

He had no clue what was going on. He needed to find out where the bleeding was coming from. "The baby," she said. "The baby, Doc said—" She was out.

Lifeless. He grabbed her wrist. Her pulse was rapid and her skin was cool and clammy. He grabbed the blanket and covered her up. The effects of her words hit him. Merry had been pregnant and she had just lost the baby.

If he did not do something quickly he could lose Merry and he couldn't have that. He removed her clothes and the bloody mess. The blood was still trickling down her legs but not flowing as it once was. The pain was still present but not as intense.

What was he going to do? He needed to go for the doctor but he didn't feel like he could leave Merry. Her eyes fluttered open and tears were pooled there.

"Merry, I need to get the doctor."

"Too late," she whispered. "Don't leave me." She was so cold.

He got another blanket and piled it on. He didn't know what made him think about it, but Hank and Melissa were the closest neighbors. He could ride over there and maybe Hank would go for the doctor and Melissa could help him. He would only be gone about twenty minutes. It seemed logical.

"Merry, I am going to get Melissa and send Hank for the doctor." She turned her head away from him and nodded. He kissed her brow and headed to the barn.

Grace was the fastest he had ever remembered her to be. In record time, they were at the Hasketts. Thad's mind was too intent on getting help to contemplate what had just occurred. He banged on the door for what seemed like several minutes. He was met by a very angry man.

"Merry's ill, I need help."

Melissa came from the bedroom. Tommy followed from his own room. Hanks stare told Thad he was not with the rest of them. Too much drink and too much confusion clouded his eyes.

"Hank." Melissa's voice was so sharp and loud even Thad was taken aback. "Go saddle my horse." The man put a coat on and without word stumbled to the barn.

"Go get the doctor, Thad," she called from the bedroom as she changed.

"Hank is useless tonight, I will go stay with Merry." She came from the bedroom ready to go.

"She lost the baby, she is bleeding a lot." Melissa recognized the fear in the strong man's face. She nodded and shewed him out the door. She was right behind him and Tommy followed.

On the way to the doctors he prayed. He asked the Lord to spare Merry for purely selfish reasons, he couldn't live without her. He prayed for Merry and for the doc, Melissa, Tommy and even Hank. He prayed for himself. This was all too much to process and his heart was breaking for Merry.

Doctor Lapp knew what had happen the minute he opened the door to find Thad Sheridan standing there. He didn't have to speak.

"Go saddle my horse, son, then go on back to Maggie, I am on my way." Thad didn't waste any time.

He was back home in record speed. Tommy was headed into the kitchen with a bucket of water. He was trying to pour it into a pot on the stove. It was a little too heavy for him and he was struggling. Thad reached over the boy grabbing the bucket and poured it in the pot. A basket caught his eye. It was full of blood soaked sheets and nightgowns. How much blood had his wife lost.

Melissa was sitting beside the bed comfortingly speaking to Merry.

"The doctor's right behind me, she still bleeding?" Thad did not take his eyes off of Merry.

"Not as bad but she does continue to bleed." Melissa did not have a good feeling about how much blood Merry had lost.

Melissa herself had miscarried multiple times, so much that Doctor Lapp had told her to stop trying. Her last miscarriage went much like this and it resulted in the doctor performing a procedure that snuffed out any chance for a baby of her own. Those painful memories came rushing back and she was afraid for the pain her friend would have to endure. Not the physical pain but the emotional pain.

The doctor's presence jarred Melissa back to the task at hand. Zeke Lapp took one look at Merry and knew his assumption during the ride here was correct. Merry Sheridan was not going to fair well.

He touched Merry and took her pulse much to rapid. She was still bleeding and had lost a pretty good amount.

"Melissa, I will need some hot water, a lot of clean towels or bedding."

She went to leave the room and he followed her.

"Are you up for this?" Dr. Lapp questioned his assistant.

"Who else would be better to help Merry than me?" he patted her cheek.

"Place these instruments in boiling water and put a little of this in the water." He handed her a small bottle of alcohol. He returned to the room.

"Thad, I want you—"

Thad interrupted. "Don't kick me out of this room, Doc."

“I want you to put something under this end of the bed.” He pointed to the foot. “Something that will elevate it just a little to get Maggie’s feet above her heart.”

Thad set to doing what the doctor asked.

In the meantime, Zeke lifted the sheet and examined Merry. She whimpered out in pain and the bleeding picked up. She then sat up in pain and fell back hard on the bed. Thad’s look was shear fear.

The doctor handed him a cloth sprinkled with what Thad guessed was ether or chloroform.

“Put this just a little above her mouth and nose and count to ten then take it away. Don’t you inhale or you’ll be on the floor too.”

Once he did that and Merry was out, the doctor began to give orders.

“Thad, you keep your hand on her wrist. If her pulse changes drastically you let me know. Understand?” Thad grabbed Merry’s wrist and shook his head.

“Melissa, I will need your help at this end.” Melissa readied herself and brought the instruments to the doctor’s side.

It took the physician well over an hour to completely stop the bleeding and remove the remains of the baby.

“Thad, I don’t see any way around . . .” He wasn’t quite sure how to say it in mixed company. “Well, she just won’t be able to carry a child.”

“I understand, Doc, you have to do what you have to do.”

Melissa knew all too well how Merry would respond to that, she had some words of wisdom for Thad if he would welcome it. She got her chance a few hours later.

Tommy had offered to set by Merry’s bed and let Thad get some coffee. The boy loved Merry and needed to see that she was improving and not going to die. Thad obliged the boy’s request. Kissing his wife’s hand, he placed it on the blanket. It was no longer cool and clammy but had nice warmth to it. Tommy picked up the hand after Thad left and rested his small cheek on it, he had missed the Sheridans.

In the kitchen, Melissa poured Thad some coffee and fixed him a bite to eat. He let out a pent-up sigh.

"Was I supposed to know she was expecting Melissa? Did I miss something?"

She smiled.

"No Thad, the man doesn't know until the woman tells him. You didn't miss anything. Nor did you do something to cause this to happen."

The woman was reading his mind.

"Thad, this is going to be devastating to both of you. Merry is going to try and push you away but don't you let her. You be persistent. You be there whether it seems like she wants you there or not. Listen to her but don't let her wallow in it all either."

He gathered by the urgency in her tone she spoke from experience. He covered her hand with his. "I won't and I am sorry."

"For what?" She asked.

"For making you relive some painful memories."

Her smile was sweet when she replied "My grandmother use to say things happen on purpose. I couldn't have been anywhere else tonight."

Melissa and Tommy left and Melissa promised nothing would keep her or Tommy away from visiting the Sheridan's on a regular basis. She also said she would be over later with some food.

Thad gave her a big hug and big thank you. He praised Tommy for all his hard work and for helping take care of Merry and the animals this morning. Tommy just smiled.

Once inside Doc Lapp told Thad in detail what procedure he had to do. Something called the uterus, which held the baby had been "not normal" and was beyond his repair. He had to remove it and with that removing any chance for the two of them to have children of their own.

"This won't be easy on her. I have to tell her as soon as possible and just so you know, she won't believe you when you tell her it won't make a difference to you. So you'd better be thinking of a more clever way to convince her. I can just about predict Maggie' s response."

Thad could too. How was he going to convince her that he would be okay without having children? Yes, he is sorrowful about the loss of this one. He felt like his guts had been kicked out but he knew his life was not his own. He had to trust God to make the right decisions in his life.

It wasn't until the following day that Merry was awake enough to fully comprehend all that had happened to her. Liddy was there when Zeke told her what he had to do. She was silent. Her eyes flew to Thad and she looked away. He asked if they could be alone and the Lapps went out onto the back porch. The blood-stained snow remained and they prayed as they removed the remains of the ordeal. Liddy with tears and Zeke with anger over not being able to mend his dearest friend.

Inside Thad sat on the bed and took both his wife's hands. She would not look at him.

"Merry, look at me."

She wouldn't. His hands moved to her face turning her head so they were eye to eye. His face just a few inches away.

"Don't you dare shut me out. What has happened is overwhelming, and I cannot get through this without you and you cannot get through this without me. So, get it out of your head any notion that this will somehow unwind any of the relationship we have weaved together over the past months."

Why was he so good? She thought. I have done nothing but mess up his life. Thad knew her mind was going on a wild trail and he wouldn't have it.

"Do you know how much I love my life with you, Merry? Every day you steal my breath. Every time you walk toward me or speak to me I can't imagine anything more miraculous then our love.

"Even when we fight," she finally spoke.

He placed his forehead on hers. "Especially when we fight."

She reached her arms around his neck and cried for several minutes.

She whispered in his ear, "I can't promise I won't be melancholy. I wanted us to have children."

She shuttered. He moved so he could see her face.

"Me too." He smiled "But we're not in control of things now are we."

She cupped his face with her palm. "I don't deserve you." She stroked his face.

"Hey, none of that." He kissed her hand. "I don't know of another woman that could put up with me."

Merry knew better. Thad Sheridan could have had his choice of women and they would have all "put up" with him. She was so blessed but so sad all at the same time.

He dropped her hand and smoothed the covers around her.

"If you're getting ready to tell me to rest or get some sleep I am going to scream." Her bluntness always caught him a little by surprise.

"What is it you want to do?"

She wanted to sit up a little and attempted to do so. Thad wasn't sure if it was a good idea but he helped her. She patted the bed next to her for him to sit down.

"Would you read to me from the Bible? Some comforting words." He snatched the Bible off the bedside table.

Leaning his back against the head board and propping up his feet he opened the Word. Merry struggled to move until she was laying on his chest her arms entangled around his free one. She eased her head back as Thad began to read. She heard the quiver in his voice and felt the tears hit the top of her head as he read. When the Lapps returned to check on the couple they found the Sheridan's just this way.

It wasn't the Christmas Merry anticipated. Instead of joy she had sadness. Instead of life she had death. Instead of snow they had a miserable freezing rain. The sky was gloomy and so was her mood.

Still stuck in bed under doctor's orders the only bright spot was Thad. He had fixed Christmas dinner and brought it to the bedroom. Surprisingly he wasn't a bad cook. Lone Eagle had left some venison in the barn for them. Thad roasted it and threw in some potatoes and carrots that had been put up from the summer harvest. Sensing her mood, he refused to let her "wallow" in it constantly.

"So, shall I pick a fight so we can fuss for a while? You can be quite entertaining when your feathers are ruffled." He forked in some venison and waited for a response. Nothing came.

"What? Where's my girl with the quick tongue?" He desperately wanted to draw her out of the somber mood.

"I don't have anything for you for Christmas. I . . . I should have planned better."

"I don't require gifts to be happy Merry. In case you haven't noticed I've been pretty happy these last few months."

"I can't understand why. Everything I go to do has turned into one big mess."

"Stop." His voiced raised a bit and Merry looked up. "I mean it, Merry. This has got to stop! What happened to *us*, not you," he pointed, "and not me. *Us* is what is called life. Things bad and good happen without any regard to what we think or plan. Did you deliberately plan to lose this baby?" Her heart lurched and her eyes widened.

"Of course, you didn't, so don't take the blame. We are either going to trust our life to God or fail and personally I hate to fail."

His voice held no furry. In an odd way it was very loving so much that Merry wasn't sure how to take it. He was looking at her intently.

"Listen, I know it is going to be rough on us for a while and I expect tears and longing to be a part of that. What I don't want to see is self-loathing." His hand stroked her cheek. "Now you better eat up. I made dessert."

"You are impossible, you know that, right?"

"You'll learn to live with it over the next fifty or sixty years, I'm thinking," he said as he left the room to make some coffee.

She had never seen him bake anything so she had a bit of anticipation about dessert. He put the coffee on and brought the packages Abby had sent. He cleared her dishes.

"Gifts or dessert?" he asked.

She opted for the gifts first. She had eaten more today than she had in the past few and she felt a little stuffed.

"You first she said as she handed him a gift marked 'for my handsome brother' he opened the package and found a pair of leather gloves and a leather-bound book of poetry.

"She's something else." He turned the book so Merry could see the title.

"Wouldn't hurt you to use that once in a while. A body gets tired of fighting all the time." She gave him a poignant look. "You never even tried to court me."

He looked at her with mirth "I never got a chance, you were so sure I was leaving no amount of wooing would warm you up."

"Don't make excuses for your lack of propriety, Thad Sheridan." He opened his mouth to speak and she reached up and closed it.

"My turn." She opened her gift from Abby. It was a beautiful crocheted shawl. She held it up to examine it. "Abby has wonderful taste."

"Looks like there is more in there." Thad reached his hand for the package and Merry tugged it away. "Those things are for me." She held the remaining articles close to her chest.

"You sure about that?" His eyes sparkled with unreleased laughter. He mouthed the familiar word "impossible."

"What am I going to do with you?"

He produced the third package and handed it to her.

"Marry me."

She opened the box and found two gold wedding bands. Tears laced her lashes as she took the larger of the two and put it on his finger then handed the smaller to him. He did the same.

"I love you, Merry." It was the first time he ever said it outright. She knew he loved her he had showed her from the first day. She never realized the formal words had yet to be spoken and she wasn't sure she had said them herself.

"I love you too, Thad." He kissed her twice and started to get up.

"Hey, what are you doing?" she whined.

"Getting dessert."

"You're just going to kiss me and walk away like that."

"Uh huh, see how it feels. Dirty trick, isn't it." He returned shortly with a dried apple dumpling and a few more kisses.

The winter was rough but by the looks of it spring would be early although you never trusted the Dakota weather. Lone Eagle believed the winter would be short according to the Indian way. Every person in town had their own old wives' fables about how to determine weather. It didn't matter to Merry because she had Thad. Maybe in the few short months they had been married she was depending on him too much. Every once in a while, she would get a measure of fear. What if she lost him, like the baby, happy and blissful one minute and devastation the next? If her husband was there to read her thoughts, he would tell her, "We don't operate on fear."

There was a break in the weather and Thad had gone into town. He should be home soon. Merry had just removed the last batch of cookies from the oven when Thad arrived. He took a deep breath closed his eyes and inhaled the aroma of cinnamon and sugar. It was this scene Merry was met with when she turned around to greet her husband.

"Sometimes I think you stay with me for the cookies."

He opened his eyes removed his coat and made a beeline to his wife. "That obvious, am I?" His arms moved around her waist and drew her to him he kissed her forehead and grabbed a warm cookie from off the table. She shoved him a way with a slap on his chest.

"You're . . ." She had to stop saying he was impossible it did no good.

"Handsome?" he said eyebrows raised, she shook her head,

"No, that's not it." He made a look as if he was crest fallen.

"You're right." He sighed. "Handsome doesn't do me justice."

"Impossible. I'll keep saying it because it is the only thing that fits." She gave him two pecks on the cheek which was the norm.

"I will say this, you're pretty cute."

"Puppies are cute Merry can't you do any better than that?"

"I'll think on it and let you know when I come up with something."

"Well, while you're thinking you can read this."

He produced a letter from Abby and Merry squealed. They had not heard from her in a while and Merry missed her correspondence. This letter was addressed to both of them so Merry told Thad he should open it. He sat down at the kitchen table with his coffee Merry leaned on the arm of the chair. Thad opened the letter.

Dear Thad and Merry,

Sorry it has been so long between letters. Mother has fallen and broken her hip. There is not much they can do for her except bed rest and you know that is killing her. As I said before she gets a little feebler every day. She asks about you a lot Thad. I know when you left Mother and Father both were pretty hard on you. If you could see fit to come and visit I think it would do Mother a world of good. I am not sure how much longer we will have her with us. She is set in having Jackson outline her final wishes. Please come. Please Thad, come and bring Merry. I long to meet her face to face.

All my love
Abby

PS. Baby number three is due in August. We are hoping for a boy this time.

Thad judged Merry's face for a reaction to the post script.

"I am sorry to hear about your mother, Thad." His eyes stayed locked with Merry's. "And I am overjoyed for Abby's expected arrival. I hope it's a boy." She smiled and patted her husband's cheek. "I am fine, for sure and for certain." She pushed the hair back from her forehead, a sure sign of her inward anxiety.

He let out a sigh, and took a drink of his coffee.

"You are going to Charleston, aren't you?" Another sigh escaped him.

"I don't see how we can go. Who would look after the farm?"

"I can do all that, I did it for years."

"I wouldn't leave you here alone."

"Well, it's not like I wasn't alone before you came along. I did fine then and I would do fine again." She was getting agitated.

"I am not leaving you here."

"Well, I would like to know why you think I have all of the sudden become incompetent of running this farm."

"I didn't say that."

"You might as well."

"You're something else, Merry. Most women would find it chivalrous that her man wouldn't want her to be left alone."

"I'm sorry if I don't see the chivalry in your actions, Thad Sheridan." He knew he was in for it when she took to using both names. "It seems to me it is practical that you should go see your mother, and since the farm requires daily tending that I stay home." She was fit to be tied.

"I guess I need you more than you need me, Merry."

Why did he have to go and say that? She was winning this argument, her mind reasoned.

"I just don't want to go without you." He pushed the hair back from her forehead and looked solemnly into her big brown eyes.

"Well, as my gallant, stunningly attractive husband would say, 'God will make a way.'"

"Stunningly attractive, I knew you'd come up with something."

God did make a way a few days later when Melissa and Tommy came over in their small sleigh. Merry was discussing the conundrum with Melissa when she offered to look after the house while the Sheridans were away.

"It would be no trouble for Tommy and me to come each day, and if there is something too much for me I will have Hank see to it." Merry wasn't sure this was a good idea as they had not seen Hank since his altercation with Thad.

"Maggie, it will be fine. Hank is pretty ashamed of himself and since he won't come around when you're here I am sure he would help out when you are not here. He owes Thad that much."

"I am not sure Thad would allow you to take on the responsibility."

"I can handle Thad Sheridan," Melissa said with a smirk.

"Could you let me know how you do that because I certainly haven't figured it out?" Merry's hands were out palms up.

"Anybody with two functioning eyes can see you have that man in the palm of your hand, Maggie."

"I don't know, Melissa. We fight an awful lot."

Melissa's covered a smile.

"I bet you do a lot of making up." Merry's face flushed. "I take it back. Anybody with two functioning eyes can see that man has *you* in the palm of his hand." The women giggled and Thad and Tommy chose that time to enter the house.

The giggles turned into gales of laughter and Thad knew he had been the object of their conversation and their laughter. He bent over to look Tommy in the eye.

"You see how they are acting."

Tommy looked toward his mother and Merry then back to Thad.

"That only means one thing." The women were eager to hear what he had to say.

"They were talking about us men. Only something a man has done can make a woman laugh like that." Not taking his eyes off Tommy's, he pointed to the two innocent looking females.

"T-That's a g-g-good th-thing, r-right?" Tommy asked his mentor.

"Yeah, that's a good thing." He winked at his wife and headed for the stove.

"Melissa has solved our problem about our trip." Merry treaded lightly.

"Is that right?"

He heated a little milk and stirred some chocolate in it for Tommy. He placed the warm beverage in front of him along with a cookie. His eyes met Melissa's.

"If it is what I think it is the answer is no."

"Just hear what I have to say, Thad, before you pass judgment."

He nudged Tommy over and sat down. "Let's hear it."

She unveiled her plan. He was pretty sure she and Tommy could handle things for the time they were gone but he didn't know how Hank would take it. What if something happened that need more attention than the two of them could handle? When she was finished, he posed that question to her.

"Hank would help." Melissa answered.

Thad's eyebrow rose in question since he had not left Hank on good terms.

"He is embarrassed about what happened. He has too much pride to come over here and apologize. He owes you this Thad."

He started to protest but her words stopped him "Tommy and I need a place to stay, even if it is just for a break."

"Okay." He put an entire cookie in his mouth and leaned back.

That was it? Okay, just like that. If Merry had suggested it, the argument would have went on for hour's maybe days and he says okay.

Chapter Six

There was a lot of buzzing around the next few weeks. Stage tickets, train tickets, packing. Thad wasn't sure how long they would be gone so they planned on three weeks.

Merry was thankful she allowed Liddy to make her a few more dresses. Ever since the Fourth of July celebration Liddy had taken it upon herself to outfit Merry every chance she got. Thad had even bought material and gave it to Liddy to surprise Merry on a few occasions. The day finally arrived for them to leave.

They caught the stage outside of Rudolph. The whole trip was exhausting. It was a very travel weary couple that exited the train in Charleston. Merry wasn't sure how her legs were going to hold her up she was so tired. Thad helped her off the train and kept his hand to her back for support. He had to be just as tired. He seemed a little unsettled.

"I can tell you I don't miss the city," he whispered in her ear.

The noise and the smell was new to Merry. So much activity whipping by her. There was a woman coming toward them that had to be Abby. She was smiling from ear to ear and was almost running. When she got to the couple her arms went around Thad's neck and he lifted her into the air.

She was a beauty to say the least. Merry had never seen hair so golden. It was all piled on top her head with lavish curls flowing down the back. Her dress was the color of russet leaves and her eyes were nearly but not quite the color of Thad's. He put her down and she turned toward Merry.

"Aren't you lovely, Merry," she said as she scanned Merry from head to toe.

It was nice of her to say so, but with Abby Lorton within fifty miles was anything else considered lovely.

"I approve, brother, but you better not let her out of your sight."

"Don't plan on it," he said.

Abby gave Merry a big hug and kissed her cheek. It was sure to look odd. Merry was about a foot taller than her sister-in-law.

"You must be hungry. I thought we could get some lunch here in town before we head out to Laurel. Now I have a carriage or you could walk. I know it's a little brisk out but I will leave it up to the two of you."

"I would like to walk but if you ladies would like to ride I can meet you there." Thad said.

All eyes were on Merry now.

"I would like to walk also but I can ride with you Abby if you like."

Abby sized Merry up. "I would absolutely love for you to ride with me but there will be plenty of time for us to chat. You walk with Thad and keep him out of trouble. Although I don't think that is possible."

Thad assisted his sister into her carriage. "I think I will stop and see if Jackson can have lunch with us." Thad just smiled and nodded.

Once the carriage had left the two stepped onto the board walk.

"Does she ever slow down?" Merry asked

"Nope, talks and walks in her sleep or she used to. I caught her sliding down the banister one night sound asleep. She'd have broken her neck if I hadn't been there to catch her."

"She is so beautiful Thad. I could just sit and look at her, but she doesn't act like she knows it."

"Some women are like that." He tightened his hold on her and kissed her cheek.

"Hey, Sheridan!" A loud booming voice was followed by a huge body mass nearly tackling Thad.

Thad had braced his body and nearly flipped the man into the street. The man righted himself and stuck his hand out.

"Heard you were coming back. When did you get in?" He was pumping Thad's hand with excitement and his face was lit up.

"Just got in about an hour ago."

The man caught sight of Merry and took a step back looked her up and down then walked totally around her ending up in between her and Thad. He let out a long lone whistle.

"I'd say you struck gold, brother."

Merry blushed fully. She even surmised that the bottoms of her feet were red.

"Merry, this is my old friend Lachlan Kennedy," he said as he moved the man and took his rightful place again by Merry.

"Lach, this is my wife Merry." Lachlan bowed at the waist and kissed her hand.

"It is a real pleasure to meet you, ma'am."

He was handsome, not as handsome as her Thad but in his own way he was a catch. He was as tall as Thad but much broader. His golden blond hair had quite a bit of curl to it but it was kept short. He had a close clipped beard and hazel eyes and his voice was so deep it was disarming.

"How long are you staying?"

"Not sure how long the town will let me stay."

"I understand, fifteen years and people still talk about it."

"I am the town traitor, the black sheep."

"Not in my book, brother. Town hero, more like it." Lachlan was reflective. "Where you headed?"

"Lunch at the hotel. Do you care to join us?"

He looked at Merry and appraised her once again. If it had been anyone but Lach, Thad would have to nip that kind of behavior in the bud but he knew Lach meant nothing by it.

"It's tempting but I have an engagement."

"Did you ever settle down, Lach? Get married?" Thad had lost touch with his old friend.

"Well, once you left I pretty much had the playing field all to myself. I think I played my way out of the game. No wife, may have to head to the Dakota Territory see if I could stake a claim like that." He pointed to Merry.

Merry took everything in. She was getting to see a little bit more of her husband's character and understanding some of his upbringing. It was far, far different than her own.

"Are you staying in town or at Laurel?" Lach asked.

"Were staying at Laurel."

"I'll come out sometime tomorrow and we'll catch up."

"I look forward to it."

"Merry," he said then whistled again and with a nod he was off.

"He is a character," Thad was saying. "I hope he didn't offend you, Merry."

"Not in the least. He is very good natured." Thad side glanced at her.

"I want to warn you not all of Charleston will be so kind, and I can't guarantee my mother will be overly kind either."

"I am sure with the lapse of time people have put those things behind them, especially your mother."

Merry felt better after lunch. Jackson Lorton had treated them to a wonderful meal. Merry had never been in such a fancy restaurant and was very nervous. If it wasn't for Thad's hand resting comfortably upon her knee she would have headed for the door.

Thankfully, Abby did most of the talking. Jackson was a very charismatic man and everyone seem to like him. People stopped by the table to chat with him. He had a genteel demeanor which accentuated Abby's vivaciousness. They were a good match.

After lunch Abby walked Jackson back to his office. Thad wanted to show Merry a bit more of the town. They strolled for a while. Thad was a relatively good historian and highlighted all the high points of this part of Charleston. He conversed with a few people that recognized him and introduced Merry to them all.

They had just crossed the street when a woman coming out of a store looked their way. "Thad Sheridan," She drawled out his name in an exaggerated southern dialect. "I can't believe you're in town and haven't come to see me." Another petite beauty was headed Merry's way but this was not his sister.

The woman was looking at him like a cat looks at a bowl of cream. She came with her hand out stretched and Thad grasp it gently.

"Hello, Jena."

"Well, is that any way to greet an old dear friend? We were practically married."

Same old Jena he thought. He hoped she would have matured some.

Merry just stood there looking at the woman with her elaborate frock, earbobs and delicate gloved hands. Her eyes batting like butterfly wings in Thad's direction.

"Jena, this is my wife Merry." Even in a situation like this her name on his lips appeased her. "Merry this is Genevieve."

"Oh, don't tell me you finally gave up the hunt, Thad. After you left and broke our engagement I was sure you'd stay a bachelor."

This is the first Merry had heard of Thad being previously engaged. She was a little shocked. Her Irish blood may be boiling but her poker face was very good.

"Seems to me Jena we both know you have the story a little mixed up."

"Thaddeus James Sheridan, you know it isn't proper to dispute what a lady says in public. You do that in a place of privacy. If you care to come by the house I will be happy to discuss it with you there."

Was she just flirting with my husband an Irish voice was whispering in Merry's subconscious? *What about that husband dear how are you going to handle that one?* She never looked away from Jena but willed her husband silently to put the woman in her place.

"That won't be necessary it's of no importance now."

She turned her eyes on Merry. "My you're a quiet thing."

"I am not one to just talk to hear my head rattle. I usually wait until I have something significant to say. Right now I don't find the occasion."

That's my girl. Thad thought.

Jena was clearly not at all happy with the way things were going. She always liked to have the upper hand and Merry just went over the top. Strolling out the door was Jena's husband. He eyed Thad with abhorrence.

"Sheridan," he said, barely opening his lips.

"Sebastian, this is my wife Merry. Merry, this is Sebastian Cross, Jena's husband."

Thad did not return Sebastian indignation but was sedately cordial.

"What are you doing here?" He just kept staring at Thad.

"Oh, now, Sebastian, don't get your feathers ruffled. You know Loraine Sheridan broke her hip it is only right our Thad come to see her."

Somehow in her own mind, Genevieve still believed she was the belle of the county. She was certain the two men were at odds because of her. Nothing could be farther from the truth.

"You have your nerve Sheridan showing your face around here." This was said with gritted teeth.

"Well, the last I knew it was a free country. That is what I fought for."

Merry did not realize just what a blow her husband delivered. Sebastian Cross didn't fight for either side but hid behind his father's money.

Thad tipped his hat, "Jena, Sebastian," and escorted Merry to Abby's awaiting carriage.

"Don't tell me. The Crosses welcomed you with open arms." Abby said in response to Thad's tight jaw.

"Well at least one of them wanted to." Thad shot Merry a look at her comment. She batted her eyes in mockery but Thad knew Merry may be joking now but later he would have some explaining to do.

The drive out to Laurel was a hushed one. Abby sensed her brother and sister-in-law needed the peace. She was certain by the look on Merry's face she knew nothing of Jena and Thad's past. It was true the two were engaged to be married until Genevieve Harrison found another suitor with more money than the Sheridan's. She tried to tell her brother Jena had an agenda and it was money but he didn't seem to listen.

While he was in law school Jena played the belle of the county. She certainly didn't act like a woman in love or engaged. When Abby confided in her mother Jena had other beaus her mother's response was for her to stay out of it. Jena was right for Thad and it would all work out *and* for her, under no circumstances, was to tell Thad. She was relieved when Jena's true colors were revealed and she and Sebastian were married.

Abby couldn't take the silence anymore.

"Did Jena say something horrible to you Merry? I just can't stand the wretched woman."

To be honest Merry couldn't remember what she had said or what Merry had said back. All she could think about was 'what was Thad thinking about?'

"Don't worry about Merry little sister she can handle herself." He chanced a look at his wife and she was pushing the hair back from her forehead. He just wanted to be alone with her and talk to her. That wasn't going to happen until later tonight when they would be dead tired.

Laurel was the biggest house Merry had ever seen. It was also the most beautiful house she had ever seen. She referred to it as a house because it was too cold to be a home.

An older man greeted them at the door.

"Mr. Thad, it sho is good to see you." The man was about in tears. If it had not been improper for house staff to engage in emotional outburst he would have hugged Thad.

"Timmons, it is good to see you. You're looking well. Let me introduce my wife Merry."

Merry was several inches taller than the man and his clouded eyes looked up at her.

"Nice to meet you, Miss Merry." He looked at Thad and smiled. "Sho is good to see you got married." The old man took the two valises they had been traveling with from Thad. "You go on in and see Mrs. Sheridan she's been asking for you."

Two sets of footsteps came running down the large staircase Anna Beth and Patience had waited long enough to see their Uncle Thad. He had won them over the few days he spent with them in Denver. They were anxious to see him. They converged on him, wrapping their tiny arms around his legs and waist both talking at once.

Anna Beth was the spitting image of her mother and Patience was a complete opposite. She had dark curly hair and brown eyes like her Father. You could tell she was very mischievous.

"Girls this is your aunt Merry." Abby said with her hand in the crook of Merry's arm.

The girls looked at their aunt standing head and shoulders above their mother.

"You're a giant," Patience said and Anna Beth quickly clapped a hand on her younger sister's mouth.

"That's not nice," she scolded the younger girl who promptly bit her sister's hand.

Merry was smiling and started to speak but Abby cut her a look to remain still.

"Patience, you apologize to Aunt Merry. She is very tall but you were rude."

"I sorry, Aunt Mawee."

Merry got down on her level and put out her hand.

"We will be good friends." Patience's little hand came out and she laid it in Merry's large palm. She started to speak but was afraid she would get reprimanded. She instead turned Merry's hand so she could kiss it like a southern gentleman would.

Thad laughed and scooped both girls up in his arm. "Let's go see Grandmama."

Merry swallowed the lump in her throat.

Abby reclaimed Merry's arm. "You will be so good with children. I hope you and Thad have a bunch. He has always said he wanted a dozen. You are getting a little late start but you're still young enough."

Merry's heart was breaking. Her sweet sister-in-law had no idea.

They followed Thad and the girls up the large winding staircase to the first room he came to. The massive door opened and Thad put the girls down to go in. He hung back and let Abby follow the girls.

They were very quiet as they entered their grandmother's room. They approached the bed but did not touch it. Mrs. Sheridan greeted her grandchildren rather formally. Once she spoke to them they were seated on the small settee next to the bed. Loraine Sheridan turned to see her son and daughter-in-law standing in the door way. She was much schooled in her reaction to seeing her son.

"Did you come all this way to stand in the doorway Thad?" He placed his hand on Merry's back and led her to his mother's bed.

"Hello, Mother." He leaned and kissed her cheek. She had aged a lot. "How are you feeling?"

"I have seen better days. This must be Merry. Hello, dear." Her eyes grazed Merry and then went to her son.

"You look just awful, Thad." Merry was astounded at the declaration.

"Thank you, Mother." Thad picked up Patience and took her place on the settee. He settled Patience on his lap and coaxed Anna Beth to scoot closer to him and motioned Merry to sit.

"So, Mother, how did you break your hip, a dance?"

She snorted. "Don't be funny. I tripped over a rug in my sitting room. I see the scar hasn't diminished any on your face. What a disgrace the whole ordeal was." She added.

"Mother are we going to spend our visit dragging up the past?"

"Merry, where are you from? Who are your descendants?" Her stare was meant to intimidate as she changed the course of the conversation.

"My father was an Irish immigrant my mother was from Pennsylvania. Most of my life I have spent in the Dakota Territory." There was an element of shock in her mother-in-laws eyes along with a bit of disdain. This was not going to be a fond memory.

She sighed. "I am very tired as I am sure you both are. Abby tell Hester I will have tea in thirty minutes then prepare to rest. "You children have a nice dinner and Thad I will see you first thing in the morning." The group had been properly dismissed.

All of this seemed to roll off Thad's back. Abby clasped Merry's hand.

"Don't mind Mother, she is so used to being in control, this lying flat on her back has made her . . . well, a little unbearable." Merry tried to put herself in Loraine's place. She supposed she may have just cause not to like Merry but she treated Thad horribly.

The trio had tea in the nursery. Thad was on the floor playing with the girls. The sound of laughter filled the large room. When he grew a little tired and stopped for tea, the girls hung on him. They sat there for a few hours just talking. Merry listened mostly. Abby and Thad reminisced telling childhood stories. They had Merry in stitches. They were very ornery children.

Thad saw dark circles forming under Merry's eyes. He knew she must be very tired. He was beat himself.

"Merry." Abby must have read the scene before her. "Could you use a soak in the tub? You are probably covered in dust."

"That is a fine idea, Abby," Thad agreed.

"I think I may fall asleep in there," Merry confessed. "It would be nice."

Abby stood and pulled a cord hanging from the corner of the room. It was only moments and a servant appeared.

"Christine, will you please prepare a bath for my sister-in-law and tell the cook Thad and Merry will be served supper in their sitting room when Merry is done bathing."

"Yes, ma'am." The girl curtsied and left the room.

"Well, look who has become woman of the house." Thad was teasing his sister.

"If you want a bath, you are on your own, Thad. I am sure Timmons can assist you."

He leaned back in his oversized chair and stretched out his legs putting his head back. He could fall asleep.

"I can take care of myself," he declared as Abby took her leave. She kissed him on the forehead telling him how glad she was he was home. Even if it was for a short visit.

He squeezed her hand. "You make the trip worth it."

She grabbed Merry's hand and started out the door. As Merry passed he captured her free hand and brought it to his lips. It wasn't long until he was asleep in the nursery he occupied thirty-five years ago.

Christine prepared Merry's bath and added some sweet-smelling crystals in the water. Once alone, Merry relaxed. The bath refreshed her mind and spirit. She leaned back and replayed the day in her head.

When she closed her eyes all she saw was Jena. She was worldly and stunning and Thad had loved her enough to make a proposal. She wasn't entirely sure how the engagement ended but neither had seemed to put it completely behind them.

Did Thad marry her because Jena was no longer available? Jena had the nerve to let Thad know the door was still open. This caused Merry to sit up. How could a woman be that frank in front of the man's wife? Sitting up made Merry shiver, or was it the thought of Jena and Thad.

She leaned back. Her mind went to Thad's mother. She was certain the woman did not think much of her son's choice of a wife. After fifteen years of estrangement, she brought up all the old hurts. Her mind went back to Jena and she decided before she became angrier she should finish her bath.

She wasn't sure how long she had been in there so she dunked her whole head under the water quickly washing the day out of her hair. Christine had returned with a dressing gown and left some towels for Merry. When she entered the bedroom, Abby was waiting on her. She asked if she could brush Merry's hair out. They sat on the bed like kids.

"I always wanted a sister, Merry, and you are perfect."

Merry smiled. "I share those same feeling, your letters have been such a treasure to me. You are extremely witty."

"I can tell Thad loves you a great deal and that makes me very happy. I have always felt Thad was penalized for doing the right thing." The brush stopped "and he was always doing the right thing."

"He is a man of great integrity," Merry added.

"It is a rare occasion a man eavesdrops and hears such praise." Thad stood leaning against the doorjamb bathed and clean shaven.

"Did I mention he's impossible?" Merry asked her sister-in-law.

"Always has been." Abby threw a towel at her brother. He caught it in midair hurled it at his wife. Before he could get out of the bedroom, every wet towel had bombarded him.

"Hurry up, I am starved," he called over his shoulder and went into the sitting room where food had been brought up for he and Merry.

A small table held a large amount of food. Abby was asked to stay but declined. She always sat with the children while they ate then dined with Jackson when he returned home.

Merry was walking about the room in her white robe and her hair half dry pulled to one side. The more she strolled the more the room filled with the smell of lavender.

"You must be hungry. Are you going to eat?" Thad asked.

"What is behind that door?" She pointed to the door on the other side of the room.

"Open it."

She looked at him strangely. She opened the door and there was another bedroom. It was decorated in a very manly décor, a vast difference to the bedroom she was just in.

"Whose room is that?"

"That was my father's room."

"I thought that was your parent's room." She pointed to the bedroom on the other side of the sitting room.

"No, that was my mother's room." A queer look came over her face.

"You mean?" She didn't really know how to put it.

"It is not uncommon in a house as big as this for everyone to have their own room. It is rather customary in the South."

"Why is that?"

"I guess people need their own space sometimes, maybe they fuss a lot." He smiled.

"I don't care how angry I might be." Her hand was on her hip. "And after the events of today, I am pretty angry with you, Thad Sheridan, but if a woman is bold enough to fight with a man, she better be woman enough to sleep with him at the end of the day."

He was speechless. He crossed the room and stood in front of her. The bath may have revived her but the dark circles were worse. He stroked her face with his thumb. His eyes caressed her face and his thumb moved to the softness of her lips. He bent to kiss her and she sighed just a little. She let him kiss her twice and then put her hands on his chest gently pushing him back.

"I'm serious, you could have told me about Jena."

He rubbed the back of his neck. "We are both hungry and tired. Can we fight tomorrow?"

They ate almost all of the meal provided for them. "It wasn't long until they retired. Lying in the stillness Merry looked at her husband. He was lying on his back with his hand draped over his forehead. She knew he was not asleep.

"I have to know one thing before I go to sleep."

He turned and propped himself on his elbow. He did not say anything but gave her his undivided attention.

"Do you still care for Jena?"

"I care." He saw a shadow cross her face. "I care that her soul is headed to hell unless she changes her ways. Other than that, I couldn't care one wit about Genevieve Cross." He returned to his original position. "And," he added, "that little act she put on today was solely for the purpose of antagonizing her husband and putting false thoughts in your head. If you allow that to happen, the fault is yours."

She reached for his hand. She knew he was right. She began to giggle.

"I can see why some men would prefer their own room." He joined her in her laughter. He knew there would be no fighting in the morning.

The next morning Merry awakened to an empty but spacious bed. Her body ached from the nearly three-day journey to Charleston. Thad had eased her mind last night and she was able to sleep rather nicely.

Thad heard her stirring and came from the sitting room with his Bible in hand. He had been up for hours preparing for what lie ahead when he would be summoned by his mother.

"Good morning." She smiled.

"Good morning. Did you sleep all right?"

"Yes," she rubbed her eyes, "but this bed is so big it kind of swallows you up."

"It is a little bigger than what I prefer." He sat down on the edge.

"I believe six people could sleep in this bed."

He tipped his head back and laughed. The things she found to focus on.

"What time is it?"

"It is close to seven. If you would like to go back to sleep no one would care."

The thought was tempting but she was ready to face the day. "No I feel pretty good. I think I will get dressed."

"Breakfast today will probably be around nine so you don't have to hurry. I will find you and we can go down together. I suspect my Mother will be sending for me soon."

"Thad, can we pray together?"

"I would love that." They gripped hands and Merry began to pray. She prayed the Lord would lead Thad in the conversation he would be having with his mother. She prayed for Abby and Jackson and the girls. She prayed for everyone but herself. If she knew what lie ahead today she would have quickly tagged her name to the list. A few minutes later there was a knock on the door. Loraine Sheridan was ready to speak to her son.

Thad threw up a prayer as he entered his mother's bedchambers.

"Close the door and come sit where I can see you." The only place where she could fully see him was on the edge of the bed. With her assurance, it would not cause any pain to her he eased himself onto the bed.

"How have you been Son, truthfully?" There was not a bit of concern for him in her face.

"I have been more than fine."

"Yes, I can see, you're smitten with that Irish woman."

"Her name is Merry mother, and it goes beyond smitten, I love her very much."

"How on earth did you ever meet someone like that?"

"What do you mean someone like that?" Thad had promised himself not to let his anger get the best of him and to guide his tongue wisely.

"Thad, she is nothing like our women here. Her clothes are . . ." She paused. "I suppose when you're that size, it would be hard to find anything appealing, does she even own a corset? It would help her cinch in her chest."

"There is absolutely nothing wrong with Merry's figure. It is very pleasing." Thad had a happy little smile on his face.

"Thad Sheridan, do not be improper."

"You brought it up, Mother."

Merry was dressed and headed downstairs. The door to Loraine's room was open a crack and she heard Loraine mention her name.

"All I am saying is Merry is not right for you. There is not an ounce of refinement in her. I see she wears the necklace I sent her. Does she wear it all the time? It is a rare stone and should be worn with the proper attire. It was meant for Jena. She was supposed to be your wife. Jena was perfect. I still don't understand what happened between you two."

Thad's mother had asked him not to interrupt so he had stayed silent. He was formulating his final words on the subject that would end anymore criticism of his wife.

Merry was stock still at the door. She knew she should not be listening but they were, after all, discussing her. She heard the pause and waited for Thad to speak after a few ticks of silence she heard Loraine say, "You know I am right." Merry headed down the stairs. She had heard and not heard enough.

"Mother," Thad's tone was very cool. His words were measured. "Merry is and will always be the right woman for me. God brought us together and I love her more than anything in this life. I will not allow you to insult her in any form, verbally or emotionally, and," he added very defiantly, "if you can't abide by that I will leave today."

His mother sighed. "This all started the first time you came home from law school, that Kennedy boy encouraged you to read those essays from that religious zealot from a century ago. What was his name? Wesley? John Wesley? After that you changed and I didn't even know my own son."

"The change was Christ in my life, Mother, not some man's writings."

"Yes, yes, I have heard it all before. When you chose to fight with the Yankees, Lachlan came to your father and me and told us about how you were making choices based on God's will not on your own. He said we shouldn't be upset. He would have been right there with you had it not been for that sister of his. He kept visiting right up until your father died."

Thad felt ashamed that he had not tried to stay in contact with his old friend Lach. The fact that he went to his folks as a peacemaker for fifteen years on Thad's behalf showed the depth of a Christian bond. He would have to thank him when he saw him today.

"A couple of times he would bring that sister with him. I just couldn't stand to be around her."

"Mother, her mental capacity was that of a five-year-old."

"Well, he should have put her somewhere after his folks died, but he insisted in caring for her. I suppose that is why he never married. It got him out of the war too. Your father had more grace with the situation. That sister loved our stables and he would take her and Lach to them. The girl always had a child's expression even as she aged, she finally died, God rest her soul."

How could his mother defy the existence of God then use such a phrase? His mother was visibly tired and Thad left the room headed to find his wife.

He met Abby in the hall. "If you're looking for Merry she went downstairs."

He started to turn but Abby stopped him with a hand on his arm. "Thad, when I came out of the nursery I saw Merry standing outside Mothers door. She listened for a few minutes and then went down the stairs rather quickly."

His eyes slid shut. How much had she heard?

He headed down the stairs. He ran into Timmons just outside his father's study.

"Timmons, have you seen my wife?"

"I believe she is in the dining room with Miss Anna Beth and Miss Patience."

Thad found them there. Merry was engaged in conversation with his oldest niece. She conversed with Merry as an adult would. They were discussing the house.

Patience on the other hand was still in her nightgown sitting at the table. Her legs were tucked under her gown. Her hair a curly mess and her eyes were still full of sleep. It was obvious she was not fond of mornings.

"Good morning, ladies." Thad kissed his nieces and went to Merry.

Bending over he kissed her on the mouth a little longer than was proper. Her response was indifferent and he knew she had left the door of his mother's room before she had heard Thad's rebuttal.

The girls giggled at their Aunt and Uncle.

"You girls don't need to act like you've never seen anyone kiss before. Your father and I do it all the time." Abby had arrived and breakfast was served.

She and Thad had never witnessed much of a loving relationship between their parents. She supposed they both decided to conduct their marriages differently. If she thought her brother a good man before, Thad's 'conversion' had made him so much more.

During breakfast Anna Beth asked Merry if she would play a game with her after the meal and Merry agreed happily. Patience perked up and clapped her small little hands.

"No Patience, you are spending the morning with me." Abby said and the little girls face fell and tears begin to form. "Remember what Daddy said this morning when you were so cross and wouldn't get dressed for breakfast. He said you could come down in your nightgown but if you did you would spend the morning upstairs with me."

The little girls head went down on the table in tears. Thad started to reach for the little girl but Abby cleared her throat and shook her head. "Jackson was firm on this Thad, do not coddle her."

Thad grinned at his sister and returned to his breakfast.

"You can see what kind of disciplinarian he will be Merry. You will have to be the stern parent."

Abby wasn't looking at either one of them or she would have seen the hurt that past between them. Anna Beth saw it.

"Uncle Thad, you can play too I didn't mean you couldn't play." She had mistaken his look of sadness for rejection. Isn't that just like the innocence of a child? She didn't want anyone to feel left out.

He stood and lifted his little niece into his arms and whispered in her ear. Whatever he said put a look of pure love on the youngster's face. Merry made a mental note to ask him later. She gave her uncle a big hug and kissed his cheek right on the scar. She ran her finger down the length of the mark.

"Uncle Thad, how'd ya get that?"

"That is a story for another day precious."

Timmons arrived then to announce the arrival of Mr. Kennedy who was waiting for Thad in the study.

The two men shook hands and Thad suggested a walk down to the stables. The morning sun made the air feel less cool. The tender beginnings of spring were all around.

"I was sorry to hear about your sisters passing. How long has she been gone?"

"Three years. It seems like yesterday." The big man looked on the verge of tears.

"After Mom died several people wanted me to put her someplace, said she would ruin any chance of a life for me. You remember her, Thad, how special she was."

Thad nodded remembering how she tagged along every time they went fishing. She would sit on the bank smiling hands deep in the bucket of worms finding just the right one for each of them. He also remembered the patience Lach had with her.

From the time Mrs. Kennedy became sick up until Lorelei's death, Lachlan Kennedy had given up his life for his sister. He couldn't enter the war because of her. Thad was certain very few women in his circle would take on the care of Lorelei if Lachlan had pursued.

Lach looked at his friend.

"I was just doing a little reminiscing she was very special."

"Tell me could you put one of your nieces 'away' just like that." He snapped his fingers to emphasize the point.

"I don't even like to think about it. You did the right thing Lach. Lorelei was blessed to have you."

"Don't kid yourself Sheridan, I was blessed. She taught me the purpose of life and it is not what I see all around me day after day." The man continued with a sincere passion. "The joy of life isn't in things. It is your grubby little hands in a worm bucket and your heart so in tune with your creator nothing else matters."

"I'm sorry Thad I just see a lost world and the limitations of being one man."

"We go to the field the Lord sends us," Thad encouraged his friend. "I want to thank you Lach for taking the time to repeatedly speak to my parents about the Lord. I wrote them several letters over the years but never once heard back."

"That's because they never opened them."

Thad wasn't surprised.

"I would come to see your folks. Your Dad and I would end up out here. He told me once he had all your letters but whatever you had to say wouldn't make a difference. I guess I am just simple enough to believe the scriptures when it says a prophet has no honor in his own country. They weren't going to listen to you but maybe they would listen to me."

A mist covered Thad's eyes. To think Lach would pick up the torch when Thad had to lay it down touched his heart. God had blessed him with a good friend.

"I could never seem to get very far with them Thad. I grieved terribly when your dad passed. I don't know what he did in his last moments but up until the day before his heart was still hard."

Anyone else would have been appalled Lach would say such things but Thad understood the gift of a free will and a changed life. He was not offended.

"A bright spot is Jackson and Abby they are eager to hear what I have to say and seem to be weighing it all up." Thad was overjoyed at this. Merry had been witnessing to Abby. They had been taken to church as children but it was more of a show than anything. It was what was expected of the family. His parents hadn't a clue what it meant to be truly saved. It was a comfort to know Lach was working on this end. There was hope.

On the way back to the house, Lach asked how Thad and Merry met. Thad relayed the whole story including the loss of the baby. He told him about Hank and Lone Eagle and how he had been trying to show them Christ. They ended up back in the study and read and prayed together for the next hour. It did Thad's heart good. He had a selfish wish his friend would someday come to the territory, but if he did who would witness to his family. God had a perfect plan of where he needed the likes of Lachlan Kennedy and Thad Sheridan.

His thoughts were interrupted.

"What is that smell?" Lachlan took a deep breath and inhaled.

Thad knew exactly what it was. "Come with me."

The two men found their way into the kitchen. The cook was sitting at the table with a distressed look on her face. Anna Beth was standing on a chair next to Merry. Patience, who had served her sentence was dressed and sitting on the countertop dotted with flour. They were baking cookies. A hot pan had just been removed from the oven and was cooling when the men entered.

"Wait till you taste one of these." Thad handed Lach a warm handful of goodness and he sunk his teeth in. Never had he tasted anything so good.

"Merry."

His mouth was full of cookie. He started to speak but Patience informed him not to talk with his mouth full. The adults laughed.

“You should taste her raspberry pie.” Thad had moved to stand behind his wife, putting his hands around her waist.

“You should taste his apple dumplings.” She motioned with her head as she worked the dough to ready more cookies.

“Uncle Thad doesn’t cook” Anna Beth stated with skepticism.

“Don’t underestimate your old Uncle Thad.” She had a look on her face and Merry knew she did not know what *underestimate* meant.

“He just means if he has to cook he can.”

“Oh,” she said and tried to picture her uncle in the kitchen. Perhaps he got the scar while trying to cook.

“What is going on in here?” Abby arrived after her nap. The cook stood.

“I am sorry, Mrs. Lorton. She wanted to use the kitchen. I—”

Abby was shocked at the tone the cook had taken. “She has a name, it is Mrs. Sheridan, and it is perfectly all right for her to use the kitchen. I did not intend to insinuate I was the least bit upset.” The cook had the good graces to leave the kitchen.

“Try a cookie momma we helped Merry make them.” Anna Beth was so proud of her accomplishment.

Abby took a bite and the thing just melted in her mouth. “Darling, they are wonderful. You did a grand job.” She kissed her daughters head. She was feeling a little remorse. She was the girl’s mother she should be baking with them, but how would she know to do that. Her mother never baked with her. Her emotions got the best of her.

Merry witnessed the tirade of emotion playing out.

“Thad, you can show the girls your skill in the kitchen. I’ll leave the rest of this to you and your little helpers. Anna Beth is more than capable of assisting.”

With that she led Abby out of the kitchen and into the downstairs salon.

“I am sorry if I overstepped my boundaries in there. I just thought it would be fun for the girls.”

“Oh Merry, I am not upset about that. I am upset because I need to be doing those types of things with them. My mother never did anything like that with me matter of fact, she did very little with me. I had a governess that saw to everything. I want to be there for my girls in a way my mother never was."

"You will be." Merry was holding her tearful sister-in-law's arm.

"You will be so good at this." Abby patted her own stomach and squeezed Merry's hand. She so wanted Thad and Merry to experience the joy her children brought her.

Merry stood and walked to the window.

"Abby, I need to tell you something and please don't be hurt." Abby got a sickening sensation in the pit of her stomach. "Thad and I won't be having any children. I . . . We lost a baby back before Christmas and . . ." Her voice was starting to crack and she shoved the hair off her forehead.

Abby was now standing beside her. "Merry, I am so sorry, and here I have been hinting and saying things that had to be so hurtful to you and Thad."

"We should have told you. I felt a little guilty not sharing with you by letter but the time never seemed right."

"Merry, I know people lose a child, but they go on to have other children."

Merry's look was far away. "I lost a lot of blood, and there was a problem . . ." She couldn't say it.

"I understand, Merry, how awful for you both." She held her sister-in-law in a loving embrace.

"Do you smell that?" Abby's nose was turned up. Merry sniffed it was the unmistakable odor of burnt cookies.

"Don't look at me," Lach was saying as Thad was shoveling the burnt cookies into the compost bin.

"You were supposed to watch them while I took Patience to . . . Never mind."

Anna Beth had been putting the cookies on the platter and Lach was supposed to watch the pan in the oven. It was quite the mess Merry, and Abby found when they entered the kitchen a little haze of smoke remained. Thad looked at Merry and instantly knew she had been crying.

He desperately wanted some time alone with his wife, but things kept getting in his way. He was just going to have to claim the time and the time was now. Stopping her from going to the stove he put his hands on her shoulders turned her around and gently nudged her out the kitchen door following behind her.

"Hey, aren't you going to clean up your mess," Lach mentioned as they were headed out the door.

"Get a wife, Lach" the phrase was thrown over Thad's shoulder. He heard his old buddy's' familiar laugh.

Thad didn't stop but guided Merry out the door. He draped his coat around her shoulders, and led her across the yard to the gardener's cottage. It was a nice quiet, empty place where they could be alone.

From her vantage point, Loraine Sheridan could see the couple step into the dwelling. If Franklin had not disowned his son things would be very different right now. Thad would have been allowed home and she was certain Jena Harrison would have been her daughter-in-law, and Thad would be here to run Laurel and the Mill. Instead, he was a thousand miles away without any controlling interest in what was rightfully his. She let out a heavy sigh. She must formulate some sort of plan.

"You've been crying."

Thad shut the door to the cottage and turned to face his wife. She was staring at him her mouth in a tight line and her eyes defiant.

"And I believe you were eaves dropping this morning. Care to tell me what you heard and when you decided to stop listening."

"I have been crying but it is not what you think and believe me I heard enough."

He noticed the familiar bite in her words. He usually liked sparring with her but today he was weary.

"Where's the necklace?"

Her hand went to her throat. She had removed the necklace after breakfast and planned to leave it behind for Loraine when they left.

"In the room, I've grown tired of wearing it."

"Uh huh." He crossed his arms over his chest and leaned back against the wall.

The snake, why did he have to be so good at this? He is going to just lean back and let me jabber on and tangle myself up in my own words. She just wouldn't talk.

She found an old crate and sat down, placing her hands in her lap. "Was that all you wanted to know? About the necklace, I mean," she said coolly.

He spoke, more to himself than her. "The necklace was about midway through the conversation right before we discussed your, uh . . ." He stroked his chin and gave her figure an appreciative glance. Her eyes popped and she stood

"My what?"

By her reaction, she didn't hear his mother's disparaging comments about her dress. This helped him speculate that she left off listening about the time his mother stopped and he had yet to begin his rebuttal.

"You didn't even defend me." She was coming toward him in a rapid manner.

He was mad.

"How would you know what I did or didn't say? You walked away."

"Lower your voice, I am sure they can hear you in the house."

If his piercing blue eyes could get any colder she hadn't seen it. He was incensed.

"I know." He pointed to his chest then aimed his finger at her. "You know that I love you Merry but this constant doubting you do is getting old. The fact that you believe I would let anyone, including my own mother, disrespect you shows the lack of confidence you have in me. A man's pride can only take so many hits before he reacts."

He headed to the door and stopped. He promised himself he would never walk away from an issue just because he was angry.

Merry watched his back when he stopped he ran his hand through his hair and rubbed the back of his neck. Without turning around, he spoke. “We are going to stay in here until we get a few things straightened out.” He turned and leaned against the door.

Merry hung her head. She ached all over. She didn’t know she had injured his pride. She had made it hard on him because of her own lack of self-worth.

“All my life,” she started “I was passed from one person to another. Once my father died my mother just let anyone and everyone take care of me. Whoever was up for the challenge?” she shrugged her shoulders.

“My uncle finally took me until he decided to get married and then I was shipped out to my grandfather. There was talk about sending me back to Ireland to my father’s folks but they couldn’t find them. I guess I have built up a kind of defense. Then when you came along and offered to take me it was just one more act of pity.”

It was all he could do not to silence her but he knew they would get nowhere until she unburdened her heart.

“But you were different. I never saw pity in your eyes. I saw a lot of things I didn’t know existed. I saw friendship, compassion and selflessness. I saw love and I got scared. Then all those things materialized in a wonderful life within me. I was going to have tangible proof of your love.”

The tears were trickling down her face and splashing on her chest. “And then it was gone.” She wiped her eyes with the palms of her hands. “I do know you love me, Thad. Problem is I can’t seem to love myself. I’ve never felt worthy. I know that is self-pity and I am trying but the lost hope of children was a devastating blow.”

He couldn’t take it anymore he needed to be touching her.

Before he could make a move, she had come to him and fell hard against his chest. Her face buried in his shoulder. He stroked her back and after a while he lifted her head. Wiping the tears from her cheek he looked intently into her eyes.

“Merry, do you believe all things work together for good to them that love God, to them who are the called according to his purpose. Do you believe you are called?”

She placed her hand on his and softly shook her head. “Then you are worthy.” His hands cradled her face.

Her head dropped and she silently prayed. Thanking God for such a gift as Thad Sheridan. He was doing much the same for his own gift of Merry Quinn.

They talked a little bit more as Merry used Thad's handkerchief to put herself back together. She made a step for the door and started to open it. Thad's large hand came above her head and closed it.

"Hold on just a minute." She turned expectantly to her husband.

"We had a pretty good fight here I'm thinking it requires some pretty good making up."

She leaned against the door and welcomed her husband's attention.

It was almost an hour before Loraine saw the couple leave the Gardner's cottage. What could they possibly have to discuss that would take that long. Her mind drifted back to her days in the Gardner's cottage. She and Franklin went there mostly to fight out of earshot from the servants but they always made up before they left. A smile graced her face. She did love that man.

She watched as Thad playfully flirted with his wife and knew she would be no match for the women in Thad's life. She closed her eyes and dreamed of her late husband.

Chapter Seven

Thad spent the rest of the afternoon with his mother. She was very somber after their morning discussion. She spent the majority of their conversation reminiscing about the old days before the war had torn them apart. Thad felt sorry for his mother and the losses she had suffered but he would never be sorry for fighting for what he believed in. He felt they cleared the air some. He knew he could return to the territory with a clear conscious.

"This came today. I don't suppose you will attend." She handed him an invitation.

The Sheridans and the Lortons were invited to dinner tomorrow evening at the home of Captain John and Lady Angela Harrison, Jena's parents.

"I can't imagine why they would want to have dinner with me?"

"Can't you son?" his mother raised one eyebrow.

He honestly didn't know.

"If you don't go it will be a reflection on me," she said.

"If I don't go it will be a reflection on Christ, Mother, not you."

She did not like that comment and started to rebuff her son. He kissed her forehead.

"Write them and tell them the Sheridan accept, that is if you haven't already." He left to break the news to his wife.

“What do you suggest I wear?” She was saying moments after he told her of the dinner plans. He was lying stretched out on the bed hands folded under his head.

“Let’s see. Did you bring that cute grey dress you wear to garden in? She climbed up on the bed.

“I am serious Thad what am I going to wear? You know everyone there will be elegant and then here comes old Merry Moogret.”

His hand came out and swatted her hip rather harshly. “None of that.”

She rubbed her hip “I can’t believe you just did that.” She looked a little miffed.

“If you act like a child you’re going to get treated like a child.”

There was a soft knock at the door and Abby’s voice was on the other side.

“Come in, Abby, and save me from this tyrant.”

“What?” She gracefully glided into the room.

“Your brother just hit me.”

Abby’s eyes were wide.

“I spanked her and if she doesn’t straighten up I’ll do it again.”

“Was he always such a bully, Abby?”

“No, I can’t imagine what has happened to him unless it would be the effects of stubborn Irish lass.” Merry was speechless and Thad was laughing his fool head off.

“Did you need something Abby?” Merry smiled at her sister-in-law enjoying the teasing.

“I came to see what you plan to wear tomorrow night?”

“I was just trying to discuss that with Mr. Impossible, which was pointless.”

“I am here to help so you may leave if you wish.” Abby looked at her brother.

“Not on your life. I’m staying.”

He did stay right there on the bed as Abby had Merry try on every dress she brought.

Abby frowned. “They’re pretty Merry don’t get me wrong. There just not eye catching.”

Thad got off the bed and pushed his sister into the sitting room and closed the door. He walked over to the closet and found the only dress that would work for the evening.

"Is there a reason you didn't show her this one." He held the blue dress she wore on the fourth of July. She had no answer except the dress held fond memories for her and she didn't want Jena Harrison Cross to diminish that in any way.

When no answer came from her he simply said "put it on." Once the dress was on, he fastened the tiny buttons.

"Where is the necklace?"

She motioned to the chest of drawers. He slipped the necklace around her neck and affixed the clasp. "A man would have to go a long way to find a woman as beautiful as you Merry." He whispered. Catching her eye in the full length mirror he winked.

He opened the bedroom door and presented his wife. Abby was in awe.

Thad chose that time to leave the two ladies. "Leave it to Mr. Impossible," he said as he bowed out the door.

Merry was nervous the whole day. She played with her nieces to occupy her mind. She knew nothing about dinner parties and social graces and she certainly did not want to disgrace her husband or his family. Abby assured her she would do fine. If she was unsure about something just copy what she was doing. It still terrified her. One thing she was not terrified about was spending the evening with Jena. She was experiencing a wave of confidence in regards to her husband ex-fiancé. She planned to take the high road.

The Harrisons had the biggest house in town. *Le palais* French for the palace was in the middle of town. The high steps led to an enormous porch with big thick columns. Lady Angela's family was of French decent and the house reflected the ornate styles of Europe. It rivaled Laurel but was not as genteel. Laurel was nestled in the out skirts of town surrounded by several acres.

The couples were escorted into a large sitting room on the ground floor where they were met by Captain Harrison and Sebastian. Thad had been gearing up for the meeting all day. He wasn't sure what to expect from the Harrisons'. He knew what to expect from Sebastian.

"Thad, it has been a long time, it is good to see you." The captain extended his hand with sincerity in his remarks.

"It is good to see you sir. I would like to introduce my wife. This is Merry."

"It is a pleasure to meet you, Merry." He smiled and kissed her hand.

He greeted Jackson and Abby and motioned for everyone to sit.

"I would say I can't imagine what is keeping the ladies but then I would be lying." This was met with smiles and he kept up the conversation.

"Tell me, Thad, do you like the Dakota Territory? I was out there once it was beautiful, I grant you but a little too isolated for my taste."

"I do like it, sir, but it takes some getting used too."

The captain turned his focus to Merry. "And do you like it, Merry?"

He wasn't at all what Merry expected he was polite and there was no condescension in is manner.

"Yes, sir, it is pretty much the only place I have lived."

"Ah, so what do you think of Charleston?"

"It is beautiful I will grant you but a little too populated for my taste." She smiled and the older man laughed.

"Touché, Mrs. Sheridan. "You have yourself a charmer, Thad."

"Yes, sir, and don't I know it."

"Who's a charmer, dear?"

Angela Harrison stood in the door way with her daughter. They were very elaborately dressed and both looked as if they had gotten hold of some of Merry's special lemonade. Captain Harrison rose to welcome his wife and daughter. Sebastian stayed near the fire place glaring at everyone.

"Why, you, of course." He kissed her hand and led her into the room. Jena entered by herself.

She slowly sashayed past Thad to stand next to her husband. Adjusting Sebastian's tie, she spoke, "Mother, have you met Thad's wife, Margret?"

She intentionally used a wrong name to give Merry the impression she wasn't worth remembering.

"It is good to see you again, Thad." Lady Harrison's tone was cool.

Thad rose to take Angela's out stretched hand "Lady Harrison, may I introduce my wife, Merry Margret Sheridan."

Jackson and Abby could not keep the mirth from their faces. Everyone knew what little Jena was doing and it backfired.

"It is a pleasure to meet you, Lady Harrison."

"Likewise . . ." Angela paused as if trying to recall her guest's name.

"Merry," she supplied, "or you may call me Margret, as your daughter prefers."

Without so much as a nod, Angela turned. "Shall we go into dinner?"

Lady Harrison led the way she took Thad as her escort leaving the captain to escort Merry. The table had tiny place cards telling everyone where to sit. Merry was seated between Sebastian and Jackson. Thad was seated across the table at the very end to the right of Lady Angela with Jena on his other side. Merry wasn't discouraged. No, her Irish blood was at a full boil, but her mind was crisp and cool. She would have the final say tonight. She would be leaving with Thad.

The dinner conversation took many directions. Merry spoke when spoken to. Captain Harrison engaged her in the discussion frequently. He was pretty taken with her. She was not self-absorbed like his wife and daughter. It wasn't until recently he noticed how haughty his wife and daughter had become. He believed his meetings with Lachlan Kennedy had something to do with his eyes becoming open.

"Have you seen Lachlan Kennedy since you've returned?" his thoughts prompted him to ask Thad.

"Yes sir, he seems to be doing well."

"I have never met a man like Lach. Most men wouldn't have taken the care with Lorelei as he did."

Jena sighed as if she was bored. "I can't understand for the life of me why he did not put her somewhere. Instead he took her all over town. He showed up at every event with her in tow. She always had some sort of accident that was very disruptive of the festivities."

Most of the table couldn't believe what was coming out of Jena's pink stained lips.

Abby was completely red. Thad just stared at her profile in disgust. Jackson nervously fidgeted with his napkin. Merry looked as if she could take her hoe to Jena's tongue. Jena and Angela didn't seem to notice.

"Ruined the poor man's chances of ever getting married." She continued.

Captain Harris leaned back in his chair and caught Jena's full attention with his eyes.

"Perhaps I should have put you somewhere, daughter." Captain Harrison's anger was acute.

"John." Angela was attempting to diffuse the situation with a glare. "I have never heard a more heartless statement. Is this what I raised you to become?"

"Let's have coffee on the veranda." Angela started to rise.

"Sit down, Angela." She immediately sat down.

"These people are our old friends and I think they deserve and apology from our daughter in regards to her rude behavior. Wouldn't you agree, Sebastian?"

Sebastian, up until this point had been a fly on the wall, was now called upon to give account for his wife. The wife he loved who held no regard for him outside of his bank account.

"It would seem she has stepped out of line."

Good for you, Sebastian, Thad thought. There was hope after all. Jena left the table in tears.

Angela rose to follow but Sebastian stopped her.

"I will handle this." He rose to leave and Angela also excused herself. Captain Harrison saw his guest to the door and made his apologies.

They didn't see Jena Harrison anymore during their visit but they did see her father. Captain Harrison came a few days later to see Thad. He came to apologize for all the trouble he had caused for Thad when he returned from the war. Captain Harrison had been one of the people who brought some tough accusations against Thad and encouraged the town to disown their native son.

"I may not have agreed with you but I now see I should have respected your decision. I made it too hard for you to stay in Charleston. I'm sorry."

The man that stood before him was not the same man he knew so many years ago.

"I am a firm believer in God's will Captain Harrison so much that I try to follow it in every aspect of life. It was his will that set me on the path I took. Your actions had very little to do with it. I am honest when I say your treatment as well as my own fathers saddened me, but they in no way broke me."

The man's eyes were intent on Thad when he spoke.

"I imagine your attitude toward the whole ordeal is the influence of religion in your life. Much like Lachs and the way he treated his sister."

"It's not religion, it is being Christ like. It's serving Christ instead of ourselves."

"So you say, as does Lachlan, but I have known you both from infancy. You were always good boys. It is just your nature."

"That's where you are wrong. My nature was sinful until I realized my need for a savior. Once I came to the understanding I was responsible for Christ death because of my sins I was able to see just how lost I was. There was no other answer to my life than to hand it back over to my creator and be reconciled through his son Jesus Christ."

"I have been meeting with Lach to learn more about all this but I am just not sure I believe it all."

"Captain Harrison, the more you hear the more you will want to hear. Until you have a child like faith to believe it won't be clear."

The man's face had hard lines in his forehead. He was searching and the Holy Spirit was dealing with him pretty heavily. Thad was silent. Captain Harris finally spoke.

"Well I didn't want you to leave without making my apologies."

"Why do you suppose you picked now, after all these years to do so?"

The man had a blank look on his face. Thad smiled.

"You think about it sir, and please keep meeting with Lach." Captain Harrison stuck out his hand and when Thad grasp it he pulled the younger man into a fatherly embrace.

That evening after dinner Thad announced that he and Merry would be leaving the day after tomorrow. He had not discussed this with his wife so it was just as big as surprise to her as it was to the others. She couldn't deny she was ready to go home. She had discovered that every town had its Liddy Lapps and its Zelma McPhersons.

"Are you disappointed?" he asked as he walked her upstairs to their room.

"Not in the least."

"Mother asked me to meet with Jackson tomorrow about some papers I need to sign. I am not sure what all of it is about since I was disinherited, but after that I am free. Is there something you would like to do or some place you would like to go on our last day?"

"Maybe just spend it with Abby and the girls. I would like to see Lachlan before we leave too."

He stopped on the stairs putting his hand over his heart.

"Should I be jealous?" he feigned being hurt.

"Well I did see him pull out a book of poetry and with that voice of his Mr. Impossible may just get knocked off the throne."

He reached to swat at her and she ran the rest of the way up the stairs and down the hall, Thad on her heels.

Christine was coming out of their room when they reached the door. Merry was doubled over laughing and Thad was leaning against the wall.

"Mrs. Sheridan would like to see you, Ms. Merry."

Merry sobered up quick. "When?"

"She said when you came up to retire to send you in."

Thad reached for Merry's hand and turned toward his Mother's room.

"Mrs. Sheridan said she wanted to see Ms. Merry alone."

Merry's hand went to her forehead.

"You don't have to go." Thad told her.

"Does she know we are leaving?" Thad nodded. Merry headed to her mother-in-laws room.

"Please sit." She motioned Merry to sit in a chair that had been placed by the bed.

"I don't know you well enough to like you, nor do I know you well enough to dislike you. The only thing I know is Thad is happy. I would guess that should make me happy."

Merry stayed silent. The woman continued.

"I had plans for Thad. Not one of those plans has come to fruition. I also had dreams for Thad and although the package isn't what I imagined the dream is what I had hoped for. Take care of my son. I leave him to you."

That was it. That was all the woman had to say?

Merry wasn't sure how she should respond. Should she be "thankful" to have this meager morsel of a compliment? Merry measured her words.

"Plans do not coincide with life and dreams are a byproduct of hope. Thad's life has miraculously and divinely intertwined with mine. So much that the entire package is perfect, maybe not in the eyes of those around us but in the eyes of our Heavenly Father. That is the source of Thad's happiness."

Loraine Sheridan closed her eyes and leaned her head against the backboard tears settled on her lashes. She patted Merry's knee affectionately and said, "Good night." Merry knew she had been dismissed.

Merry caught sight of Thad just as he entered their room. He had been listening.

Sad faces stood at the train station. Abby and the girls were near tears. They had grown to love Merry and hated to see her leave. It took Thad almost fifteen years to return would it be another fifteen before they reunited? He promised it wouldn't be as he kissed his sister good-bye.

"You're always welcome to come see us," he offered. The girls were all for that and it eased the sad look on their face.

Lachlan had come to see his friend off as well.

"Thanks again Lach for all you're doing here." Thad's hand was almost swallowed up in Lachs.

"We all have a job to do Thad, we just need to keep doing." Thad smiled at his good friend.

Lach turned his attention to Merry, shaking his head he whistled.

"I can see where a man would leave all this and head west if he knew that was waiting on him." He pointed with a nod toward Merry.

Thad smiled. "Read her a little poetry and she might stay."

Merry gave Thad's arm a hard pinch then stood on her tiptoes and kissed Lach's cheek.

"It was nice to meet you, Lachlan Kennedy"

"The pleasure has been all mine."

The couple boarded the train. They were going home.

Thad was a little quiet on the way home. Merry wasn't sure if he was sad or if his meeting with Jackson was bothering him. He didn't mention much about the details of his meeting just that Franklin Sheridan may have disinherited him but Loraine hadn't. He promised they would talk about it when they got home.

He also seemed very tense. When she laid her head on his shoulder to rest a bit she felt the tightness of his muscles.

"Are you okay?" she asked, his eyes were roaming around the train car and he didn't hear her."

"Thad."

"What?" he asked, not looking at her.

She tried to survey the car to decide what had captured his attention but she couldn't figure it out. "I will be right back. I think I recognize an old friend."

So that was it. Thad rose and exited the car. He stood on the platform in between the cars speaking with a man smoking a cigarette. Merry watched the men shake hands and then the other gentleman flick the cigarette into the open air.

"I thought that was you, Sheridan." The man smiled.

"You working for the railroad now, Carter?"

"Yip, it is a lot less stress than the rangers. You still Bible thumping?"

"I am still following Christ if that is what you're asking."

Carter just shook his head. "Who's the little lady? Don't tell me someone finally roped you."

Thad just smiled. "It happens to the best of us, I guess."

The man winked at Thad's smile.

"I noticed a couple of men on the train I am not sure I trust." This got the man's attention.

"Go on."

"About a year ago, I was following a trio from Laredo. They had stolen the payroll of a rancher friend of mine and had moved on to a little bit riskier take. I spotted two of them when I boarded. I have been trying to find out if the third one is with them but I haven't seen him. They seem to be taking inventory."

"Right now, I'd say they are taking inventory of your wife."

Thad's head shot around and sure enough one man was sitting across from Merry and the other had sat down in Thad's vacated seat. He started to move but the older man stopped him. "You go rushing in there they may get wise. You got a plan?"

Merry was looking out the window and didn't hear the two men approach. It didn't take long to find out it wasn't Thad who sat beside her. The smell was unbearable.

"Ma'am." He tipped his hat.

"I am sorry, sir, this seat is taken."

"Yes, ma'am, by me." His eyes roamed her face and neck and she could feel the heat from her blush. He kept his gaze on hers. The other man sitting diagonally from her smiled showing a mouth full of blackened teeth. The man next to her fingered the sleeve of her dress. She pulled her arm away. He was saying something but her head was buzzing. She could see Thad still talking to the man but his back was to her.

The man moved his hand to lay on her knee. His hand was moving and she slapped it. This only made the man bolder. About that time, Thad walked past her. Her eyes flashed terror. Could he not see what was going on? How could he just walk past her? He had been preoccupied with something. This was ridiculous.

She wanted to scream but nothing would come out. It was happening all over again. She began having flashbacks of her previous encounter. If she hadn't witnessed the death of the two perpetrators she would swear they were the same two men.

The barrel of Thad's Colt revolver was flush against the base of the man's skull. Carter was stationed in the same position behind the man with the horrid teeth.

"Gentlemen, put your hands in the air."

There was a collective gasp from the passengers.

The man sitting across from Merry shot his hands up in the air immediately. Carter, without removing his gun from the man's head, reached around and disarmed him. Pulling him to his feet he escorted the vermin out of the car.

The one sitting next to Merry wasn't moving. He looked at Merry and saw her watching Thad. He knew she was the man's wife. He was going to have a little fun.

"I intend to keep my hands right where they are." He looked down and Merry realized his hand was still on her knee. She pushed at it but his grip got tighter.

"Last chance," Thad said coolly as he pulled the hammer back. The man leaned over and whispered in Merry's ear. Thad's gun came down hard on the man's head and he was out.

Everything became dark. Why was that? It was as if someone were slowly blowing out the lamps. Wait, it's a train. What was going on? Merry was confused.

"Merry, Merry."

Why was Thad yelling at her and why was he shaking her? Her eyes fluttered and realization hit. She had fainted. Thad was leaning over her. She tried to sit up. He helped her.

"You all right?" He cupped his hand around her cheek lifting her head to see her eyes.

"Yes, I'm all right."

He had witnessed the whole ordeal so he knew she wasn't physically hurt. He did feel with some certainty the old haunts came flooding back. He moved to sit beside her and took her hand in both of his.

"Is that the reason you were so preoccupied for the better part of the day?"

He leaned his head back to rest it on the train seat. "Those were the men who were tormenting Spotted Hawk."

Merry gasped. "Those are the men that shot you." Her fear was anger now.

He pulled his hat down over his eyes "It's over now. They are wanted for robbery. Carter will turn them over to the authorities.

Just like that, it was over. It wasn't over. Merry had dozens of questions for her husband but the hat over his eyes told her answers wouldn't come anytime soon. He wasn't asleep she knew that because he still had both hands wrapped around her left hand and the grip was snug.

They rode in silence until they stopped for the night. When the train stopped Thad and Merry were the last to get off. Merry felt very light headed when she stood and nearly passed out again. Thad had caught her just in time.

"You sure you're okay?" He was a little worried. No, he was extremely worried.

"I don't know what is the matter with me? Maybe it is all this sitting."

"We will get a bite to eat. Maybe that will help." They left the train and headed straight for the hotel.

While eating Merry asked her husband those "dozens" of question and he answered everyone.

She didn't want to tell him that she wasn't feeling any better. She just felt "woozy." She had to stop on the middle of the stairs to catch her breath.

"I'm going for the doctor, Merry." Thad's voice had an urgency to it.

"That isn't necessary."

He started to speak.

"If I still feel this way in the morning, I will see a doctor." Her look was firm so Thad agreed. He helped her up the stairs and to their room. He was pretty certain he would get no sleep tonight. He was worried about his Merry.

The hotel room was small but clean. Thad didn't waste any time getting out of the suit he had on. He removed his shirt and shoes and poured water in the bowl to wash the grit off his face. He was wiping his face with a towel when he caught sight of Merry.

"What is that?" his tone was rather harsh.

Merry had been undressing and had gotten down to the new corset Abby had given her.

"No wonder you've been swooning all day. Get that thing off."

Merry was a little stunned and she didn't move. He walked over took out his knife and split the back lacing. The garment fell to the floor. She was shocked at his behavior. The thing was ruined and she was sure Abby paid good money for it. In one fell swoop he picked the garment up and tossed it out the window. Merry's eyes were big.

"Y-y-you j-just . . ." She pointed to the window.

"Yes," he answered her unspoken question, "and that's the last one you'll ever own. I don't like them and you don't need it. No man likes to hold his wife and be greeted by that armor." He was walking around the room on a rant about a corset.

Merry had to admit she immediately felt better once she was freed from the confines of it. She chanced a peek out the window to see what happened to the spurned item. Two mangy dogs were fighting over it in the alley. Thad looked over her shoulder and saw the show the dogs were putting on.

"They'll break their teeth." He laughed. He slipped his arms around his wife's waist. "You have to admit this feels a whole lot better."

She leaned against his chest. "Yes, it does."

The stage only stopped briefly to let the Sheridans off in Rudolph. The town was covered in white from a spring snow. The air was crisp as they made their way to Zeke and Liddy's the fourteen days they were gone seemed like a life time. It was supper time and Liddy had anticipated their arrival perfectly with a sumptuous meal. They told the Lapps all about their trip and asked about the town happenings. As usual nothing exciting happened in Rudolph. Melissa and Tommy had stayed at the house during the day and went home at night. Liddy had been out to the house yesterday. Everything was in fine order. Thad went to the livery to retrieve the team and wagon. He loaded their trunks and they headed for home.

There was a warm glow coming from inside the house and tinny puffs of smoke were coming from the chimney someone was in the house. Perhaps Melissa and Tommy were staying all night. Merry thought for sure Liddy would let them know they would be home tonight. Maybe they decided to stay and welcome the couple home. After the events on the train Thad wasn't that optimistic.

"You stay here." He reached for his gun.

"It could be Melissa and Tommy you know."

His voice was low. "If it were Tommy he'd be out on the porch already." Good point she thought.

Thad got out of the wagon and quietly made his way up the steps and on to the porch. He peered through the window. The fire place was a full blaze. A lamp was burning on the table. There was a cake in the center. Coffee sat steaming on the stove. A note hung on the door.

He put his gun away and retrieved his wife. "What's going on?" She was a little cranky from the ride. Okay, she was more than cranky and her tone was harsh.

"You'll see."

Merry stomped up the steps and was on her way to barreling in the door when Thad caught the hem of her coat. "What are you doing, what's wrong with you?"

She looked at him as if he had lost his mind. He pointed to the note on the door. By the light spilling out of the window Merry was able to make out the words. It was Tommy's hand writing. Her hand lay on her heart at the sweetness of his words.

> Mama and me baked a cake and made coffee and made the fire. Mama wanted you to have a nice coming home. We took real good care of the animals and Pa cleaned the chimney, but not when the fire was there. Gus was sad all the time. I reckon he missed you. Mama and me did, and Doc and Liddy too, miss you, that is.
>
> Love,
> Tommy
>
> PS Doc Lapp said to tell you I would be over in the morning to feed the animals so you can sleep in.

Merry was almost in tears at the adorable letter with misspelled words and such kind thoughts. The post script brought a smile to Thad's lips. Doc was a character.

Thad opened the door. They were met with a nice warm home and the smell of freshly made coffee. The Hasketts must have just left. From behind the curtain Gus came bounding toward the couple he nearly knocked Thad over.

"Hey, boy." He scratched the dog's ears.

"Right past me, as if I don't exist, I was good enough until you came along, fickle dog." Merry tried to be displeased with the animal but his cuteness got the better of her. She turned to rub his belly.

Merry went into the bedroom to take off her coat. She pulled back the curtain and stopped. Someone had put beautiful curtains at the window. A new lovely quilt graced the bed along with crocheted doilies on the nightstand. There was a framed picture of Thad and Merry from the July Fourth celebration on the dresser. She had forgotten about that, Liddy had insisted they get it taken but Merry never knew what happened to the photograph. There was a drawing that Merry surmised was supposed to be Gus propped up next to the picture. Tommy must have felt that Gus needed his picture added.

Thad came up behind her to open the curtain back further. "Somebody has been busy. This is real nice."

There was a washstand and mirror in the corner with a bowl and pitcher and nice towels. The room was crowded but it all seemed to blend together perfectly.

Thad sat on the bed. "Somebody has done some work on this mattress." Merry sat beside him. She still didn't say a word. The mattress had been re-stuffed. "It's going to make sleeping in easy." Thad nudged his wife but she was deep in thought.

Someone thought enough of her and Thad to do these kind acts. Melissa, and she was sure the Lapps had a hand in it. They had done a very special thing. She was so tired from the trip all she could do was cry.

Chapter Eight

The weather had finally broken. Thad and Merry could get into the fields to prepare the ground for the crops. It bothered Thad that Merry was working so hard next to him. When he had met with Jackson back in Charleston he found out his mother had left Laurel to Abby and was in the process of selling the mill. The money received from the mill would go to Thad.

Thad didn't want the money. He had done fine for fifteen years and felt certain he could maintain a nice living for he and Merry. Jackson estimated the mill would be worth a great deal of money. Thad could be set for a long time if he managed it properly. He doubted money would make Merry stop working on the farm but maybe it would help get her out of the field. Until then he needed her help. The money would arrive someday. Thad needed to decide how he was going to handle it. He never expected it so he never planned for it.

"That's a worrisome look on your face." Merry was looking at her husband, streaks of sweat traipsing down her face.

"I was just thinking."

She rolled her eyes. "Yes, I figured that much out."

He half smiled and took a drink of water she had brought him.

"You thinking about the mill? Thad if you want to go back and run the mill, I will go."

He had no desire to run or own the mill.

"I appreciate that but that is not what I was thinking. I was just thinking about the best way to use what we will be given."

"I thought we were supposed to be praying and waiting? She put her hand on her hip and raised both eyebrows in condemnation.

"I just don't like you working out here like a field hand."

"This isn't Charleston, Thad, and I am no southern belle." She picked up her bag of seed and started back where she left off planting.

"No, but you are a woman and you should be doing—"

She whirled around. Fire lit her brown eyes. "Women's work, is that what you think? What is women's work?"

"Hold on, I just meant there are things a man doesn't like to see his wife do, things that will wear her down or overtax her."

"Like doing the laundry?" She waved her hand to the line of clothes flapping in the gentle breeze.

"I am just saying, you shouldn't have to do both."

"It is just your stubborn male pride, which is all in the world it is."

"Pride that a man wants to shelter his wife a little, not put her through more—"

She cut him off again. "More than she can stand." She was nearing him now fit to be tied.

"Stop putting words in my mouth," he snapped back.

"I don't have to put words in your mouth because I can read them all over your face. I did all this on my own for a few years. It may have been hard, but I did it."

"Yes, I know you did, you make sure I know it's *your* farm."

"What is that supposed to mean?"

"It means every time I try to make things a little easier on you as far as the farms concern you get your back up like an old cat and get very territorial."

"This isn't the south, Thad, and women don't sit inside all day doing needlework."

"I'm done talking about it." His body stiffened.

Whoa, that was not like him at all.

He flipped the reins and the old mule plodded ahead as Thad steadied the plow. His pride had gotten the better of him.

How ridiculous the whole argument was Merry thought as she dropped seeds into the turned up ground. Her back was beginning to ache and she was so hot and sticky. It did make a body miserable. Suddenly an overwhelming guilt lay over her soul. This is what Thad was getting at. He didn't want her to feel this way, back aching, arms numb from dropping seed into the ground then covering it up with a weary foot. He was thinking about her.

The sun was just above them. Merry told him she was going to go start lunch. He nodded and said he would finish the row. On her way back to the house, she noticed Lone Eagle and Spotted Hawk headed her way. She waved and the two eased their mounts up beside the garden. They had seen the whole argument and Lone Eagle had an amused look on his face.

"Night Wolf give you what for?" Merry blushed.

"I have a temper. Lone Eagle and you know it."

"Best keep tongue in head or Night Wolf leave."

She smiled, shielding the sun so she could see the Indian's face. She asked the question that had always been at the back of her mind. "What made you dump him at my door step that night?"

He spoke to Spotted Hawk in their native tongue and the boy turned his horse and left.

"Night Wolf saved son. Morning Dove saved son. Same spirit in you that in him. You one." He crossed his forearms over his chest to emphasize "one" then turned to look at Thad laboring in the field.

"He make you happy?"

"Yes, very happy."

"Keep tongue in head." The Indian turned his palomino and left.

Merry went into the house. She couldn't get what the Indian had said out of her thoughts. He had identified the very marks of a marriage orchestrated by God. Two people sharing the same spirit and becoming one. She realized there were times in the marriage she wanted to break away and assert herself instead of considering she was half that made a whole. It wasn't who could get the upper hand or win the argument it was who needed to bend to get through the rough patch. She recognized the fact Thad was thinking of her. He initially had tried to tell her what he was thinking, what was in his heart. She had turned the conversation into an argument about her. How self-centered was that?

Thad walked to the outside pump and stuck his head under. He washed the dirt and sweat from the back of his neck and face. Turning his face toward the sun he asked his heavenly father to forgive him for his anger and for help in saying the right words to apologize to his wife. He didn't mean to belittle her. Perhaps it was his pride that ruled his words.

Inside the house Merry sat a plate in front of him and poured him a cold glass of water. He started to speak but she beat him to it.

"I was thinking today would be a good day for some of my special Lemonade but I figured you've had enough sour words to swallow."

She stood behind his chair and rested her hands on his shoulders. "I'm sorry I was so hateful. I know you were thinking of me and I appreciate it." She double kissed the top of his head and moved to get the coffee pot.

"Well you were provoked and you were right my pride was taking a beating." She poured his coffee and he grabbed her hand

"I am sorry, Merry."

She moved her hands to cup his jaw.

"Just so you know for sure and for certain you make me very happy, Thad Sheridan." She kissed him then sat down to her own plate of food.

The couple headed back out to the field hand in hand. They were stopped by an unexpected surprise. Spotted Hawk was walking behind the plow making very straight rows.

"Would you look at that? The boys good with a plow." Thad had dropped Merry's hand and started in the direction of Spotted Hawk. Merry didn't follow but returned to the house. Thad didn't notice.

Thad planted while Spotted Hawk plowed they made a good team. Merry took them some water and told Spotted Hawk he was staying for supper tonight. She had asked him to stay before when she was teaching him to read and write but he would always decline. She gave him no room to refuse. It was some hours later when the two returned to the house.

A very silent Spotted Hawk sat as the fried chicken, green beans and potatoes were passed his way. When Thad grabbed Merry's hand and began to pray, the boy's eyes darted back and forth from Thad to Merry. When she opened her eyes, she saw Spotted Hawk's black eyes staring at Thad. The Sheridans had been trying to witness to both Lone Eagle and Spotted Hawk but Lone Eagle was so steeped in the Indian way, it made it difficult. He, of course, was raising Spotted Hawk to follow in his footsteps.

Thad wasn't sure just what it was that woke him up. Perchance it was his wife's snoring. She had been fighting a spring cold. At night, she would have trouble breathing. He walked into the kitchen to get some water when he saw a fiery haze from the kitchen window. He knew instantly it was coming from the vicinity of the Hasketts.

"Merry!" he shouted as he raced to get dressed.

"Merry!" He shook the bed. She sat up, heart beating, eyes wide.

"Looks like a fire over at the Hasketts." When the words soaked in she sprang out of bed.

"I will go on Grace. Can you bring the wagon?"

"Yes, go." She was dressing as quickly as she could. He passed her on Grace as she went to hitch up the team.

It took Merry some time to get the team hitched up. The barn was dark except for the one lamp Thad had left and the horses were not cooperating at this time of night. She heard the faint sound of the town bell that alerted of an emergency. She finally got the team hitched. She filled the wagon with buckets and quilts and anything else she could think of. Gus jumped in the wagon and she tried to get him out. The dog hunkered down so she didn't waste any more time. She lit out not sparing the horses.

Thad was first to make it to the Hasketts. He felt as if hot steel had been laid in his stomach. The house was totally engulfed in flames. If anyone was inside, he doubted they could get out. He doused himself with water and wrapped a handkerchief around his mouth and nose. He headed toward the inferno. He didn't make it in very far when he nearly tripped over the charred body of Melissa Haskett.

The smoke was so thick Thad's eyes began to burn and he was coughing. He could hear the cracking and popping of the beams overhead. The roof was going to collapse. He couldn't go any farther in or he would be surrounded by flames with no way out. Reluctantly he stumbled out of the house. He was met by the Hasketts neighbor on the other side Jim McPherson. He had spotted the flames about the time Thad did.

Town's people were beginning to arrive. McPherson, Elmer's younger brother helped Thad to the pump where others were filling buckets of water. Thad's throat was spasming and he couldn't stop coughing.

"Let it burn," he rasped.

He had seen this awful sight before. When a dwelling was that engulfed, nothing survived. He heard the sound of wagons coming from town and he heard the wagon coming from his home.

Merry.

He turned as Merry flew off the wagon seat surveying the small crowd for the three people who were not there. Not seeing them she headed for the burning house. Thad jumped up and picked up his pace. As Merry began to run he knew he had to circumvent her from getting any closer. His hands caught her shoulders and she tried to push past him, her face in utter fear. She became stronger as she shoved against him. She didn't say anything she just fought against his strong frame. He finally lifted her off her feet and moved her back.

"There's nothing we can do, it's too late," he whispered in her ear. His lungs spasmed again and he began coughing. Merry slid to the ground in tears.

The fire had been subdued and those from town who came to help headed back. What a tragedy!

Dr. Lapp was tending to Thad. Merry sat still beside him hanging on for dear life. Sheriff Bullock was walking around what use to be the Haskett place. He was trying to determine how the fire started.

Melissa's body was just inside the door frame and Hanks was found at the back door. The roof had totally collapsed over what was little Tommy's bedroom. He was not looking forward to uncovering all that lay beneath. They would have to wait a few more hours until the sun came up to continue.

"Thad you're not out of the woods." Doc Lapp was concerned Thad inhaled too much smoke.

Merry felt sick to her stomach. She pushed the hair back from her forehead and Thad moved to wrap his arm around her. He pulled her to him and rested his chin on the top of her head. He knew she was crying. He felt like crying himself.

The soot was so thick on Thad's shirt that Merry started coughing. She didn't know if it was the cold she had or the smell of smoke. Thad released her and moved to tie Grace to the back of the wagon. He needed to get Merry out of the night air. He helped her in the wagon and whistled for Gus. The dog wouldn't move. He called the dog by name. The animal bent his ears back but would not come. He walked toward the dog and something came to him. The dog had been in the same spot since he arrived. Right on the cellar door.

Thad wasted no time running to the wooden door, throwing the heavy door open.

"Tommy," his hoarse voice broke the silence. "Tommy, are you in there?" Merry had gotten out of the wagon and headed toward Thad. In a few split seconds, Tommy emerged from the cellar right into Thad's arms. Tears were flowing from the grown man's eyes as the boy sobbed, his arms wrapped tightly around Thad's neck.

As Thad carried the boy to the wagon Tommy opened his eyes for a brief second to view what was his home. He shut them tightly he knew his ma and pa were somewhere inside. His tears flowed unhindered.

Merry placed a blanket around Tommy as the doctor briefly examined the boy.

"Take him home with you. Here is some medicine that might make him sleep if he needs it. This is for Thad it will help the lungs. See he drinks it tonight and in the morning. Liddy and I will be by sometime tomorrow." He kissed Merry's forehead.

Tommy sat in between Thad and Merry on the ride home. His little body shook. Merry piled on the quilts and Thad had his arm around the boy drawn up as close as he could get him. Gus had finagled his head between Tommy and Merry so that it lay on Tommy's lap. No one spoke on the ride home.

Once they reached the Sheridan cabin Thad suggested Merry and Tommy go on in and he would take care of the horses. He also wanted to get some of the soot off of him. It may help his breathing. He told Merry as much so she urged Tommy in, Gus on his heels. She led Tommy to a chair and washed his face. He blankly stared at her his eyes so red from crying and his little heart breaking. She wasn't sure if she should say anything so she just kept silent.

She poured a little bit of the medicine in some water and gave it to Tommy. She moved behind the curtain to find one of Thad's shirts for Tommy to wear. His clothes were muddy from sitting in the cellar. Tommy turned his head to watch her. The action didn't go unnoticed. He wouldn't let her out of his sight.

"Here Tommy put this on." He did as she asked and stepped behind the curtain and slipped on the shirt.

When he reappeared, she had him take the medicine. He drank it down without emotion. Tommy sat there until Thad entered. Thad had left his clothes in the barn and came in wrapped in a quilt. He put his hand on Tommy's shoulder. "You're going to be okay."

The boy laid his head on the table and cried. Gus jumped up on the table and covered the boys head with his own. Merry didn't have the heart to get the dog off the table. She felt like crawling up there herself.

Thad went to dress and when he came back, Tommy's head was still on the table. The medicine had started to work. He lifted the boy in his arms and carried him to the bedroom. Merry pulled back the covers and Thad laid him down. As soon as his head hit the pillow his eyes flew opened. There was panic in them.

"Shh. Tommy, it's okay, we're here," Merry whispered, smoothing the boy's blond locks away from his face.

The little boy grabbed Merry's arm and pulled. "S-stay." A sob escaped his lips

"Of course." She wasn't sure if he wanted her to stay there with him or if he was asking if he could stay.

He pulled on her arm until she lay down beside him. His arm wrapped around hers he laid his head on her shoulder. His other hand clutched whatever part of Thad was closest. He did not want either one out of his sight. Guardian Gus stationed himself at their feet.

Tommy's body would jump and twitched while he slept but never once did he break his hold with the couple.

Thad was sure his coughing was keeping Merry from getting any rest. He broke away from Tommy's grip and went into the kitchen. Merry heard him leave and Tommy began to move. She was afraid to rise herself lest she wake Tommy.

Thad made some tea and sat looking at the floor. He couldn't get the sight of Melissa and Hanks bodies almost burnt beyond recognition out of his mind. What would Hell be like? He thought. Could he have done more to help Hank? Should he have reached out after their fight? He always relied on the Holy Spirit to guide his directions and now he was second guessing himself.

He prayed for a while confessing his thoughts and fears to the Lord. He hadn't been praying very long when he felt a small hand on his arm. Tommy stood in the dim light with Gus at his side. The boy was shaking. Thad turned in his chair and opened his arms Tommy dropped his forehead on Thad shoulder and Thad's arms encircled him.

"It's okay to cry, Tommy." The boy had been holding back a little. He didn't want everyone to think he was a baby. He had cried at first but to keep crying wasn't right.

Thad pulled the boy back and looked him in the eye. The dam was about to burst and Tommy was doing all he could to stem the tide.

"This wasn't your fault and there was nothing you could do."

"W-Why d-did he do it?" The boy had muttered through a launch of tears.

"Who, Tommy?" Thad questioned. The boy didn't answer.

No one knew how the fire was started. Sheriff Bullock would be out there later this morning to investigate. Thad planned to be there.

He held Tommy as he cried and after a little while the boy had cried himself to sleep. He placed him back in bed and went to do morning chores it was a little early but he wanted to get to the burn site and do some investigating of his own. When he returned from the barn Merry was up.

"What are you doing up?" he scolded.

"I could ask the same question of you."

"I couldn't sleep," he said as he put her eggs on the table. "I thought I would turn the tables on the chickens and wake them up." His smile was followed by fit of coughing. It worried Merry.

"You shouldn't be out in this early morning air or in that chicken coop with all the dust."

"I'm fine." His voice was hoarse and raspy

"Yes, it sounds like it." She frowned at him. "I will get breakfast started."

"Merry, I am really not hungry so don't bother. I think you should rest today and take care of Tommy." She turned around to face her husband. Her hands crossed over her chest.

"And what will you be doing?" She knew he was up to something. He peeked beyond the curtain to ensure Tommy was asleep. His voice was low.

"I want to go back and help the sheriff clean up." He was being vague and moving around the kitchen aimlessly.

"Uh huh, what else?"

He grabbed his hat and kissed her cheek. "I'll be back later." She decided not to push it.

Thad took the wagon over to what used to be the Hasketts. He wasn't sure what all the sheriff had planned. When he got there, Sheriff Bullock and his deputy already had placed Melissa and Hank's body in pine boxes. Sheriff Bullock was not surprised to see Thad headed his way.

"I thought you might need help." Thad offered his hand.

"Uh huh and what else?"

"Am I that obvious?" Thad asked.

The sheriff shook his head. "What's bugging you?"

"Just interested in what started the fire."

"Go have a look."

Thad walked all around the edges of the fire then methodically made his way into the heart of the rubble. About twenty minutes later he returned to Sheriff Bullock.

"What's the verdict Ranger?"

Thad looked into the still smoldering debris. "The fire was definitely intentionally set."

Sheriff Bullock's eyes narrowed on Thad "what makes you think so?" Thad headed to the edge. He outlined his evidence for the sheriff.

"Tommy know anything?" the sheriff asked. "

I think he does but it has to be the right time when you question him." The sheriff nodded in agreement.

"Pastor Gray's going to hold the services when you and Maggie think Tommy's ready."

Thad took a deep breath "I probably need to go into town and talk with him." Thad had a coughing spell and the sheriff encouraged him to stop by Doc's too.

The mercantile was a buzz when Thad entered. He wanted to pick up a few things for Tommy. He had lost everything in the fire.

"I bet the fire was set by that Indian." Elmer McPherson had his back to Thad and was talking to one of the men Thad had occasionally seen at church.

"You know that's how they settle matters. My brother said the Indian is on the ridge behind his house about every day. Probably headed to Merry Sheridan's."

The man in front of McPherson went ashen at the sight of Thad.

Thad's fury had gone to his fist. He wanted to beat the man and he hadn't felt that way toward another person in a very long time. He unclenched his fists and counted to ten. McPherson had stopped talking and slowly turned around. The store was full of people this morning. They were all waiting to see how Thad would handle this.

"I was wondering," Thad addressed the crowd, "if anyone would be willing to provide some things for Tommy Haskett?" He continued turning his piercing gaze toward McPherson.

"Perhaps the McPherson Mercantile would donate a couple sets of clothes seeing they are such pillars in the community." The crowd was still.

"Well, I . . . of course, Mr. Sheridan, take what you think the boy will need." McPherson moved around the store gathering things for Tommy, never making eye contact with Thad. A few people in the store added what they could.

"Much obliged." Thad tipped his hat to the crowd.

He then leaned in so only McPherson could hear him. "Best be careful talking about another man's wife. Talk like that could get you . . ." Thad didn't finish, he just let the thought hang there and left the store with a box full of supplies for Tommy.

He headed over to the Lapps. He wanted Zeke to let Sheriff Bullock know what was being circulated. This could spell trouble for Lone Eagle.

"Thad, you look just awful." Liddy was saying as she escorted him into the living room. "Have you slept at all?"

"Not much." He plopped down in the nearest chair.

Doc Lapp came from his office at his wife's bidding. "Well, I can see you followed my orders son to stay home and rest."

Thad's lungs chose that time to attempt to clear themselves of the remaining soot.

"Have you even taken any of the medicine I left for you?" Thad nodded his head in the affirmative.

"I am surprised that wife of yours let you out of the house."

Thad kept coughing.

"Stop chastising him and do something," Liddy spoke harshly to her husband.

"Come with me, son."

Thad followed the doctor into the kitchen. The doctor poured steaming water in a bucket and added some liquid. He pushed Thad's head just above the rim and covered his head and the bucket with a large section of cloth.

"Vat vasnt efer bas fit." Thad was saying something but it was muffled by the heavy cloth. "What's that?" the doc asked and Thad lifted a corner of the cloth.

"I said 'that wasn't ether, was it?'"

The doctor pushed Thad's head down again and put the corner of the cloth down.

After the water had cooled and the steam evaporated, Thad was allowed to show his face. His hair was damp and his face glistened. The coughing had subsided and he actually felt like he could take a deep breath. He sat on the couch and did just that. Liddy had fixed some tea with herbs to help sooth his throat. She had also put a little something extra in it at her husband's order to relax Thad.

He told the doctor about the conversation he overheard and asked him to relay it to sheriff Bullock. A yawn escaped Thad's lip and he tipped his head back. Doctor Lapp made eye contact with his wife and the two went into the kitchen.

"That was pretty sneaky, Dr. Lapp," Liddy was saying.

"The boy needs to rest and he wasn't going to do it any other way. I need to go check on Tommy. I will let Merry know Thad won't be home for a while and I will try to find the sheriff."

Doc Lapp passed the dozing man as he went to gather his bag. Thad was still audibly wheezing when he breathed.

Merry was a little worried. She had expected Thad home by now. It had been at least four hours since he left. Tommy was up and looked expectantly at the door about every fifteen minutes. He had followed Merry everywhere she went still in one of Thad's shirts. She had washed his clothes and they were hanging on the line not yet dry.

They were working in the garden when she heard the wagon. Tommy beat her around the corner of the house. It was not Thad. Doctor Lapp exited the wagon and came toward the two.

"How are you this morning, Tommy?" He placed his hands on Tommy's shoulders and looked him in the eye.

"Ohhkay." The boy's sad little face peered up at the doctor.

"You will be, son." Doctor Lapp took Tommy in an embrace.

Anyone who knew Tommy and anyone around him just wanted to hug him, this only intensified the emotion.

"Thad isn't here," Merry said when he released Tommy.

"Yes, I know that is what I came to tell you." Merry had a twinge of fear at the moment.

"He's fine, Maggie." He recognized the look on her face and wanted to ease her mind quickly. "He is at the house taking a nap." Merry looked at him with astonishment.

"He stopped in to see me and started coughing. I gave him some different medicine. I was a little surprised you let him out of the house today, Maggie."

"You think I could stop him? The man does what he wants. Stubborn as that old thing right there." She pointed to the mule just on the other side of the fence who on cue bellowed out a he-haw and went kicking across the corral.

"Exactly," she yelled at the mule. "How on earth did you get him to take a nap?" she asked her friend.

"That's physician privilege."

Doctor Lapp had examined Tommy to make sure he was still okay physically. He gave Merry some herbs for her spring cold and was headed back to town when he ran into Sheriff Bullock.

"You been to the Sheridans? The sheriff wanted to know.

"Yes, I wanted to check on Tommy and tell Maggie that Thad was at my place taking a nap." The sheriff thought this peculiar and indicated so by scratching his bald head.

"He wouldn't slow down any other way but a little extra shot of something in the herbal tea. I am not convinced his lungs will return to normal."

"Hmm he was out at the Hasketts early this morning tromping around."

"That explains his coughing spells intensifying. You're not going to keep him down. Stubborn as a mule." Dan agreed and headed his stallion toward the Sheridan's.

"Oh, Dan." Zeke stopped the man and he returned to the wagon. "Thad wanted me to tell you word is going around town that Lone Eagle started the fire that burned the Hasketts."

"It doesn't take long for speculations to start circulating. I'll tell you this Sheridan thinks it was intentionally set."

"By Lone Eagle?"

"No, but I think he thinks Tommy knows what happen. Do you think he is up to talking Doc?"

"You'll know if he is or not. I trust your judgment Dan." The sheriff tipped his hat and turned the chestnut stallion around.

Tommy saw the sheriff coming down the road. The boy had understandably been quiet for most of the day. He kept within sight of Merry and helped her with all her tasks. Gus hadn't been far from Tommy. He did not go off as usual but stayed close to the boy.

"S-Sheriffs c-c-coming. S-Suppose he w-wants to t-t-talk to me." Merry tried to gauge the boy's thoughts on the subject by reading his face. It was blank.

"Are you all right with that? You don't have to." The boy who was back in his own clothes now walked out the door and met the sheriff as he got off his horse.

"Hello, Tommy." Tommy nodded and took the sheriff's hand. They walked through the pasture toward Tommy's fishing hole. Tommy was having to grow up fast, Merry thought as she prayed for the boy for the hundredth time.

"That was a low-down stunt you pulled, Doc," Thad said as Ezekiel Lapp entered his own kitchen. Thad was sitting at the table eating a piece of pie Liddy had recently pulled from the oven.

"Bad boys get punished, Thaddeus. Heard you were out early this morning traipsing around in the smoldering embers. You were supposed to take it easy today and certainly not aggravate your lungs by cool damp air and smoke." Thad began to speak but the Doc didn't notice.

"Thad, if you don't do what I say you could have long term effects and," he pierced Thad with his grey eyes, "I told Maggie as much so she can put the hammer down on you." They all knew once Merry got something in her head there was no dissuading her.

"Thanks a lot," he said as he started on his second piece of pie.

"Good to see there is nothing wrong with your appetite." The Lapps chuckled and Thad feigned embarrassment.

"I ran into Dan on the way back, told him what's been going on here in town. He was headed out to check on Tommy."

Thad didn't waste any time leaving. He felt responsible for Tommy and didn't want to be gone if he was needed. When he arrived home Merry met him just outside the barn. She began unhitching the team.

"Merry, I can do that."

"Haven't you done enough today? Doc said . . ." He rather forcefully took the horse's bridle out of Merry's hand.

"I know what the doc said. As soon as I am done here I'm going to go in the house and I would appreciate a glass of lemonade."

She reached for the bridle and he stepped to cut her off. He bent his face a breath apart from hers.

"I like a lot of sugar," he whispered as his lips found hers.

"You think a couple of kisses and I will just do your bidding?" she said as he turned to remove the bridle from the horse. "I have found that it works rather well on you." He winked.

She playfully smacked his face and pranced into the house. Leaving Thad shaking his head.

Merry had to admit to herself the nap at the Lapps had done wonders for Thad. He looked refreshed as he drank his lemonade on the front porch. They were waiting for Tommy and the sheriff to return.

"I don't think we should ask Tommy any questions about what he saw," Thad said while looking out at the horizon.

"Why is that?" Merry wanted to know.

"I have a bad feeling about this, Merry." He told her about the talk in town.

"It only happened a few hours ago and already there's talk. I hate that town." She pushed her rocker a little harder.

"Past issues with the Sioux still have people on edge."

"Lone Eagle wouldn't do such a thing."

"We know that, but the town folk don't."

"I think Lone Eagle was leaving food for Melissa like he did for me. She said she would find rabbits and venison here and there, buckets with honey in it. She didn't know where it came from but I knew. Thad, do you think we should warn Lone Eagle?"

"I am in hopes this talk will die down or Sheriff Bullock will be able to curb it. Let's wait and see if it is still being circulated on Sunday if it is I can talk to Lone Eagle."

It was late afternoon when Sheriff Bullock returned with Tommy. When they reached the porch Merry started to get up and give Sheriff Dan her seat.

"Have a seat, Sheriff. I have some lemonade. Would you like some?"

"Yes, ma'am, that would be nice." She smiled as the man perched himself on the rail.

"Tommy?" she questioned.

"Yes, ma'am. Th-Thank you."

He had sat on the first step tossing a ball to Gus who was faithfully bringing the thing back and dropping it at the boy's feet.

"Tommy's a fine young man, Thad," the sheriff was saying looking at the back of Tommy's blonde head. "He has faced a lot of hard trials but was very brave today in talking with me." He knew the boy was listening and wanted him to know just how proud he was of his willingness in the midst of all his pain to tell what he knew.

"That doesn't surprise me a bit, that's how his parents raised him. They would be proud," Thad added.

Tommy looked over his shoulder at the two men. He thought he had lost everything last night but there on the porch was a small piece of his life. A piece he could hold onto. At least for a little bit.

The sheriff would not stay for supper. He asked Thad to walk him down to the barn to retrieve his horse.

"You were right Thad. Hank started the fire. He was not in his right mind from what I gathered from the boy. He thought he was still fighting the war. Tommy said he saturated the place with alcohol and lit it. He ordered Tommy and Melissa into the cellar. Melissa tried to stop him but he knocked her down. Must have knocked her out because Tommy thought she was dead. When he tried to stop his pa, the man shut him up in the cellar."

Thad could not imagine what the little boy had been through. Not just last night but night after night.

"I am counting on you not to disclose anything I've told you, not event to Maggie."

Thad gave his word.

"What happens to Tommy now sheriff?" Thad didn't feel he could just assume that he and Merry could have the boy outright.

"Judge would have to rule in favor of someone taking him. I don't see a problem if you and Maggie are up for it."

Thad extended his hand "We are most definitely up for it."

Merry and Tommy had supper on the table. It was good that Tommy was kept busy. It was obvious his mind was on the events that had changed his world but Thad and Merry wanted to provide all the comfort they could.

"Tommy, I know it isn't much but some of the town's people sent some things your way, clothes and shoes and a few other things." Thad drug a box from out of the sitting room. Tommy knelt on the floor and went through the box.

"W-What will h-h-happen t-t-to me?" There was such sadness in his question even Gus looked as if he was going to cry.

"For now," Thad started looking over the boy's head to Merry, "and hopefully forever you'll live with us, but the law has to be involved. That is if you want to live with us." He did not say anything but stared into the box.

"Tommy, Thad and I know how much you loved your parents and how much you will miss them every day. We can't take their place but we can continue the love they had for you."

Thad gazed at his wife. She never ceased to amaze him. She had just made Tommy's burden a little lighter.

Tommy's head rested on the box ledge. He didn't want to cry anymore but he just couldn't help it. Merry knelt beside him and gathered him into her harms. When his silent tears subsided, he looked his long-time friend in the eye. "I w-want to l-live here."

The night air was very damp and Thad began coughing again. So violently if she didn't know about the fire Merry would think he had consumption. Doc Lapp had sent medicine with Thad so he could do his own steam treatment as he had done earlier in the day. Merry helped him and he sat under the cloth at the kitchen table. When the water had cooled, Thad appeared from under the cloth. His face was shinny but his eyes were so red from the coughing he looked a little spooky. She and Tommy fixed him some peppermint tea which seemed to help.

"I think I will head to bed." Thad stood and stretched his back. "Tommy, Merry has fixed the room up in the loft for you if you would like to sleep up there. If not, you can sleep down here. It makes no difference to us."

Tommy grabbed the shirt he had slept in the night before and started toward the loft. He turned and ran to the Sheridan's hugging them for a brief moment then scooted up the ladder.

Merry had a few more things she wanted to get done before retiring, so she sent her husband off to bed with a kiss on the cheek.

"You're not going to be much longer are you," he wanted to know. He didn't like going to bed without her. It just wasn't right.

"I'll be along in a minute. By the looks of you, you'll be asleep when your head hits the pillow." She didn't know her own husband he thought. Lavender was the only thing that put him to sleep at night.

He had just started getting undressed when he heard a rather strange noise coming from the kitchen. There it was again. "What was that?"

He reached the kitchen just in time to see Gus attempt to climb the ladder to the loft. He had jumped and missed and was trying again.

"He's going to break his neck." Merry shook her head.

Thad lifted the dog and hoisted him up to the loft. This was not done without a cough or two. Merry was afraid he would start the spasming cough again. When he walked past the last lit lamp, he blew it out and grabbed Merry's hand on the way.

"I don't care what you were doing it can wait until tomorrow we're going to bed."

She was too tired to argue with him and that was saying a lot.

It was late morning when Thad's eyes suddenly opened. By the full sunlight coming through the window he knew he had slept way too late. He felt very groggy as he tried to lift his body to the side of the bed. Someone had put something in his tea again, and he was about to unleash his ire on her.

The subject of his thoughts then appeared looking breathtakingly beautiful. How was he going to yell at that! Her hair was swept to one side and she was wearing a new yellow day dress. It was like summer just wafted in. She had in her hand a cup of coffee.

"Good morning." She smiled and handed him the cup.

"Uh huh, no way am I drinking anything I don't pour myself." He was sitting on the side of the bed hair on end and a good growth on his jaw and chin. He flopped back on the bed his feet still touching the floor. Merry snickered.

"This isn't funny," he groaned out. She sat the coffee down and took a seat beside him.

"It was for your own good." She patted his chest. He opened one eye.

"What time is it?"

"Close to ten." The eye closed.

"Why are you so dressed up today?" His hand went through her hair.

"Tommy and I are headed into town. All the morning work has been done so you can take it easy today."

"What good is taking it easy when I will be home alone?"

"Gus will be here." He sat up and shook his head trying to wake himself up. His eyes were slits when he looked at her.

"Thanks."

She smoothed back his hair then reached to open one of his eyelids a little wider "You'll be fine." She kissed his forehead and she and Tommy left for town.

Thad didn't know what to do with himself. He didn't really feel up to working and all the easy chores of the day had been done. He got cleaned up and ate the breakfast Merry had left for him. He decided Grace probably needed a good run, so he headed to the barn. As he was leading her out, he came face to face with Lone Eagle.

"I want to know your God."

Thad was shocked. His meetings with Lone Eagle had tapered off. The Indian just stopped coming.

"Sure, let me put Grace up and we can go into the house."

"I put horse up. You go get book. We talk out here."

Thad prayed his mind would clear as he went into the house to get his Bible. This was the opportunity he had been waiting for Lone Eagle seemed to really be searching.

"Inside man in raging battle," he pointed to himself. "No peace."

"Why do you believe that is?" Thad questioned.

"Your God torment me."

Thad shook his head no. "God reasons with man."

"How so?"

"God shows each person their sinful nature. He tells you the reward for serving sin. He also says I gave my son to die for your sins, if you love my son I will love you and forgive you of your sins and you can be reconciled to me and there is no punishment." The Indian wasn't grasping it. Thad would have to try another approach.

"Let's say you were the chief over all the Sioux. The only way you could save your people was to allow Spotted Hawk to be killed. In doing so, the Sioux had to make a choice to accept that you gave your son for their life and become part of you or they walk away and disrespect the offering you gave of your son. Those who accepted the sacrifice became a great tribe and those who did not wondered around with no peace, yet you repeatedly offered and some saw the value in your son's life and returned to your tribe asking forgiveness. Eventually there will be no more opportunity and you will have to destroy those who did not accept your offer."

The Indian was in deep thought, so deep Thad thought he was in a trance. After several minutes, Lone Eagle spoke.

"A son is ultimate gift. Great love Father has for Son."

"Yes, and the scriptures say if you love the son you love the father and the father loves you."

"I accept son, will God accept me?" There was a longing in the tan face.

"Absolutely, if the inner man is sincere and has a broken heart." Thad pointed to the heart of the man.

"Inner man surrender," he said with a smile and a mist in his black eyes. He reached for Thad's outstretched hand.

"Brothers," the Indian said.

"Brothers." Thad hugged the huge man. They spent another hour discussing parts of the Bible. Lone Eagle promised to come twice a week and meet with Thad. It was a happy Indian who scaled the ridge.

Thad was so happy he couldn't wait to tell Merry what happened. He literally jumped off the porch when she pulled up. This brought a laugh out of Tommy and a snort from Merry.

"What has gotten into you?" she said. He didn't wait for her to get down out of the wagon but lifted her out and whirled her to the ground.

He grabbed Tommy and threw him over his shoulder like a sack of feed and whirled around. Tommy was hysterical with laughter.

"Thad Sheridan put that boy down. You're going to make him sick." He put Tommy down as she demanded and turned toward her. She could tell he was coming after her and she took off running. "Thad." She skirted behind the wagon. "What on earth is going on?"

"Can't a man be overly happy without his family thinking he's crazy?" He hoisted Tommy on his shoulders and reached for Merry's hand. "I have some pretty exciting news for you." He put a huge kiss on top of her head.

She reached the steps standing on the first one so she could be eye level with her husband. "Please share so I can act like a raving lunatic." That didn't damper Thad's enthusiasm.

"Guess who came to visit while you were gone?"

"I haven't a clue." She put her hands on her hips acting a little bit impatient.

"Lone Eagle."

"You know, Thad, he has been here before and you weren't this excited."

"Okay your right Merry he has been here before but he's never left here before with the Lord."

He waltzed into the house lowering Tommy off his shoulder just before he went through the door frame. It took a minute for what he said to sink in.

"Wait, Thad, did you say—"

Thad told Merry the entire story about his conversation with their friend. Merry was as happy as Thad although she didn't show it in such a demonstrative way.

The three sat down to supper and the couple noticed Tommy's very somber mood. Tomorrow after church they were going to have the funeral services for Melissa and Hank. It would be pointless to ask Tommy if he was all right. The boy lost his parents, of course he was not all right. His world was turned upside down.

"Something on your mind, Tommy?" Thad asked as he watched the boy shove his food around his plate.

"I-I'm g-g-going t-to hell," the boy blurted out rather loudly. Merry was taken aback. Thad thinking of an appropriate response.

"What makes you think so?" Thad asked as he took another bite of food in displaying some normalcy with the conversation.

"I c-caused the fire."

Merry gasped a little and Thad stopped eating. He knew that wasn't the truth but Tommy had something he needed to get off his chest.

"How so?" Thad responded.

"T-That n-night I t-told God I w-wished you were m-m-my Pa."

The little boy was in torment.

"G-God t-took 'em c-cuz of m-me."

Merry reached over and rested her hand on Tommy's. "God doesn't work that way Tommy. God knew you loved your Pa. He also put Thad in your life to help your Pa. He understood your feelings. The fire was an accident."

"W-Wasn't no accident, was it, Th-Thad?" Tommy turned to Thad.

Merry's eyes also turned to her husband.

"It doesn't matter son what happened was out of your control. Nothing you did caused anything."

Tommy hung his head.

"Look at me, Tommy." Thad's voice was stern but loving. The boy obeyed. "Wanting to be here with us is not a sin. Life has to go on. It will hurt a lot but it is okay to be yourself and be happy.

Laughing and playing does not mean you don't miss and love your parents, got it?"

His large hand rested on the lad's shoulder and gave it a playful shake.

"G-Got it," Tommy answered in a low tone.

"Good. Now eat up because I made dessert while you were gone today.

Both Merry and Tommy's head shot up.

"And don't look at me that way Merry Sheridan. You're not the only cook in this house."

"This ought to be good." She nudged Tommy and rolled her eyes. Thad scooted back his chair in a huff and went out the back door. Merry moved in her chair to try and see where he was going and what he was doing. When he returned, he had made frozen custard.

"How did you—"

He cut her off. "Mr. Impossible strikes again." He scooped some out for Tommy and then a bowl for himself. "You don't get any." He looked at Merry and licked the spoon.

"What?" she cried.

"I saw you rolling your eyes."

She got up and went to where he sat. "Please, husband dear, I am sorry I rolled my eyes."

"I don't know. Tommy, she doesn't sound too sincere. What do you think?"

Tommy, taking this all in, realized his parents never shared such joy. He was taking what Thad said to heart. He could have fun and still miss his folks. "M-M-Make her b-b-beg."

Thad howled with laughter.

"Thomas Aaron Haskett," she turned on him. "First Gus and now you. Isn't anyone on my side?" She reached for the boy and started to tickle him. Thad grabbed her around the waist to save Tommy. Pulling her back she fell in his lap. The house was filled with laughter as it should be and Thad shared his custard with his unrepentant wife.

Chapter Nine

"I must say what a privilege it is to be escorted to church by such a fine-looking man." Tommy had come down the ladder dressed in a new suit. Merry was straightening his tie.

"Why, thank you, dear," Thad's baritone voice came from behind the curtain of their room. Merry rolled her eyes. Thad came from around the curtain.

"Oh, I just assumed you were referring to me. I keep forgetting this house is over ran with handsome men." He winked at Tommy.

"W-We a-are p-p-pretty h-h-handsome." Tommy tried to wink back at Thad but he was having difficulty.

"See what you've started." Merry's finger came out to point at Thad.

"No fussing on the Lord's day." He went to open the door for her.

"Ma'am." He bowed at the waist as she went through the door. Tommy followed and the three left for Sunday services.

After his sermon, Pastor Gray announced the funeral services would be held for the Hasketts immediately following closing prayer. They had already been buried but pastor was going to say a few things at the cemetery.

The Sheridans were exiting the church when John McPherson called Thad over. The big redheaded man always seemed to have a wad of tobacco in his mouth and every time he spoke a little of the spit ran into his beard. He was a widower with no children and could be rather cantankerous.

"Just so's you know, I don't believe Bullock's report 'bout ole Hank startin' that there fire. The Indian been hangin round. Saw him goin into Hanks barn a time 'er two. Wudn't shore what he was up too guess we know now."

Thad just turned and walked away.

"Your place is safe, that there is a fact. That Indian was pretty cozy with your wife 'foring you come along, seen him myself many times on the ridge headin that way he won't be a burnin' you out lessen he gets her out first."

Thad wasn't sure he had ever experienced such a flash of anger. He turned and with just a few quick strides he was in McPherson's face.

"Seems to me Hank said something about you being after him to sell his property to you. He said at times your request had a hint of a threat. It would appear you had more motive to burn them out then the Indian." Thad didn't raise his voice but Sheriff Bullock knew something was going on.

"Is there a problem here McPherson? Sheridan?"

"No problem, Sheriff," Thad said has he backed away.

"What about you, John?"

"Nothing the United States Cavalry can't fix."

"And what does that mean?" The sheriff had taken Thad's place of being in McPherson's face.

"I sent a telegram askin' them to have a look into the Haskett burnin'. I'm not so shore ole Hank did it, as long as that Indian is still around."

"I did my investigation McPherson the case is closed."

"We'll see." The man strode off.

The sheriff lifted his hat and wiped his bald head. "He's going to stir up a hornets' nest." Thad had heard the whole conversation.

"Yup, he has already got the town stirred up. There is still gossip going around about Lone Eagle's involvement. They say you and Maggie are protecting him with the story of Hank's illness."

I hate this town was the thought that ran through Thad's mind with the accompaniment of Merry's voice. He understood her feelings.

"You got something to say, boy?" The sheriff looked at Thad.

"Nah, not just yet."

Merry motioned for Thad it was time to head to the cemetery. The little cemetery just on the outskirts of Rudolph had two freshly dug graves. Tommy stood between Thad and Merry. Pastor Gray read from the Bible and spoke the words the Lord had given him. The sheriff was just off to his right and Doc and Liddy Lapp stood to the right of Merry. Not one person from town had come. No one was surprised as Rudolph had become a very cold place. Pastor Gray closed in prayer with his final word came a beautiful song from the lips of Merry.

What a friend we have in Jesus,
All our sins and griefs to bear!
What a privilege to carry
Everything to God in prayer!
Oh, what peace we often forfeit,
Oh, what needless pain we bear,
All because we do not carry
Everything to God in prayer!

Who knew she could sing like an angle. Thad could barely hear her during the church service and she only hummed at home. He closed his eyes and let the words of the Hymn wash over him. When she stopped, Tommy's voice picked up where she left off. There was no stutter in the boy's voice.

Have we trials and temptations?
Is there trouble anywhere?
We should never be discouraged—
Take it to the Lord in prayer.
Can we find a friend so faithful,
Who will all our sorrows share?
Jesus knows our every weakness;
Take it to the Lord in prayer.

Together they sang the last verse. Their voices blended in perfect harmony. Thad had a huge lump in his throat.

Are we weak and heavy-laden,
Cumbered with a load of care?
Precious Savior, still our refuge—
Take it to the Lord in prayer.
Do thy friends despise, forsake thee?
Take it to the Lord in prayer!
In His arms He'll take and shield thee,
Thou wilt find a solace there.

When the song ended, Tommy buried his face into Merry's sleeve. She gently wrapped her arm around him smoothing his hair then kissed the top of his head. She caught Thad out of the corner of her eye. He was wiping his own tears.

They ate dinner with the Lapps then headed home. Once there, Thad told Merry he wanted to take Grace for a run. She thought about asking him to take Tommy with him but something made here hold her peace. Something was bothering her husband and he needed time to think.

Tommy was worn out and actually asked if he could take a nap outside. Merry threw an old quilt under the shade tree just to the side of the house. She watched him a minute as he lay on his back looking up into the heavens hands folded behind his head. It wasn't long until he yawned, turned on his side and went to sleep.

She sat in the chair rocking as Thad came out of the house. He smiled at Tommy "did you know he could sing like that?" he asked his wife.

"No, I have never heard anything like it. It was just beautiful. He kept that a secret."

"You kept a pretty good secret yourself Merry." His hands rested on the arms of the rocker and stopped it. Leaning over to kiss her on the cheek he smiled at her. "When I get back, I'll read some poetry if you will sing."

"When you get back you better tell me what you're up to." He frowned for just a fraction then set her to rocking.

"See, you can't be wooed?" he said as he loped of the porch. "It's hopeless," he said with a smile in his voice. She stood up and leaned over the railing.

"Giving up so soon, Mr. Impossible?"

He continued into the barn to saddle his horse when he finished he rode out of the barn and up to the porch "I don't give up, I'm pretty sure we'll be fussing when I get back and I know that's the quickest way to your heart." He turned the mare around and headed down the road.

He was going to do something she wouldn't be happy with. Where was he headed? She began rocking a little faster. The more she thought about it the more worked up she got. Over What? She didn't know. Then why was she letting herself stir this furry. She decided no matter what he was doing she was not going to get mad. She would show him she can be cool headed. But why would he goad her that way. He could be infuriating at times. She got up went into the house and started baking.

He felt dishonest but he knew Merry would not understand. He wanted to survey the Haskett home or what was left of it one more time. There was the chance of rain in the air he wanted to do one last survey before any evidence was washed away. He knew Dan Bullock was good at his job but he suspected he had seen more evidence of arson than Dan. He also had a deep gut feeling that if McPhersons boast were true this whole ordeal could get ugly.

He wasn't exactly sure what he was looking for but he knew he would know it when he saw it. That is the way it always was with him whether he was commanding a regiment or leading a man hunt he was driven by his inner instincts.

He knew Hank probably started the fire but he was asking himself "Could that be proven?" He knew Lone Eagle did not start the fire but he was asking himself if that could be proven. Tommy knew what happened. Would he be asked? Would they take his word? It just seemed Thad was loaded with questions he had to answer. It was the old fires of a love for the law that drove him. He walked around the ashes looking, digging, measuring and documenting.

When he finished at the Hasketts he headed toward Lone Eagle's village. He felt he needed to warn his friend about what was being said in town. He pushed Grace over the ridge into Indian Territory. He knew this wasn't the brightest thing he ever did. It was not a good thing to go into an Indian settlement without the accompaniment of someone from the tribe but he took his chances.

The thought had just left his mind when two braves came from the trees and stopped him. Their hands were on their weapons so Thad didn't move. The brave known as Two Winds eyed Thad narrowly while the other circled around them.

"You Morning Dove's man."

Thad chose to nod.

Two Winds turned his horse and escorted Thad into the settlement. Seeing his friend, Lone Eagle emerged from his dwelling.

"You not here to visit, what trouble Night Wolf?" Lone Eagle held Grace's reins as Thad dismounted. There were a group of people around him, mostly women. They were intrigued with his eyes and just kept staring at him. He felt a little uncomfortable and Lone Eagle dismissed them in the native tongue.

"We walk. You distract women," he said as Spotted Hawk took the reins from his father.

Thad and Lone Eagle stood a ways off and Thad explained what was happening in town. Lone Eagle was silent for a few minutes. He was looking out on the horizon.

"I do what you say, Night Wolf. Trust God."

"Yes, we will trust God. I just wanted you to know." They spoke a little longer. Lone Eagle had some questions for Thad regarding some scripture Spotted Hawk had read to him. The clover they were standing in and the trip to the Hasketts had irritated Thad's lungs and he began to cough.

"You ill Night Wolf?" the concern in the big Indians voice was genuine.

"No, just this." He raked his hand through the clover. The act brought on more coughing. Lone Eagle offered to have one of the

Indian women make him some herbal medicine to "fix cough" but Thad politely refused much to the woman's chagrin. Thad let out a shrill whistle and Grace pranced toward him. He was headed home.

Supper was just about ready when Thad entered the door. He had another coughing spell in the barn and wanted to make sure it was over before he entered the house. Tommy was setting the table and Merry was dishing up the food.

"Did you sleep well, Tommy?" His voice was hoarse and raspy. Merry's angry eyes pinned him to the wall. "Something sure smells good." He went to wash his hands.

Well, it is not you, Thad Sheridan. She chewed the words in her mouth and swallowed them. She wasn't going to fuss. The man reeked of ash. She knew exactly where he had been. She sat down, "Tommy, would you like to say grace?" Thad's hand engulfed Merry's as Tommy said a short prayer. Merry tried to retrieve her hand but Thad held it tight.

"Tommy, I was very impressed with your singing voice. You should sing more. Don't you agree, Merry?"

She knew what he was doing taking control of the conversation so she couldn't question him. She can play this game. She would just talk to Tommy.

"Tommy, I don't recall ever hearing you sing. When did you discover you had such a voice?"

The boy shrugged his shoulders. "M-Mama and I used t-to sing in th-the cellar."

That hurt. Merry's mind saw the picture of a scared boy and a mother who did all she could to protect him.

"Don't be surprised if the pastor asks you to sing a special sometime at church." Tommy's eyes were as big as half dollars. "I think," Thad finally released Merry's hand so she could eat, "that he will ask you and Merry to sing a duet." Merry's eyes were now as big as half dollars. Thad stifled a cough.

After dinner Thad engaged Tommy in a game of checkers. He was avoiding Merry to a certain degree. She could feel it. She took Gus and went out to her garden. It wasn't like him to keep secrets from her. She reckoned he had a right too but it bothered her. Maybe he was protecting her. What did Tommy say that night "it wasn't an accident." The more she thought about it the more she hoed and the harder she hoed. Something was going on and she was being kept in the dark. She stopped to pray, *Help me, Lord, to trust the man you have given me, help me to trust you.*

She had worked a good hour in the garden when her back began to hurt. She had ascertained such a grip on the hoe she almost had to pry it from her clenched hands. She did not realize how deep in thought and prayer she had been.

The smell of coffee drove her in the house.

"We were hoping you would come in soon. That pie is just begging to be eaten, right, Tommy?" The boy smiled widely. She got plates and forks and handed the knife to Tommy.

"Will you do the honors?"

Tommy was thrilled and he cut the pie as careful as he could but the pieces were all different sizes. The look on his face showed his disappointment.

"You know, Merry, I never thought of cutting a pie this way. So many different sizes make it easier to choose what your stomach could handle. See this piece here?" He pointed to a smaller one. "This piece here is what you might want after a big meal. You know just enough to fill the sweet tooth. This piece here, this big one well that's a piece you get when your hankering is as big as outdoors. Then there is these in between pieces I call them just right pieces. They're just right if the bigger ones are gone."

The boy's face was lit in wonder at Thad's analogy. Thad's words held purpose for the youngster. He had a very unique gift of making people feel treasured. She couldn't fuss with him in fact, she couldn't take her eyes off of him.

He felt her staring at his profile as he ate. It took him a few minutes to look back. She was probably still upset with him. He figured her eyes would reveal the igniting ember of a spat. Instead he was met with a look he had seen earlier from the Indian woman. He knew he was off the hook.

Nothing was said about where Thad had been that afternoon and the two went to bed in a comfortable silence—that was, until

Thad began coughing in his sleep. At first it was a cough every so often then it became spells of coughing. He woke up and sat on the side of the bed. Merry moved to sit next to him. Her hand went through his hair her voice was a whisper.

"Thad, for my sake, you have got to take care of yourself." He coughed. "Doc Lapp says you could do permanent damage to your lungs if you don't do what he says. Whatever you did today was it worth all this coughing and misery?" Her words were soft and gentle and the tone tore at his heart. He hadn't been thinking about her worries. He leaned on her and put his head touching hers.

"I'm sorry," he rasped. He began coughing again and she rose to heat some water.

In the lamp light of the kitchen she could see Thad had coughed so much there were blood vessels broken in his beautiful eyes. He poured the water into the bucket and Merry added the medicine the doctor had prescribed. While he was leaned over the bucket Merry fixed some tea.

"When you're done drink this." He lifted the side of the cloth and she could only see his raised eyebrows. "I didn't put anything in it I promise. It is just chamomile tea."

Once the steam dissipated, Thad emptied the water. He sat and drank the tea arching his back and rubbing his chest. All this coughing was stretching his muscles. He propped his elbows on the table and rested his face in his hands he had a headache to boot. Merry had gone back to bed thinking her husband would return when he was through drinking the tea. When he did not return, she rose to check on him.

"Thad, what is it?"

He massaged his eyes and temples. "All this coughing has given me a headache." She went to the cabinet and got some lavender oil she had put up last spring. She put a small drop on her finger tips and rubbed it into Thad's temple working her way to the back of his neck and shoulders. She felt his tense muscles began to relax. She wished she had put a little of doc's secret remedy in his tea again but he wouldn't have forgiven her a second time.

"That helps, thank you." He reached up to touch her hand. "And thank you for not questioning me about today." She kissed the top of his head a couple of times.

"Who knew I could hold my tongue?"

He leaned back to look up at her and just smiled. "Go on to bed, Merry." His voice was still raspy.

"I can't go to sleep without you next to me. I'll wait." He got up and walked her to bed.

Things had been pretty still for the Sheridans over the past few weeks. Tommy had become comfortable in his role as a part of the family. Thad had written the circuit judge to petition for the adoption of Tommy. He prepared both Merry and Tommy that it may take a while.

Thad continued to have an occasional cough. He was feeling better and was able to work without the coughing fits. He was showing Tommy the workings of a farm and giving the boy responsibilities he embraced the opportunities.

They watched Merry come from the house and head to the barn.

"What do you think she is up to?"

Tommy shrugged his shoulders. It wasn't long until they saw her pull the horses out and start to hitch up the team to the wagon. Thad's first inclination was to rush to help her. His head talked him out of it she was capable. He would let it go. It didn't take her long and he watched her meticulously double check all her steps. She pulled the wagon up to the two.

"I am headed into town. You two need anything?" They both said no, smiling at one another.

"You two are up to something, you might as well spill it."

"I thought Tommy and I might sneak off and do a little fishing."

"Catch enough for company. I'm going to invite the Lapps out for supper." She was off.

The Lapps were happy to be invited for dinner and would head out after the doc finished up. She had stopped by the post office to get the mail there was a letter addressed to Thad with no return address and one from Abby. It was addressed solely to her. She felt compelled to stop and read the letter. It was usually addressed to both her and Thad.

April 30, 1881
My Dearest Sister,

I am writing to let you know Mother has passed away. You are probably wondering why I have addressed this letter to you instead of Thad. I am doing this for Thad. You will tell him and share his sorrow and he will not have to go through the pain of re-telling the details. I hope you understand. She passed away peacefully in her sleep. The hip never healed properly and she developed pneumonia. I will write more when I have the chance.

All my love,
Abby

Merry's heart was breaking for her husband. He had carried some guilt over being so far away. Their visit earlier had been good but he still felt as if he let his mother down. She prayed as she slowly pushed the team home.

As she neared the house she spotted Thad and Tommy walking on the road with a string of fish. She slowed the team. "You fellas need a ride?"

"Yes, ma'am, if you are headed our way." The two jumped in the back of the wagon laughing and arguing with each other about who caught the biggest fish. When was she going to find the right time to let Thad know about his mother? She couldn't just blurt it out, could she?

When she stopped the team, Thad jumped off the wagon and came around to help her down. "Merry?" he questioned in regards to her worried look.

"I need to talk to you."

"Did something happen in town?"

Her eyes darted to Tommy who was trying to get the fish out of the wagon.

"Here, Tommy." Thad helped the boy with the fish. "Can you take these to the back of the house and put them in the bucket?" The boy struggled to hold the line of fish.

"I-I c-can," he said as he walked carefully toward the back of the house.

"Put some water in the bucket and I will be right there." Thad assured him.

Thad turned to look at Merry. He didn't move but stood directly in front of her his arms resting on the wagon seat. "I got a letter from Abby." Her voice cracked and Thad knew it wasn't good news.

All sorts of things went through his mind. "And?" he prodded his wife to continue.

"Your mother, she . . . she's gone." His head begin to nod a little as if acknowledging the fact would somehow help.

"How?" His throat was tight with emotion.

"Abby said she developed pneumonia and went very peacefully in her sleep." His head nodded again. He swallowed hard and looked down the road. Merry reached out and touched his arm.

"I'm okay, Merry," he said and headed around the house to help Tommy clean the fish.

She watched them through the kitchen window. Thad was patiently teaching Tommy how to clean the fish, allowing the youngster to make mistakes and learn from them. The sadness was evident in his manner. Tommy noticed it too. After they were done cleaning the fish Tommy took the bucket to wash it out. Merry noticed him stop and head back to where Thad set on the back porch. She didn't know what the two were talking about but it ended in Tommy's arm sliding around Thad's shoulder and patting him on the back. He must have told Tommy about his mother. Merry reached in her pocket for a handkerchief when she found the other letter for Thad. She figured a few more minutes wouldn't matter so she laid the letter on the table for when he returned to the house.

Thad and Tommy handed over the fish to Merry.

"I almost forgot, Thad. There was another letter for you on the table." Thad picked up the letter and opened it.

Mr. Sheridan,

The written petition you submitted was reviewed by Judge Jamieson Carlisle. He will take it into consideration and make the decision when he is in your area the week of May 23, 1881. Judge Carlisle will be presiding over the inquiry involving a Sioux Indian and an arson case. Please be prepared to meet with the Judge during this week.

Sincerely
R. J. Pratt
Legal Secretary

He folded the letter and placed it back in the envelope. "A judge is going to be coming to Rudolph the week of the twenty-third in regards to the petition for adoption." Thad shared with his family.

This was good news. Tommy and Merry were all smiles. Thad's smile was strained. It was good news but the fact an inquiry was going to be held in regards to the Haskett case was not. Thad's mind was racing. He was afraid of this. He wondered how long it would be before they got word Lone Eagle had been placed in custody.

The Lapps had arrived for supper noticing a mixture of emotion in the house. Tommy seemed particularly happy but Thad was preoccupied and his usual happy disposition was missing. Merry was frequently looking at her husband as if surveying his well-being. Doctor Lapp at first thought Thad may be ill but he knew Maggie would blurt that out.

Over the meal, Thad caught Zeke and Liddy glancing at each other.

"I received word today that my mother has passed away."

"Oh, Thad, we are so sorry." Liddy's hand flew to her throat. "How did it happen?"

Thad told the couple how his mother passed and accepted their condolences and concern.

After dinner Thad asked the physician to take his coffee out on the front porch. He went to the bedroom and retrieved the letter he received earlier. There was something else in the letter that he hadn't shared with his wife. At first it hurt Merry's feelings but she checked her emotions and allowed the spirit to direct her thoughts and actions. If she needed to know Thad will tell her.

It was pretty late when the Lapps left. Tommy had fallen asleep on the floor where he had been playing with a set of wooden animals the Lapps had brought. Thad lifted the boy and carried him up the loft then returned for the dog. Once he completed the task he went and opened the front door and motioned for Merry to join him on the porch. He rested his hands on the railing and leaned a little over looking up at the sky. She joined him her frame leaning against the rail facing him.

"What else was in that letter?"

Thad let out a slow sigh and lifted his head to the heaven. "They're going to hold and inquiry regarding the accusations against Lone Eagle. Judge Carlisle is a pretty tough Judge to convince especially if he already has his mind made up."

"What was Tommy talking about when he said it wasn't an accident?" Thad sat on the railing

"You're an intelligent woman Merry what do you think happened?"

She was still for a few minutes. "Well it is obvious it wasn't an accident seeing as we found Tommy in the cellar and not in the house like Hank and Melissa. If it was accidental Tommy would have been at the pump getting water and Hank and Melissa would be fighting the fire. I suspect Hank was reliving the war and things got out of hand."

Thad just looked at his wife.

"Are you telling me this is what Tommy told the sheriff happened? She asked

"I am not telling you anything."

"Do you think they will want to question Tommy?" her stomach started to knot up. She didn't want the poor boy to have to try and get through such an emotional ordeal. It was difficult enough for him to speak without feeling embarrassed.

"Not if I can help it?" Thad jumped off the rail and sat in the rocker. "They will probably try to hold Lone Eagle for questioning."

"We should get word to him." Even in the dark she saw a look cross her husband's face. "Unless you have already done so, have you already done so?"

"I have."

She shook her head. "Please tell me you didn't just ride into Indian Territory on your own?"

"Okay, I won't tell you." He had a grin on his face.

"You delight in doing things like this, don't you? You can't go in there without an escort. Lone Eagle told you that, but do you listen. Mule headed." As if the mule could understand the human language, the animal let out another hehaw. "Oh, sorry, girl, she yelled toward the barn, I didn't mean to insult you."

She was flitting around on the porch like a mother hen and Thad was just watching her. "Aren't you going to say anything?" She stood in front of the rocker.

"There's nothing to say."

"How about 'I am sorry, Merry. I should have told you. I shouldn't have gone to Lone Eagle. I should have waited for him to come here.'"

"I would gladly say all of those things, Mrs. Sheridan, if I was sorry but I am not and if that gets your feathers ruffled further that would be fine by me."

Oh, he had that look on his face, that face that says he is enjoying himself. Merry was too easy of a target. She knew that and his smile just drove the point home.

She plopped down on the bottom porch step and put her elbows on her knees like a child. He moved to sit behind her on the top step and wrapped his arms around her.

"You make my life worthwhile Merry. I hope you know that." She leaned her back against him. She had a lump in her throat.

"This has been the happiest year of my life, I hope you know that," she whispered back. They spent another hour just this way. Thad had opened up and mourned his mother's death.

It was a few days later when there was an early morning knock at the door. Thad heard the light knock coming from the back door. He rose and peeked out the window Spotted Hawk was standing nervously looking all around. Thad had a pretty good idea what brought the boy here at this time of the morning.

"What is it Hawk?"

"They have come and taken Lone Eagle." The boy had been learning to speak proper English from Merry and had done rather well.

"Who was it?" Thad motioned for the boy to come in.

"It was the United States Cavalry."

Thad shook his head. "Do you know why they took him?" Thad was trying to determine how much Lone Eagle had shared with his son.

"They think he burned the Haskett home."

"Where were they taking him?"

"Sheriff Dan said he would be taking him to jail and not to worry. He would be taken good care of."

"The sheriff will make sure your father is fairly taken care of. I will head into town after breakfast and see your father and the sheriff."

Thad put some coffee on. "This will get the cook up. You hungry?" The boy was fourteen years old of course he was hungry.

Thad was right. It was only a matter of minutes and Merry appeared hair a mess and her robe half on. She was a little taken aback to see Spotted Hawk sitting at her table.

"I didn't know we had company. Hello, Hawk." She tightened the robe around her and smoothed back her hair. Her appearance did not phase the boy. Thad handed her a cup of coffee.

"If we go get some eggs, will you make breakfast?" he asked her as if he had to barter for meals. He was doing this teasing for Spotted Hawk.

"Don't pay him any attention, Hawk, he gets at least three meals a day without so much as lifting a finger." Thad laughed and Spotted Hawk just looked between the two. These people had strange ways.

Thad went to finish getting dressed and Merry was making some biscuits. Tommy had come down and was surprised to see Hawk. He smiled a sleepy smile at the tan skinned boy wearing only trousers made from deer hide. Spotted Hawk raised a hand to return Tommy's greeting. When Thad returned the three men headed to the barn.

After breakfast, which was totally consumed, Thad made the trek into town with Spotted Hawk. This was Spotted Hawk's first trip to town and Thad had warned him the people would not be kind. It didn't take long for him to figure this out. As soon as one of the town's people spotted him they would cross to the other side of the street or sneer in his direction.

Thad kept his hand on Hawk's back as they made their way to Sheriff Bullocks. Sitting outside the office were two US Cavalry soldiers. They surveyed Thad and the boy and opened the door so they could enter the Sheriff's office. One of the officers stepped inside.

"Judge Carlisle will be here next week and some big fancy lawyer from back east will be in on tomorrow's stage or so I am told." The sheriff's eyes landed on the solider and he affirmed the information.

The sheriff led Spotted Hawk and Thad to the cell where Lone Eagle was staying. He had finished breakfast. Sheriff Bullock opened the door to retrieve the tray and let Spotted Hawk in. The man embraced his son.

"I am good, not to worry." He patted the boys back.

"He's going to need representation," Dan was speaking to Thad in the outer office.

"Isn't there an Indian agent assigned?" he asked the officer standing outside of Lone Eagle's dwelling.

"He refused, he is asking for a Thad Sheridan to represent him."

Thad's eyes went to the Indian who was talking to his son in his native tongue.

"Do you know this Thad Sheridan?" the officer asked the men.

"Yeah, I know him," the sheriff said, slapping Thad on the back revealing to the young cavalryman just exactly who Thad Sheridan was.

Lone Eagle and Thad talked for a few minutes. The Indian said he trusted Thad with his very life and knew whatever happened Thad would do his best. He also asked Thad to look after Spotted Hawk while he was incarcerated.

"He can stay with us if he would like."

Lone Eagle turned to his son and began to speak the native language. Thad had picked up a word here or there and knew Lone Eagle was encouraging his son not to be angry.

Thad picked up a few supplies from the new mercantile in town. A man had opened up a small store on the far end of town. It was worth it to Thad to go the extra distance to not have to buy from McPherson.

The new mercantile owner had not yet been tainted by the town. Thad prayed the owner would never get to that place. Still the town was what it was and when Thad entered with Spotted Hawk the people inside filed out, some of the women gasping and some men muttering under their breath.

The owner, Mr. Tyler, waited on Thad politely and efficiently. He made no moves to discourage Thad or Hawk from returning. This would be the Sheridans' new place to trade.

"You are more than welcome to stay with us Hawk." Thad stated as the two neared home. The boy had not moved his gaze from straight ahead since they left town. Thad wondered about what was going through the boy's mind.

"My father did not burn the Hasketts out," he said bluntly.

"I know that." Thad turned to look at him.

"It does not matter that you know it, it matters what judge knows and he will hear what town's people tell him." His face set like a flint turned to Thad.

"I will do my best to show him the truth" was all Thad could promise.

"He will not go unharmed through this journey?" Spotted Hawk's face was back toward the horizon. Thad studied the boy's words. He was probably right.

"Lone Eagle wishes for me to stay with you. I will do so, in the barn."

"No." Thad was shaking his head. "No guest in my house sleeps in the barn. Besides, you know, Merry wouldn't allow it."

"Morning Dove have head like rock." Thad smiled. "And," the boy added, "heart of angel."

"That's my girl," Thad said and pushed the horses to pick up the pace.

Thad stood just out of eye sight when the stage came in. He wanted to see just who the big fancy lawyer was from back east. The man got out and sure enough it was a former classmate of Thad's. Grover Whinsted was a year behind Thad but he had no trouble recognizing him after all these years.

Elmer McPherson was there to meet him and ushered him down to the town's only hotel. He continued to watch the two men when he heard a familiar voice coming from the stagecoach.

No, his mind was playing tricks on him. It couldn't be. He turned toward the voice just in time to see Abby step down from the stage followed by Anna Beth, Patience and Jackson. He blinked to make sure what he saw wasn't an illusion.

"This is it," he heard Jackson say as Abby dusted off her dress and fanned her face. She was dressed in such a way you could barely tell she was expecting.

"Look, there is Uncle Thad." Anna Beth had spotted him and ran to meet him. He scooped her up in his arms and she gave him a big kiss.

"What in the world are you doing here?" he grabbed his sister in a huge embrace. He shook Jacksons hand and took Patience out of her father's arms.

"She had to see you." Jackson pointed toward his wife.

"Now stop it," she scolded Jackson. "I did want to see you. I had to see you, Thad. Please don't be angry."

"Angry! I am thrilled, although I am surprised the doctor let you travel in your condition."

"See?" Jacksons hand was resting on his wife's lower back. "I am not the only one who is questioning the doctor's sanity."

"I am going to say this for the last time." Abby nailed both men with a glare. "I am fine and the baby's fine. He has done nothing but kick the whole trip."

Thad took the Lortons to the Lapps for tea. He knew it would be more comfortable for all of them. He wanted Zeke and Abby to meet just in case she would need him during the visit. Thad also wanted to catch the doctor up on what was going on with Lone Eagle and asked the physician to pray with him. No offense to the doctor but Thad couldn't help thinking who he really needed was Lachlan Kennedy. He could pray the house down.

When everyone was rested a bit, Thad decided they should head for home.

"Merry will be beside herself." Thad said as he put Patience in the back of the wagon. Thad started to plan where everyone was going to sleep. Oh well it would all work out. If ever there was a time he needed family, it was now. He couldn't keep the smile from his face or the prayers off his lips.

When they reached the house Tommy and Hawk came out to unload the wagon. He motioned for everyone to be quiet as he helped Patience and Anna Beth down from the wagon. He lifted both in his arms and went through the door. Merry had her back to him and was blacking the stove.

"Merry, honey could you give me a hand." Merry rose and straightened her back.

"Help with what?" she said as she turned around.

The look on her face was absolutely priceless! She opened her mouth and the cutest squeal floated out.

"Where did you come from?" she ran to take Patience from his arms and gave Anna Beth a kiss.

"Where is your Momma?"

Abby and Jackson entered the cabin. Patience was handed back to Thad as Abby and Merry embraced, both women were crying. Merry turned to Jackson.

"I can't believe you let her travel in her condition." She was staring at him expecting an answer.

"You're married to a Sheridan, Merry. Have you not come in contact with their stubborn side? Once their mind is made up, you might as well be talking to a mule."

Merry waited a brief second. She was sure she would hear the hehaw from the one outside. She and Thad laughed and told the story of the mule's knack for commenting just at the right time.

The Lorton's were introduced to Tommy and Hawk. The Lorton's being genuinely kind people treated both boys with the utmost respect and kindness. Patience was so in awe of Hawk's long black hair she just wanted to touch it. Spotted Hawk was good natured about it. He even took Tommy and the girls out to play in the yard.

"Merry, I am sorry. I just had to come and did so without even thinking about where we would stay if you didn't have room. What a terrible imposition."

"Nonsense. We have—" She stopped. They didn't have plenty of room but they had enough. "We may not have plenty of room but we have enough."

"Sure," Thad added. He had been thinking about this. It would work out. "Jackson, you and Abby can take our room." Abby started to protest but Thad threw his hand up. "I doubt you would be able to climb the ladder." He pointed and she smoothed her ruffled feathers.

"Merry and I will sleep in the loft. The girls can sleep on the floor up there with us."

"He doesn't know our girls does he Abby?" Abby giggled "They won't be on the floor they will be right in the bed with you. Anna Beth isn't so much of a problem but Patience ends up long ways across the head of the bed some nights."

"We'll manage."

"The boys can sleep on the floor in the sitting room," Merry added.

"The boys live with you?" Jackson asked.

"Yes. Is that going to be a problem?" Merry queried with a hint of dread in her voice. Those were her boys as much as Anna Beth and Patience were his girls.

"Not in the least. I guess I didn't realize they lived here

"In our excitement, we probably left out a detail or two," Thad added. "Sit down and we will explain."

With the full explanation being given on how Tommy and Hawk came to be staying with the Sheridan's the Lorton's sat in awe.

"So that was Grover Whinsted on the stage with us." Jackson questioned. "I thought he looked familiar. I worked a case with him a couple of years ago. Pretty ruthless."

"I am not surprised to hear that," Thad commented.

"I know your knowledge is more on the banking end of the law but I would like to get your thoughts. Maybe after supper we can talk through some things."

"Be glad to help any way I can, Thad."

"How long are you staying?" Merry looked to Abby. "And might I add I hope it is a long time."

Abby looked to her husband, smiling. "We thought a couple of weeks, maybe three."

"I know that look, Jackson." Thad slapped his brother-in-law on the back. "You said two weeks and she's going to try and get more just by smiling and being sweet." Jackson laughed. Thad hit the nail on the head.

"Well, it happens to the best of us," Thad added.

"I don't think that was what Abby was trying to do," Merry interjected, irritated that Thad would insinuate she had used feminine wiles to get what she wanted.

"It happens to the best of us," she mocked him. "When have I ever tried to get what I wanted by cozying up."

"I wish you would try it just once. It sure takes less energy than quarreling." He was antagonizing her. He winked at her just to add fuel.

"Thad Sheridan, that is no way to talk to Merry. You're just being a bully." The women had united.

"Jackson, have you ever noticed the way a woman uses your full name as a switch when she's angry." Abby and Merry gasped and Jackson felt empowered.

"I am reminded weekly that my name is Jackson Lorton." he put emphasis on the name. "Who could forget?"

Thad cackled. Merry and Abby were both standing now.

"Look at them, Abby, two grown men acting like children." The reprimand didn't faze the two. They both sat there with huge smiles on their faces. It never occurs to a woman just why a man likes to see her all riled up. The age-old secret was still safe.

The women were still a little miffed at their men when they put supper on the table. Anna Beth and Patience were chattering non-stop. This was literally a different world to them and they couldn't stop asking questions. Merry and Abby were unusually quiet. When Thad asked for the bread to be passed Merry handed it to him rather roughly. He reined in a smile as he dipped his head but Merry saw it. He just couldn't help himself. She was annoyed.

Spotted Hawk was a very observant young man and he saw the whole interaction.

"Are you two fighting again?" Hawk said as he elbowed Tommy who was sitting beside him. Thad had a grin on his face as his head came up to meet Hawk's black, smiling eyes.

Merry was red with embarrassment.

"F-Fight now, k-kissing later," Tommy added and Merry's blush extended.

"Do they kiss a lot too?" Anna Beth asked like it was something disgusting.

"They kiss all the time." Patience was pointing to her parents.

"That's enough, girls," Jackson said as he threw a wink in his wife's direction. How could they scold any of the children? They had the grownups dead to rights.

Merry and Abby had retired to the small sitting room with some tea. Jackson and Thad were at the table talking about the upcoming inquiry. The girls were on the front porch with Tommy and Gus. Hawk was on the back porch getting a break from Patience. Her father had forbid her from going out the back door.

"Can you believe those two?" Merry said as she moved her head in the direction of the kitchen. "I didn't realize I had married a man so much like my brother," Abby said as she looked toward the kitchen. "I do love him, so very much," she added wistfully, referring to her husband.

"I get so angry at Thad sometimes I just want to put my hands around his neck, but I know in the same instant I would be fighting the urge of smothering him with a thousand kisses. How can a woman's emotion run such a course? You know Abby, this is exactly why they do what they did earlier. It drives us right into their arms."

Abby smiled. She would like to be in Jackson's arms right now.

"Are you tired Abby, I don't want to keep you up if you would like to rest. I have made the trip from Charleston it wore me out and I didn't have two children in tow."

"I am a little tired but to tell you the truth Merry I can't go to bed without Jackson I just can't rest." Merry nodded in understanding. Abby shifted on the settee.

"Are you all right, Abby?"

"Yes, it is this corset I am wearing for expecting mothers. It is the most uncomfortable thing."

Merry began to chuckle. "Let me tell you what happened to my corset."

Thad and Jackson had been working for over an hour. Tommy and the girls had come in from outside and was playing with Tommy's wooden animals. There was some low laughter from the sitting room. It was good to hear Merry and his sister laugh. Suddenly there was a huge loud round of laughter causing everyone in the kitchen to raise their head.

Tommy turned to Thad. "W-Wwhat d-did w-we do t-this time?"

Tommy was right, women only laugh like that when they were laughing at a man. Abby was astonished at her brother's disposal of a perfectly good corset.

Chapter Ten

Thad went into town a few days later to see Lone Eagle. The man was doing well. He talked openly with Sheriff Bullock about his recent conversion. The sheriff was touched by the man's humility in the wake of what was going on in his life.

Judge Carlisle would be here on the Monday stage just three days away and the inquiry would start Tuesday Morning. Lone Eagle asked Thad again to take care of Spotted Hawk and "teach him not to be angry." The words haunted Thad. How could he teach a young man not to be angry when someone takes his father off without just cause? His anger was justified.

Thad was just a few miles from home when he was ambush by the Indian brave that had helped Two Winds escort him into the village. The young brave approached Thad's horse so quickly it startled Grace and threw Thad off balance.

In a split second the Indian had knocked Thad from a top the horse. The two went wrestling to the ground. After several minutes the Indian had pinned Thad to the ground and held a knife to his throat. Thad lay still crystal blue eyes locked on the Indians. The Indian raised the knife and Thad's timing was precise. His elbow came up knocking the knife out of the man's hand sending it flying. He turned on the Indian and had him face down with both arms restrained behind. The more the brave struggled the tighter Thad's hold.

The tall shadow that fell over the pair caused Thad to look up. Two Winds stood with his hands across his chest. He did not move. Thad rose bringing the Indian with him still restrained. He positioned the brave between himself and Two Winds. When the brave was up right Two Winds reached out and slapped the young brave across the face.

Thad's first inkling was to release his hold but it might be a trick. Two Winds spoke in the native language to the young brave who lowered his head. Two Winds put his hands gently on Thad's and pushed them releasing his hold. The brave immediately jumped on his horse and raced away.

Two Winds stood face to face with Thad.

"I will not harm you, nor will I protect you. I am not as Lone Eagle. I have no loyalty to you." The Indian started to walk away.

"I have not bothered you. Why the ambush?" This surprised the Indian. He turned slowly. His eyes narrowed on Thad.

"To see if you are what you appear?"

"Am I?" Thad wasn't sure what he was supposed to be.

Two Winds went and picked up the braves large knife that had been discarded. Coming back to Thad he handed the weapon to him. "Night Wolf strong warrior." Two Winds left.

Thad was pretty dumbfounded by the whole scuffle. Were they trying to scare him? Thad was a fighter whether he liked it or not and they had better not mess with him or his family. Still he wasn't quite sure what to make of it.

He hid the knife in his boot. There was no need scaring Abby, or Merry for that fact, with the story. The whole scrimmage had given him a mouth full of dust and the coughing began. That was all he needed. If the cough didn't subside before he reached home, Merry would be giving him what for. He raised his arm to cough into his sleeve and noticed a tear and some blood. He must have been cut by the knife.

Grace was pretty lathered up from the ride home. This could work in Thad's favor. It would take him longer to groom her and he could attend to his slight wound and ease his lungs. Tommy who had been waiting for him to come home came racing into the barn.

"Y-You must have r-rode h-her hard."

Thad had a guilty feeling. Why was he trying to keep something like that from Merry? They were supposed to be one. He would be hurt if she kept things from him.

"I did in fact. Tommy, do you think you can rub her down and take care of her for me?" The boy was very happy to do so. He had been helping Thad and learning just the right way to do it but to be responsible for doing the whole job set the boy over the edge. His smile was huge.

"First will you go in and tell Merry I need to talk to her and have her come out." Tommy wondered why he just didn't go in there and talk to her. Adults did strange things at times but he did as he was told.

Merry came out of the house and saw Thad going around to the side of the house. That man, she thought is always up to something. She headed around the corner and heard the cough.

"Don't say a word." He was rather firm so she said nothing. He grabbed her hand, "Let's go for a walk."

She walked silently beside him as they traveled a good distance from the house. He was in deep thought. Merry wondered when he was going to begin speaking. He had told her not to say a word and she was determined he would be the first to talk. They ended up next to the creek.

"I am astounded that you have not lit into me yet," he said, dropping her hand.

"You rather commanded me not to say anything so I haven't."

"I didn't command anything."

She shrugged her shoulders and walked a bit down the creek. When he didn't follow her, she turned. She hadn't noticed his sleeve so when he rolled up the garment and removed the makeshift bandage her eyes went wide.

"What on earth happened?" she rushed to look at the wound. It was small but deep and trickled blood. He reached into his boot and pulled out the Indian's knife. She looked at him in bewilderment.

"This needs cleaned and probably a few stitches. Why didn't you come into the house so I could take care of it instead of dragging me out here?" She was assessing the wound on the back of his upper arm. "How did it happen anyway?" her worried brow was all Thad could see.

"I didn't want to explain to Abby and Jackson that I was ambushed by an Indian and about got my throat slit." He gave Merry the details of what occurred.

"I was going to try and keep it from you Merry but that's not right. A man and a woman shouldn't have secrets even if it appears to be the right thing to do." His eyes traveled her face. "Besides with all the extra people around how else was I going to get you alone?"

She snuffed "Who are you fooling? If you wanted to be alone with me nothing would stop you from going right in the house and saying so, and let me tell you I have been waiting for you to do just that." She was pretty sassy it was one of his favorite qualities about her.

They decided to hide the wound as much as possible and later after supper when Merry was going to cut Thad's hair she would stitch up the wound. Maybe they could pull it off.

They sat by the creek bank talking. It seemed since the house had been full they had no time to just talk. Merry loved the sound of Thad's voice. She loved to hear the rich deep baritone of his words.

"Merry."

She especially loved hearing him say her name. He seldom called here anything else and she liked it that way. Everyone wants to hear the sound of their name.

"Merry?" Thad had stopped talking when he realized Merry wasn't paying attention. He had asked her a question and when she didn't answer, he turned to see a far-off look and a tender smile.

"Care to share what's going through that mind of yours putting that wistful look on your face?" "Oh." She blushed. "Just thinking. Did you say something? I am sorry, I wasn't listening."

"So I gathered. It wasn't as important, at least not as important as the reason behind this blush that has your ears aglow." He reached out and tugged on her ear and she swatted it away.

"A lesser man might get jealous."

"Never mind." She rose to head back to the house but he did not follow.

Assuming he was behind her, she walked a ways before she noticed.

"Are you pouting?" She stomped back to the creek edge.

"Your allowed to sit and think but I'm not?" he placed his hand over his heart.

"You may sit and think all you want." She flipped around a little peeved. Before she knew it, he had her in his arms and tossed her into the water.

"Oh!" she screamed her face in total surprise. "You!" She couldn't get any words out and struggled to get up but fell back down. "Don't you dare laugh at me, Thad!" She was pointing at him.

"Don't you mean 'Thad Sheridan'?" He was mocking her.

"Why would you do such a thing?" She was standing in the middle of the creek hands on hips.

"I thought you needed a little cooling off."

She made her way to the edge and started up the side. "Will you give me a hand?" she asked.

He shook his head no. "I don't trust you."

"Some southern gentlemen you are."

He laughed as she started up the bank. She started to slip in the mud and he reached out to catch her. She grabbed his arm and pulled with all her might. He fell face first into the creek. When he stood covered in mud she could not hold her laugh. He sprang out of the water and she took off running toward the house.

The two came running and laughing on to the porch wet and muddy. When they opened the door, they were met with stares.

"What happened, Uncle Thad?" Anna Beth asked

"I will tell you what happened," Merry spoke before Thad had opportunity. "Your Uncle Thad threw me in the creek."

There was a chorus of "Thad," "Thad Sheridan," and "Uncle Thad" all at once from the group. Before anyone could reprimand him, he put his hand up to stop them.

"Tommy, you are a smart man. Looking at Merry and I, what would you say occurred?"

Tommy's surveyed the couple. "S-She got you b-back." Thad nodded and winked at Tommy and headed up the loft to change. Merry trailed behind.

The group didn't know what was going on but there was a lot of good hearted laughter coming from the loft. Minutes later the two appeared in clean clothes.

They were always so happy Jackson thought. He and Abby were happy but there was something different about Thad and Merry. How could Thad go from Laurel to this place and be happier? This home had something he and Abby didn't. He was in deep thought when he caught his wife staring at him. He would like to discuss it with her but was afraid she would think he was unhappy with her.

"One of us is missing." Thad asked as he looked around the group, "Where is Hawk?"

"He left right after you did this morning." Merry turned to the kids. "Has he not returned at all today?"

Patience who made it her personal job to keep track of Hawk spoke up.

"He hasn't been 'round all day and he promised I could brush his hair today." The girl was put out, that was obvious.

Thad knew a little twinge of anxiety. Hawk was angry about his father being held in the town jail. He had tried to talk with him about it but Hawk shut him out. "If he isn't back by supper I will go look for him."

After supper Thad went to saddle Grace. Hawk had not come back yet and he and Merry were getting worried. Merry met him in the barn.

"I just saw Hawk on the ridge. He is just sitting up there." Thad finished saddling the horse.

"Let me go." Merry placed a hand on Grace's neck. He didn't want to let her go but he knew if anyone could reach Hawk it would be his mother Morning Dove.

Life was so remarkable. A person could fill a void for another in so many ways. He didn't argue with her and helped her onto his horse.

"If she gets a little rambunctious remember you set the pace."

"I know how to ride a horse, Thad."

"I was talking to the horse." He stepped back just in time for Grace to blaze past him. "Slow down," he hollered as he watched her take off through the pasture.

When she was a short distance from Spotted Hawk, she dismounted and walked to where the young brave was sitting. When he first heard her footsteps, he knew they were the footsteps of a woman. He never moved as she sat down beside him.

"It is terrible what is happening to your father, Hawk. I believe Thad can help him."

"He is already guilty in the eyes of the town. That will not change no matter how strong Night Wolf is."

"Thad is strong. He also is strong up here." She poked the boy's temple with her index finger. "Oftentimes this is stronger than this." She took her finger from the temple to the muscle in Hawk's arm.

The boy would not look at her. His eyes stayed on the setting sun.

"Running Creek and Two Winds attacked him today. It was a test of this and that." He poked her temple and the muscle in her arm.

"Why would they want to test him?" she asked.

"Because Lone Eagle trusts him, they had to prove him."

It didn't all make sense to Merry but she did not press the matter. "We will do our best to bring the truth to the people," she promised.

"The truth did not save the man Jesus you talk about. They killed him anyway." This surprised Merry. Hawk had never seemed interested in hearing about Jesus.

"This is true, Hawk. The truth was all around the people. Jesus himself was the truth and they refused to see it. You say the town does not believe the truth of your father's innocence. Does that make the truth about your father untrue?"

He turned to look at her not saying anything.

"Does the truth become untrue because of what you think?" He was silent but paying close attention. "Jesus is the way, truth, and the life no matter what man says. Your father will be innocent no matter what the judge decides. Don't be like the town Hawk and judge the life of Jesus as untrue when it is all true."

Spotted Hawk's stomach began to growl.

"Help me up," she asked and he stood to help her. "I saved you some supper. Let's go home."

"Where did you learn to sew like that?" Thad was asking Jackson as the man pulled the thread through Thad's skin meticulously.

"I got in on the tail end of the war, worked with a doctor did a lot of stitching." Thad never knew that about his brother-in-law. They had fought on opposite sides but that didn't matter now.

Jackson had noticed the injury when Thad went up the loft to change and waited until they were alone to ask about it. "And," he added, "I know a knife wound when I see it." He raised his eyes from his work to look at Thad. Abby, Tommy and the girls had gone for a short walk so Thad felt free to tell Jackson the story behind the wound.

Merry and Hawk arrived upon the scene as they entered the back door. Merry looked at Jackson's work. "Not bad."

Thad came down the loft Tuesday morning in his best suit. His face clean shaven and his hair recently trimmed.

"Can my lawyer husband be any more handsome?" Merry asked as she helped straightened his tie. There was no clever comment as usual. She knew her companion was nervous.

"Thank you." He smiled. She took both his hands in hers and began to pray with her husband.

Abby watched from behind the curtain of her bedroom. The scene did so much to her within. She felt empty all of the sudden.

When Merry finished praying Thad gathered her in an embrace. Stroking her silky hair and kissing her forehead Abby overheard him speaking.

"Could a man be any more blessed to have his wife pray for him?"

The emptiness turned to a feeling of guilt. Was she that type of wife?

Thad helped Merry into the wagon. Jackson and Hawk rode in the back. When they made it to town a crowd was forming outside the schoolhouse where the inquiry was to be held. Merry, Jackson and Hawk went into the building and Thad headed to the jail to see Lone Eagle. The man was in good spirits and told Thad he had been praying and put it in hands of God. Thad prayed with his friend then left to prepare for opening statements.

Grover Whinsted was sitting in the front seat talking with Elmer McPherson when Merry and Hawk took their seats. He looked at Hawk with a smirk on his face it angered Merry. She stared at the man until he had the decency to advert his eyes that was until Thad entered the room. When he saw Thad, he looked to Elmer and pointed at Thad.

"Thad Sheridan is the 'bully farmer' representing the Indian? Do you know who Thad Sheridan is?" The man's face was red and his eyes were bulging at McPherson.

"That," he was still pointing at Thad, "was one of the best law students at Cambridge." This was all said in a slightly elevated whisper.

"He's a lawyer?" McPherson choked.

"Not officially, but it does not matter." The man took out his handkerchief and wiped his brow, taking a deep breath.

Judge Carlisle entered and the day began. Whinsted presented his opening statements to the judge. He was very convincing. Thad's opening statements were just as impressive. Merry had no idea people could debate issues with so much complexity. When the judge called for a recess for lunch, Merry felt as if she had worked all morning in her garden. Her whole body was stiff and hurt. She was so tense she didn't realize until she stood.

Thad approached her and offered his hand.

"Liddy went home to fix us some lunch if you are interested." He rubbed the back of his neck and massaged his eyes. She knew he probably had a headache. She had developed one.

"Let's go." He let her step in front of him. He reached and put his arm around Hawk's shoulder. Hawk's eyes searched Thad's for answers.

"We're fine, let's get some lunch."

Outside the Lapps' house, Thad stopped.

"Merry, you and Hawk go on in. I need to talk to Jackson for a minute." When the door shut, Jackson spoke.

"You have to put her on the stand if that is what you want to talk about."

"You read my mind, Jackson. I have to show Hank's potential to harm."

"But." Jackson added. "once you put her on the stand, she is open game for Whinsted to question her relationship with Lone Eagle, and he will."

Thad rubbed his chin. "I know. She can handle it." It was said as if he was trying to convince himself.

"She can handle it," Jackson confirmed.

Merry watched her husband come through the door followed by Jackson. She met him in the hallway and took him into the doctor's office.

"Let me tell them what happened at the house." He started to tell her he planned to but she wouldn't let him.

"Don't try to protect me. You know it will help the case. You have to let me speak."

"If you would let me speak." He grabbed her chin and kissed her. "I have already decided to put you on the stand." She smiled.

"I want you to be ready because Grover will go directly to your relationship with Lone Eagle." She looked a little shocked.

"I will be fine."

He hoped she was right.

The full schoolhouse heard Merry recount the evening Hank Haskett knocked out the kitchen window and ordered everyone to take cover. Whinsted rose to ask a few more questions. Just as suspected they had nothing to do with the Haskett case.

"Mrs. Sheridan, what is your relationship with Mr. Lone Eagle?" Before she could answer Thad rose.

"Your Honor, this question has nothing to do with the testimony provided by the witness."

The judge turned to Whinsted. "Give me a reason to allow this question."

"I am trying to ascertain if there is reason for Mrs. Sheridan to perjure testimony. There is a known previous relationship with Mr. Lone Eagle." Merry wasn't sure what perjure meant.

"I will allow the question." Thad knew he would but he had to try.

"Your Honor, may I explain to the witness what the word perjure means." The judge motioned with his hand for Thad to instruct his witness.

"Mrs. Sheridan, Mr. Whinsted is calling you a liar." Merry's eye's flashed anger. Thad knew that would ease her anxiety. She was at her best when she was mad. Grover also had a flash of anger directed toward Thad.

Merry coolly recounted the birth of Spotted Hawk and the death of Yellow flower. She relayed the fact Lone Eagle would provide her with food and game by leaving it in the barn for her. She left out the outlaws buried in unmark graves somewhere east of her property. Thad was relieved she did not tell the encounter as it could cause further problems.

"Was there any type of payment made for this food the Indian delivered?" there was a murmur in the crowd.

"Your Honor, the witness is not on trial here," Thad objected.

"I want to answer." Merry shocked even her husband.

"Go ahead, Mrs. Sheridan." Merry looked at the town of Rudolph.

"Yes, there was payment." The crowd was silent.

"I taught his son to read and write. I gave his people help whenever he requested, I paid him in friendship and kindness. Something he would never find in this town."

Thad couldn't help but smile "Mr. Sheridan, do you have any questions for the witness."

"No, Your Honor."

"You may step down." Thad stood to assist Merry down from the chair she had occupied.

"Will council approach the bench?" Thad and Grover made their way to the judge.

"I appreciate and enjoy good litigation as I have observed. However, if I do not have a concrete statement from someone, this case will have to go to trial, Sheridan."

"I do have a witness, but I was trying to keep the eight-year-old off the stand."

Grover looked at Thad. "If you have a witness, put him on the stand."

"Your Honor, there is a little problem." Thad was attempting to appeal to the mercy of the court on Tommy's behalf. "He is the Hasketts' son."

"Your Honor, if this will put an end to this inquiry, Sheridan must make the boy testify."

"Your Honor—"

Thad was stopped by Judge Carlisle. "Have the boy here tomorrow at ten to tell his story." He looked at Thad giving him no option to dispute.

"Present your closing arguments, gentlemen.

Grover did his best to put doubt in the judge's mind that Hank Haskett would burn down his own home. He also wanted to raise suspicion that Lone Eagle had some sort of grudge against the Hasketts and burned them out. Thad knew Tommy's testimony would be enough to convince the judge, so he took this opportunity to do something else.

Thad stood to the side of the judges table facing both the judge and the town.

"The person responsible for the death of Melissa and Hank Haskett is in this courtroom." He turned to face the full room.

"It is me," a large gasp was heard, "and it is you, and you and you." He pointed to several people in the room.

"It is the town of Rudolph for shutting out one of their own and not loving and helping the Hasketts. If just a few people had reached out to Hank, he might have been able to overcome the traumatic aftereffects of war. You can try to shove the blame onto an outsider but it does not negate the truth lies at your doorstep along with the guilt."

Not a peep was heard when Thad took his seat. For several seconds, all he could hear was his own beating heart.

"Court adjourned until tomorrow morning at ten when we will hear the final witness."

Lone Eagle was very pleased with Thad's ability. The Indian was very content as he took his place in the Rudolph jail. Spotted Hawk was going to stay and have supper with his father. He would be to the Sheridans later. It was a very tired bunch that arrived home that afternoon. Thad had to get with Tommy and let him know he had to testify in the morning, but right now all he wanted to do was lie down. His head was pounding.

Abby met them at the door. "How did it go?" she asked her husband.

"Your brother has not lost his abilities in the courtroom, fine work today Thad." Jackson praised his brother-in-law.

Thad gave a weak smile and kissed his sister on the cheek. "I had a lot of help," he said as he went up the loft.

For some reason, Merry stayed down stairs. She felt Thad needed some time to wind down. She didn't like the strain she saw on his face or how all this was affecting him. He wasn't her good natured jovial husband, and she understood why. When he didn't come back down for a while, Merry decided to go up.

Thad was lying on the bed with his white-sleeved arm draped over his eyes, a sure sign he wasn't asleep. His suit jacket and tie were thrown on the chair, and his boots were beside the bed. Merry hung up his suit and tie.

"You really did a good job today. I know Lone Eagle could not have had anyone better to represent him."

"Thanks," he said in a tired, ragged breath.

"Why don't you take a nap and I will wake you for supper."

"That's not going to work unless you come and lay down too." He never removed his arm from his face but patted the other side of the bed with his other hand. Merry willingly lay down next to her husband, resting her head on his shoulder and her hand on his chest.

"I am so proud of you, Thad." She nuzzled a little closer enough to kiss his neck. His arm went around her and brought her closer to him.

"I was pretty proud of you as well. I guess we didn't make any friends today." His hand methodically and repeatedly went through her hair. If he didn't stop she would be asleep in no time and they both were.

When she woke, she was a little disoriented. Where was she and why was she asleep in the middle of the afternoon. It all began to dawn on her, and she started to sit up. Her husband was lying there watching her.

"Hello," she said, stifling a yawn. He stretched the arm she had been laying on and wrapped it around her waist bringing her within kissing distance. One long kiss followed by a second when little eyes peered at the top of the ladder.

"They're awake," Patience shouted back down to whoever was in the kitchen. "They're kissing again."

"Patience Lorraine Lorton, you get down here this instance. You were told not to go up there," Abby was heard reprimanding her daughter. The curly dark hair was suddenly gone when Jackson swooped her off the ladder and out to the woodshed for a spanking.

The couple giggled and Thad started to get up.

"Let's lay here a little longer." She snuggled down next to him again. She didn't have to ask him twice his head went back on the pillow.

"When do you plan to talk to Tommy?"

"I don't know. Do I wait until morning so he won't worry all night or tell him this evening and give him a chance to think about it?"

"Either way it will be difficult for him. I know you worked extremely hard to keep him from having to testify. I don't like Grover Whinsted very much I can tell you that."

"He is a good lawyer Merry." She leaned up to look him in the eye.

"Do you regret it?"

"Regret what?" his finger went down her nose tapping her on the chin.

"Charleston, being a big fancy lawyer, a woman like Jena."

"I will admit, I love the law but I couldn't do it day in and day out. After a while, it would lose its purpose. As far as Charleston it's not where you live it's who you live with and with that comes no regrets.

Abby had attempted to start supper. It was a good thing Merry came down when she did. She was trying to follow the recipe for biscuits Merry had written out but when she opened the lard bucket and got a whiff of the awful stuff she nearly vomited.

"You get used to it." Merry said as she reached a clean hand in the bucket and scooped out enough to add to the flour. Abby decided to stick to preparing the vegetables she felt sure she could handle the task.

A teary-eyed, red-faced little girl accompanied her father back in the house. She walked to her mother and laid her head in her lap. Abby sweetly rested her hand on the child's curls.

"Abby, don't pacify her. She has some apologizing to do."

There was a sudden ache in Merry's heart. It was that empty space in her heart just below Thad. The place only a child can fill. She squelched the thought and swallowed hard. It never seemed to get easier.

Thad was behind her looking over her shoulder. He seemed to sense her thoughts. She reached her hand up to stroke his cheek. He was a sweet man.

"Are you going to kiss again?"

"PATIENCE!" her father's rage was evident "What did we just talk about outside."

Thad lifted the girl into his arms. "It has occurred to me the reason you are so interested in people kissing. You feel left out."

He just started kissing her all over her face in little short kisses and she giggled. He then aimed her at Abby who put a few on her face and then toward Jackson who in spite of his ire kissed her check then kissed his wife.

When Thad aimed her toward Merry he intercepted Merry's kiss with his own lips and slid the girl to the floor. When Anna Beth, Tommy and Hawk walked in there was a whole lot of kissing going on. They turned and walked out.

A few minutes later there was a knock on the door.

"Is it safe to come in?" Hawk was asking and the other children were laughing. Merry and Abby decided to catch each child at the door and include them in the kissing. This was met with tolerance by the kids until Thad headed toward Hawk and Tommy. The boys sprang back with their hands out. Thad's rich laughter echoed throughout the house as he put some type of hold on the boys and gave the top of their heads a rub with his knuckles. For all that was going on in their individual lives there was a time of laughter.

"I-I-I s-suppose I w-will h-have t-to tell w-what h-happened to the j-judge," Tommy said after prayer was said over the meal.

It was an answer to prayer. Merry had prayed there would be some sign to guide when to bring the situation up. She said a prayer of thanks deep in her heart.

"Not just in front of the judge, Tommy, but the whole town. You think you can do that?"

The boy squirmed in his seat. "Y-Yeah, I-I-I c-can d-do that." Thad smiled at the boy. There was an emotion Thad had not seen on Hawk's face. If he had to describe it he would say it was admiration for Tommy's bravery.

"You know," Merry was saying as she sat on the bed brushing her hair, "Abby was telling me in Charleston boys like Tommy would end up in an asylum. Can you imagine our Tommy in a place like that? A boy like him does not belong in such a place."

"No, they don't but it happens. People won't adopt children that are . . . I am not sure what would be the best word to use."

"Special," Merry suggested.

"Yes, special."

He was motionless on the bed and Merry thought he had gone to sleep. As she put her brush on the bedside table he abruptly sat up.

"Merry, you're unbelievable, a beautiful, unbelievable genius." He was now standing beside her side of the bed grabbing both her hands he pulled her out of the bed.

"Thank you but I don't understand what's going on."

"It's wonderful." He kissed her hard and quick on the mouth.

"Jackson!" he yelled as he redressed.

"Thad stop yelling you're going to wake the children." He looked at the two girls sound asleep on the floor and nearly jumped out of the loft.

"Jackson, Abby, get up."

"Thad, what is it?" Jackson peered around the corner of the curtain tucking in his shirt.

"Merry has a great idea."

"I do?" she said and he yanked her from the ladder and whirled her around.

"What's going on?" a sleepy Hawk and Tommy came from their makeshift room.

"Nothing. Go back to bed, boys." The boys obeyed.

Abby appeared and looked at Merry "Mr. Impossible has finally snapped."

Thad had them all sit at the table while he told them Merry's great idea. She had no idea what it was so she was just as excited as the others.

"The money, I know what to do with the money from the sale of the mill. Merry and I will start a boy's home. You know for children like Tommy." He lowered his voice and looked toward the sitting room.

"If I know you Thad you have a whole plan already formulated let's hear it."

"It will take time and I . . ." He looked at Merry. "We will need your help."

Thad excitedly laid out his plan. The plan was to build accommodations for around a dozen boys. The boys would be taught to farm and other useful skills while going to school. It would be for those who had no other place to go and would keep children out of places they didn't belong. They would be given a loving home and a good foundation.

He looked expectantly at the trio.

"Well, I think it is a wonderful idea," Abby said with tears misting her eyes.

"I am having some thoughts rolling around in my head as well, Thad," Jackson added. "Since my father and I bought the mill, maybe we could be benefactors."

You would have thought Thad was going to kiss Jackson he was so happy. Merry had been very quiet. They all now turned to her. The lump in her throat was the largest one she had ever had. The emotion that edged from her heart was like a river challenging the banks. Thad wasn't sure what emotion was playing across her face until she rose putting her arms tightly around his neck she wept. Could a man give anymore of his self away? She loved him so.

Chapter Eleven

Jackson couldn't sleep. He was staring at the rough-hewn ceiling of this modest dwelling. He and Thad had grown up in the same stream of wealth. How could Thad be happy in this setting? Yet he was, very happy and thriving. He had never met a man like his brother-in-law. He constantly made decision based on what was best for those around him. Rarely thinking about the effects it would have on him. There was a twinge inside of Jackson. He had been strategically planning his ascent into the political world. Everything he did, everywhere he went was in the light of this overshadowing dream but people like Thad Sheridan and Lachlan Kennedy made him second guess what the pursuit of happiness was.

Abby knew her husband was not asleep because he had not kissed her nor the baby growing inside of her yet. It was a nightly ritual. A kiss for his wife and then a quick kiss and a word to the little one about to make his or her appearance into their lives.

"What is going through that thick head of yours?" Abby turned to face her husband.

A smile played at his lips. To say 'nothing' would be a lie she would see right through.

"Just thinking about you and the girls."

"Thinking about us with such a concerned look on your face, I'm worried." He laughed a bit a strained laugh and Abbey picked up on it right away she sat up in bed.

"What is it Jackson?"

How did he tell her he, all of a sudden, was miserable inside without her thinking he was unhappy with her?

"Could you and the girls live like this?" his eyes never left the ceiling.

"No, I mean I suppose we could if we had too. We have been accustomed to the way we live. It would be difficult. What are you getting at?" There was a little panic in her voice.

"I am not suggesting we move here don't worry. I can't figure your brother out. Thad could have any law job he wanted, he could run and win any political race he entered. He is just that type of man but he chooses to live here and do this." His hands spread out into the air to emphasize the "here" and "this."

"Thad is just a different type of man Jackson, he always has been. He was always helping the under privileged and those in need."

"Yes, he is a good man."

"You're a good man too Jackson. Your aspirations for office proves that."

"Ah, yes, but men like Thad and Lach don't have to prove anything."

"You are just as good as either of them. You are just using your talents in a different way." She was beginning to feel uneasy about the conversation.

Jackson turned and kissed her on the lips then bent his head to kiss the baby. "Your papa will do his best, child."

Abby couldn't shake the emptiness within her. She felt helpless and she knew nothing she said comforted her husband. Had she been Merry she would have grabbed his hands and prayed for her husband. The guilt was thick in the air.

Everyone was up bright and early. Today Tommy would tell his story and this whole ordeal would be over. Merry was a little worried about Tommy. She overheard Thad talking to him in the sitting room.

"Don't be afraid. Just take your time. If you get frightened or nervous you just look at Merry and keep your eyes on her. I am not sure what Grover is going to ask you but if you tell the truth all will be fine." The boy nodded at Thad. "I am proud of you, Tommy." Thad's hand rested on the boy's shoulder. "Let's go get the chores done."

The old building was full to capacity. The judge was eager to get this over with. Tommy was put immediately on the stand. Tommy, in his Sunday best and hair fixed exactly like Thad's sat in the chair next to the judge.

"Son, you do know what a lie is, don't you?" Tommy shook his head yes. "I expect the truth." Tommy shook his head again. "Mr. Whinsted, you may proceed."

"Son, do you know this man?" Grover pointed to Lone Eagle.

"Y-Yes, sir."

"Have you ever seen this man around your parent's property?"

"Y-Yes, sir." The crowd began to murmur.

"When?"

"H-He would b-bring f-food to the b-b-barn s-sometimes." Whinsted was not expecting this.

"Ever see him with some type of jug or bottle?"

"N-No, sir."

"Did he ever talk to your mother or your father?"

"N-No, sir."

"Did you see him the night your folks died?"

Tommy's little face had a wave of emotion. "N-no, sir."

"Suppose you tell us what happened on the night your place burned."

Merry wanted to spit in the man's eye. Couldn't he see how torn up Tommy was? They all knew the story needed to be told but to go about it in such a cold heartless way was ruthless.

Tommy's stuttering became worse as his emotions got the best of him. He began telling the story of how his father had been very quiet at supper and had sent Tommy to bed early. He could hear his mother trying to plead with his father about the war being over. Tommy was awakened in the middle of the night by his father. Taken outside he was pushed to the ground. His father asked him to crawl to the cellar and open the door.

Melissa tried to reason with him but a fight ensued. At this point, Tommy's tears made the stuttering more difficult to understand.

Whinsted's patience were running thin. "Your Honor," he said and shook his head in the boy's direction.

Thad bolted up. "No, you wanted him to testify, now let him finish."

A righteous anger flared in Thad. Tommy needed to tell the story and needed everyone to hear it. The judge's head made a motion and Thad asked Tommy to continue. The boy finished his story. Thad reached for the sobbing boy intending to hand him to Merry. Spotted Hawk intercepted him and taking the boy in his arms carried him out of the schoolhouse.

The silence in the courtroom made the judge's gavel sound like thunder as he declared Lone Eagle innocent and the inquiry was dismissed. He was free to go.

Lone Eagle shook Thad's hand. "Night Wolf have many talents. Thank you."

"Don't thank me. Thank Tommy, he's the hero in all this."

Thad put his hand on the Indians back and headed out the door. They were joined by Merry, Jackson and the Lapps.

"Come on over to the house and get a bite to eat before you all head home." Liddy was urging. Lone Eagle gave her a questioning glance.

"I mean you too." She pointed at the man. "I'll not take no for an answer."

"Better come, she means it." Merry smiled and Lone Eagle smiled at Liddy.

The sudden pop and Lone Eagle's body dropping to the ground surprised everyone. The men were shouting for the women to get down. There were a few other pops as gunfire was exchanged but from who?

Lone Eagle had a gaping hole in his chest. Every time his heart beat the blood spurted out like a spring. The man was pale, clammy and dying you could see it in his eyes. Thad had taken his suit coat and pressed it over the wound with all his weight. The blood was pouring from the man.

The gunfire had ceased. In the middle of the street lay Lone Eagle struggling to breathe as the blood trickled out of his mouth. Spotted Hawk had rushed to his Father's side just in time to say goodbye. The Indian grabbed his sons arm and with what little strength he had linked it with Thad's. He spoke to his son in the Lakota and his eyes fluttered then closed in death.

Everyone was in shock. Thad, covered in blood slowly got up to assess the situation. Scanning the surroundings, he saw another body down. The gunman who had shot Lone Eagle had been shot off his horse by Ezekiel Lapp. The man lay writhing in pain in the dusty road from a gunshot wound to the leg. The cavalry officers had him in custody.

Spotted Hawk fighting tears was doing some type of ritual over his Father. Tommy was as white as a sheet. Where was Merry? He spotted her, Liddy and Jackson headed toward the Lapps front door.

"Jackson," Merry asked. "Is anyone watching?"

Jackson turned his head to see everyone huddled around Lone Eagle's body.

"No, Merry."

"Good, because I think I am going to—" Jackson caught her just before her knees completely buckled and lifted her into his arms carrying her into the doctor's house. One of the bullets had lodged in her upper arm. Liddy sent Jackson to get the doctor and Thad.

No one but Jackson and Liddy realized Merry had been hit in the action. She had just stepped behind her husband when the fatal shot was heard. As the two men hit the ground Merry was in open range for the next shot.

Thad ran to the doctor's house. He never touched the stairs as he flew through the door. Merry was sitting on the exam table with her arm wrapped in a clean towel.

"I'm fine," she said in a much louder tone then she knew. Her dirty face was streaked with tear stains and she was very pale. Thad's heart was beating out of his chest. There was an anger in Merry's eyes that made him tread lightly.

He walked toward her and kissed her forehead. The doctor arrived just then and looked at the wound.

"It's going to take a bit to get that bullet out. It is pretty well lodged in there." He looked to his wife. He started to rattle off a list of things he needed.

"I need to go check on Hawk and Tommy. I will be right back."

The few minutes he was gone Liddy helped her change into a gown leaving her left arm out. "Are you in much pain, Merry?" Liddy asked. "You've not said two words."

"I am fine," she said, in a matter of fact tone. Liddy wanted to argue with her but she decided not to.

Thad returned and she unloaded on him.

"Don't come in here and tell me things are going to be okay." He blinked and started to speak.

"The last thing I want to hear right now is Thad Sheridan's words of wisdom and comfort. This year has been nothing but death first the baby, Melissa, Hank your mother and now Lone Eagle. Don't you stand there and give me all the reasons why I should handle this like you do. I want no part of it."

He understood it was part of her grief but he had a little grief himself.

"I—" He once again started to speak but she cut him off.

"I mean it, Thad. I have no interest in what you're about to say." She wanted to fight and he would oblige. His tone was cool.

"Be that as it may, I have two boys out there that need to see you're all right. So you better get yourself together before I return." He left abruptly.

Tommy and Hawk peeked around the door.

"Come in, boys." Her hand went out and Tommy clutched it.

"I am going to be just fine," she reassured the small boy.

"Hawk, I am so sorry about your father." The boy's stoic face showed no emotion but his eyes were keenly on Merry's face. "He was such a good man. I don't understand who would do this." Still no response. The Indian people had a way about them. She knew inside Hawk was hurting and she had no way of helping him.

The boys were sent home with Jackson. Hawk promised he would stay until Thad and Merry returned the next day. Hawk was not going to open up about what happened to his father he would grieve his own way. Thad just wanted to be there when he needed him.

The doctor was preparing to put Merry out while he worked on her arm. He was sure she would be fine but he would have to work a little harder at getting the bullet out.

Thad was all prepared to stay by Merry's side but the doctor would not allow it. Liddy had fixed water for Thad to take a bath. He was covered in the dried blood of Lone Eagle and looked horrible. One look at Merry who adverted her eyes from him and he knew he wasn't wanted at this time. He took the towel and a set of clothes from Liddy and disappeared.

The bath felt good he couldn't deny it. He thought about the shooting. He was pretty certain the bullet that struck Merry was meant for him. Had he not gone down with Lone Eagle, the shot would have hit his head, killing him instantly.

The man who did the shooting was a paid killer. Someone had paid him to kill Lone Eagle. Who, the man was not saying. It all happened so quickly Thad's head hadn't stopped spinning yet.

By the time he finished his bath and emptied the water, the doctor was through with Merry's arm. He had given her some laudanum to help with the pain. Thad cautiously approached the makeshift operating table. He stroked her face and her eyes opened. The anger was gone and there was a gloss over her eyes.

"Hi," she said as a lazy smile lay on her lips.

"How are you feeling?" he asked as he pushed the hair away from her eyes

"You are so handsome," she whispered, her speech a bit slurred. The doctor chuckled under his breath.

"It's amazing how that medicine affects people in different ways." He looked from Thad to Merry. "Some sleep it off and some get sentimental or downright mushy."

Her eyes fluttered open and they landed on her husband. She smiled again. "You're mine," she said in the form of a declaration. Her good hand patted his arm.

"Yes, always." He laid his hand on top of hers.

"You're handsome," she said again.

"Yes, I think we have established that." He smiled again.

"Aren't you going to kiss me" He had to laugh. His Merry would not ask to be kissed in front of people.

Doctor Lapp laughed out loud this time.

"Could I have some of that medicine to take home for later?" Thad questioned, grinning at the doctor.

Merry, who was disgusted because Thad had not kissed her, pinched his arm. He bent his head and kissed her tenderly.

"I guess that will have to do," she said as a yawn escaped. Her eyes slid shut.

Liddy approached the table. "I have the spare room ready why don't you take Merry on up. She will rest better there.

Thad picked up his wife and with Liddy's guidance placed her in the bed. Something dawned on him. In the wake of all that happened he had neglected to talk to the judge about adopting Tommy. Being assured his wife was asleep he bolted from the door.

"Have you heard the stage leave?" he asked the Lapps.

"No, but I haven't really been paying attention," Liddy spoke.

Thad headed out the door.

The stage door was being shut and the driver was climbing to the top when Thad reached the door. "I need to talk to the judge." The driver did not look the least bit happy. He spoke around the cigar in his mouth.

"Make it quick," he uttered.

"Your Honor, with everything that transpired this morning the matter of Tommy Hasketts adoption got forgotten. I would hate to have the matter drug out."

Judge Carlisle reached across the seat and opened his attaché case. Quickly going through his stack of papers he pulled two documents and laid them on top. His assistant produced a writing instrument.

"Sign here and here," he pointed to where Thad's signature was required.

"I will have these completed and submitted. The boy is yours."

Something good was coming from this day. Thad smiled and shook the judge's hand.

"And Sheridan," Judge Carlisle would not let go of his hand, "if you're ever in need of a job, come see me. You are a worthy opponent in the courtroom."

"Thank you, sir." Thad retrieved his hand and shut the stage door.

For all the tragedy that happened the physical day was beautiful. The afternoon sun was making its way across a cloudless sky. Thad was transfixed with the world around him as he headed back to the Lapps. He really needed to stop and process everything that occurred in the past few hours. He was just on his way to do so when the sheriff beckoned him from the porch of his office.

Thad made his way over.

"How is Merry?" Dan asked his face showing true concern.

"Physically she will be fine, emotionally I am not sure?"

"She's a tough one, that girl is."

Thad smiled. Yes, his wife was tough and strong and sometimes people spoke those characteristics to describe her as if that was all she was. She was a loyal person to her friends. She was a giver and a protector. When she loved you, it was a deep love and when she hurt, well, let's just say you hurt as deep as you love. This day had not been easy on her.

The sheriff began talking again and Thad had not stayed up with the conversation.

"I'm sorry Sheriff what did you say?"

"I said the gunman was not paid to kill Lone Eagle, he admitted he just shot the Indian because he could." This sobered Thad.

"So, he was here to kill me?" The sheriff nodded.

"You don't seem too surprised, Thad."

Thad took a seat and stretched his legs out.

"Sheriff, I have had a lot of people threaten me over the years this isn't the first time someone has taken a shot at me. I just never had someone pay money to try and kill me."

"You have any idea who that might be?"

Thad thought for a minute. Half of Charleston probably had the money and motive to do so but he didn't think his home town would go that far.

"No," he answered.

"You going to tell Merry?" the older man searched Thad's face.

"Sure, you don't keep something like this from Merry. You know that."

"We have another little problem." Thad's eyebrow raised in question.

"The undertaker refuses to do anything with Lone Eagle's body."

Prejudices even at the death of a man. *Can the human race stop long enough to give a man a proper burial?* Thad was thinking.

"I don't suppose the town would let him be buried in their cemetery?" Thad voiced knowing all too well the answer. "Where is Lone Eagle?"

"In a pine box I keep. He is in my wagon."

"I will ride out and talk to Hawk and see what he would like to do." Thad stood and stretched his back.

"I will ride out and talk to the boy Thad. You go see to Merry and yourself."

"Thanks Dan, and I would appreciate it if you wouldn't spread the word about me being the target today."

"None of anybody's business."

Thad checked in on Merry she was still asleep. Liddy motioned for him to leave the room. "I have some food put back for you if you're . . ." The growling of Thad's stomach seemed to anticipate her next word.

"Hungry," Thad said as he patted his stomach. "I think it's obvious."

Liddy smiled and placed her hands on both sides of Thad's face.

"You did real good today, I'm sorry it turned out the way it did. You are a wonderful addition to our life Thad Sheridan and don't you forget it." She kissed his cheek and headed for the kitchen.

Thad knew he deserved none of the credit. That belonged to the Lord but it was nice to hear all the same.

Thad decided he should share with the Lapps the information he had received from the Sheriff. He also told them about the undertaker's decision not to assist with Lone Eagle's body.

"I presume the Lakota will want to give him a proper burial," Dr. Lapp surmised.

"Since Lone Eagle's conversion I believe there has been tension in the camp. I am not sure if they will take him. Sheriff Bullock was going to go out and talk to Hawk."

The trio was just finishing coffee when Dan arrived. He wasted no time in telling them Lone Eagle's tribe had moved on early this morning.

"The whole bunch of them gone. Not a trace left. Spotted Hawk said he would find a place to bury his father. I told him I would bring the body out tomorrow."

Thad's heart was very heavy. "We can bury him up on the ridge, I know a good place."

Death, it seemed to be following him, hovering over him like a great cloud. He knew what Merry was feeling he felt it too.

It wasn't long after the sheriff left when Thad retired to his wife's room. He brought her some food and she admitted she was hungry. He helped her sit up a bit and fixed her tray so she could use her good arm to eat. Gone was the Merry who thought he was handsome. The Merry who was angry and wanted none of his thoughts was back. Now was not the time to discuss the gunman's true intent.

He sat on the edge of the bed his left hand resting on the other side of her legs. He dipped his head to be eye level with his wife. She would not look at him.

"Are you in a lot of pain Merry?"

"Yes." The answer was curt.

"Would you like for me to get the doctor?"

"No." Another short answer.

"Do you need help with your tray?" She had yet to attempt to eat. She raised her head.

"I meant what I said." Her eyes were red and bloodshot evidence of the day she had.

"I never doubted you thought I was handsome." He hoped the best course of action was to be himself. Although the comment came without his usual mirth. She began eating.

"You know what I am talking about." She managed to get out between bites. He stood and sighed.

"Good night then," he said as he turned on his heels and left the room.

As Thad passed the doctor on his way out the back door he informed him of Merry's pain. The physician rose and headed to his patient's room.

Thad headed out the door and just kept walking. He needed time to pray. The Lord had answered so many of his prayers today. Tommy was able to testify without much trouble. The boy did well even in the midst of all his raw emotion. Spotted Hawk's action to take Tommy into his arms and take care of him made Thad proud. The look on Lone Eagle's face when his son made the gesture was priceless.

Spotted Hawk was softening that was until a total stranger gunned his father down. Lone Eagle's death was a result of Thad's life. He found it hard to pray when he thought about it. He just kept telling God he was sorry. There was comfort in knowing Lone Eagle had given his heart to Jesus and heaven waited for him.

He had not been paying attention to where he was walking. He had gone quite a ways. The evening sun was setting. He knew he should head back but he didn't want to head back he had a weight on him he just couldn't take. He dropped to his knees and began to pour his heart out to the one who could lift the load.

The more he prayed the better he felt. The more he called out to God the more God seemed to answer him. All the things that had come to pass today needed to be sifted through to find the purpose. His divine purpose. He knew Merry did not want to hear those things but it was the way Thad was made. He had to find the meaning, the reason and the next course of action. He decided if that was the way his creator made him then that was the way the creator would teach him. He waited and he listened and slowly the Lord was speaking.

Lone Eagle was a good friend and Thad's heart grieved the loss. Since God was in control of both of their lives he chose to take Lone Eagle and spare Thad. It was clearly meant to be the other way. Thad couldn't live in guilt and vowed not to let it destroy him.

It was also clear to him the idea for a boy's home was the way to proceed—that is, if his wife is still in agreement with the arrangement. Tommy was legally theirs now and he would offer Hawk a home and family as well. He knew this may not go over well with Hawk but he would offer the young man just the same.

A dim light was on when he returned to the Lapps. The couple had retired to the small living room. He hadn't realized how long he had been gone and went to apologize to the couple.

"Merry has been asking for you," Liddy spoke first.

"Oh." He looked toward the upstairs. "She okay?"

"I just gave her something for the pain. She just wondered where you had gone. She was afraid you went home." Thad started to speak but Liddy stopped him.

"Goodnight, Thad."

He tipped his head in a nod and took the stairs quietly.

His wife lay motionless in the bed. The medicine already taking affect. He hated she thought he would leave her but he was glad for the time away. He took off his boots and laid on the other side of the bed. Before long he was asleep.

The soft weeping from the other side of the bed woke Thad. It took him just a minute to realize where he was and what the sound was. He raised up and turned toward Merry.

"Merry are you in pain?" Her head went from side to side.

"Merry." His soothing voice was a whisper and his hand came up to wipe away her tears. "Please don't cry."

Her good hand went up to trace his lips. "Say them," she choked out. "Say those words I didn't want to hear earlier." He kissed her fingers. "Please, Thad, I need to hear them. I have to hear them." There was panic in her sobs. He laid his face next to her ear and began to whisper.

Merry thrashed about all night, crying out reliving old haunts. Thad was glad when the first lights of dawn broke through the Lapps spare bedroom. His wife had finally fallen into a somewhat peaceful sleep just as the sun was coming up. He was wide awake. He wanted to get Lone Eagle home and he felt desperate to see and speak with Spotted Hawk. He also knew Tommy hadn't fared well with all of this and he wanted to reassure the small boy that life at the Sheridan's could return to normal.

He ate a quick breakfast then rode with the sheriff home, leaving Merry in the care of Liddy. He would come back for her later in the day.

"It doesn't seem to be bothering you that someone put a price on your head." Sheriff Bullock never minced words.

"It bothers me," Thad said rather sternly. "I will get to the bottom of it, but right now I have a few other things higher on the list."

"You have a lead?" Dan asked.

"Not a clue, and that's the way I like it."

"Have you told Merry yet?" Thad was not in the mood for all the questions Dan was asking.

"Are you always this nosy or is it just me?" Thad had a smile on his face.

"Son, until you showed up I nary asked a question? You've plumb worn me out the past year."

Thad knew he was teasing but it did seem like a lot had happened since his arrival.

Merry was not happy Thad left without her but she understood. Liddy helped her dress and brush her hair. The pain in her arm was tolerable. The pain in her heart was not.

Her close friend had been murdered. If she stopped to think about all Lone Eagle had done for her over the years she reckoned she couldn't remember it all. He always made sure she and her grandfather had plenty to eat. During the winter when she would get low on food and the bitter cold and snow kept her grandfather from hunting Lone Eagle would drop off some rabbits or deer. How many times he kept them from starving she couldn't count. She loved him as only a friend could love and she would miss him.

Her thoughts went to Spotted Hawk. If her heart was grieving, she was sure Hawk's was breaking. He loved his father and tried so hard to be the man he was. She also knew he was stubborn and very determined to be a man even before his time. His adjustment to life without his father would be a difficult one. She was sure Thad would offer him a home with them but she wasn't sure he would take it. She really just wanted to get home and take care of her boys. She spent the morning in prayer preparing for what might lie ahead.

Spotted Hawk wanted to bury his father alone. He asked the sheriff and Thad to help him get the body up to the ridge under a huge tree that grew there. This was not an easy task as a wagon could not make it up to the ridge. Grace was used to drag the pine box to the appointed spot.

Once there, Thad helped Hawk dig the grave and then was asked to leave. Thad, sensing the boy's need for time, mounted Grace and headed home. Spotted Hawk's eyes stayed on Thad's back until he was out of sight. When he could no longer see him, the Indian boy slumped in tears across the pine box.

Spotted Hawk had not returned by the time Thad was ready to leave to pick up Merry. He did not like this as his tribe had gone and Spotted Hawk had admitted he wasn't sure where they had relocated. He was somewhere alone and that bothered Thad. It certainly would distress Merry. She was sure to ask about him.

Tommy, Anna Beth and Patience were insistent on riding into town with Thad. He finally relented. They would bring cheer to Merry. He supposed Abby needed a break. She had been managing the house during the inquiry and had taken care of Tommy and Hawk like they were her own. He meant to tell her how much he appreciated her but he hadn't seen much of her today. When he stopped to think about it he hadn't seen her at all.

Jackson loaded Patience into the wagon with strict instructions not to be a pest. He stopped Thad before he reached the wagon.

"Thad, could you ask Doctor Lapp to stop by tomorrow and see Abby?"

Thad's mouth went dry. Jackson immediately read the man's eyes.

"I don't think it is serious it is just that she had some swelling problems when carrying Patience and it looks like her feet are starting to swell a bit. I just thought it would be good for him to see her before we leave."

Thad found his tongue. "I'll make sure he comes. Jackson I'm sorry I have put a lot on her the past couple of days. I should have come home yesterday."

"Her feet would have swelled whether you were here or not. It is nothing you did. Please don't say anything to the girls, they worry over everything." Thad clapped Jackson on the back and headed to the wagon.

Worry started to creep up the back of his shoulders and into his neck. How dangerous would the trip home be for Abby and the baby? He began to pray.

It wasn't long before two wagons headed to the Sheridan's. Liddy Lapp insisted she bring supper when she accompanied her husband out to see Abby. The woman was a Godsend. She and Dr. Lapp had all three children with them and they headed out about twenty minutes before Thad and Merry. The couple was thankful for the time alone. They needed to have a conversation. Thad felt he needed to tell Merry the truth about what happened as soon as possible. She had just rested her head on his shoulder giving him liberty to speak. Now was the time.

"Merry I need to share some important information with you about the shooting." Her head raised and she calmly took in her husband's profile. When he neither spoke nor looked at her, she grasped his chin and turned his face toward hers. Inducing him to speak.

"The gunman was a paid man."

"A bounty hunter? Who would want Lone Eagle killed?" she asked.

"It wasn't Lone Eagle they were after." Her arm tightened around his in understanding and her face was fixed looking straight ahead.

"W-Who do you think," she swallowed, "it was?"

"I don't know and I can't think about it right now. I have too much going on to give it the thought it needs."

Her eyes were icy as she stared once again at his profile.

"Well, may I think about it since it doesn't seem to be that high of a priority for you." Her tone was familiar to him.

"Don't get upset. I am sure the man will finally reveal who paid him then the law can handle it."

"But in the meantime—"

He cut her off. "In the meantime, we have two boys who need all of our energy and support." She released her hold on his arm and moved a little bit away from him. The motion annoyed him and he took it out on the team.

"Tell me, do you ever get tired of being right?" she inquired her chin resting in the palm of her uninjured hand.

"It's my burden."

He moved just as her hand came out to swat at him.

Doctor Lapp broke the bad news to Jackson. He felt for the good of Abby and the baby she should stay until after the birth. This was a crushing blow to Jackson because he had to return to work. He dreaded the thought of leaving her here but he wanted the best for his wife. For some reason, he totally trusted Ezekiel Lapp.

Abby was near tears when Jackson entered the bedroom.

"Don't start crying or I may too." He sat and took his wife's hands in his.

"Jackson, we shouldn't have come. I shouldn't have forced the issue. This is all my fault and if we lose . . ." He gathered her into his arms.

"You know me well enough to know if I hadn't wanted us to make the trip we wouldn't have made the trip. So stop crying, it will all work out." He produced a handkerchief for her and she dried her eyes.

"What are we going to do about the girls?"

"They can come home with me and the nanny can see to them until we are all back together."

Abby knew this would never work. As much as the girls adored their father they would never leave her.

"Are you trying to convince yourself that will work Jackson?"

"I was hoping you would at least let me try before I had to give in." He kissed her forehead.

Life at the Sheridans had not settled down one bit. Jackson had left for Charleston. Abby was on strict orders to take it easy and Anna

Beth and Tommy had become best friends. This left Patience a little, well, thin on patience. She seemed to be always whining. The only time she was happy was when Spotted Hawk played with her.

Hawk had accepted Thad and Merry's offer of a home but the boy was different since his father's death. He was quite an angry young man. Thad planned on giving the boy ample time to adjust to life in a home but there were times Hawk was defiant.

A month had passed since Merry had the bullet dug out of her left arm. There was a nice scar forming and the pain returned if she over used it. She was still supposed to be doing only light work but light work was not getting the wood in. Thad had been so busy with the crops there were chores he couldn't get too. Chores Tommy was not big enough to do and chores Merry shouldn't be doing. She was getting low and no wood had been chopped recently.

She placed the wood in the proper place and raised the ax with both hands, just as she went to bring the ax down she felt the ax stop in midair.

"What do you think you are doing?" The ax was removed from her hand. Her husband's tense face was hawkishly staring down at her.

"Now what does it look like I'm doing, silly?" she reached for the ax and Thad moved it out of her reach.

"Get in the house." He was so angry it came out between clenched teeth. She had learned one thing during her first year of marriage when his teeth were clenched like that she let it be. She obediently went into the house.

The sound of wood splitting lasted for a good two hours. Thad was late coming in for supper. When he did arrive, his eyes were locked on Hawk. There was tension between the two. It was so thick no one seem to be talking except Patience. She was trying to tell her Uncle Thad about something she had done. He was only half listening until she mentioned Hawk.

"Hawk is going to teach me how to braid rope." She said. This got his attention.

"I am afraid that will have to wait until another time sweetheart. After supper Hawk is helping me out in the barn."

The girl was crushed and her little lips started to quiver.

"Now no crying Patience. He can show you tomorrow besides I hear Merry is planning on baking cookies. She will need your help." This perked the girls' spirits up, but it did nothing for Hawk's, who ate with his head down.

"I asked you two nights ago to chop more wood for Merry. Is there a reason you didn't get to it?"

The boy stared directly into Thad's eyes not saying a word.

"I see, there was no reason, you just didn't do it." Still no emotion from the boy.

"Hawk one of the rules in my home is that I will not tolerate anyone disrespecting my wife. Tonight, I found her getting ready to chop wood, a chore I asked you to do. How much disrespect did you show by not doing that for her?"

The boy flinched.

"That act is disrespectful to the person who feeds you three meals a day, washes your clothes and loves you. The next time and there better not be a next time, I will take you to the woodshed."

The boy bristled at Thad's threat.

"When we discussed you staying here it was with the expectation you would abide by the rules of a family. I would be saying the same thing to Tommy if needed. You understand?"

The boys' slight dip in his head was not overly convincing to Thad but he let it go. Turning into the nearest stall, he added fresh hay. Hawk was in the adjoining stall silently working.

Thad left the boy in the barn and went into the house.

"I hope you weren't too hard on him," Merry spoke softly to her husband. He took her elbow and escorted her to the back porch.

"I will not allow him to be disrespectful. I have let a few things slip giving him the benefit of the doubt but there comes a time when it has to stop." Her husband was very serious.

"His whole life has been turned upside down Thad, he is just trying to fit in."

"True but he is also testing me and eventually this will have to be settled."

"I will love them and you can discipline them." She said and headed into the house.

He stopped her "I don't like the inference that I don't love Hawk because I discipline him. Discipline is a part of love you know that Merry."

Merry had not intended to hurt his feeling but it was clear she had. They had better figure it out if they were to provide a home for young boys.

It didn't take any amount of time for Hawk to push Thad's buttons. Hawk had been brooding and not watching where he was going when he plowed into Merry causing her to drop her basket of eggs. The runny yokes were all down the front of her dress. The boy never stopped and Thad had seen the whole thing. He headed toward Hawk with quick long strides. He grabbed the boy by the collar and shoved him toward Merry. When they got to Merry Thad asked if she was okay. When she indicated she was, he proceeded on pushing Hawk to the woodshed.

Inside the woodshed Thad removed his belt and whipped Hawk. The boy never flinched and when Thad was done the boy headed toward the door.

"Oh, no, Hawk, we're going to talk. You're going to talk." He led the boy to a stack of wood and made him sit. He sat across from him.

"I will never hold you here against your will. I want you to stay because Merry and I love you. Part of love is respecting one another. Now I believe Merry and I have shown you respect but I have yet to see the respect returned." He paused and waited determined to stay in the woodshed until Hawk responded.

Hawk bent over and put his face in his crossed arms. There was no noise but Thad saw the lad's body begin to shake as his grief spilled out. Thad rose and squatted beside the youngster placing his arm protectively around him.

"Why him?" the boys voice was soft and broken. How would Thad tell him the bullet was meant to be his? Should he tell him the complete story? He decided to tell him everything. They spoke for some time. Hawk apologized to Thad. He couldn't promise he would always be good but he would promise to abide by Thad's rules.

"You know, Morning Dove has been outside the door listening this whole time," the boy whispered.

Thad motioned for Hawk to keep talking as they each moved to one side of the door. When Hawk opened the door, Thad grabbed Merry and pulled her inside.

"Eavesdropping has always brought you nothing but trouble. What do you have to say for yourself, young lady?"

"Well, I . . . oh." She started to leave but Hawk blocked her way. He leaned forward and kissed her cheek. She returned the gesture with a stroke to his face. He smiled and turned to leave.

Merry's intent was to follow but he turned to face her. He tossed the belt to Thad

"Eavesdropping is disrespectful is not so?"

"That is so." The old Thad was resurfacing and headed toward his wife. While Hawk blocked the door, Thad turned Merry over his knee. Thad and Hawk left the woodshed laughing. If Merry weren't so happy with the smile on Hawk's face, she would be miffed. She smiled as she headed to the house rubbing her backside.

Chapter Twelve

Liddy Lapp coming to visit was always a treat. Today she brought candy for the kids and a letter from Jackson for Abby. Abby had been given strict orders to rest and not overdue it. She had borne her confinement with a good-natured attitude but she missed her husband something terrible and longed to be home. The baby was due the first of August and it was just the end of June. She wasn't sure she would make it.

"What brought you out, Liddy?" Abby asked from the chair on the porch. Her feet propped up.

"I had to see how my favorite patient was doing and to bring you the best medicine." She produced the letter and Abby smiled wildly. She tore into the letter and never saw Liddy enter the house.

Dearest Abby,

How I miss you and the girls. I hope this finds you well. Your last letter gave me great comfort that you are being taken good care of. My worries are few knowing how well Thad is taking care of things. I hope the girls are being helpful and Patience is leaving Hawk alone.

Tell Thad things on this end are happening rapidly for the boy's home. Father is on board and surprising enough Captain Harrison has asked to help out. He has changed so much Abby. He and Lach and I are meeting once a week. Captain Harrison has given his heart and life to Christ. I am not sure I fully understand what it is all about but I do like to hear what Lach has to say. There has to be more to this life than what we have. I love you and the girls but there is an emptiness I can't explain. It is an emptiness I have not been able to fill. You know me well enough to know this is not a slight to you and the girls. If I am not mistaken you feel the emptiness as well. Lach says to keep my mind and heart open. I am asking you to do the same.

Until we are together again,
All my love,
Jackson

Tears streamed down her face. She felt the emptiness he was talking about. Every time Thad or Merry speaks she feels it. Every time they prayed or sit on the porch holding hands reading the Bible, oh, yes, she feels it. Was Christ the answer as she had been told?

Thad happened on the porch in time to see Abby wipe the tears away.

"Abby, you okay?" He rushed to her side. She waved her handkerchief to signify she was.

"Something has upset you. Has one of the kids done something?" she handed him the letter. He read the short note. He stood and kissed the top of her head.

"I'm here when you're ready, little sister," he offered as he went to seek out his wife. Abby closed her eyes and leaned her head back.

Thad found his wife in the kitchen visiting with Liddy. He was a little disappointed. He had a few free minutes and had something he wanted to show his wife. Merry didn't notice his countenance as she poured his coffee but Liddy did.

"Merry, I really stopped by to visit with Abby. If you don't mind I will have my tea out on the porch."

Merry handed her the mug and started to go out on the porch. Liddy stopped her.

"If I am not mistaken your husband wishes to spend a few minutes with you. Better take advantage of all the stolen minutes you can." She winked at Thad and moved Merry in his direction. When Thad smiled, he lit up a room. Their small home was a glow.

"Mrs. Sheridan, would you do me the honor of taking a walk with me?" Thad asked with an exaggerated southern drawl.

"Mr. Sheridan, I would be delighted." She moved to leave but he flew up the ladder into the loft.

"What in the world?" she hollered up "Are you getting your book of poetry?"

He jumped out of the loft not using the ladder. Grabbed her hand and sailed out the back door. Gus enthusiastically followed the two.

They walked a little ways just enjoying the warm day. It seemed like a long time since they had quality time alone.

"I've missed you." She said as she wrapped both arms around his. She was looking for all the world like she wanted to be kissed and he indulged her. She sighed heavily and laid her head on his shoulder.

"What's that you're carrying? Doesn't look like your book of poetry." He stopped and sat down.

"I have something to show you."

She knelt beside him. He unrolled the papers he brought.

"I have been working on the plans to expand the house I wanted your thoughts."

He wants her thoughts? No one ever wanted her thoughts or opinions? Her mother, her uncle, her grandfather they all did things around her not with her.

"See here Merry." His hand was resting on the edge of the paper. "I want to extend the kitchen, make it bigger, then put a door here and build a glorified bunkhouse for the boys." He was pointing and moving his finger around. "And here, here will be our room and it will be big enough to hold anything your heart desires." She was silent and he looked at her.

"You're all my heart desires." It was said so soft he almost missed it.

"Now that's what a man likes to hear, although most women wouldn't admit it so freely." He kissed the tip of her nose.

"You better put a big closet in here," she pointed, "to store your impossible ego." She shoved him, knocking him off balance. He stretched out propping himself on one elbow.

"Go on and look it over."

She bent her head and her hair fell covering part of her face. The sun was dancing on each strand making all the colors gleam. She was his Angel. God had blessed him abundantly. She was beautiful, strong, sweet. The list lengthened in his head and he thanked his maker for making such a woman.

He watched as her eyes surveyed the document. When she felt his gaze, she turned her eyes to meet his. His life would be nothing without her. He didn't ever want to be away from her. Do all men feel this way? He continued to blatantly stare at her unashamed. She returned his intense stare. No words were said. No words needed to be said. They simply declared their love with their eyes. After a few brief seconds, she broke the spell.

"May I make a few suggestions?"

Liddy and Abby were sipping tea on the porch.

"I have a little plan I need your help with." Liddy leaned up in her chair.

"This sounds serious, Liddy. What's on your mind?"

"Thad and Merry's anniversary was a few weeks ago, and I am certain they did not celebrate."

Abby's face fell. "I had no idea. Everything has been such chaos. This is just awful."

"Yes, but we can fix it."

"What's the plan?"

"The plan is to send those two away for a few days. If you don't mind me moving in with you."

Abby thought to protest saying she could watch the children with Hawk's help but the truth was she was tired all the time and knew she couldn't do it.

"I would love it."

"Let's try to surprise them in some way," she added. "But how?"

"I have an idea." Hawk with Patience on his shoulders had been at the side of the porch and heard the whole conversation.

"Well, let's hear it," Liddy urged him up on the porch.

"I know a small little cabin on the banks of the small river. We could fix it up, lay in supplies."

The two ladies looked very skeptical.

"Indian women say it's a most beautiful place, Morning Dove will love it."

"How far is this cabin, Hawk?" Liddy asked. He shrugged his shoulders and Patience went bobbing up and down.

"I could show you on your way home." Liddy still wasn't sure but she agreed to let Hawk take her.

Patience was placed next to her mother and the two were off.

"This is a secret Patience so you must not tell your Uncle Thad or Aunt Merry." The little girl was all smiles happy to be a part of a secret. Abby just hoped she wouldn't spill it before they worked everything out.

Liddy was in shock. The view from the cabin was spectacular. Indian women had a good eye for beauty. The cabin was tiny but situated just perfectly. A little cleaning and fixing up and it could be a nice honeymoon cottage.

"Who owns this, Hawk?"

"Lone Eagle built it for Yellow Flower."

Liddy stood and stared at the boy. "This is perfect, Hawk. I am sorry I doubted you."

The conspiracy to surprise the couple was in full swing. Hawk who had not accompanied the Sheridan's to church had promised to go with them tomorrow. His job was to take the couple to the cottage after church. Tommy and the girls were going to spend the day with the Lapps.

It was rather shocking when Hawk asked Merry to cut his hair. No one had suggested he cut the long inky locks. He confided to Merry he planned to make Patience a doll with his hair. Merry was careful to keep the hair from hitting the floor of the porch. Thad and Tommy both opted for a trim. Three very handsome men escorted the women to church the next morning.

Hawk had borrowed one of Thad's white dress shirt to wear to church. He was truly a handsome young man.

"Hawk, you're going to turn the girls' heads one day." Merry smoothed his collar. If an Indian could blush she was certain Hawk was. Patience had not seen Hawk with his new haircut and she was not happy. She cried all the way to church on his shoulder. The tears would soon be forgotten when she saw the doll he was making.

"It's a good feeling having a wagon full of family." Merry looked over her shoulder at the people she loved the most in the world.

"We do make a fine-looking load if I do say so myself," Thad added.

Anna Beth raised up behind her uncle and wrapped her arms around his neck "We are something ain't we?"

He had to laugh Abby would not let her get away with the use of ain't. Sadly, the people of Rudolph Community Church thought the same thing, the Sheridans were something taking in that "heathen."

The Sheridans entered the church and sat in their usual pew. No one spoke to the group as all eyes were on Hawk. The young man sat stick straight and stared ahead. The service held so much tension Pastor Gray had trouble delivering his sermon. He ended it rather abruptly.

Merry was fit to be tide but she was not shocked. This town ran low on good manners. Thad's anger was at a fever pitch. When the group filed out Pastor Gray tried to do a little damage control but Thad was not buying any of the rehearsed words. It was a good thing the younger kids were going home with the Lapps it would give time for Thad to speak with Hawk.

Hawk took the reins from Thad "I drive." Merry sat in between the two men. She turned to Hawk.

"Hawk I want to apologize for the way the church behaved today."

"I am use to it. What made you think the building would change the people?"

He had a good point. Thad was afraid this would push Hawk farther away from the Gospel.

"Are they Pharisees?" Hawk asked stunning the couple. "Standing at the door not letting one in or out?" Hawk was a very smart young man.

"Yes, I believe they may be, but please Hawk don't put us all in the same corral."

"Hawk, this isn't the way home." Merry and Thad had been so upset they had not noticed all the turns Hawk was making.

"We are not going home."

"What are you up to?" Merry looked at her husband accusingly.

"Don't look at me, I haven't a clue what is going on?"

"Hawk, you want to let us in on what's going on?"

"No, sir." He kept his smiling face toward the horizon.

Hawk pulled the wagon as close to the dwelling as he could but the trio had to walk to the cabin. The small porch was decorated with flowers. Tommy and Anna Beth had made a sign that read "Happy Honeymoon." When the stunned couple turned to inquire of Hawk he was gone.

Thad opened the door and lifted Merry into his arms. Carrying her across the threshold felt like the right thing to do. He kissed her as he put her back on her feet and she clung to him returning the kiss. When he sighed, she began to giggle.

"What's so funny?"

She declined to answer. Wasn't the woman supposed to sigh after a kiss?

Thad looked around the two-room cabin. It was very well made. Merry was walking around the room.

"I had forgotten this was here." There was something in her voice that caused Thad to turn. The look on her face was reflective.

"Whose place is this?"

"Oh," she stuttered when she saw him looking at her. "I am not sure who owns the land but Lone Eagle built the cabin."

Why did the statement trouble him?

His mind went back to his first sight of Lone Eagle standing at the edge of the garden with Merry. He wanted to ask her a few questions but he realized it was jealousy on his part. He couldn't let that emotion get a foot hold. He rubbed the back of his neck.

Merry saw his hand go to the back of his neck and knew she should explain.

"You hungry? It looks like someone has packed a feast . . ." He was looking in the baskets sitting on the table. She could feel the tension in the room even if Thad was doing his best to fight it.

"Lone Eagle built this cabin for Yellow Flower. Yellow Flower was not and Indian."

Thad's surprise was obvious.

"She was given to Lone Eagle in trade for horses by an Asian man headed to California for the gold. She was a pitiful creature Thad." Merry wrapped her arms around herself as if to shield herself from the memory.

"Lone Eagle built the four walls to give her a form of security." Thad was quiet. She continued, "When Yellow Flower died he left our home and for two days I did not see him. I at first thought he was leaving the baby with me and I would never see him again. I found him here on the third day." He did not love her but he wanted to protect her. He had a tender heart. Merry couldn't help remembering the kindness of her friend. The only comfort in her heart was that he reconciled with his creator before his death.

The happy mood in the cabin had taken on a melancholy tone. Thad felt responsible due to his own feelings rising to the surface. He couldn't hide his emotions from her.

"Since we are discussing such gloomy topics let's go ahead and argue about your lack of concern over being the target of murder." Merry suggested.

They had not mentioned the attempt and he had hoped Merry had put it out of her mind. He hadn't planned on doing anything about it.

"I don't plan to do anything so can we move on?"

"No! We cannot!"

He thought he had seen Merry at her angriest it was evident he had not.

She pivoted walked straight out the door and slammed it behind her. He watched her storm toward the river bank, picking up a stick and wielding it like a sword. He knew better than to follow her. If he was honest he didn't want to. He was too tired to battle. There were too many emotions intertwined to sort them all out. He was angry with the town. He was jealous over a past friendship. He was anxious to get the building project started and he was overwhelmingly in love.

Back at home there was excitement. When the Lapps brought Tommy and the girl's home they found Abby alone and in labor. She was pacing in the kitchen stopping to lean over the chair. This was the scene when Liddy entered.

"Oh, good heavens, Abby, how long have you been in pain?" She helped the woman to the bedroom, calling for her husband in the process.

"It started right after the family left," she panted out. "It's too early." There were tears forming in her eyes.

"Now, now, sometimes babies have a mind of their own. Let's just get you into bed so Zeke can examine you."

Jackson was sitting looking out his office window at the people filing out of the church across the street. His mind was in Dakota Territory. He woke up early this morning with an uneasy feeling about his wife and daughters. He couldn't shake the notion that they needed him. He decided to go to the office and get his mind off his feelings.

Perhaps he should have gone to church. He saw Lachlan Kennedy exiting the church and he thought of beckoning him to come in. He didn't have to. Lach was headed his way.

Lach waited for Jackson to unlock the door.

"Jackson, I came to pray for you. May I?"

The lump in his throat and the knot in his stomach tightened. "Yes, please." He preceded Lach into his office.

"I can't rightly say why I feel this so strong but I had to seek you out." Jackson nodded and Lach began to pray.

If you were to ask Jackson at that moment what Lach was saying, he would not be able to recount it. When Lach was finished, Jackson was a mess. He slumped in his chair his face drained of color.

"I can't do it anymore Lach." Jackson ran his hands down his face.

"Can't do what?" Lachs normal vibrant voice was a compassionate whisper.

"Live like this." Tears dripped off the mans face "I am miserable, Lach. All this and I am empty." He spread his arm out indicating the bank.

"There is only one thing in life that makes a man truly happy Jackson. A relationship with the Lord. Until you have that you have nothing."

The man's head went down on the desk and he sobbed. Lach's hand rested on Jacksons shoulder.

"Work it out Jackson, just ask, it's there."

Lach prayed silently while the man cried. After some time, Jackson's head came up. The weight of the world lifted off his shoulder and peace settled upon the man. He had asked forgiveness and received it.

Jackson and Lach sat and talked for well over an hour. Jackson was able to pray for his wife and children now and it relieved his anxiety. The empty feeling he had written to Abby about was instantly gone.

How was he going to explain to her what happen to him? Would she understand? Would she leave him, taking away his children? He didn't think she would but you could never predict what one might do. He learned that the hard way a time or two. He confessed his thoughts to Lachlan. The man assured him that Christ grace was sufficient for whatever lay ahead. He felt the peace in the promise.

Thad changed out of his Sunday clothes. Someone had gone to a lot of work to make this special for he and Merry. They had provided clothing and supplies for at least two days and here they were fighting. They had perfected the art in the short year they had been together.

He opted to feed his growling stomach than to soothe his wife's ruffled feathers. She needed to understand he just couldn't leave to pursue the attempt on his life. He had responsibilities. Her for one but there was Tommy and Hawk who needed stability right now. Abby and the girls needed his protection. He made a promise to Jackson that he could never keep if he went out in search of his attempted killer. Merry would just have to understand.

Merry expected Thad to follow her. When he did not, she was surprised. He always met her head on when they disagreed. This was not typical Thad Sheridan behavior. Maybe she is asking too much. He should understand his safety is the most important thing to the family. His safety would always be her first priority but it goes beyond just her there is Abby and the girls to think about. Not to mention Hawk and Tommy. He must realize how much he is needed and needed alive. He is just too stubborn.

"Doctor Lapp, I want to push," Abby let out in a short, winded burst.

"I know, dear, but I don't want you to just yet."

Ezekiel Lapp did not have to tell his wife what to do. She knew by the crease between his eyes this was going to be a breech birth if he didn't intervene. Liddy helped her husband position Abby in such a way to promote the infant turning. If the baby did not turn on its own Dr. Lapp would have to assist. He informed Abby of the plan.

"I trust you, Doctor," and she did, but she was overcome with great fear. She needed Jackson here or at least Thad. She needed strength.

Hawk was in charge of the children, so he took them fishing. He knew enough to know they did not need to be under foot. He let Liddy know where they would be going. The soft cries coming from the bedroom were frightening Anna Beth and Patience. It was a difficult task for Hawk to get them to consent, but finally, the four left the cabin.

The baby was not turning. Dr. Lapp with the help of his wife manually manipulated the baby successfully. "You can push now Abby, giver all you got."

With Liddy supporting her back Abby raised up and pushed with all her strength. She fell back on the bed her face red and damp with perspiration.

"One more just like that one and will have this dark headed baby delivered."

She geared up and gave it all she had. The infant appeared hearty and healthy. With a good vigorous rub, his lungs opened up.

"He's a healthy boy, Abby A *big*, healthy boy. When did you say you were due?"

"August." She sighed as he lifted the little one for her to see. Her eyes were huge when she surveyed her infant son. He was so much larger than either of her girls had been. A laugh escaped her lips.

"Another month, this baby wouldn't have made it," the doctor made note. "You're blessed to have gone early."

Blessed. Yes, she was blessed. She didn't deserve to be she reasoned. What have I done to receive any blessing? I have been so selfish all my life. Never really giving God the time of day but expecting a healthy child to arrive.

Tears flooded her face as the baby was placed in her waiting arms. The thick dark hair was definitely Jackson's, but when the babe's eyes fluttered open they were ice blue like his Uncle Thad. The baby immediately wanted to nurse and had no difficulty filling his tummy. Mother and son were left alone to get acquainted.

Thad stood and looked out the window. He figured it was time to confront Merry. Hopefully she had calmed down, and they could discuss this reasonably.

He found her at the river bank, feet turning circles in the water. She heard him approach and he sat beside her. He was so close that his arm rested on the ground behind her. His face was close to hers and he looked at her profile. She looked straight ahead. He leaned to kiss her check and she abruptly moved. He was dazed.

"You're not going to come out here and attempt to diminish the situation by soft talk and smooth lips." Thad tried to hide his mirth and rubbed his hand over his lips. Her fury was acute.

Why did he insist on igniting her anger then laugh at her?

"Why do you always laugh at me, Thad?" His countenance changed but he did not move.

"Merry, I—"

"Don't tell me you don't—"

"I was more laughing at the fact that you pegged me pretty good."

"What?" Her look was puzzling.

"I was trying to win you over by being sweet. I can see it was not the right path to take."

"What does that mean?" she was yelling.

"Okay." He tossed a stone into the river and stood. "Let's just have it out." His hands were on his hips. "Ladies first." Silence hung in the air. He stood there waiting and she stood there thinking. He cleared his throat and put his palms up in wonderment of her silence.

"I need you, your family needs you for our sakes I don't understand why you are not trying to get to the bottom of this. Are you going to let Lone Eagle's death be in vain? You owe Hawk that much. Yes, the man who killed him is in custody, but who sent the man? All of that was meant for you and you cannot understand why it bothers me so much? It is a very selfish action on your part."

He had been dressed down before by someone he loved as much. His father had used the exact same argument when he made his decision to fight for the north. He had a responsibility to his family, he was being selfish. It hurt then and it hurt now.

The emotions of the past had risen to the surface. "I have had some experience with this type of situation would you not agree?" he was amazed at how calm his voice was.

She didn't speak.

"What if I went after this person and what if that was his plan all along. To draw me away so he could hurt my family. What if he doesn't want to kill me but wants to torture me? What better way than kidnapping my wife, kids, sister or nieces?" She hadn't thought of that.

"How often is that truly the case Thad? Are you sure you're not drumming up excuses?"

First of all, Thad Sheridan did not make excuses. The very scenario he gave her had happened to a fellow ranger. Thankfully Thad had stopped by the Rangers house to check on his wife and daughter and prevented the plot from unfolding.

If he could have someone that he trusted stay with Merry and the boys he might search for leads.

"Merry, in some cases, if you lay low, the person will expose themselves. I trust in the law."

"What are you afraid of, Thad?" He could have sworn she slapped him. If she had it would have hurt less. He wasn't sure what his next move should be but he knew he wasn't going to run from this fight.

"I will hunt down the person who wants me dead when I can be assured some *male* person will be here to protect you and the boys. Not before."

Her eyes consumed her face they were so large. "*I do not* need a protector. I can take care of myself and you know it."

"I know you *believe* you can," he countered, "but these people never work alone."

She was flabbergasted with the argument.

"Don't ask me to do this under any other circumstances Merry." His words had a finality to them. She wanted to speak but he had sat back down and put his feet in the river and laid back.

Anna Beth and Patience approached their mother's bed. Her face lit up at the sight of her girls.

"Come meet your brother." She turned the sleeping infant so his sisters could touch his tiny hand.

"What is his name, Mamma?" Anna Beth asked.

"Unless your father has changed his mind his name will be Thaddeus Jackson Lorton, but we'll call him TJ." The girls smiled.

"I like it. Uncle Thad will like it too," Anna Beth commented.

“Is Hawk going to go get Uncle Thad and Aunt Merry?” Patience asked her mother, secretly hoping she could ride with Hawk to get the couple.

“No, no, honey, they will be back soon enough. We don’t need to bother them.”

Hawk and Tommy was standing just outside the curtain and Abby beckoned them to come in and see the baby. Hawk surprisingly asked to hold TJ.

“He has Night Wolf’s eyes. I will call him Little Wolf.” The baby grinned at Hawk and the boy’s face sparkled. Abby felt that old nagging that something was missing. She talked herself into believing it was because Jackson wasn’t there to share in such an occasion but deep down she felt the knocking on her heart.

The “happy honeymoon” was anything but. There was a thin veil of tension hanging between Thad and his wife. Each spent the rest of the day on their own. Thad went fishing and Merry sat on the porch rocking. He was polite when he asked if she wanted to go and she was polite when she declined. When he returned, she cooked the fish and they ate in relative silence.

When the sun had set and the stars poked through the black sky Thad headed to bed. “Goodnight, Merry,” he said as he kissed her in the same manner he did every night only this night it didn’t have the warmth to it.

“I will be in in a minute,” she said. She had done a lot of talking to herself but she hadn’t actually spoke to God about the problem. She wanted to do so before she went to bed. What was that verse about not letting the sun go down upon your anger? She didn’t want to go to bed angry at Thad.

A half hour later Merry climbed into bed Thad had his back to her so she wasn’t sure if he was asleep or not although she was pretty sure he was not. When she was situated with her back to him he turned and put his arm around her waist and buried his face in her hair. This was how he went to sleep every night and he wasn’t going to stop now because of some hurtful words and differencing opinions. Merry took great comfort in his gesture.

Hawk, Tommy and the girls arrived to pick up the couple. They were astonished at the happy news of the baby that had arrived. Abby had given them strict instructions not to tell Thad and Merry the sex of the child or the name. This was very hard for Patience to do but Hawk had promised her a surprise if she could keep the secret. Thad tried his hardest to get it out of one of them but even his closest side kick Tommy wasn't uttering a peep.

Thad literally flew into the house when Hawk pulled up to the door. Abby and the baby were in the sitting room. He stopped at the door watching Abby rub the baby's head. She noticed him quietly at the door.

"Come meet your nephew," she spoke softly. Thad entered and squatted next to the chair.

"He's so—"

"*Big*," she finished for him. "And over a month early," she added.

Thad was mesmerized by the infant.

"Here," she said as she stood and handed the baby to him. "Thaddeus Jackson Lorton meet your uncle Thaddeus James Sheridan. His eyes met hers. Just as she hoped he was pleased. "We plan to call him TJ."

"I like it." His smile was wide. Standing at the door Merry saw a joy on his face she had never seen before.

The rock in the pit of her stomach was too much. She quickly turned before she was seen and headed to the outhouse. It was the only place she could be alone. Once inside she allowed the tears to flow. Seeing Thad's face reminded her of what they could never have, what she so inherently wanted. She knew this day would come but she wasn't prepared for the hurt she felt on the behalf of her husband.

When she had gotten herself together Merry left the outhouse only to be met by Liddy.

"I know this is difficult for you Merry. Believe me I have been in your shoes and it doesn't get any easier. What you have to remember is your grief is your grief. Don't knowingly or unknowingly put that on another person."

Merry was pretty stunned. It was if cold water had been thrown in her face.

"When a woman cannot have children and all her friends are having babies it is easy to allow our grief to diminish their joy. Don't do that to Abby."

"But did you see Thad's face?"

"I saw a man very happy for his sister. Not a man swallowed up in self-pity."

Ouch did that sting. Was that how she was acting? Merry searched her heart. Yes, that was exactly how she was acting.

Merry entered the sitting room. "Hand him over, Thad," she said as she stood with hands on hips. "And I don't want any comparison about how he looks like Ole Uncle Thad."

"But, Merry—" Abby began but Merry wouldn't let her finish.

"Abby, you know how impossible he is in situations like this." Thad kissed his nephew and handed him to his wife. When she pulled the cover away from his face the boy's eyes opened bright and wide.

"I don't believe it," Merry said as she looked from Thad's eyes to the baby's eyes.

"Amazing, isn't it, how much he looks like Ole Uncle Impossible?" Thad had no other comment as he left the sitting room.

Jackson had just received the telegram from Dr. Lapp. He was so excited he felt like running up and down Main Street. He had a son! Instead he quickly headed home to pack. He was taking the first train he could get to the Dakota Territory.

The Sheridans had a strained relationship. Thad was himself most of the time but there was something gone from him. Merry chastised herself for being the cause but she still felt she was right and once they were able to bring justice to the person trying to kill him the better off everyone would be. She would just have to endure this rough patch.

The telegram said Jackson would be arriving sometime between the third and sixth of July. Abby could hardly wait to see him and for him to see their son. The girls were jumping up and down even Tommy was getting excited to see Uncle Jackson. Jackson had been teaching Tommy all about the banking system and how to manage all the money he would make some day.

Thad saw Merry headed toward him and he knew what was on her mind. He and Hawk were mending fences on the other side of the corral. She approached and smiled at Hawk.

"I have chocolate cake in the house Hawk with some cold milk. I just sent Tommy and the girls in to get some why don't you join them." He looked to Thad and he nodded his approval. The boy loped into the house.

"I take it you wish to talk to me about something or you would have offered me cake too." He turned to keep working on the fence. "Hope you don't mind if I keep working."

"Do you need help?" she asked.

"What I need is for you to get whatever it is you have to say off your chest." The words came out hitting there mark just like the hammering that drove the nail he had just placed.

"Well you don't have to be so smug about it."

"What is it, Merry?" He stood to face her. "Or do I really need to ask?"

The hammer hung loose in his hand and he faced her. His eyes shaded by his hat. His shirt damp from perspiration. She should have brought him out some water it was the first of July and very warm. That would have been a kind thing to do but after his display of a poor attitude she would have just thrown it in his face.

"I have a lot of work to do, Merry, so if you don't mind, can we move the conversation along?"

What a tongue he has today. She was good and mad.

"Jackson is coming here and the doctor said Abby and TJ won't be able to travel for a while. Now would be a good time for you to do some investigating." She stopped and braced herself for his reply.

"Is that all?" he asked and when she nodded in affirmation he went back to work.

The Fourth of July celebration was fast approaching. Tommy had talked so much about it both of the girls had worked themselves up into a frenzy. He would take his yearly trip with the Lapps. He was looking forward to some time away from Patience but he would never say so.

There was the speculation Hawk would not be welcomed at the celebration in town. Merry felt torn. Hawk eased her mine when he offered to stay behind with Abby and the baby. Abby did not protest. She admired Hawk's strength of character.

Chapter Thirteen

Something woke Merry up. It was pitch black except for the moonlight shining through the window. She caught motion from the corner of her eye. Thad was dressed and filling his saddle bags. His gun was strapped to his waist.

"What are you doing?" She sat up in bed.

"What you want me to do." He kept digging through the top drawer of the dresser. "I don't know when I will be back. I'll drop you line or send a telegram when I can."

She climbed across the bed and rose to stand beside him.

"Don't leave like this." Her hand rested on his chest.

"Like what?" His eyes scanned hers.

"Mad," she whispered.

"You think I am mad, Merry? I thought you knew me better than that."

A sob caught in her throat. He gathered her in his arms rubbing her back he kissed the top of her head twice.

"Make sure the boys mind," he said and headed down to the kitchen. He was very quiet as he moved out the door careful not to wake anyone else in the house.

She cried from the front porch as he saddled Grace and headed out. She had a sinking feeling in her stomach. She watched until he was out of view. It was a little pass two so she went back to her bed full of sorrow and regret. Somehow all her reasoning for why he should go seemed like a heap of ashes. She asked him to leave now she had to pay the price. She cried into his pillow. The lingering smell of him only made her cry harder.

Thad rode in the darkness. There was a time when he enjoyed this part of being a Texas Ranger the hunt, but since he met Merry his life in the Dakota Territory was all he needed. Merry – his thoughts were on her. Most women would have begged and pleaded for their husbands not to set out after a killer, but not his Merry. She practically pushed him out the door. He tried very hard not to let his attitude affect their relationship but he knew it had. He prayed about it. He never felt the spirit convicting him of being in the wrong. He had feelings and those feelings he was justified in having. He truly wasn't mad. He tried to put a name to how he was feeling the only thing that came to mind was wounded.

"Where is Uncle Thad this morning?" Anna Beth came in from helping gather the eggs. "He is usually out in the barn when I gather the eggs is he sick?" The little girls face showed great concern.

Before Merry could answer Tommy came in with the same question.

"Is Thad still asleep? He usually comes in and steals TJ for a few minutes in the morning." Abby joined the inquiry.

Merry felt overwhelmed with all the questions. She was desperately trying to not let her grief spill over to the others.

"Night Wolf needed to take a journey. He will be gone for a while but will return as soon as he can." Hawk saved the day. All participants in the conversation just stared at him. Merry's eyes met his in quiet assurance.

"Can we still go to the celebration?" Patience little heart was setting itself up to be shattered. Hawk picked her up and set her on his hip before the pouting could start.

"Tommy will take you," he said and bounced the little girl. "Right, Tommy?"

"R-Right, H-Hawk."

"And," Hawk added, "I bet Morning Dove could use some help baking cookies after breakfast."

He sat Patience down with a squeal and went back out to the barn. *What just happened?* Merry thought to herself. Hawk had taken over the entire situation. He had the whole family doing his bidding. He obviously felt he needed to fill Thad's void.

Everyone was cleaned and dressed ready for the Fourth of July celebration. Hawk hitched up the wagon and loaded all Merry's treats in the back. He helped Anna Beth into the wagon and then placed Patience next to Tommy.

"Tommy, you watch out for the girls, and you girls stick with Tommy, understand?" Three heads bobbed up and down. Tommy was proud to have the honor of protector bestowed upon him by Hawk.

"Any words for me, Thad . . . I mean Hawk?" Merry said with a mischievous smile as she climbed up on the wagon set.

"Don't get into trouble, Morning Dove." He handed her the reins and they were off.

Abby enjoyed the day with Hawk and TJ. Hawk worked most of the day outside and Abby cleaned the small dwelling from top to bottom. Something Merry would not let her attempt had she been home.

She and Hawk sat down to supper when the door open. Jackson stood in the door way and his wife flew into his arms. Tears were in both their eyes as Jackson held his wife's face in his hands. "I have missed you," he said, kissing her again. She clung to him as if he would suddenly disappear.

Hawk made himself scarce as Jackson and Abby went into the small sitting room. Jackson reached into the cradle and picked up his sleeping son. He showered kisses on his son and took a seat. Abby positioned herself next to him.

"I can't believe how big he is, the girls were so tiny in comparison." His eyes were washing over his son looking at toes and fingers. When the baby opened his eyes, they focused on his father's.

"Well, I'll be." He looked at his wife. Abby and Anna Beth both had similar colored eyes which were a less intense color than Thad's but TJ had the exact mysterious eyes.

"What are you calling him?"

"TJ. Is that okay?"

"It is what we last talked about. Thad like it?"

"Of course, you know Thad."

Jackson smiled. "Where is everyone?"

"Merry took the kids to the Fourth of July celebration."

"Where is Thad?" Abby's silence caused Jackson to lift his head and move his eyes from his son to his wife.

"What is it, Abby?" He shifted the infant up to his shoulder.

"He left this morning. Merry hasn't said anything. Hawk actually is the one who told us he would be gone for a while."

"Something's going on. Have you talked to Merry?"

"No, I got the feeling he did not leave on the best of terms."

"I will talk to Merry." Jackson's voice was very matter of fact.

"Jackson, it may not be any of our business."

He looked out the window. "Thad would not leave without good reason, and he wouldn't leave Merry in anger." His wife had a worried look on her face. His worried look had to do with how she would take his news.

"Abby, have you been thinking about what I wrote to you?" She shook her head.

"I've done more than thinking. I have given my life to Christ."

Panic went through her body. She knew this was where his life was headed and she feared the change that would take place in their family.

"I'm happy for you, Jackson."

He grabbed her hand and kissed it. "The emptiness is gone, Ab. I can't believe how good this feels. I didn't realize how little I loved you and the girls until I received God's love. Don't get me wrong I loved you and the girls more than anything but it was just a natural love. Now the love goes through God first and it's pure."

She abruptly stood and left the house her tears threatening to spill. Jackson began to silently pray for his wife.

Thad had been on the back of Grace for most of the day. His first stop would be the cavalry. He would attempt to speak to the officers who transported the man Sheriff Bullock identified as Clive Gunderson.

He stopped and let Grace rest as he took out a biscuit and some cheese he had packed in his saddle bag. His mind went to his family. He prayed Jackson would arrive soon. He hated the thought of leaving the women alone but he put them in God's hand. He had a measure of trust in Hawk. He prayed he would find the person who wanted him dead quickly. His desire was to get started on adding on to his house. The crops were planted and he long to spend his time constructing the boys home.

It was almost dark when Merry pulled the wagon in front of the house. Hawk appeared coming from the barn. Patience had fallen asleep. After lifting Anna Beth out of the wagon, he tenderly picked up Patience and carried her into the house.

Anna Beth was talking nonstop to her mother when she caught site of her father. She practically climbed the man to get her arms around his neck. He had such a different look in his eyes when he looked at his daughter.

"Daddy, you look different." Anna Beth patted his cheeks.

"I am different, sweetheart." He rubbed his nose on hers. She giggled and he put her down.

Patience had awakened when they entered the kitchen. Jackson took her from Hawk. Her drowsy eyes flashed open when she realized it was her father who now held her. She rested her head on his shoulder and snuggled his neck. His heart was overjoyed.

It was no use Merry couldn't sleep. In Thad's absence, the girls had asked if they could sleep with their aunt. She obliged only to be pushed out of her own bed. She didn't care. They were such sweet girls.

Without Thad, she was restless anyway and this was just the first night. She prayed he would be home soon. There was an element of guilt that blanketed her. She pushed him into this and she was beginning to feel the pressure from her decision.

Merry scurried down the ladder only to be met by Jackson who was sitting at the table with a brand new bible opened.

"I suspected as much," she whispered. "You were a different man when I saw you today. I had a feeling it was more than TJ's birth."

He smiled brightly. "I had a little birth of my own."

"Where are you reading?" she questioned as she got a drink of water.

"Lach and the pastor suggested the book of John." Merry agreed it was a good place to start.

They conversed a little while. Jackson telling her of his conversion. Something he had yet been able to share with his wife.

"Why did Thad leave, Merry?"

The question was asked point blank. There was no heading in that direction he just asked the question. It was really none of his business and that particular fact made her a little antsy.

"The reason I am asking," he filled in her silence, "is because Thad made a promise to me he would take care of my girls until I returned. I returned and Thad wasn't here. It is not like my brother-in-law not to keep his promise."

He couldn't see her face. If he had he would have run for cover. How dare he blame Thad. He left the same day Jackson arrived. He did keep his promise.

"He just left this morning. I hardly see that as a breach of promise." Her words were terse.

"He didn't know I would be home today. My telegram said my expected arrival would be the third through the sixth. What was so important he had to leave?"

"Jackson, why are you so insistent on knowing something that is none of your business?"

"Because I know Thad Sheridan wouldn't leave you behind unless he was in some kind of trouble." She sat down across from him and pushed the hair back from her face.

"At least tell me when he is coming back." He asked.

He had arranged for a shipment of pine to be sent so Thad could start building. It would be here in a week or two. He thought to surprise Thad but this wasn't working out as he had planned. Something was wrong and he felt he could help if Merry would open up.

"I don't know," she said in a soft voice. "The man who killed Lone Eagle was sent here to murder Thad, not Lone Eagle. The bullet that hit me was meant for him."

There was a gasp from behind the curtain and Abby appeared.

"I didn't want to worry you all. Thad and I thought it best not to tell you."

"So Thad has gone looking for this person. Why now? It has been over a month."

"He didn't want to go." Fresh tears pooled in her eyes. "I made him." A sob caught in her throat and her hand covered her mouth.

"No one makes my brother do anything, not even you, Merry." Abby put her arm around Merry's shoulder.

Jackson suggested doing the only thing he knew to do pray. As he, Merry, and Abby joined hands he prayed. Abby felt as if she was being left out. She felt helpless a feeling she did not care for.

"Gunderson told us he was paid in cash. He collected half before and would collect the other half once word had been gotten back that you were dead." Thad had been able to track down one of the cavalrymen.

"He said a third party paid him and he never saw the man's face. Gunderson is still in custody if you would like to speak with him it could probably be arranged." Papers were drawn up to give Thad privileges to question the man. He was on the next train.

"I hope the little gal that took your bullet is faring okay," Gunderson said smugly. If he didn't need information he would have retaliated. "I had you dead." The man put his hand up in the form of a gun and aimed it at Thad's head.

"You missed and that landed you in here. You killed a man and you will pay for that. It is not going to make any difference for you so you might as well tell all you know."

The man sized Thad up. "I would if I knew anything."

"You didn't know the man?"

"A man got in touch with me in Missouri said he had a job if I was interested. When I saw the price, I was interested. Somebody paid real good to have you six feet under. Why are you so special?"

"What did this man look like?"

"Don't know. He talked to me from behind a curtained coach. He slipped a piece a paper with all the information on it to me and half the money up front. When I had proof you were dead, I was to go back to where we met and the bartender would have the money."

"What was the saloon name?" The man hesitated. "Please," Thad asked.

"The Silver Lady."

Thad got the town and directions from the man. As he started to leave Gunderson stopped him.

"The man had the same drawl when speaking as you do. Wasn't a Texas drawl. You boys are from the South."

Merry wasn't faring too well with her husband gone. She felt very short tempered and had to apologize several times to Tommy and Hawk for growling. Her own disgust with how she handled things was eating her up. She should have trusted Thad to do the right thing let him lead like the scripture taught. Instead she pushed her wants and wishes on to him and now she saw what the results were.

Jackson felt obligated to stay until Thad returned causing him to be away from the bank longer than expected. There was a load of lumber just waiting to be made into Thad's dream but Thad wasn't here. He was out doing her bidding.

"I s-see s-someone c-c-coming," Tommy hollered from the porch step.

There was a bit of excitement in his voice. Thad, Merry thought, it must be Thad. She rounded the house shielding her eyes to look down the dirt path. It wasn't Thad.

There was something vaguely familiar with the way the man moved but she wasn't sure who it was. Jackson joined her on the porch. "We have company." She motioned to the form making its way closer.

"It couldn't be?" Jackson said with a grin on his face.

"Who is it?" Abby asked, her height preventing her from seeing the man.

"Looks like Lachlan Kennedy to me."

The arrival of Lach added yet another person who would want to know where Thad was. Merry would have to say she didn't know and then all those miserable feelings would pile up on her again. Her mind was going in circles. When he got closer to the house you could hear him singing at the top of his lungs.

"What on earth are you doing here?" Jackson asked.

"I thought Thad might need some help with the carpentry. I have a whole summer to waste. I thought, why not?"

Merry stepped from the porch. There was no long whistle from his lips as there had been at the first meeting Lachlan just wrapped her in a big hug.

"Where's that man of yours?" he asked when he released her. I wish I knew was the words she wanted to say. She had not heard one word from Thad since he left three weeks ago.

"He isn't here, Lach, had some leftover ranger business to take care of." Jackson saved Merry from an awkward explanation.

"Listen, Mister, I told you. A fancy man came in here ask me to hold the cash until Gunderson picked it up. I had my suspicions as to what Gunderson did for a living but I mind my own business. I just handled the money."

The bartender was telling the truth. Thad could tell when a man was lying.

"When you say fancy, what do you mean?"

"You ever been down south? He was a southern gent type all prim and proper. His way of speakin gave him a way. I knew he was a dirty reb."

One thing Thad had learned was his assailant was a southerner. He was starting to believe his journey would end back in Charleston.

As Thad started to leave one of the girls who worked at the Silver Lady made her way over. He was in hopes he could get out the door before one of them noticed.

"Hey, honey, why you leaving so soon?" she asked in a sugary sickening tone.

"Ma'am." He tipped his hat and continued to the door.

She got in front of him. Her cologne was so strong it nearly made Thad's eyes water. She leaned in close.

"Bartenders aren't the only ones who know what goes on around her." She had something to say, but was it going to benefit him?

"Suppose you tell me why I might want to hear what you have to say."

"Come upstairs and we can talk." She smoothed the collar of his shirt.

He walked out. He felt certain he could find the person without her help. It may take a little longer but he would trust the Lord.

"She must be pretty special to make you walk away, cowboy." The painted lady had followed him outside.

"She is," he said affirmatively, "and what you're doing is sin."

The lady wasn't ready for that. She was caught off guard. For the first time in her life she felt ashamed. No man had ever refused her advances. When this one did she needed to know why. She found out in a hurry and her anger dissipated into humiliation.

"The man who brought the cash was from Charleston. Went by the name of Maxwell Alexander, at least that is what he told me. Funny, he dropped a piece of paper on the way out that had the name Sebastian Cross embossed on it. I kept it. I always keep things that might bring me some extra money."

Sebastian Cross. Why after all these years would Sebastian want him dead?

"I say, I kept it and there was some writing on the back side might interest you. I would be willing to give you a good price for the information." She leaned on the saloon railing.

He hated being in this place it made him feel so unclean. This was one of the reasons he got out of the Texas Rangers. This was no place for any man to spend his free time and it was definitely not a place for a Christian man anytime.

"Do you want it or not?" She was a little curt.

"No, I am sure I can figure it out without the note." He wasn't giving her any money. Whatever the note had on it he was confident the Lord would lead him to the proper conclusion without her help.

He stepped off the saloon porch to the other side of the street. He was hungry and the little cafe was still open. He sat down and the waitress poured him a cup of coffee.

"What'll it be?"

He was the only one inside and by her tone he figured they were getting ready to close.

"Just bring me whatever you have left over. It doesn't have to be hot."

The waitress sobered at his request. "You're serious?"

"Yes, ma'am."

"He's an odd one." Thad turned when he heard the woman from the saloon behind him.

"Came to the saloon for information and couldn't get out of there fast enough. Never had the first drink, played the first game of poker and never gave me the first look. So yes Mae, he's serious."

She threw the piece of paper on the table and left. The stationery was Sebastian's. On the back was the word Rudolph Dakota Territory and Margret Quinn. His next stop would be Charleston.

Merry fixed a large dinner. She was so happy to have Lach here. If her husband was here they could get started building. But her husband wasn't here thanks to her and the building would have to be postpone. In her anxious state cooking was her outlet.

Lach took Thad's seat which made Merry miss her husband that much more. Hawk and Tommy were slightly enamored with the visitor. Tommy with Lach's constant singing and Hawk with the man's size.

Lach continually smiled and was perpetually happy. Just what this crew needed. His personality was such that no matter who was talking and in this case all the children were talking at the same time, Lach paid attention to everyone.

"Lach, you said you had the summer free. I guess I never knew what employment you held."

Merry asked after Jackson blessed the meal.

"I am a teacher at the local university in Charleston."

The boys looked a little crestfallen. Such a stature of a man wasted on education, so they thought. Merry's face showed her astonishment.

"Lach taught me how to read," Anna Beth told the group. Her face beamed at the big man across the table.

"That's right, honey, one of my best students," then he added the word "ever" and you could see Anna Beth sink into utter happiness.

"Hawk, maybe Mr. Kennedy could help you with your math. I have taught you all I know." Merry turned to her . . . son, yes, he was her son. Not by birth but it didn't matter. She couldn't believe she would love her own flesh and blood any more than she did Hawk and Tommy.

There was a sparkle in Hawk's eye. He had a drive to learn and was already passing Merry in some subjects. Maybe Lach could take him farther in study.

"I would be happy to help if I can," Lach confirmed.

After dinner, the children tore themselves away from Lachlan to go outside and play.

"I was hoping to be able to help Thad. I should have sent a telegram. Merry I am sorry I just showed up. My mother would reprimand me on my lack of propriety would she not Abby?"

Abby giggled. "Yes, she would."

"Don't think a thing about it, Lach. I love that you're here. You'd be welcome anytime."

She placed a large piece of raspberry pie in front of him. He sniffed in the aroma and took his first bite.

"That right there," he pointed to the pie with his fork, "was worth the trip." He tucked into the rest of the piece and never looked up.

Merry had disappeared up to the loft. When she returned, she had Thad's drawings for the renovation of the cabin.

"Lach, Jackson would you look at these drawings and tell me if you think we could get things started for Thad."

Merry unrolled the plans and the men stood to study them. A frown creased Lach's brow.

"This here won't work." He was pointing to one of the drawings. Jackson leaned in

"I think your right. What if we went about it the other way?"

Merry tried to follow what they were saying. She felt a little sad they were critiquing her husband's work.

"If we went that way then this would work."

"We could start at this end expand the kitchen first create this room. Is that going to be a bedroom?" They were all looking at Merry.

She bent over the plans "yes, he wanted to move us out of there." She pointed to behind the curtain.

"I say let's get started first thing tomorrow." Lach was all smiles.

After a huge breakfast, Jackson, Lachlan, Hawk and Tommy started laying the foundation for the addition to her grandfather's humble home. Her home. It was surreal what was happening before her in the absence of her husband. Someone else was building his dream. The old pang of guilt resurfaced.

She asked if she could help and they all just looked at her. Taking pity on her Lach promised when he found something he thought would suit her skill he would call on her.

"Like making lunch," she said snidely. He laughed that booming laugh of his.

"I was thinking more of a keen eye when we start lining these boards up and an extra hand with the hammer, but I will take lunch if that is what you had in mind."

Was he serious? Did he really think she was capable of doing manual labor on this project? She could tell by his eyes he was serious.

Thad drug himself into Charleston. He was dirty and had a full beard. He was in need of a bath and a shave. He had spent two days deciding how he was going to approach Sebastian. Did he need to involve the law? Sebastian had no idea Gunderson was going to kill an innocent man so he wasn't guilty of murder. He was guilty of hiring a man to do his killing for him. If Gunderson had succeeded they both would be going to jail. He needed a good night's sleep along with that bath.

He checked in to the Charleston Hotel. The owner didn't recognize him and was reluctant to give him a room until Thad laid the cash on the counter.

"I'd like water brought up for a bath and a shave."

Within the hour, Thad was his old self. The bath and shave revived his spirit and he couldn't wait another day to confront Sebastian. He had to put this behind him. He had been gone almost six weeks and he was ready for this to be over. When he went passed the front desk he nodded to the clerk. He then recognized his old classmate, Thad Sheridan.

Thad made his way down Main Street. Sebastian dealt in properties and if Thad wasn't mistaken his office was at the end of Main. It was ten till five and Sebastian was getting ready to lock the door when he saw Thad approaching. He opened the door and let the man in.

"What do you want Sheridan?" This was not the interaction Thad had expected.

"You don't look surprised to see me?"

"This is your hometown. You have a right to return. I am confused as to why you would seek me out."

For a man who wanted him dead Sebastian acted as if he was preoccupied. Something wasn't adding up.

Construction was coming right along. Merry felt sure Jackson was putting his job in danger. He had stayed way past what he originally intended. She had inconvenienced so many people her misery was hers to reap.

She had a letter from Thad. He was in Kansas and he was fine. He still didn't know how long he would be. The letter was posted a week and a half ago and she had no idea where he was today. He had been gone exactly five weeks, three days, and fourteen hours. The time chipped away at her heart. She prayed continually.

Of an evening Lach, Jackson and Merry would discuss the Bible. Abby would sit and listen only because she felt left out if she didn't. She couldn't understand some of the things her own husband was saying. He had added a whole other facet to his character. She felt there was now a part of him she didn't know and that made her uneasy. Hawk would also sit and listen. He seemed to have the same look on his face as Abby. He was an outsider too.

"I will get right to the point." Thad laid the stationary on Sebastian's desk. "Somebody tried to kill me."

Sebastian picked up the paper which had his name at the top. He flipped it over and read the scribbling.

"How did you get this?" he asked as he fingered the piece of paper.

"Belonged to a man named Maxwell Alexander, you know him?"

"I know him very well, he is my solicitor."

"You seem pretty calm about this, Sebastian." Thad wasn't sure what to think when Sebastian started laughing.

"You think I hired someone to kill you." He threw the paper back to Thad.

"Does that handwriting look familiar to you?" he asked Thad. "Did she never pen letters of love to you?" He hadn't noticed but the script was feminine looking. "If I am not mistaken, that is my wife's penmanship," Sebastian confessed.

Thad sunk into the nearest chair. Jena had tried to kill him, but why? It had been fifteen plus years since the breaking of their engagement. What reason would she have? The questions were written on his face.

"Trying to figure out why after all these years she wants you dead?" Thad still wasn't sure he should believe the implications Sebastian was proposing. It could be a diversion off of himself. "She didn't want you, but more than that she didn't want anyone else to have you."

"What?" Thad was scratching his head. He still wasn't completely sure Sebastian was being honest.

"The only reason Jena married me was because my family had more money than yours. Among all her beaus, I believe she truly loved you." He slumped back in his chair. "As long as you were not around, she convinced herself you never married due to the torch you still carried for her."

"When you brought Merry here, she was livid. Believe me, I have been married to her for fifteen years and that was the angriest I have ever seen her." Sebastian had been staring at his wife's writing. He looked up to Thad's stunned face.

"You seem shocked. I have lived in your shadow all my married life. You see, Jena does not love me, nor has she ever." There was a real sadness in his words.

"But you love her."

"Yes, much to my detriment, I do. It is time I come face to face with the fact she is not capable of loving me." He tipped his head back and sighed. If this was a farce, Sebastian was a good actor.

Jackson and Abby both felt they should stay until Thad returned. Jackson was sure Merry could take care of herself. She was probably a better shot than he was. He knew Hawk could cunningly take a man down with no problems but there was Lach. Lach was sleeping in the barn without complaint but it still would not be proper for him to be here without Thad. Thad would not want his wife's reputation soiled so Jackson would stay. He just wished Thad would return soon. He needed life to return to normal. At least his new normal.

Merry was pleased with everything but herself. She missed Thad. The whole year they had been married they had rarely been a part for the day. Six weeks was an eternity.

She prayed daily and worked hard on discovering her rightful place as the wife in their home. She realized she imposed her will and used his love to get her way. She vowed she would never do that again. He once asked her to trust him. She recognized now the trust was continual not circumstantial.

"Jena's parents are coming to dinner tonight why don't you join us and see what kind of reaction you get?"

Thad thought that was a pretty good plan. He was good at reading people.

"I think I will invite Max as well. Be at the house around seven." Thad nodded and started to leave.

"I have never liked you, Thad, but I never hated you enough to kill you."

"Understood." Thad put his hat on and headed to the hotel.

Thad arrived just a little before seven. He was placed in the study with Sebastian and Captain Harrison. It was good to see the Captain. He was a changed man and Thad saw it the minute their eyes locked.

"Good to see you again, my boy, but you're looking a little lean."

"Good to see you too, sir." He let the comment about his appearance lapse.

"What are you doing back in Charleston?"

"I had some loose ends to tie up, sir."

Maxwell Alexander was escorted in and Sebastian directed the gentlemen to the dining room.

The men were seated. Thad had his back to the entrance when the ladies arrived. When Jena and her mother arrived to their places the men stood. Jena in her own world of making an entrance took a few seconds to recognize Thad. When she did there was a brief look of shock. She recovered quickly.

"Why Thad darling what brings you to Charleston?" she approached him with her hand out. As a southern custom he barely brushed his lips atop her cool knuckles.

"Yes, Thad to what do we owe this pleasure." Lady Angela continued she looked around "Where is," she paused and looked to Jena, "your wife? Assuredly she wouldn't let you come to Charleston without her." She gave a haughty laugh until her eyes locked with her husband who reprimanded her with just a look.

"Yes, tell us, Thad, what brings you to Charleston?" This was Sebastian's way of giving Thad the go ahead.

"A few months ago, someone tried to kill me."

Angela gasped as did Jena, rather insincerely.

"I have traced him back to Charleston."

"Oh my! Why would anyone want to have you killed?" Jena exclaimed. "How dreadful," she added.

Sebastian's eyes were trained on his wife. He and Thad had both caught her slip when she used "have."

"You say you tracked him here?" Captain Harrison asked.

"I found out, as Jena so aptly stated, that the man who did attempted to kill me was a hired man. When I spoke to him he told me he received money from a man named Maxwell Alexander."

All eyes turned to Maxwell. Maxwell was ghostly white and perspiring.

"But," Thad added as he put a reassuring hand on Maxwell, "Maxwell here was just a delivery boy, isn't that right?" The man was too upset to speak.

"A friend of Maxwell said he left this behind." He produced Sebastian's stationary and handed it to Captain Harrison.

He noticed the name and turned to his son-in-law. The anger flashed in the captain's eye and he started to speak. Before he could form a word, Sebastian flipped the note over.

"There is more details on the back. Do you recognize the script?"

Captain Harrison's eyes flew to his daughter. "What is the meaning of all this?"

The captain was standing flailing the paper toward his daughter.

"I don't know what you mean, Daddy."

"Is this your handwriting?" She perused the note

"No, Daddy," she lied. Sebastian's eyes willed Maxwell to speak up.

There was silence. You could hear the clock in the hallway ticking.

"Thad, if you are suggesting what I think you are, I am going to have to ask you to leave." This came from Lady Angela.

"Did you not hear her slip of the tongue? She said why someone would want to have you killed. How did she know that fact when Thad had yet to reveal the information?" Sebastian's eyes remained on his wife as he spoke.

"Sebastian! How dare you accuse me of such a thing?" Jena was putting on a show crying without tears. "I would never do such a thing."

"Yes, you did. Yes, you did," Maxwell had found his voice. Everyone's head turned except Thad's. His attention was on Jena. He saw a crack in her facade.

"You blackmailed me. You said if I didn't deliver the money you would tell Sebastian I was skimming off the accounts." He looked at Sebastian. "I did one time, Sebastian, to pay off a gambling debt, but that was it." Sebastian nodded and turned to his wife.

"You are lying!" she screamed. "You hired Gunder—" Jena stopped when she comprehended she outed herself.

Her father fell back in his chair.

Lady Angela was stock still and staring at her husband.

Jena was in a rage. "I hate you." She leveled her eyes on Thad. "You had to go to Boston, you had to fight for the North. You ruined my whole life. I hate you." If she could, she would have flown across the table at him.

"Why now? Why after all these years?" Thad asked.

"Because you came back married!"

When Captain Harrison found his voice, he looked to Thad.

"What happens now?"

Thad stood and walked toward Captain Harrison, putting his hand out to shake the man's hand. "I will leave that up to you and Sebastian."

"What is right will be done. You can trust you will not have another attempt on your life."

With that Thad thanked the man and turned to leave. He wanted to be on his way first thing in the morning. Sebastian followed him to the door.

"I am sorry, Thad, for everything."

"Thank you, Sebastian, and if you don't mind, I will be praying your marriage can sustain this."

He shrugged "What marriage?" he asked as he walked out ahead of Thad. Calling over his shoulder, he said, "Go home to your wife, Thad, and live in peace."

Thad had the urge to follow Sebastian to see if he somehow might help but it was clear by his fast pace he wanted to be far away and alone. His prayers would have to suffice knowing Sebastian had the support of a father-in-law who could spiritually help. The weight of the world was off his shoulders. Now maybe he and Merry could get down to the business of living. He missed that woman. Sun up couldn't come fast enough.

Lach had suggested the construction start with getting Thad and Merry's bedroom basically out of the kitchen. He had worked hard the last four weeks to make sure the room fit the plan Thad had designed. Once the room was done they could expand the kitchen and be ready to branch out with the housing compartment. He would stay and do as much as he could. Fall classes would be starting before he knew it.

Lach was a teacher from the time he entered the cabin until he retired to the barn. He had taught Anna Beth some math, helped Patience with her patience. Tommy he taught some carpentry skills and a few new songs. It was Hawk he had the most influence on.

He opened up a whole new world by books he had brought with him. Hawk had read Moby Dick and was already half way through Great Expectations. Hawk worked right alongside Lach through every step of construction and seem to soak up anything the man taught. He however got annoyed with Lach's constant humming and singing. One would think Lachlan Kennedy was trying to teach the boy some tolerance. He would just grin when Hawk would ask him to stop. The two teased and wrestled around like family. He would be missed when he returned to Charleston. Merry just hoped Thad returned in time to see his old friend.

Nearly seven weeks now Merry woke up alone. She had forgotten how it felt. It seemed as if Thad had always been with her. How did one's heart get so completely saturated with another person so quickly?

There was always this under current of fear that something had happened to her husband. The thought keep her nerves raw and she was on edge. She went down the ladder and started breakfast. Her nerves getting the best of her she cooked enough food not even Gus could eat all the leftovers.

The cool breeze of the afternoon felt good against the lingering effects of a hot midday. This was the perfect time to work in the garden. Gus who had been laying in the cool up turned sod perked his ears and shot out of the garden at lightning speed.

"W-W-What do you s-suppose got into him?" Tommy's stuttering had gotten better thanks to some tips from Lach.

"Who knows. Probably caught wind of a rabbit."

Tommy's face was turned toward where the dog had left. His face longing to follow his best friend.

"All right, go on, but if it is a skunk your both in trouble." The boy took off running and it wasn't long before you could hear Gus barking in the distance.

Merry went on about her hoeing and Gus went on barking, something wasn't right. She took her hoe and went to the front of the house. She stopped in her tracks when she saw Gus literally jump into Thad's arm practically knocking the man down. Tommy was following with Anna Beth close on his heels. Even Hawk with Patience on his hip trotted toward Thad. Merry watched from the porch.

When Thad righted himself from Gus's embrace he was nearly knocked over from Tommy's hug, He lifted the boy into the air and threw him over his shoulder tickling his ribs.

"How's my boy?"

"Good," Tommy said without a pause. Anna Beth was hanging on his belt. He pulled her up on his hip and gave her a kiss.

"How are you love?" she gave her uncle a big squeeze around the neck. He sat the children down and reached for Patience. She gave him a big sloppy kiss and laid her head on his chest. He put an arm around a smiling Hawk's neck and kissed the top of his head teasing the boy. For as tired and weary as Thad was he wouldn't have traded this moment for anything.

The group walked Thad home chattering all the way. When Merry came into view his heart leaped. She was his home. Not any structure or piece of land or deed. His home consisted of one incredible woman. He watched as her hand went up to her forehead to push her hair back. He had hoped his coming home with answers would wipe the worry off her face.

As he made his way up the steps with the children he stopped in front of her. His free hand reached out to stroke her face and he leaned in close.

"You can go ahead and put all those little worries out of your head and move on now." His eyes melted her and she couldn't speak.

"I am warning you, kids," he said as he put Patience down, "there's about to be a lot of kissing." Moans and groans were heard from the children as he cupped her face in his hands and their lips met.

When Merry opened her eyes she and Thad were alone on the porch or so they thought. Lach had perched himself in the doorway leaning on the door jam.

"I see you finally found a woman you could woo."

"Lach!" Thad said with excitement.

He turned his body to greet his old friend but Merry stopped him by tightening her grip she pulled Thad's face back toward her and with a flick of her hand waved Lach back in the house. Lachs hearty laugh resonated as he retreated through the door. Merry kissed the grin from Thad's face.

All Thad wanted was a bath a biscuit and a bed in that order.

The seven weeks on the road had drained him. He greeted Jackson and Abby. Instead of shaking his brothers-in-law hand as he customarily did the new Jackson embraced his brother. There would be no in law anymore it would be in-Lord. This caught Thad a little by surprise but he just returned the gesture.

Abby was all tears. She just kept commenting on how "thin" he looked. He supposed he lost about ten to fifteen pounds. He really didn't feel like eating while he was traveling but now, he was sure he would be able to put those pounds right back on. In Abby's defence, she had seen Thad when he came home from the war. He was very emaciated then and it took him months to get back to where he should be.

After some brief conversations, Thad excused himself. He grabbed a clean pair of clothes his soap and razor and head toward the creek. He was trying to decide whether or not to tell his family the whole story or just simply say he had taken care of the issue. He would have to tell Merry but was it necessary to tell those who live in Charleston, yet the word would eventually get out. His family needed to hear his side.

The bath did little to revive him if anything it made him more tired. When he reached the house, he could smell the aroma of Merry's cooking. It reminded him of his first days in the cabin with her.

"Supper will be ready soon."

He looked over her shoulder and into the skillet filled with sizzling chicken.

"Smells good, what is everyone else going to have to eat."

"Same old Thad," Abby said with a smile.

"I did manage to bring some gifts home for the children. Where did Hawk put my things?"

"Up in the loft, I think."

He kissed his wife's neck and headed up the ladder.

Thad did not come back down and Merry was certain he was probably resting. When supper was ready she sent Tommy up to get him. Tommy returned.

"I-I-I tried to wake him, h-he just rolled over." Tommy had a sad little look on his face.

"We will just let him sleep, he can eat when he gets up."

They all sat down at the table and Lach blessed the food. Jackson and Abby immediately discussed their departure plans. Abby and TJ had seen Dr. Lapp earlier in the day and he gave them his blessing for traveling back to Charleston.

Thad never appeared and Merry found him sprawled out on the bed sound of sleep. She lay down beside him the rhythm of his breathing lulling her to sleep. She was so thankful to have him home and in one piece. He had not spoken about the trip and she was determined not to ask. She had caused enough trouble. Soon she was asleep.

The room was pitch black and Thad could feel the warmth of his wife beside him. The last thing he remembered was fried chicken. Did he eat? He couldn't remember. He was beginning to wonder if

Merry hadn't slipped something in the glass of water he had drank when he came back from the creek. He felt that groggy.

His stomach gave evidence that he had not eaten and drove him out of comfort to search for some food. He found a plate in the oven piled high it wasn't hot but he didn't care. He took the food out on the front porch. With his bare feet resting on the railing he tipped back in the rocker and began to eat. Gus at his side slightly begging for a bite.

Merry moved and Thad was not there. She sat up and looked around the room. She listened and heard nothing from the downstairs. She put on her robe and climbed down the ladder.

The plate in the oven was gone. She tiptoed to the front door and saw his feet on the railing and heard him quietly talking to Gus. The screen door squeaked as Merry made her way out and leaned on the railing facing her husband.

"I am sorry I woke you." He said.

"Don't ever be sorry for giving me the option of being awake with you." She tickled the bottom of his feet. "I did a lot of thinking while you were gone, Thad. I want you to know how sorry I am for pressuring you to go. I should have trusted your judgment and been a better wife."

His feet came down and his hands clasped hers.

"You are right you should trust me, but I am glad I put an end to it. Now about you being a better wife I don't see how you can get much better." He kissed her hands.

She pulled him up. Her hand caressed his face. He looked so tired and his face was gaunt, remorse filled her heart.

Thad slept a good part of the day. The house was still when he exited the loft. A plate of cinnamon cookies sat on the table with a note, "Gone fishin', come join us." A smile spanned Thad's face. He grabbed a cookie and headed to find his family.

You could hear the noise of a loving family echoing through the trees. Thad stood back and watched the people he loved the most in the world. Merry turned and caught him watching. The sun bathed her in light and his breath caught in his chest. This was the life he had longed for this was a life of purpose.

Epilogue

The sun was just setting as Thad hammered the last nail in the spacious room filled with twelve individual sleeping quarters. He and Merry's dream was soon to be a reality.

They had turned the small cabin into a larger home with a massive kitchen to accommodate what they hoped would be a large family. The town thought them crazy and tried to block the completion of the home for boys but Thad did everything by the legal book. Soon they would welcome their first guest.

"Do you think we will be sorry?" Merry asked as she breathed in the deep smell of pine.

"Some days it might seem so. You having second thoughts?" he was standing behind her surveying the work. He, Merry and the boys had nearly built the whole thing.

"No, it's the right thing to do. Besides taking in strays is something I am good at. Look how well you turned out." He wrapped his arms around her resting his chin on her shoulder

"Now who's impossible?"

The End

About the Author

Sarah Hale was born and raised in rural Central Indiana. The defining moment in her life was when she answered the knock on her heart's door at age five. Since that time, she has dedicated her life to following the will of the Lord. The journey led her to the field of nursing in 1993. She currently is a staff development coordinator and nurse educator. In addition to writing, she enjoys cooking, traveling and is an avid University of Kentucky basketball fan. She lives in the country near the small town of Mooreland, Indiana.

CPSIA information can be obtained
at www.ICGtesting.com
Printed in the USA
FFHW02n0039191018
48826607-53011FF

9 781640 79445